Midnight

Born in Copenhagen, Lene Kaaberbøl published her first book at the age of fifteen. She has worked as a secondary-school teacher, a copy-writer, a literary translator and a literary editor, but she is now a full-time writer. She has published many books in Denmark and has translated her own work into English. *The Shamer's Daughter* was shortlisted for the Marsh Award for Children's Literature in Translation, and *The Serpent Gift* was distinguished for excellence on the IBBY Honour List 2006.

Also by Lene Kaaberbøl

SILVERHORSE

Midnight

Lene Kaaberbøl

MACMILLAN CHILDREN'S BOOKS

First published 2009 by Macmillan Children's Books
a division of Macmillan Publishers Limited
20 New Wharf Road, London N1 9RR
Basingstoke and Oxford
Associated companies throughout the world
www.panmacmillan.com

ISBN 978-0-330-44487-3

A CIP catalogue record for this book is available from
the British Library.

Typeset by Intype Libra Limited
Printed and bound in the UK by CPI Mackays, Chatham ME5 8TD

CONTENTS

RAVEN

Essford was filled to bursting with the Spring Market crowds. The dense press of carts, wagons, animals and people moved through the gates in stops and starts, watched by sleepy guards. It was early, and the air was still cold enough to cause steam to rise from muzzles and mouths and the warm bodies of horses, donkeys and steers. The grey pony in front of Kat raised its tail and let a couple of yellow balls of manure plop on to the paving stones before it was willing to walk on. Finally, she and Rane could move forward too. She pressed her legs against the flanks of her old horse, but he hardly needed the signal. This was by no means Rane's first market – he had probably been to more than Kat – and he trudged on in happy confidence that a water trough and a filled manger awaited him soon. Perhaps even a roof and a cosy stall . . . Now that he served the Bredani of all Breda, the most powerful figure in the country, and was no longer a humble innkeeper's hack, he had taken a liking to the finer things in life.

The bredinari post station was located conveniently close to the city walls in Essford, but today Kat had to stay far away from such amenities. Nor was she wearing her grey apprentice uniform. No one was supposed to notice that the Essford Spring Market was receiving a visit from one of the Bredani's very own hellhorse Riders (well, a hellhorse Rider *apprentice*). This was also her reason for riding Rane – he was a nice, robust and unremarkable brown gelding and would cause no heads to turn.

'It doesn't matter if they see you. Just don't let anyone *notice* you.'

That was the first thing Kat learned about being a spy. Well, not a spy exactly. Covert courier, more like. She had been sent quite often to contact people who could under no circumstances be seen talking to a real bredinari, because no one was supposed to know that they were working for the corps. They called it *being discreet*, and the first time it had happened, Kat hadn't quite understood why anyone would pick her for that kind of assignment. She had asked Simon about it – he was the one who had brought her to Breda and seen to it that the bredinari Academy had accepted her, and she still thought of him as the one who *knew*, the one who could answer all her bewildered questions if he wanted to.

'You're about the least discreet person I know,' he had said, laughing. 'But you do know how to keep your mouth shut when it matters. And they could hardly send someone like DiCapra, now, could they?'

No, they couldn't. She knew now that they sent her instead because she was what the city people called 'a rustic' and used to dealing with 'the common sort'. By which they meant that she did not expect her boots to be polished for her every time she stayed at an inn, the way some of her fellow apprentices such as DiCapra did. Nor did she sound as if she had spent her entire life giving orders to city servants every time she opened her mouth. Sometimes, though, she thought her masters were not entirely aware that common people in Essford did not talk exactly like common people in Three Valleys, where she had grown up. To the high and mighty, anything that wasn't Breda posh was probably just 'peasant-like'. When she had to be *discreet* in Essford and other places, she tried to talk as little as possible. A girl who sounded like a stranger was automatically considered no-good travelling trash and treated accordingly. Such girls were not thought decent. How could they be? Decent girls stayed at home, never venturing more than a day's journey from the place they were born. It was often easier for Kat to pretend to be a boy, the way she had done two years ago when she first left her mother's inn. But she was fourteen years old now, a grown-up, more or less, and it had become harder and harder to hide the fact that she *was* a girl. Should she tell her superiors about this difficulty, or would they only laugh?

She would have liked to ask Simon about that too. But he was posted to Three Valleys now, and absent most of the time. She felt bereft without him.

A small wiry man shoved past her, forcing Rane to sidestep so that Kat's knee brushed a whitewashed wall.

He threw her a belligerent look in passing, as if daring her to complain.

'Hey . . .' she began, and then thought better of it. It doesn't matter if they see you, as long as they don't notice you, she reminded herself. Starting a quarrel at the city gates was perhaps not the best way to stay unnoticed. She reined in her temper and held back a tart remark. Let the man take her place. She would still get there, wouldn't she?

Suddenly, there was a commotion at the back.

'Make way,' someone shouted, rather desperately. 'Make way!'

In this crowd? thought Kat. Where are we supposed to make way *to*? But people did move, and with surprising speed too. Horses tossed their heads in sudden panic, frantic carters shoved their own carts into the gutter. And then she saw it.

A silver phantom rushing nearer at great speed. A horse, yet not a horse . . . too slim, too fast, too dangerous . . . too *shiny*.

It was a hellhorse, its Rider bent across its withers, barely slowing as he reached the edges of the crowd. The pair clattered down the path that had suddenly opened up for them, and Kat could feel the stillness, the fear and fascination that held the crowd. Despite herself, she stared. Despite nearly two years of working with the creatures, nearly two years of learning their ways, still, she stared.

They were beautiful.

Beautiful enough to stop the breath, deadly enough to

smash and tear the packed and vulnerable human bodies lining the narrow trail. But the Rider's control did not waver, and Kat felt a burst of fierce pride and hope. This was her world too, this beauty, this speed! And one day, one day soon, perhaps . . . one of these brilliant creatures might be hers.

The hellhorse halted. Its orange-golden gaze caught Kat's, its nostrils flared in curiosity. She knew it had sensed the fierceness of her hope amidst the general buzz of fear – sensed it, and wondered at it. The bredinari froze on its back, eyes flickering over the crowd and finally coming to rest on Kat too.

Oh, damn, thought Kat. So much for staying unnoticed!

The Rider opened his mouth, and she ducked her head rapidly. Shut up! she urged him silently. Ride on! Don't make it worse than it already is . . .

She knew him from the Castle – not to talk to, just one of the elite group of older experienced Riders she wanted to belong to one day. Zenith was the name of the hellhorse. Flustered, she couldn't at the moment remember his.

Had he recognized her? There were few enough girls at the Academy, and she had gained some unwanted notoriety in her time there.

If he had, he was too clever to show it. He urged the hellhorse onward, not quite at their earlier breakneck pace but fast enough to be gone from Kat's sight within seconds. She breathed again.

'Damn demons,' muttered the man who had taken Kat's place in the line. 'A hazard to decent folks, they are.'

A big florid woman turned and glared at him.

'Shut your mouth,' she snapped. 'They are the Bredani's own messengers. Her word, her law. Show some respect!'

The man shifted uneasily.

'I'm just saying—'

'Well, you go say it somewhere else. This town is loyal to the Bredani *and* to her Riders, and you had better be too!'

The man muttered something under his breath, but apparently decided that discretion was the better part of valour. Looking at the set of the woman's mouth and the size of her forearms, Kat didn't blame him.

The crowd began to move forward again, more slowly even than before. Kat sighed. She thought with envy of Zenith's Rider, who would probably be at the bredinari post station already, helpers swarming to care for him and his mount. No such luxury for her. Once she got past the gates, she would have to find somewhere to leave Rane. Probably a tethering post, which meant she had to pay some horse keeper to watch him, or he might not be there when she came back. She squinted at the sun. At this rate, it would be midday before she found the meeting place where she was supposed to hand over the sealed orders she carried. If she could find the man they were meant for, of course. What if he had gone by then?

*

Finally she found the part of the market where caravan masters hired men for the summer's journeying. There was a gravel track where men and boys could show off their riding and driving skills, and a small rope-circled ring for the fighters – those who were trying to impress the masters into hiring them as guards.

A sizeable crowd had gathered round the fighting ring, and Kat could hear the bell-like chime of sword against sword. There was an impressive rapidity to the sounds – strokes were given and parried, it seemed, with quite amazing speed. Curious, Kat wove her way through the crowd until she could see what was going on.

Both of the swordfighters were young, and they had the same very pale flaxen hair. Probably they were brothers; in any event, they were clearly used to training together. They whirled round the ring, raining blows on one another, with a throwaway recklessness that made Kat draw in her breath, half-expecting the blades to bite into an arm, a chest or a neck. Yet the parry always came just in time, and the brothers continued unscathed. It was a breathtaking display even to Kat, who was used to watching some of the best swordfighters of the realm every day. She was reminded of Lusiana Ceuta, her best friend among the apprentices at the Castle. Lu was incredibly good, but could she hold her own against such dazzling speed?

The brothers (if that was what they were) finally broke off, and there were people in the crowd who began to clap and stamp, as if they had just seen a group of jugglers perform. One of the brothers, the tallest one, gave a little bow;

the other seemed to be more indifferent to that kind of applause. He dabbed the sweat from his brow with the end of his blue sash and rolled his shoulders as if to rid them of some stiffness.

Not far from Kat, a man snorted.

'Well, that was a fine show,' he said, somehow making the word *show* stand out, and suddenly Kat saw the brothers in a different light. The man was right – what she had seen *was* a show, a carefully orchestrated performance designed to show off. Somehow she doubted that her Swordmaster at the Castle, Master Haryn, would have been much impressed. And perhaps Lu would not have done so badly against the brothers after all.

The one who had bowed turned his head quickly to see who had spoken.

'Perhaps you can do better?' he asked, and from the way his eyes shifted, Kat could tell that he still wasn't sure who the speaker was.

'I can certainly give you a real workout instead,' growled the man, ducking into the ring. 'If you want to, of course . . .' The challenge in his voice made it sound more like *If you dare*. But actually the brothers' new opponent did not look too fearsome. He stood only about shoulder-high to the taller of the brothers, and was probably twice his age. His beard was grizzled, and the width of his shoulders not terribly impressive.

The taller brother laughed. 'Aren't you a little old for this kind of dancing?' he asked. 'Are you sure you can keep up with the music?'

'Try me,' said the oldster. 'Who knows? I might have a

few moves you've never heard of.' He drew his sword, and that appeared to be it. No blade-swishing or shoulder-rolling, or any other kind of warm-up. He just looked ready. And Kat could tell from his stance that he had been properly taught at some point in his long past, because not even Master Haryn would have faulted his balance.

The brother noted this, and gave a small nod of recognition. Then he launched his first attack – a sweeping slash at the neck, followed by a feint at the chest, then the neck again, then a low thrust, and finally a long, beautiful lunge at the heart. It was done very smoothly and at a ferocious speed, but it was a pattern the oldtimer had just seen the brothers use with one another. He parried the first four blows with no apparent trouble, then stepped out of the way of the lunge in a quick turn that brought him side to side with his opponent. With his free hand, he grabbed the tall fighter by the back of the neck, then kicked his legs from under him and slammed him into the gravel. The young man barely had time to stretch out his arm so as not to fall on his own sword. The old man stepped on his wrist, and that was the end of that duel.

The other brother watched with expressionless intensity.

'What's your name, old man?'

'Horsa. But most people call me Raven.'

'You don't exactly fight by the rules, Raven.'

'You know what? Neither do highwaymen,' said Raven.

*

Kat followed Raven carefully when he left the ring, heading for the beer tent an enterprising innkeeper had set up at the edge of the caravan area. She bought herself a mug of beer, as he had done, and when he sat down, she sat down at the same table. There were other beer-drinkers aplenty, but this early in the day the place was not yet completely crowded. They had the table to themselves.

'Trivallia,' she said.

'Yes, I remember you, greyling. What have you got for me today?'

Under cover of the table she slid him a sealed pouch and a leather tube of the kind couriers used for written messages. Like the pouch it had been sealed so that the recipient could be certain no prying eyes had seen the letter inside.

'Wages,' she said. 'And new orders.'

He weighed the pouch in his hand, but let it disappear inside his shirt without opening it. The sealed orders followed, but he did not appear very satisfied.

'That's all very well,' he growled, 'but the high lords and ladies of Breda seem to think I can read. I can't'. He looked at her sideways. 'Can you?'

'I suppose so,' she said hesitantly. She did not read as fluently as the other apprentices, not yet, though she was improving. But why did he ask? She couldn't – he couldn't think that –

'Oh no. You can't mean . . .' she began.

'Why not? Better you than some crook of a market-clerk.'

'But . . . they're your *orders* . . .' Never look at what you are carrying. *Never* read a sealed order. Though she had only served as a courier for a year, the rules were practically engraved on her skin, and she had never before even glanced at the messages she had carried. Reading ordinary mail could cost her her place at the Castle. Reading sealed orders . . . The punishment for that was *years* of hard labour in the mines, or so she had heard.

'Relax,' said Raven, emptying his mug in one long swallow. He wiped his mouth with the back of his hand and burped with obvious pleasure. 'It's not like you broke the seal, now, is it? You brought me my orders right and proper and by the book. If I ask you to read them to me afterwards – well, that's really no concern of the lords and ladies. Come on, finish that beer and let us find a quiet corner.'

Kat looked dubiously at her half-full mug. She was not at all sure that her commander-in-chief, the austere Dom-Primus Alvar Alcedina, would agree with Raven's casual view of such things.

'Come on,' said Raven once more. 'Who's to know? I won't tell if you don't . . .' He smiled at her, and his brown eyes suddenly held a glint she was more used to seeing in the glances of younger men. For some reason she was reminded of the tale of the Sea Witch who lured a fair-haired youth into very perilous waters with much the same words. But Raven was hardly a witch of any kind, and this was, of course, completely different. Wasn't it?

She finished her beer. It was a shame to gulp it down like that – it was very nice beer. Not as good as her mother's, perhaps, but not bad at all.

'Where are we going?' she asked, and knew in her heart of hearts that she was agreeing to this because she was curious. What might such 'discreet' orders contain? And who were they from? The pouch had been heavy, so Raven was evidently paid well for his services.

'Let's just take a little walk. Find some place where there are not quite so many people about.'

It wasn't easy to escape the market crowds of Essford. Luckily, Raven knew his way around and led her away from Market Square, down a side street to the banks of the River Ess. There were people here too, loading and unloading the squat-looking barges, or offering their goods for sale directly from the boats. There was a sharp, mildewed odour in the air, a smell of river and fish and things that have been in the water too long. She followed Raven down some narrow slippery steps to the towpath. This was where the chunky, powerful barge horses walked, towing the barges and their loads upstream, but right now she and Raven had it almost to themselves. They walked downstream a bit, until the river traffic thinned and the shouts of the vendors faded behind them.

'Right,' said Raven, squatting down to sit on the low wall bordering the river. 'Won't find a better spot anywhere inside the city walls. 'Here. Sit. Pretend you're admiring the pretty boats.'

Kat did as she was told, even though she did not feel entirely comfortable dangling her legs above the slow olive-green waters of the river. She wasn't about to admit her unease to Raven, though. Raven fished out his orders and broke the seal with a small folding knife.

'Here you go,' he said, handing her the papers. 'Now, if you would be so good as to let me know what my lofty masters wish me to do this season . . . and afterwards you can help me write a few things down for you to take back to them.'

'Isn't it a little impractical not to be able to read for a man who . . . a man in your profession?' said Kat, picking at the papers without unrolling them.

'Hell, yes.' He cleared his throat noisily and spat into the river. 'I did have a partner, you see. He took care of all the paperwork. But this winter he went and got himself a dose of lung fever. Six days, and that was him done for. Hell of a way to die, heaving and gurgling and turning blue in the face. Like drowning very slowly.' He shuddered. 'It's why I do this, you know.' He glared at her angrily, though she didn't quite understand why. What was she supposed to have done? 'So that one day I won't have to travel the roads in winter. So that one day a man might have a home somewhere, with a wife who wouldn't toss me out in the morning, and maybe even a couple of kids I could be sure were my own . . .'

'But you can't buy things like that . . .' said Kat hesitantly.

'No? You'd be surprised how much affection a man encounters when his purse is full. And at the very least I would be able to pay for a roof over my head, and a decent fire when *I* want one. No way am I going to end up in the back of a two-wheel cart, coughing my lungs out!' Again that furious look – and this time she got it. All she had done to deserve his anger was to be born a girl.

She was female – like the maestras, who controlled the land and every house on it, and who held the power in Breda. Female like the women – probably quite a few – who had taken Raven to their beds for a night or two, only to 'toss him out' in the morning. That she was no maestra and in a sense had no more home than he did probably did not count in Raven's way of reckoning things.

She gazed into the murky waters of the river. So many men felt the way Raven did. Even her stepfather Cornelius suffered a constant nagging dread that one day Tess would throw him out on his ear, despite the fact that Tess had actually *married* him, contrary to all Bredani decency and custom. Kat knew that fear very well indeed. She had used it, again and again, whenever she had wanted to hurt Cornelius. And again and again, he had become shaken and furious and lost his grip on his temper. That was when he had hit her, if he could catch her. Finally it had reached a point where Tess had had to act. And her solution had been to send her eldest daughter away, again contrary to all Bredani decency and custom. So in a way, Cornelius's fear of becoming homeless had made *Kat* homeless. Oh yes, she knew it well, that fear.

And yet she could not think ill of the women who had sent Raven on his way those many mornings. That was the way it was done. Maestras were supposed to have no other mate than the spirit of the land they ruled. And if one were to go against custom and risk the wrath of the Locus priestesses . . . well, few women would pick someone like Raven. There was a glint in his brown eyes, to be sure, and though he was no athlete to look at, still, one could see that he knew how to use his body, for work, for fighting, and perhaps for other things as well. But apart from that . . . he certainly was no beauty, with the bulldog set of his mouth, and the nose that showed signs of having been broken. He spoke rudely, and tended to spit, burp and scratch himself with little delicacy. Kat doubted that he owned a handkerchief. And while he didn't stink – not quite – there was still that certain ripeness to his smell that was usual among people who did not have easy access to hot water every day.

'Well?' he said, still with that angry look. 'What are you waiting for?' As if that was one more thing for him to hold against her: she could read and write, and he couldn't.

She smoothed the paper and began to read.

'To Horsa Guardsman, given this Spring Month of the seventeenth year of the rule of Our Blessed Bredani Cora Duodecima, that he may know his duties to the Bredani and be—'

'Skip that bit,' muttered Raven. 'All that muck about "serving faithfully", and so on. Where do they want me to take hire?'

Kat skimmed through the introductory sentences as quickly as she could.

'It is the will of the Bredani that he take hire this season with a southbound caravan, and that he observe and mark down his observations, his reports to be delivered at the following post stations . . .' She broke off. 'How are you going to do that?'

'I'll have to get a new partner, then, won't I? Damn it

all.' He spat into the river once more. 'So, southbound. What else?'

Her eyes returned to the paper.

'And that he be especially mindful of any mention of the following persons . . .' A list of twenty-three people followed, most of them men, with descriptions of their appearances and, in most cases, the crimes they had committed. Most were listed by name – one of them had three, it appeared, and switched between them. It was a lot to take in, thought Kat.

'Can you really remember all this?' she said. 'Just . . . in your head?'

'Just because I can't read doesn't mean I'm stupid,' said Raven in an offended tone, and rattled off the string of descriptions like some sort of weird street rhyme. He did not miss a single name and made very few mistakes in the descriptions.

'Wow!' said Kat. 'I couldn't have done that.'

'In my "profession", as you so daintily call it, it pays to keep stuff in your head instead of on paper. And they don't pay me just for my good looks, you know.'

All the same, he had Kat read the list to him once more before she went on.

'If he encounters any of these persons, he must without delay ride to the nearest post station and send word to Breda by fast courier. If a bredinari Rider is present, immediate arrest may be made of the following . . .' and the first eleven names on the list were mentioned again. 'In addition, as regards the Southland, the following is of particular concern to the Bredani: all military movement, any civil unrest, the price of iron (ore and worked iron both), the price of bread and other victuals, any foreign presence whatsoever, as well as marriages and rumours of marriages in the families Bartelin, Martlin, Horsalin, Pavlin, Arlin, Karelin, and Sibast-Mikélin. Of most particular interest, any rumours regarding Madalena Bartelin, any word of ill health or deaths among the ruling families, especially Regent Jakobus Martlin and his Queen, must be reported. Given by his hand and seal, Alvar Alcedina, DomPrimus Bredinari.'

'Military movements, civil unrest, food prices, iron prices, foreigners, and marriages, death and illness among the high-borns . . .' muttered Raven. 'Right. Think I've got that. Is that it?'

'That's it,' said Kat, feeling dizzy. Alvar Alcedina. She had just read a set of sealed orders given by the Dom-Primus himself. Oh, no. She could almost feel his glacial blue eyes boring into her from more than ninety miles away. Oh, Sweet Our Lady, let him never, ever, ever find out. He didn't like her as it was, had called her 'the insubordinate little Vale girl', and the fact that he had had to take her back after having once expelled her probably had not made him any fonder.

'You got anything to write with?' asked Raven.

She nodded. That was another thing that was drilled into the apprentices: no matter how short the trip, some items *had* to be carried on your person. Ink, pen and paper were three of the must-haves.

'Good. Now, write this down for me . . .'

And she did, with a barrel-lid for a desk and her very

best handwriting. She knew there would be spelling errors. Try as she might, she was still not up to Academy standards when it came to reading and writing. But then, who said Raven's late partner had been so perfect?

A gull cried out somewhere above the river, and from time to time a couple of fishwives or a sweaty, bare-chested bargeman passed by, but other than that, they were left undisturbed. It was only just after midday when Raven rolled up his newly written report, pushed it gently into the leather tube, and sealed it with a small lump of wax he warmed in his hand. He had no fancy signet ring, but he took a small wooden stamp from his purse and impressed his mark into the wax: a somewhat clumsy bird-shape, not all that raven-like, but equally effective for all that. The recipient would be able to tell that the tube had not been tampered with since leaving Raven's care. That the courier had written the whole message for him was a fact that Kat hoped devotedly would remain a secret between him and her.

'That's that, then,' said Raven in a satisfied voice. 'I'd better get back up to the caravan grounds and get myself a southbound hire while there are still people up there who remember my little show in the ring.'

He grinned, spat into the waters one last time, and got up to leave.

'See you around, greyling girl. Behave yourself . . .'

'Goodbye,' she said, but he had already dodged into an alley between two merchant yards, and she wasn't sure he had heard her.

*

On her way back to get Rane, she discovered she had a list of wanted people in her head: Carter Betran Annas, battery and death. Georgi Northman, alias the Bear, murder and highway robbery. Oline Ellisdaughter, robbery, blackmail and grievous bodily harm . . . and so on, and so forth. She was not at all sure she could rattle off the entire list of twenty-three, like Raven could, but quite a lot had stuck in her mind without her willing it. Not all were criminals; there were some missing persons too, and others who were sought after with no reason given – an entire family troupe of entertainers, for instance. They could hardly all be robbers and murderers, thought Kat – the youngest child was only nine . . .

'Forget about it,' she told herself under her breath. It was none of her business. It was knowledge she should never have had. But trying to forget it only made the litany stick more thoroughly in her mind, it seemed. It rattled through her brain like some tune she couldn't get out of her head, even while she paid the horse keeper his money, saddled Rane, and headed for the gates. Jehan 'the Mole' Elfors, grievous bodily harm. Unknown man, aged about twenty, called the Blazer, harassment, arson and murder . . .

Stop it, she hissed silently at herself, and urged Rane into a reluctant trot, as if leaving Essford behind would make forgetting easier. You are not supposed to know this; you shouldn't have read those damn orders; just *stop* it.

Once again, she thought of Alvar Alcedina and the blueness of his ice-cold glare. She bit her lip. Please, please. *Don't* let him ever find out.

SIMON

The trip from Essford to Breda was a six-day ride for a robust but not particularly fast horse like Rane. On the evening of the sixth day, Kat rode in through the North Gate and let her tired bay gelding lumber up the Ridderway, the shortest route to the Castle itself. The weather had been horrible for two days straight – one shower chasing the other so quickly that nothing had time to dry out in the short clear spells in between. Trees and eaves were still dripping from the last one, and in the gutter, ice-grey lumps of hail were slowly melting. Now, when it hardly mattered one way or the other, the sun broke through the cover of blue-black cloud, streaking the sky with gold and purple. The wet leaves glistened, and even in the gutters the melting hail was touched with a sparkle of colour, as if it were pearls or rare gemstones.

Shutters were flung open on both sides of the street to catch the freshness of recent rain. Cooking smells wafted past Kat's nostrils, and her stomach growled hungrily.

'Come *on*, Rane,' she urged the gelding and prodded

him slightly with her heel. Rane hung his head and looked put-upon, but he was a sturdy little horse, and Kat knew that a day's travel at moderate pace had not exhausted him as thoroughly as he would like to have her believe. 'We're nearly home!'

Home. Odd that the word now came so easily – there had been a time when she would have sworn she would never learn to call this city and its Academy home. When she had first come here, a year and a half ago, she had been plain terrified of the place. And for many months she had rattled around, unable to get her bearings, not just in the castle and the city but with the people too.

'Why, it's little Trivallia! Good evening to you, my girl.'

The cheerful greeting came from Agnes Tailor, standing in the doorway of her small red house, shaking out a tablecloth. She had a son in the castle guards and regarded anyone from 'up there' as family of sorts.

'Good evening, Agnes,' answered Kat. 'How is the knee?'

'Oh Lady, in this weather? Not good, child, not good. But I get by.' Agnes shook out the blue-chequered cloth with such vigour that Rane's head came up with a jerk. Momentarily, he forgot to look like a worn-out, ill-treated, put-upon old hack.

'And where did they send you this time? Spring Market in Essford?'

Kat smiled. 'How did you know?'

'Six days out, six days home. Where else would you have been? But they might have given you one of the silver devils to ride for such a long journey. You would have been back days ago, now, wouldn't you?'

From her house on the Ridderway Agnes kept a busy eye on everything that passed through the North Gate, and Kat sometimes wondered whether she did not have a better picture of what went on in Breda, or at least in Breda's northerly districts, than even Alvar Alcedina himself. She certainly didn't miss much.

'It would have been quicker, yes. But I'm still just a prentice, so I have to make do with an ordinary horse most times.'

She rubbed Rane's withers, which inspired him to raise his upper lip and make horrible faces from sheer pleasure. Agnes chuckled.

'Ordinary he is not, that one. He's a better actor than Marduke Monkeyface, so he is.'

'I have to get on, Agnes. I hope your knee gets better soon.'

'Wait a minute, child. Let me get you a glass of my good cider, at least. I know they let you have neither food nor drink until after your reporting is all done. And after such a ride too! Six days in the worst of spring weathers. That's no way to treat a growing child.'

'Thanks, Agnes.' Kat emptied the glass in two draughts. It was fresh and cool and apple-scented, and it eased her faintly aching throat. 'This is very good. And now I really do have to go.'

'You're welcome, child. Give my love to Alvin if you see him . . .'

'I will.' Kat squeezed Rane's warm belly with her

frozen legs, and this seemed to remind the gelding what an abused horse he really was. He grunted and staggered on. Perhaps Agnes was right, thought Kat. Rane really might be a better actor than Marduke Monkeyface. It wasn't till they reached the last sharp rise leading up to the castle gate that he dropped his monkeying, picked up his pace and pricked up his ears, intent on the prospect of a good feed, a warm stable and a good rubdown.

'Glory be,' said one of the guardsmen at the gate to his partner. 'Have you ever seen such sorry-looking riff-raff? Are we really supposed to let in this scarecrow?'

'Oh, shut up, Claudi,' snarled Kat. 'What do you think you would look like if you had been soaked to the skin seven times in two days?'

'That's no scarecrow,' said the other guardsman as if Kat hadn't spoken. 'That's just Trivallia in her civvies. Always looks like that on her days off.'

'Veeeery funny. Now, will you let me in?'

'Better let her pass, Claudi. She's a real terror when she gets angry. Or do you want to end up like Ermine?'

The guardsmen both laughed, but this was no laughing matter to Kat. Ermine – Tedora Mustela – was dead. That he had wanted it, that he himself had leaned on the blade until it pierced his emaciated body – all this did not change the fact that it had been Kat's hand holding the sword. Her stomach turned into a hard frozen lump every time she thought of it. She would never be able to forget it; there were nights when she woke up crying because she had been back in Ermine's valley in her dreams, with the night full of screams and blazing fires, reliving it all, and in particular Ermine's strange little smile when he leaned forward, forcing her to pierce his heart . . . She hated it when people reminded her of it, and even more so when they did it like this, casually, with a grin, as if Ermine had been a joke and not a real human being full of dreams and pain and cruelty and longing. A human being who had been alive and was now dead.

She couldn't say all this to the guardsmen. So she just sat there squarely on Rane's back, waiting without expression until they finally tired of their joking and let her through the gate.

Rane made straight for the stone trough in the middle of the forecourt and sank his muzzle thirstily into the cool water. Kat could feel his flanks moving for each long, deep swallow. She swung down off his back and loosened the girth so that he could drink more freely. A boy who looked to be no more than ten or so emerged from the stables, and Kat was reminded strongly of her own younger brother Nicolas.

'You're new, aren't you?' she asked.

He nodded. 'But I know my business!' He gave her a belligerent glare, as if daring her to question him. But she didn't doubt him. Back home in Three Valleys, she herself had looked after the horses coming to her mother's inn from the age of seven or eight.

'Good,' she said. 'This is Rane. Look after him, will you? He has had a long ride.'

She watched as the boy took the gelding's reins and led him into the stables. Normally she preferred to see to her mount herself, but the Masters accepted no delay when one came in off an assignment like this one. She crossed the yard and wearily ascended the staircase that led up to the bredinari guardroom.

'Prentice Trivallia, returning from Essford,' she said. 'I'm to report to Master Aureus.'

The Duty Officer looked at her across the top of the report he was reading.

'Have a seat, Trivallia. There's a bit of a queue, but it won't be too long.'

The guardroom was far from luxurious. The floor-boards were bare and dusty, and the only thing decorating the whitewashed walls was a blackboard on which the duty roster was noted in chalk. There was a good cast-iron stove giving off enough heat to make the air shimmer, a bench for the waiting Riders to perch on, a desk and chair for the Duty Officer, and a lamp in severe need of a trim. Three doors led off to other rooms. Kat watched the one on the left most keenly. Behind it, she knew, was Master Aureus's office.

The bench was no marvel of comfort, but it was still better than a saddle. Next to her sat a Rider she didn't know. His grey leather breeches were spattered with mud, and his cloak smelled of wet wool. Probably he too had been caught by the spring showers. He leaned back against the wall with his eyes closed, and she did not disturb him.

Some minutes later, the door she was watching opened gently.

'I'm ready for you now, Rider Tales,' called Master

Aureus. 'Come on in. And good evening, Trivallia. You will be next.'

The bredinari opened his eyes, and it seemed he had actually managed to fall asleep, upright on the wooden bench. He looked dazed and he stumbled as he rose to his feet.

'Good evening, Master,' said Kat politely, hoping the sleepy Rider would not be too slow in his reporting. She was almost envious of Rane, who was no doubt already halfway through his dinner and tucked away in a stall full of good clean bedding. The bredinari followed Master Aureus into his office, and the door closed behind them. It was a heavy door, and not so much as a murmur could be heard once it was closed.

Aureus was not a name as such, it was a title, meaning simply Ear. It was a good title, thought Kat, because that was exactly the Master's job: to be the ears of the Bredani and listen to everything that went on in Breda, from the loudest of conflicts to the most secret whispers. There was a Master Oculus too, the Eye of the Bredani, but his office dealt mainly with cartography and mining. It was Master Aureus and his people who did all the 'discreet' work in Breda.

One of the other doors opened, but no one came out. Then there was a sharp voice from inside.

'That is my final word on the matter, Jossa. You may go.'

Kat straightened as if someone had pricked her with a needle. Jossa! Was it Simon? He was not the only one in the corps who came from Jos, but—

Why didn't anyone come through the door?

There was a pause, much, much too long – no proper bredinari ought to hesitate so long before obeying a direct order to leave. Then, at last, a familiar form filled the doorframe. Tall but not all that wide. Dark hair, looking wet and dishevelled at the moment. And a gliding, careful way of walking, as if he was holding something that might explode. He had grown a beard, she saw, covering the scar on his chin where she had once bitten him. But it was most definitely him.

'Simon,' she said hoarsely, getting up. She wanted to throw her arms around him and hug him, but it wouldn't do – not here, not now, with the Duty Officer watching and an open door behind which was that sharp voice, the one that had said *That is my final word* as if it was the end of an argument.

It was almost as if he didn't see her.

'Kat,' he said. And that was all. He was always so good at hiding his feelings, was Simon, and his face was perfectly expressionless. But his anger, his utter fury, shimmered around him like the heat from the stove.

'What's wrong?' she said, without thinking. Because of course he couldn't give her an answer right now. The Duty Officer had given up any pretence of report studying and was watching openly.

'Nothing,' said Simon. And his anger overwhelmed his defences after all. 'Nothing except the usual – that the corps doesn't give a damn about the borderlands. I don't know why it keeps surprising me. I ought to know by now!'

'That will do, Jossa!' The sharp voice cut the air like a whiplash, and Kat's heart skipped a beat when she saw to whom it belonged. In the door behind Simon stood DomFelix Lisabetta Strigius, Alvar Alcedina's second-in-command 'to the right', as it was called. Apart from Alcedina himself, Simon could not have picked a higher ranking officer to show his rebellious fury to.

Simon held his tongue, but the silence cost him and the effort showed. DomFelix Strigius watched him with a narrowed eye.

'The courage and intelligence you showed in the Tedora Mustela case has given you the chance of a new and better start in the corps,' she said, her voice only slightly less sharp. 'I would advise you not to jeopardize it with a string of black marks for insubordination.'

'Yes, DomFelix,' said Simon without opening his mouth very much. It was almost as if he was afraid what else might slip out.

'Goodnight, Jossa,'

'Goodnight, DomFelix.' Simon offered her the small bow prescribed by regulations – the bredinari never saluted anyone, not even the Bredani herself. Salutes were for guardsmen and ordinary soldiers. He left the guardroom with only a brief sideways glance at Kat. Lisabetta Strigius stood with her arms crossed and watched him leave. Then her glance fell on Kat.

'You are the Trivallia girl, aren't you?'

'Yes, DomFelix,' said Kat, wondering when she would lose that irritating 'girl' thing.

'Step into my office for a moment, Trivallia.'

'Yes, DomFelix.' Why? Because of the things she had just heard Simon say?

The room was as simple as the guardroom, with just a table and two chairs. No doubt Lisabetta Strigius's own office was more elaborate, but if she was aware of the lack of comforts she certainly didn't show it. She sat without ceremony behind the table, but made no move to offer Kat the other chair.

'Trivallia,' she said consideringly. 'You played quite a notable part in the Mustela affair yourself.' For the second time that evening, Kat was reminded of Ermine's death. She nodded slowly.

'How do you see Jossa? As a friend?'

'Yes,' said Kat. 'He's my friend.'

'Then you will wish to help him?'

'Yes.' Why did she ask? Of course Kat would help Simon if she could, but what was that to DomFelix Strigius?

'As you saw, Rider Jossa was not as composed as he ought to have been. He was angry and dissatisfied with his given orders.' There was a pause, as if the woman behind the desk was waiting for Kat to say something. But what? Kat had no idea, and thought it wisest to keep her mouth shut. Lisabetta Strigius had been born into one of the Seven, the handful of powerful families that ran almost all that was worth running as far as the capital was concerned. It showed in her manner. Authority came easily to her; trust and openness, on the other hand, were near impossible. Kat began to feel the same sort of wobbly insecurity she had felt the couple of times Alvar Alcedina or Felicia Capra-Mustela had spoken to her. You could never be certain the words meant what they seemed to mean. Lu would have known. Lu came from a fairly elevated family herself, and she knew how to read beneath the surface, though she often made a joke of it. 'You have to be careful,' she had once said. 'If you ask them the time, they think you want to negotiate a deal with them. And if you say it looks like rain, they take it as a declaration of war!' No, Kat felt safer saying as little as possible.

'People from the Borderlands often have difficulties fitting in here,' DomFelix Strigius finally continued. 'I'm sure you know a bit about that yourself.'

Oh yes, she knew that song. 'Scarecrow' and 'peasant brat' were among the more pleasant things she had been called. But surely this was not what had aroused Simon's anger so? It was a song he was quite familiar with himself, and he had taught her a lot about how to handle it. She threw a quick look at Lisabetta Strigius's face and still didn't say anything.

'Many people say that borderers are ignorant and uneducated, that they have difficulty in taking orders, that they lack proper discipline and loyalty to the Bredani.'

Yes, or that they are stupid, that they lie and steal, and that they smell bad, thought Kat. More or less like Travellers. There was a bitter taste in her mouth, and she wished that the DomFelix would get on with whatever it was she wanted to say, so that Kat could get out of there.

'I do not side with those who feel that borderers are not fit to be bredinari,' declared Lisabetta Strigius. 'On the contrary, we have many fine Riders that were born in the border regions. But Jossa must understand that it is unwise for a borderer to talk as he talks, and with such lack of temperance. I hope you can make him see that, Trivallia.' There was just the slightest emphasis on the name at the end, just a hint of a sting.

'Yes, DomFelix,' said Kat, hoping that that was all. And apparently it was. Lisabetta Strigius dismissed her with a nod, and Kat bowed and left.

Anger roiled inside her, almost as strongly as in Simon. Whatever it was that had caused Simon's fury, it would hardly have been soothed by listening to a hoity-toity Strigius noble-mindedly explaining that she had absolutely nothing against borderers as long as they knew their place. And that little sting at the end had not gone unnoticed by Kat. Trivallia was no posh old family name. It simply meant 'from Three Valleys', the way 'Jossa' meant 'from Jos'. Borderer, in other words. The message was clear: it would be just as unwise for Kat to open her mouth in the wrong places. The whole fancy rigmarole could be boiled down to two things: Keep your trap shut, and do what you can to shut Simon up too.

'Simon?'

She had looked for him at dinner in the refectory, but he wasn't there. Nor was he with Grizel, though she knew that he usually looked in on the hellhorse mare whenever he had had to let someone else stable her. Perhaps he was so angry still that he didn't dare get too close to her. Show fear and anger around the hellhorses and it was like pricking them with a knife, and Simon was much too experienced and responsible a Rider to inflict his uncontrolled emotions on Grizel.

So where? His old rooms had been taken over by another bredinari when he left to be permanently stationed at the old Resting Place in Tora's Vale, and the few times he had been back since then, he had stayed in the guest wing above the library. That was where she found him in the end.

'Simon, what happened?'

He turned, and she could see that even though he looked calmer, the anger was still there, guttering inside him. Only his careful self-control prevented him from pacing the floor and kicking the furniture.

'They called us home,' he said. 'Remus and me both.'

At first, Kat didn't see why that should anger him so.

'But isn't it nice to be back for a little while? If you never came to Breda, I wouldn't get to see you at all.'

'Oh, you'll see plenty of me now. This is no temporary leave. They closed the Resting Place. Or rather – they gave it to the Lodge Brothers.'

'To . . .' Kat was too stunned to finish her sentence. To the Lodge Brothers? But it was a Resting Place, meant to be a sanctuary for everyone who had to travel the roads. Shelter, rest and healing, the way it said above the door. To the people of the roads, the few Resting Places that remained were the difference between life and death sometimes. How could anyone give such a place to the Lodge Brothers? The lodges were basically just secret societies for men who wanted to run about in silly masks and feel important, thought Kat. There were seven of them, one for each of the Seven great families, and they enjoyed a lot of covert support and protection from people in high places. She began to understand Simon's anger. When he and Remus Varas had come to Tora's Vale a year and a half ago, the place had been a bleak shell, derelict and empty. They had worked like demons to restore it and bring it back to life, to fulfil its ancient purpose. In these difficult times, with more and more gangs and robbers harassing the border regions, the Resting Places were needed more sorely than ever. Breda provided her most distant regions with only the skimpiest protection. Kat had grown up without ever seeing a bredinari until the day Dorissa had ridden into the yard behind Crowfoot Inn, on a fabled beast the colour of silver, glowing even in the heavy autumn rain.

Many people never got to see such sights. To them, Breda was a city far away, and the Bredani a sort of fairy-tale figure with very little meaning in everyday life. When starvation, disease or robber gangs struck, you had to struggle through on your own or with a little help from you neighbours, because by and large, Breda didn't care. Except for people like Simon and Remus Varas, who tried to insist on the old-fashioned idea that service as a bredi-nari meant service to the people, not merely running messages for the high and the mighty of Breda.

'What happens now?' said Kat. 'To you, I mean. Where are you going next?'

Simon shrugged.

'They haven't made up their minds yet. After my

interview with the honoured DomFelix, I have been suspended from duty until further notice. She was kind enough to call it strain rather than insubordination.'

'Oh, Simon.'

'I should not have lost my temper like that. Normally, I am in better control.' He rubbed the bridge of his nose with two fingers, and looked tired. 'Perhaps she is right. Perhaps I am a little out of balance.'

'I don't think so. You had good reason to be angry.'

'Thank you. But I'm afraid your judgement doesn't really count. You're an ill-mannered border peasant yourself.' It was as if he saw her properly for the first time. 'You've grown, haven't you? And your hair is longer. But still as red . . .' He tugged gently at one of her ungovernable curls. 'Is everything well with you?'

'Well enough. Bruna says he thinks I might be ready for the Binding this year. So *maybe*, just maybe . . .' She didn't finish the sentence. It was as if saying it out loud might mean it wouldn't happen. It was almost time for this year's crop of foals to be weaned from their mothers. Seventeen silvery yearlings, on spindly long legs. Six were colts and had to be released on to the Mountain. And of the eleven fillies some would go to older Riders whose present mounts were due for retirement. But some . . . some would be given to the prentices, on Master Bruna's say-so. So *maybe* . . .

'Congratulations. You must have worked very hard.'

Kat nodded. Oh, yes. Hard work had certainly been needed. It was of course essential that Bruna approve of one's hellhorse skills. No prentice embarked on his or her

Primanotte – the first night of the Binding – without the Hellhorse Master's mark of favour. But the other Masters had their say as well, both the Arms Masters and those who taught letters and science. And Kat's book learning left much to be desired, at least compared to prentices who came from wealthier homes and had had the benefit of tutors practically since birth.

She was immensely proud that Bruna had passed her. And her heart beat faster every time she thought about the tantalizing possibility that soon, very soon, she might be allowed to attempt to bind a young hellhorse of her very own. A moment ago, that had seemed the most important thing in the world.

'Simon . . . will they . . . I mean . . . will they do anything to you? The DomFelix said . . .' She stuttered to a halt. She suddenly realized that she did not really want to tell him exactly what the DomFelix had said.

Simon watched her with his grey eyes, noting the signs of her reluctance, probably. She had never found it easy to hide things from him.

'So. She talked to you as well.'

Kat nodded. 'She said something about borderlanders . . .'

'Yes. I think I can imagine the rest of it.'

'Simon. Perhaps you should be . . . more careful. About what you say, I mean.'

Suddenly, Simon lost his anger. It felt like someone had just doused a bonfire with a bucket of water. He smiled.

'Imagine that. Words of caution out of your mouth, Firehead.' Again, he touched a lock of her hair with that same fond gentleness. 'You're right though. I gain nothing by losing my temper in the wrong places. And don't fret yourself – our Ermine catch still counts for something with the high and mighty. They'll let me cool my heels for a week or so, I imagine. And then they'll give me another assignment. And if I behave myself for a while, there may be another chance later, to start again somewhere else and make a Resting Place worthy of the name. But not, I'm afraid, in the Vales.' He slumped down on the bed that was temporarily his and reached for one of the saddlebags slung across the headboard. 'Here,' he said, fishing out three letters. 'They were lying around waiting for the next post Rider to Breda. I had no idea that Rider would be myself.'

They were all from Crowfoot Inn. A fat one – many pages from Tad, the mild-mannered cook who had taught Kat her letters, and many, many other things besides. Often she had wished that Tad might be her father, but she knew it wasn't so. Daughters weren't really supposed to concern themselves with fathers, seeing that they belonged to their mothers and to the land. But Kat had asked, once. Not Tess – she hadn't dared ask Tess – but there was nothing intimidating about Tad. 'Wish it were so, kitten,' he had said. 'But no. No such luck.' And she knew he wasn't lying, because Tad never lied. She fingered the thick bundle and felt a sharp pang of homesickness.

The one from Tess, typically, was much shorter. Tess was a practical woman who believed in getting to the point.

And then there was a third, addressed 'To Kat' in a hand she didn't recognize. A rather shaky hand, she thought. Whose? She opened that one first. And had to sniff and smile all at once, because this one was from Nicolas . . . Little Nicolas, who of course would not be quite so little any more – now that she thought about it, he was all of eleven years old and certainly no baby – not-so-little Nicolas had written his first letter.

'Have you seen them?' she asked Simon. 'Are they well?'

'Yes. They are all fine.'

But she knew him too well. Cold fingers touched her spine, because she heard the unspoken 'but' in his voice. He was holding something back.

'But what?' she said, sharply. 'What's wrong, Simon? Has something happened?'

'No, I told you. They are fine.' He looked at her and could probably tell that he would have to explain.

'It's just . . . Tess asked me to look into something.'

'What?'

'She said there were too many Southerners in the Vales.'

'What does she mean, too many? There are always Southerners in the Vales.' The Caravan Road to the South-lands, or Kernland as the Southerners themselves called it, cut straight through the Vales and right past Crowfoot Inn. Traffic was generally lively, and some Southerners stayed and settled in the Vales. It had always been that way. Kat's own stepfather Cornelius was one of them.

'I don't quite know what to make of it. But she is right.

Suddenly there *are* a lot more Southern men this spring. I reported it to Master Aureus, but I never heard anything. And then I was called back.' Anger flared up once more behind his careful equilibrium. 'What happened last winter, with Ermine and the hostages he took . . . When I think how I flew at Tess and yelled at her for not *saying* anything, for not letting the rest of the world help her. And now, when she finally does confide in me – I'm not there. I'm just *gone*.'

He flung his saddlebags across the head of the bed again. Being Simon, he didn't just throw them there, but put them carefully in their place. Kat knew he really wanted to kick and scream because he felt he had let Tess down, and it tore at him almost unbearably. She put a tentative hand on his shoulder.

'Simon . . . You didn't – I mean, it's not as if the Inn is on fire and you made off with the fire hose.'

For a moment he looked simply nonplussed. Then a faint smile curled his lips.

'I'm making too much of it, you think?'

Kat nodded. 'I don't rightly see how it matters. There are always Southerners in the Vales. What's a few more?'

Simon ran his fingers across the worn leather of the saddlebags, as if he were stroking a dog or a horse.

'You're probably right. But I still wish I was *there*.'

THE BLUE WAGON

Merian showed her pass to the guard, who merely waved them through with a yawn. It was early – so early that grey pre-dawn mist still softened the outlines of the Castle's stone walls. As Kat and Merian slipped through the gate, Kat had to hold back a giggle. Why did she feel like a child about to misbehave? They had done nothing wrong. It was Memory Day, they were off duty, and they had a perfectly legitimate full-day pass. Yet she still had a sense of treading a forbidden path.

'We have to hurry,' said Merian. 'I promised my cousin we would be there by sunrise.'

They ran down the Ridderway towards the North Gate, past the walls surrounding the grand estates, and then past less imposing red and yellow crafters' houses like that of Agnes Tailor, past workshops and merchants' yards and across Charcoal Market, where black-clad men were already arriving with their handcarts and their wares. Memory Day morning trade was the best of the week, but also short-lived; come noon, all the stalls would shut up shop and people would go to their family gatherings to sing the Memory Song and eat their Memory Day dinner in the place where they belonged.

'Please,' gasped Merian, hugging her sides and breathing hard. 'I need to – catch – my breath.'

'I thought you said we had to hurry,' Kat grinned, trying to disguise the fact that she was breathing nearly as hard.

Merian grimaced. 'Unlike you, I am not made of rock and mountain air.'

They continued at a more moderate trot through the North Gate. Here, outside the city walls proper, between the Caravan Road and the Grana River, it was as if the city had overflowed its bounds and deposited a flotsam neighbourhood. By and large, the people living here were not among the more well-to-do. Living outside the walls was not a thing to be boasted of. The streets were mostly unpaved, and when it rained, they turned into muddy gutters afloat with things that should have been more properly consigned to the middens. Kat and Merian turned into a narrow alley called Old Man's Street. On both sides of the throughway houses rose to as many as five storeys. They were hostels where men, if they could afford it, might rent a small room. They were cheaper than the inns, though not much, and men who had become too old for life on the roads had few other options. Here they might stay, at least till their money gave out. There might be a sour smell of pee and soot and offal, and not much in the way of light and fresh air, but it was better than putting up a shack on the riverfront among rats and thieves and seeing it torn down by the city guard every other month or so.

'Phew, what a stench!' said Kat. 'Are you sure this is it?'

'Yes . . .' said Merian, looking none too confident. 'He said Old Man's Street. Isn't there a gate down there at the end?'

There was – a heavy oaken gate with cast iron bosses above and below and around the lock. It bore a shield with the head of a beaver on it, a sign that this was the property of the Castor family. Kat looked up at the rodent face.

'They say a rat would have been more suitable,' she murmured under her breath. The Castor fortunes were made from Old Man's Street and other such miserable lodging houses, and it was hard to approve.

'Shhh . . .' said Merian. 'What if the gatekeeper hears you? And the wayfarers would be even worse off, wouldn't they, without people like the Castors?'

'Maybe.'

Merian pulled at the bell rope, and a small spyhole window opened in the gate.

'Yes?' A pair of suspicious eyes glared at them through the narrow slot.

'My cousin invited us,' said Merian and presented a wooden token to the guard. 'Abel Carter from Ormark. He is with Felis.' Felis was the leader of one of the largest caravans.

The glare did not soften.

'This is no place for Rider spawn,' said the guard. 'Why don't you stay up at the Castle where you belong?'

'I told you we should have changed,' muttered Kat.

'My cousin invited us,' repeated Merian in her stubbornest voice, and finally the guard accepted her token and closed the spyhole. They heard the bar sliding back, and then the gate opened.

'Come in, then,' said the gatekeeper. 'But no trouble, or you'll get your butts kicked, Rider spawn or no. This is private property, understand?'

'Yes, all right,' said Merian. 'May I have my token back? You might not be the only one with a suspicious mind.'

The gatekeeper scowled, but passed the small wooden badge back to Merian.

'Down the path and through the five-barred gate,' he said. 'Stay to the path and touch nothing before you are through the next gate. Anyone who as much as looks sideways at the house is in for a warm welcome. Understand?'

'Such hospitality!' said Merian. 'Yes, we understand.'

At the five-barred gate waited still more guards, dressed in the green and white colours of the Castors. Once again Merian presented her token, and they were grudgingly allowed to pass, although their grey apprentice uniforms drew yet more glares and suspicious comments.

'Sweet Our Lady, it's easier to get in to see the Bredani herself,' said Kat.

The object of this watchfulness seemed hardly worth

the guarding. Just a wide, empty field, shielded by a tall wooden fence. Well, not perhaps quite empty. In orderly rows stood forty or so wagons, some beautiful caravan homes, others more lowly baggage carts, mostly loaded with canvas, poles, planks and other building materials. Heavy draught horses grazed peacefully among the vehicles, and a large group of people, mostly men, were gathered in an uneven circle around a bright yellow caravan, yawning, chatting, and obviously waiting. Merian joined the throng, and after a bit of searching found Cousin Abel.

'Good morning,' he said. 'And high time, if I may say so. We're just about to begin.'

The words had barely left his mouth when the door of the yellow caravan opened and a tall dark-haired man came out to stand on the steps.

'Good morning, all,' he said. 'I won't keep you hanging about for any long speeches. The sun is up already, and we all want to get started. But there are a few changes in the plans from last year, so make sure you see your foremen before you begin. And the foremen this year are . . .' he ran off a list of names and responsibilities – fences, paving, east corner, west corner, latrines – 'or conveniences, if you prefer the posh version . . .', water supply, cooking sites, and so on. Merian's cousin was a foreman, it seemed, with the north corner stables as his special duty.

'And that's all, really. If you have a question, ask the foremen, or me, or one of the other four in the camp council. Right. Go to it!'

He hopped down off the steps, and as if that had been the starting signal for some sort of race, a frenzy of activity began, lasting well into the evening. And though Kat and Merian were part of it, heaving, hammering and lifting with the rest, running errands and pounding nails, digging and sawing and generally working as hard as they could, still they were left to stand open-mouthed and awestruck when evening fell and the lights came on in a city that had not been there that morning.

'It was a field,' said Kat, as if trying to make herself believe it. 'It was just a field.'

'Yes,' breathed Merian. 'And now look at it!'

There were streets lit by coloured lanterns. There were houses, castles, and palaces. That the walls and cupolas and towering spires were made from wood and painted canvas somehow did not lessen the miracle. Summertown had come to Breda, and here it would stay until autumn fell. Here, the crowds came to be amazed and bewildered, wined and dined, cheated and conned in the most entertaining fashion and picked clean of every copper they had to spend. Summertown was for everyone, high and low, traveller and city-born. And not until the autumn festival, when the last of the great caravans had passed through the City of Breda on its way to the northern seas, not until then would castles, grottoes and pagodas turn back into canvas again. In a single day all would disappear as quickly as it had arisen, and the wagons would split up and depart for cheaper winter quarters than might be had in the country's capital city.

'My poor body!' moaned Merian. 'I'm one big ache, and I don't think I have any actual skin left on my palms.'

'Your cousin knows how to keep a girl busy,' said Kat and stretched to ease her own aching back.

Merian snorted. 'A regular slave-driver, that's what he is.'

'Ungrateful wench,' grinned Abel. 'I seem to recall a different song when you were begging to be allowed to come. Dear Abel, Sweeeeet dear Abel . . .' he crooned in a falsetto voice meant to sound like Merian's. 'And when out of the goodness of my heart I give you what you ask for, this is the thanks I get? Slave-driver indeed!' He snapped his scarf like a whip and hit Merian across the back of her neck. 'But don't let me keep you. If you want to go on home, be my guest.'

'Are you crazy? Now comes the reward!'

Because this was the night when Summertown's inhabitants feted each other. They cooked for each other, poured the best beer and wine they had, they showed each other the most exquisite of the acts and tricks they had been practising all winter. Kat and Merian gaped in awe as magicians, acrobats and animal handlers vied to outdo each other in cleverness and courage. They listened as some of the best musicians in the land performed for the sheer love of music, and they cried together as Santerre of the Velvet Voice sang to them of distant cities and unrequited love. To these celebrations no outsider had access. The great public gate facing the Caravan Road was kept barred, and only those who could show a token could enter through the back door in Old Man's Street. It was dawn before the party slowed its pace.

'You know,' said Kat in a somewhat indistinct voice, 'I think I may be just a little bit drunk.'

Merian didn't answer. She was asleep.

Abel laughed. 'You two had better go and sleep it off in my caravan,' he said.

'Are you crazy?' gasped Kat. 'We have to get back to the Castle. I'm due back on duty at nine. Come on, Merian. Wake up!'

'I'm awake,' said Merian, and went back to sleep.

'Oh, no. Damn it, Merian!' Kat shook the sleeping girl so that her head lolled up and down.

'Ztop zat,' muttered Merian without opening her eyes.

Kat looked at her friend in exasperation. Resolutely, she grabbed the nearest carafe, which happened to contain water rather than wine. Merian coughed and sputtered as the contents splashed into her face, and finally sat up.

'What did you have to do that for?' she cried indignantly, water dripping from her hair and off the tip of her nose.

'We have to get back. We're due back on duty in . . . in . . . well, really soon now.'

'Sweet Our Lady! What time is it?'

'I don't know, but it's nearly day.'

On uncertain legs they hurried through the almost empty Summertown streets. The lanterns had long since been extinguished, but here and there on the steps of a caravan or at a beer house table little groups of revellers still clung to party mood, muttering the sort of deep thoughts and sentiments to each other that were best forgotten come morning. A guitarist and three other singers were trying for a four-part harmony, but kept collapsing into fits of laughter when one of them got it wrong.

Suddenly Kat came to a halt.

'What is it?' said Merian. 'Come on!'

'Wait a minute.' Kat stood staring at a caravan. A blue one, with a black roof and with the sign of a kingfisher painted above the door. Where had she . . .? And then she knew. Raven's orders. The orders she should never have seen, and which she had done her best to forget. But among the calls for information on the whereabouts of thieves and murderers and frauds, she remembered this one. She had wondered about them, because what could they possibly have done? A family troupe of entertainers, Sardi by name, travelling in a blue wagon with a black roof, under the sign of a kingfisher. And the youngest child only nine.

There were many blue caravans in Breda, most of them with black roofs. And in all of Breda, surely there was more than one family who had painted a kingfisher over their door. It was, after all, one of the Seven Original Beasts. But still . . .

'Come on,' said Merian, pulling on her arm. 'I don't know about you, but I absolutely have to have a bath and an hour in my bed if I'm going to make it through this day.'

Kat let herself be pulled along. What else could she do? She couldn't report this to anyone, because she wasn't properly supposed to know that her commander-in-chief was looking for a wagon like this one. And it might not even *be* this one. But still . . .

DANIEL

'I never want to get drunk again *ever*,' hissed Merian, and let her forehead sink down on to her arms.

'Just look at you,' said Lu. 'One more sickly than the other. Pathetic wrecks the pair of you. And you are supposed to be Breda's finest!'

'You're just jealous,' muttered Kat, leaning back so that she could rest her head ever so gently against the whitewashed wall of her room. It had been a *very* long day.

Lu grinned. 'No,' she said. 'Yesterday I was jealous, today I'm profoundly grateful.' Lu's family lived in Breda City, so she had to spend her Memory Days with them. This was not normally such an onerous duty, but the day before she had begrudged Merian and Kat their free and parentless condition quite a bit. Today, of course, was a different matter. Just to prove how healthy she was feeling, she swung up into an easy athletic handstand.

'Will you stop that?' said Kat. 'A person can get sick just by looking at you.'

Lu folded her well-trained body back into a head-up

position, narrowly missing the empty brazier on the way. Kat's room above the hospital ward was not exactly spacious, but it had a wonderful view of the fields where the hellhorse brood mares grazed. The only adult keeping an eye on her was Angia the Archivist, who was rather distant and absent-minded but generally well intentioned. She would usually let Kat make tea on the small hearth, and so it was mostly in Kat's room that the girls met once the chores of the day were over and done with.

Trying to look slightly more like 'Breda's finest', Kat straightened and sipped at her tea. She let her gaze fall first on one of her friends, then the other. Lu, with her frizzy black hair braided close to the skull and her nut-brown arms bare as usual, despite the evening chill. Merian, slouched uncharacteristically across the table, so that all that could be seen of her was her fine, straight blonde hair. They were so very different, her two best friends. Lu was really Domnessa Lusiana Ceuta, scion of one of Breda's foremost families; she had defied her mother to join the corps and become an apprentice bredinari. Merian, on the other hand, had been sent here from Ormark by her merchant parents as an emergency solution – it had been the only way to avoid marriage to the forty-five-year-old son of a Colmontian Matriarch without causing deadly offence. To Lu, wielding a sword or a crossbow was as natural as breathing. To Merian, it was an exotic art she had never before attempted. The hellhorses, such an endless source of fascination for Kat, were the stuff of nightmares to Merian. If you asked Merian, the very best thing about Breda was the castle library and its endless rows of books.

Lu and Merian. She felt lucky to have them. Although at the moment, she might wish she had never met Merian's cousin . . .

'Merian?'

'Mmmmh?'

'Your cousin Abel – does he know a lot of people in Summertown?'

'Mmmmh.'

'Most of them?'

Merian raised her head slowly. 'What are you up to, Kat? Why do you want to know?'

'No reason.'

'I know you. Have you managed to get yourself into trouble again?'

'No. Not really . . .'

Merian sighed. '"Not really" . . .' she mimicked, rolling her eyes at Lu. 'Is it me, or have we heard that before?'

'It sounds awfully familiar,' said Lu. 'Kat, do bear in mind that the yearling lists are due to be posted in just a few weeks, all right? This is no time to do anything stupid.'

Kat looked into the field below her window, at the leggy silvery fillies, one of which she wished so fervently to own.

'I won't do anything stupid,' she promised, hoping frantically that she hadn't already done so.

*

Six days went by before she had a chance to pay another visit to Summertown. Springtime was foaling season, and the apprentices were kept busy. She barely had time to snatch a moment with Simon now and then, although he was still kicking his heels in the guest quarters. But maybe that was just as well. He had a way of picking her secrets out of thin air, and she did not want him to pick this one. Reading forbidden orders . . . She could just imagine what Simon would have to say about that. She comforted herself with the thought that the orders had not said that the kingfisher caravan family had been criminals. She was probably worrying for no reason, and anyway, the wagon was in plain sight less than a stone's throw outside the city walls, so if Alvar Alcedina had his men out looking for it, someone else was sure to report it and let her off the hook. She would have another look, and maybe ask Abel a few questions, that was all, and if the owners of the blue caravan did not match the description Raven had been given, then, once again, she was off the hook. And if they did match . . . well, she would worry about that when she had to.

A lot had happened in Summertown in those six days. She realized now that the fantastic edifices she had seen on the night of the party had really only been the rough and ready outline of what was to come. Thousands of finishing touches had been added and the last and most vital ingredient in the magical potion had finally arrived: the audience. It was the evening of Waiting Day, and tomorrow most people had a day of rest. The crowd was so dense that Kat felt she was pushing through a sea of other people's elbows, bellies and rumps.

'We had better agree on a meeting point,' said Lu, 'else we'll never find each other again if we are separated.'

'Look,' said Kat, pointing. 'There's Merian's cousin's stall, the one with the giant music box on the roof. Let's meet there.'

'What is he selling?' asked Lu, craning her neck to see.

'Music boxes,' said Kat dryly. 'What else? And silk ribbons, and mirrors, and bells and other knick-knacks. Most of the stuff comes from Colmonte, Merian says. But the music boxes, those he makes himself.' She waved at Abel, but he was selling a pair of yellow ribbons to a pretty dark-haired girl, a task that seemed to take all his concentration.

'Oh, look!' breathed Lu. 'Sword dancers! Let's go and see them!'

'Can't we take a look around first?' Now, where was it she had seen the blue caravan?

'But the show is about to start! Oh, come on, Kat, I'll pay for both of us . . .'

'No need,' said Kat a little stiffly. She knew that Lu's family was rich and that the penny it cost to see the sword dancers was nothing to someone like her. But Kat had ended up in more than one fist fight because some of the other prentices mocked her for a peasant pauper, sponging off the posh Ceutas; accusations like that bit deep and were hard to forget.

'Don't be silly, Kat,' said Lu, who didn't understand. 'I'm the one who wants to see them. Come on!'

She tugged at Kat's arm, and Kat let herself be drawn into the sword dancers' tent.

Afterwards, she was glad of it. It was a stunning performance. The two brothers she had seen at the Essford Spring Market were clumsy farmers in comparison. There were three young girls and three young men, dressed in nothing except a bit of silk and pearls in the most necessary places. Their bodies, smeared, Kat thought, with some kind of oil, glistened in the footlights. On the wooden dance floor a star had been painted, and in the beginning the dancers stood stock still, each at a point of the star, breathing quietly and waiting. Then the music began – drums, then fiddles and tambourines, slowly, draggingly at first, and then suddenly lightning fast. There was a ringing blow on a brass gong, and then the dancers moved. Following the rhythms of the music they were sometimes so exquisitely slow that it was hard to see how they could possibly keep their balance, and sometimes so whirlingly fast that Kat 's own drumming fingers could hardly keep up the pace. And the swords – oh, the swords! Hissing and singing and clashing, with a high metallic clamour that became part of the music too, a brash and perilous sound like that of no other instrument.

Kat held her breath and clutched at Lu's hand, because it seemed so impossible, so dangerous. Surely a blade must slip and bite into a dancer's naked skin? Yet each time the stroke was blocked at the last minute in some surprising manner – behind the back, perhaps, or by some other dancer in the ring – or else there was a final improbable lithe evasion so that the blade slid past, with less than a finger's breath to spare, yet never biting, never causing the blood to spill.

Lu sat with stars in her eyes throughout, following each move. And when the music finally died and the dancers stood poised, their bodies gleaming now with sweat and rippling with the need to breathe deeply enough, Lu clapped harder and longer than anybody else.

'They are so *good*,' she said, incredulity and awe mixed in her voice. 'Sweet Lady, if only I were half that good.'

'It was a show,' protested Kat. 'You can't compare it to real fencing.'

'I know that, silly. But have you any idea what it takes to move like that? One tiny mistake, and it costs you an ear or a finger. And six of them in the ring at one time! I once saw three dancers together, and I thought that was pretty good. But six! And just think of the trust they must have in each other . . .' Lu looked as if she wanted to leap into the ring then and there and demand to be shown how it was done.

Kat had other plans. Now it was her turn to take Lu by the arm and drag her along. Now, a right turn by the Eastern Tea Pagoda, and then . . .

No blue caravan.

Had she misremembered? She might not have been entirely sober, but the Tea Pagoda was one of the most impressive building in Summertown, all of three floors, though the top one was for show only, with red and gold dragon heads at the corners of the three tiered roofs.

In the place where she thought the blue caravan ought to be, there was now a hexagonal wooden building with a strange-looking little glass turret at the top. On each of the three walls facing the road, scenes from faraway places had been painted – one from Colmonte, one from Koronberk in the Southlands, and one apparently representing 'the great wild jungle of Katai', as it said on the sign. Another sign above the entrance proclaimed: 'Panorama Extraordinaire: Around the World in 20 Minutes'.

'What's a panorama?' asked Kat.

'A very large picture, I think. So big that it goes all around you.'

'Do you want to take a look?' It cost a penny, like the sword dancers.

'I suppose so,' said Lu, not sounding too enthusiastic. 'Are you sure there isn't something else you'd rather do? What about the carousels?'

'I think I'd really like to see what a panorama is,' said Kat thoughtfully. It had struck her that the wooden walls of the building were blue – much the same kind of blue, in fact, as the caravan had been. So perhaps her memory had not deceived her after all.

They each paid a penny, and went in. In the middle of the building, benches had been set up, facing the walls. As yet it wasn't much of a view; as a matter of fact, it was almost too dark to see anything. A single oil lamp gave enough light that Kat and Lu could find a seat without tripping over a leg or a bench, but that was all. Most of the audience was female, Kat discovered. She supposed that made sense. This, to most women, was the only way to see a bit of the world, since no decent self-respecting woman could go traipsing across the countryside, travelling as if she were a man. The tiered benches were filling quickly, and it was obvious that the panorama people had no intention of starting the show until there was a full house. Meanwhile, a small curly-haired boy made the rounds, selling lemonade and salted almonds. Kat couldn't help smiling. She remembered what one Summertowner had told her during the party banquet: 'People come here to spend money. Why not let them spend it with me? Each time I sell them a salted pretzel they get a little more thirsty and buy a little more beer.' She declined the salted almonds, but Lu bought a cup of lemonade.

Finally the house was full. The lamp lighting the seats disappeared upwards into a shaft of some kind, and total darkness fell. Then there was a sudden blazing flash of light, and a man appeared in front of them – no, wait, six men, one for each wall. Six completely identical men . . . Even though Kat could figure out that it had to be some kind of mirror trick, it still startled her completely.

'Welcome,' said the man in a dramatic voice, bowing to the crowd. He was wearing a turquoise turban and a long turquoise robe, covered with gleaming silver stars. 'I take you now on a journey . . . a magical journey to faraway lands . . .' He raised his arms, and music began to play, softly, mysteriously. 'We begin in the east, like the sun. Come with me, my friends, to a city far beyond the borders of Breda, to a place where the sun burns hotter and the fruit tastes sweeter, where the scorpion lurks, waiting to sting the heel of the unwary . . . Ladies and gentlemen: I give you Colmonte . . .'

The man disappeared, and for a moment there was

utter blackness. Then the walls lit up, and Kat gasped. A city did indeed spread out across the horizon – a city of domes and spires glinting gold in the sun, of roofs agleam with copper and verdigris. Flowers cascaded down the balconies and trellises, blooming in colours more brilliant than those she was used to, and lining the busy streets were trees of a kind she had never seen before. She was in the middle of it, she was *there*, and she didn't even have to turn her head, because the city was gently turning around her, north, east, south, west, all the compass round. Though unseen now, the man's voice reached them easily, telling them about the marvels they were seeing. About the seaport where the merchant ships came in with their loads of silk and spices. About the mountains from whence came such silver riches. About the magnificent palaces from which the matriarchs ruled the land. About the zoological gardens where one might see lions and tigers and beasts even more strange: a dog with eight legs and a carapace like a turtle, a monkey who could count and calculate better than most men, and yes, a horse with fangs and venomous spurs, more dangerous even than the hellhorses of Breda. The city turned before her eyes, and the light changed from the blush of dawn to the glare of midday heat and finally to night, with the walls and domes black shapes merely, except for the coloured windows shining like jewels, and the stars bright pinprick lanterns above . . .

And then it was over. The oil lamp was lowered to light the audience in their seats, and the walls became blank and dark once more.

'Ladies and gentlemen, that was Colmonte. But if you wish to experience also the breathtaking sight of the castled walls of Koronberk and the flaming leaves of the Marten Tree, merely remain in your seats. The price is a penny – and a cheaper journey to Koronberk you cannot find. On top of which, ladies, it is safer and more comfortable than the real thing, and of course entirely respectable!'

The curly-headed lemonade boy was back, joined this time by an older boy who looked to be his brother. They began to move among the benches, collecting money from those who chose to keep their seats. Kat stirred uneasily. She really wanted to see more, but that would mean no carousels – in fact no more treats whatsoever, because if she wanted to see both Koronberk and the Dangerous Jungle, she would be flat broke and penniless as a pauper.

'Do you want to stay?' asked Lu.

'I don't know,' said Kat. 'I . . . can't really afford to. I thought it would be a penny for the lot.'

'Three wonders of the world for one penny?' said a voice just behind her. 'We're very reasonably priced, but not that cheap.'

Kat turned in her seat. It was the elder of the two boys. Fifteen or sixteen, she thought, with curly dark brown hair held back in a small ponytail at the nape of his neck. He was dressed in black pants and a white shirt and a scarlet waistcoat with gold trimmings. He smiled at her, and his teeth were so white they seemed to light up his tanned face. Without quite meaning to, Kat smiled back.

'Where are you from?' he said. 'The Castle?'

'Yes,' said Lu. It was pretty obvious after all, from their apprentice uniforms.

'I didn't think they had girl guards.'

'We're not guards,' said Lu. 'We are apprentice bredinari.'

'Silver Riders?' He was clearly impressed. 'So you two ride the dangerous hellhorses for a living?'

'Sometimes,' said Kat. Truth be told, they did not after all have a hellhorse of their own yet. 'But they're not so dangerous if you handle them properly.'

'Rather you than me, girl,' he said, giving her another of those dazzling smiles. He looked across his shoulder quickly, then leaned forward. 'Look, it's all right if you want to stay here and enjoy the rest of the show. Just don't tell anyone, ok? My father would throw a fit if he knew.'

'Thanks,' said Kat, somewhat taken aback. 'We'd love to. But what if your father . . .'

He patted her reassuringly on the shoulder.

'Don't worry your pretty head about it. What he doesn't know won't hurt him. Enjoy the show. I have to move on, but perhaps I'll see you later.'

He moved forward to the next row of benches, and Kat followed him with her eyes. So did Lu.

'What a nerve!' she said under her breath. 'Coming on to you like that.'

'What do you mean?' said Kat, feeling her cheeks heat.

'"Don't worry your pretty head about it,"' Lu mimicked. 'And that gipsy smile.'

'He was just being nice.'

'You think? Just wait and see. He's not done with you yet.'

Kat enjoyed her 'Journey to Koronberk' as the turbaned man called it. Koronberk was the capital of the South-lands, or Kernland as the Southerners themselves called their country. But while the man was talking about 'vines and rippling cornfields, stony mountains and proud men' and about 'the Marten Tree with its blood-red leaves still marking the site of Marten's martyr's death' Kat couldn't quite stop thinking about the boy in the scarlet waistcoat.

When the lights came up after the Koronberk panorama, he came by again and pretended to take a penny from each of them.

'If you stay here for a few moments after the Jungle is over, I'll show you something even better,' he promised, giving them a bright-eyed, bright-toothed smile.

'Really? I wonder what that might be,' said Lu dryly, once he was out of earshot.

'Oh, Lu, don't be like that. He's just being nice.'

'I'm not hanging around,' said Lu. 'There's so much else to see. And what about the carousels?'

'But I want to see what he wants to show us. We can go on the carousels some other time.'

'Suit yourself, then. But I'm not waiting around.'

'That's not fair, Lu. I went to see the sword dancers with you.'

'Yes, well, that didn't take all night, did it?'

'How I spend my time is up to me,' snapped Kat hotly.

'If I happen to want to stay here, it's none of your business. Or perhaps the wants and wishes of the likes of me don't count when the Domnessa Ceuta has other plans.'

Lu's face tightened, and she rose to her feet.

'You're the one not being fair,' she said. 'But if that's the way you want it, then go ahead. I hope you enjoy it.'

She made her way to the exit as the lights were dimmed once more. Kat sat in the darkness, biting her lip. She and Lu did fight every once in a while when Kat's temper got the better of her, or Lu's did – the Domnessa Ceuta was no shrinking violet either. And occasionally it was just too much, Lu knowing everything and being so good at everything. It was easy to get the feeling sometimes that Lu looked down on you for being so ignorant.

But even if Kat was none too sure which fork to use when several were provided, it didn't mean she was stupid! And even if Lu always thought she knew what people were 'really' up to, it didn't mean she was right.

The jungle panorama was accompanied by a lot of sounds meant to be the cries of the animals and the rustling of the trees. Some of it worked really well, and Kat nearly leaped out of her seat when the elephant 'trumpeted'. But the cicadas were plainly just someone rubbing a stick against a comb of some kind, and even though the plants looked really great, some of the animals looked oddly stiff and nowhere near as lifelike as the people and the scenery from the cities. Probably it was a lot harder to get a tiger to hold still and pose for you while you painted it, thought Kat.

'Did you like it?' The boy in the red waistcoat was back.

Kat nodded. 'Especially the cities. It was almost like being there . . .'

'What happened to your friend?'

'She . . . had to meet someone,' lied Kat, hoping he hadn't seen how angry Lu was when she left.

'I'm glad you stayed,' he said. 'Come on. I'll show you something really exciting . . .'

He took her arm gently and with great politeness, like she was some fine lady with lace on her sleeves, and she followed him towards the exit. Outside was another smaller tent one had to pass through, and a lot of people had stopped to gaze at some pictures exhibited there. Kat could hear them murmuring and exclaiming.

'They look *alive*,' said a young girl to her mother.

'Much too alive,' said the mother. 'It's not natural!'

The pictures were of people and animals and landscapes. And Kat almost agreed with the mother. They were too lifelike. How anyone could paint like that, so precisely, so exactly what a soldier or a dancer or a horse really looked like . . .

'Those aren't the best ones,' said the boy, lowering his voice. 'The Mother Houses will only let us show a few, and we have to paint on top to make them look like paintings.'

'What do you mean, *look* like paintings?'

'This way,' he said, 'and I'll show you.'

Once again, he took her elbow lightly and gently. He held the canvas at the back of the tent aside, and let her into the evening dark, and a place that was not meant to be seen by the eyes of the crowd. Here there was no glitter and no cunning deceptions, just a patch of grass surrounded by the backs of tents and wagons and a low fence. One of the wagons was blue with a black roof. And it was towards this blue wagon that he led her.

'No one at home right now,' he said. 'They are all busy setting up for the next show.'

'Won't they miss you?'

He looked uneasy for a second, then clearly shrugged it off.

'Not right away,' he said. 'Come inside.'

The wagon's interior was dim, lit by the thin blue flicker of a lamp that had been turned down very low. He raised the wick, and soft golden light spilled across a long slim table, benches, and a cooker at one end. He waved at one of the benches.

'Please,' he said. 'Sit.'

The wagon was like many others she had seen – a small house on wheels, with everything built in such a way that it could serve several functions. Under the table a sleeping mat lay ready to be unrolled, and the benches were clearly made to be used as beds as well. The firewood box by the little stove had a lid and a pillow on top so that it provided an extra seat. There was an almost obsessive tidiness everywhere, the same neatness she had seen with every other wayfarer she had ever met. Simon had it too. Carelessness carried a high cost on the roads, when one never knew where something could be fixed or replaced if it broke down.

'Look,' said the boy, taking a picture off the wall. 'This is what they really look like.'

There was no colour in this picture, only shades of white and grey and black. And it was not painted on canvas but on a thin cold metal plate. In it were a man and a woman, and despite the lack of colour they looked even more real and alive than the people and animals and places in the other pictures she had seen. The woman sat on the steps of a wagon, and the man standing next to her had his hand on her shoulder. They looked as though they were both dressed for the occasion. She wore a white blouse and a long embroidered skirt, and her long curly hair had been brushed and arranged to fall forward over one shoulder. He wore a striped waistcoat with silver buttons, and on his head a small cap decorated with a feather. They both looked very solemn.

'It's my mama and my papa,' said the boy. 'My uncle Isak made it – it was one of his very first.'

'He must be a brilliant painter,' said Kat, awe in her voice. She looked at the woman's curls – every hair was visible, just about.

The boy smiled.

'It's not a painting,' he said. 'It's real.'

'What do you mean?'

'The light makes it,' said the boy. 'No one has to use a pencil or a brush – this is made with a few chemicals and reality itself.

Kat eyed him carefully. If he was trying to fool her, there was no sign. He looked quite earnest, as if he believed every word he said. But how could it be true?

'You've looked at yourself in a mirror, right?'

She nodded. What did that have to do with anything?

'Imagine one could coat a mirror with something that made your image stick to the mirror, even after you had gone. You'd get something like this, then, wouldn't you?'

'Is that how it's done?'

'No, not quite. We use a box . . . If you come back in daylight, I can show you.' He looked at her very intently, as if trying to make sure he would remember what she looked like. 'I would like to make a picture of you,' he said. 'A picture like this.' His voice was so low it was nearly a whisper. 'It would be lovely to catch your mirror image, so one could keep it always . . .'

A shudder went through Kat, and on her arms all the little hairs prickled and rose. That had sounded . . . scary. Eerie, certainly. He wanted to trap her mirror image in a box and keep it – would the mirror then be empty the next time she looked? Yet at the same time, there was something about the way he looked at her that felt . . . lovely. Like he had said. He looked at her as though she were beautiful. She wished right now that she had a skirt like the one the woman wore in the picture. Or a velvet robe like Lu had for Memory Day dinners with her family. Anything would be better than this stupid uniform that made her look like a boy.

'One thing, though,' said the boy, touching a lock of her hair gently. 'This will be missing. That colour – like a sunrise. I can't get that in a picture.'

A familiar heat rose in Kat's cheeks and she knew her

face was practically scarlet. She ducked her head a bit, to make it less noticeable.

'You haven't even told me your name,' she said.

'Daniel.'

'Really? I have a brother called Daniel . . .'

And I'm sure he is thrilled to know that, she told herself acidly. Couldn't she at least try to come up with something interesting to say?

'And you? What about you?'

'Katriona. Though most people call me Kat.'

'Katriona . . .' He looked as if he meant to say more, but at that moment they both heard an irritated male voice outside.

'Daniel? *Daniel!* Where is the damn boy?'

Daniel put the picture back on the wall.

'Come back in daylight, Katriona,' he pleaded.

'So you can trap my mirror image in a box?' she said.

He smiled. 'If Papa will let me. We have to use a little silver for every picture, so they are quite expensive.'

This sudden talk of costs and practicalities made her feel better. The last of her goosebumps faded and she felt like herself again.

Or nearly so. There was still something about Daniel and his dark eyes, and the way he looked at her. As if she were beautiful.

'Tomorrow is my day off,' she said. 'So perhaps . . . perhaps I can come.' She had promised Lu to go home with her for the Memory Day dinner, but she might have time to visit Daniel first. Or if not, there would be plenty more

Memory Day dinners. One every week, in fact. Surely Lu would understand.

Daniel turned the lamp down low again. Then he took her hand and led her down the steps of the wagon, as if she might fall if he didn't support her.

'I'll see you tomorrow then,' he said, giving her hand a little squeeze.

'Maybe,' she said. 'If I can.'

Back in the crowded streets of the Summertown, she couldn't help smiling to herself. Daniel. Daniel and his magic box that was going to capture her image, with no pencil and no brush, only the light itself.

And then she suddenly came to a halt, so suddenly that two slightly drunken farm boys bumped into her.

'Hey!' said one. 'Watch your step, li'l lady.'

'Sorry,' she muttered, and walked on. But her step was slower and less certain. While she had been with Daniel, she had entirely managed to forget about the reason why she went to see the panoramas in the first place.

The blue wagon. Daniel and his whole family were on Alvar Alcedina's list of people he wanted found. Why? What possible interest could the DomPrimus have in a traveller family like Daniel's? She hoped fervently that they had done nothing illegal. Probably it was her duty to report their whereabouts to Master Aureus immediately. But if so, she really, really didn't want to do her duty.

*

There was a note on her door when she got home. At first she thought it might be from Lu, but the writing was Simon's. 'Come by when you have a moment,' was all it said. It was a bit late to go calling, and she was so tired that she felt her bed shouting her name. But Simon didn't write little notes every day. Actually, she couldn't remember it happening before, and despite the offhand wording she had a feeling it might be important.

In the guest wing a single lamp was still burning, but the curtains had been drawn around most of the beds and the sound of gentle snoring could be heard. Simon, luckily, was still awake. He was seated on his borrowed bed, mending a strap on one of his saddlebags, his gear spread out around him.

'Simon?' She hovered in the doorway, uneasy about intruding on the territory of the sleeping men.

He looked up. 'It's late,' he said. 'I'd almost given up on you.' He put down the saddlebag and rose to his feet. 'Let's go down into the Stone Gardens so we can talk without waking people.'

The stone seat under the peach tree was cold and moist with dew, but a lovely scent made it a pleasant place to sit all the same. The fruit trees in the gardens almost all had blossoms, and the smooth dark flagstones were dotted with pale, fallen petals.

'I didn't want to leave without saying goodbye,' said Simon. 'They've put me on the long Northern run, so it'll be some weeks before you see me again.'

Kat felt a pang of sadness. She had known he would have to leave eventually, but it had been so nice to have him there for a while, even if the reason was not a good one.

'Take care,' she said.

One of his brief, sudden smiles flashed across his face.

'Actually, that was pretty much what I wanted to say to you,' he said. '*You* taking care, that is.' The smile had vanished, gone almost before she had had time to see it. 'Kat, I ran into Lu and Merian coming back from Summertown. I was surprised that they came home without you.'

Kat felt her cheeks heat, and at the same time irritation rose inside her. What had they been telling Simon? Merian probably wouldn't tattle, but if Lu had been angry enough . . .

'I just stayed on to see something they couldn't be bothered with,' she said.

'I see,' he said. He sat there for quite a while, occasionally rubbing his boot heel across the petal-strewn flagstones. Simon, who *never* fidgeted. It occurred to her that he – that wise, composed grown-up Simon – was actually embarrassed about something.

Finally, he broke his silence.

'Kat, you know that you don't have your mother nearby . . .' he began, then ground to a halt again.

'Simon, just say it. Whatever it is.'

He looked up at the peach blossoms then nerved himself up to look her in the eye.

'Kat, if she *had* been here – your mother, I mean – there might be some advice she'd give you at this point. About men, I mean. Boys.'

In a minute he'll start telling me about the birds and the bees, she thought, and had to hold back a splutter of laughter.

'Simon, I do know how—'

He waved her off. 'Yes, I know you're not ignorant of the . . . practical side of things. I was thinking more of . . . of feelings. Kat, you are so . . . headstrong. You rush into things, never mind the consequences. You never hold back. And I'm afraid that you might get hurt. That some stupid, inconsiderate lout might do you real harm.'

Anger stirred in her, a familiar prickly yellow anger. She nearly hissed at him, the way she might have hissed at Cornelius: You're not my father! Don't tell me what to do! And Daniel was no lout.

'Have they been telling tales?' she said in a voice that stung and chilled at the same time. 'Did Lu tell you . . .' Tell him what? That a traveller boy had smiled at her? Not much more had happened.

Simon shook his head. 'No. They didn't tell me anything. You did.'

'No, I didn't! I haven't – there isn't –' she spluttered and stammered, until he put a hand on her arm to still her.

'Kat, I'm not telling you to . . . to not do it. Whatever it is you are up to. I'm just saying be careful. Try not to get hurt.' He looked down again, at his boots on the flagstones. 'And even though it is boring and wrong . . . you do have to be careful, just a bit, about what other people think and say. If you still want to be a bredinari. If you still want to see your name on the hellhorse lists in a few weeks' time.'

That knocked the breath out of her. She wanted that, she wanted it so very badly: to see her name on that list. Every night when she looked down into the south field she hoped so very fervently that one of the long-legged yearlings grazing there might soon be hers.

'But I didn't do anything wrong,' she said in a very small voice, trying not to think about blue wagons and confidential orders.

Simon gave her arm a tiny squeeze.

'Of course you didn't.'

THE PICTURE MAKER

Kat turned slowly this way and that in front of the mirror, twisting her head in an attempt to see how she looked from behind.

'Are you *sure* this is a good idea?' asked Merian, not for the first time.

'That's why I want to leave early,' said Kat impatiently. 'So I can do both. What do you think?'

'You look very nice. This is so unlike you . . .'

'Thanks very much!'

'No, you know what I mean. Normally you don't – I mean, clothes don't seem to matter to you. You're hardly ever out of uniform.'

Kat didn't say that that was because the prentice uniform was the only decent clothing she had. The skirt that was swirling gently around her legs was one Merian had lent her. Black velvet, decorated with green and blue ribbons at the hem. She wore it with her white uniform shirt, with the sleeves rolled up so that it looked at bit less regulation-like. For once, her curls had been let free of their customary strict braids, and her hair was now long enough to fall past her shoulders and down her back in copper-coloured cascades. Like a sunrise, he had said.

She peered at the mirror, hoping this was how he would like to 'catch' her. There was nothing more she could do. She possessed no earrings or necklaces, and until recently had not cared.

'Thank you, Merian,' she said, stroking the black velvet of the skirt. 'I won't forget this.'

'You're welcome. Only . . . take care of yourself, will you?'

'I always do. And we cats have nine lives, you know.'

Merian didn't smile, and didn't answer, and the worried frown stayed on her face as Kat said goodbye and turned to run down the stairs, in an unfamiliar swirl of skirt.

There was heavy traffic through the castle gates, with crowds of off-duty men and women heading for their families and Memory Day dinners, and Kat made it through without notice, despite her unregulated appearance. The city, too, was brimming with market crowds, and it took longer than usual to reach the North Gate and the Caravan Road. She entered Summertown through the wide public entrance, waving at Abel as she passed his music box stall. This time, he saw her and waved back.

By the Panorama Palace it was the turbaned man who was manning the entrance, taking pennies from the people queuing to get in. Kat came to a hesitant halt.

'Step up, young lady! Only a penny to see the world!'

'Er . . . yes, but I've really just come to see Daniel,' Kat said.

'I see,' said the turbaned man, eyeing her without much welcome. 'Well, I can hardly charge you a penny for that poor privilege. But my son is busy at the moment. You'll have to wait until the show is over.'

'How long will that be?'

'About an hour. Come back then.'

And Kat had to leave, feeling thwarted and ill at ease at the same time.

Fortunately, Abel had time for her. His booth was not too busy at this time of day.

'Do you know Daniel and his family?' asked Kat. 'They have the Panorama Palace.'

'The Sardis? Yes.'

'Do they come here often?'

'Once or twice a year, like most of us. But this is the first time they've made themselves part of Summertown. They usually have their long summer stay elsewhere. They've been based in Koronberk for a couple of years, and I'm a bit surprised that they settled here this year.'

'Why? I mean, why are you surprised?'

Abel stirred his tea. 'They can't show their best stuff here. They'd make heaps more in Koronberk.'

'That's what Daniel said. That they can't do what they do best here. But why not?'

'The Mothers are against it.'

'Yes, but *why*?'

Abel sipped his tea, studying her all the while. She

could tell he was making up his mind how much to tell her. 'Do you know what they do – apart from the panoramas, I mean?'

'Pictures. Daniel says they make pictures. By . . . by catching what is in the mirror.'

Abel nodded. 'You could put it that way, I suppose. It's called photography. And the Motherhouses have decided that this art is part of the seven plagues that led to the Catastrophe. They say the evil power of Media may reside in a photograph.'

Kat shuddered. Was this why Alcedina was looking for Daniel and his family?

'What do you think?' she asked. 'Is it really dangerous?'

He shrugged. 'I've never seen people take any harm from it. But then, I'm no expert on such . . . matters of the spirit.'

Daniel was waiting for her at the entrance when she got back.

'Welcome,' he said, with an oddly serious formality. 'I'm glad you came.'

Kat smiled and felt a rush of shyness heat her face.

'I was curious,' she said. 'How does one catch a mirror image?'

'Come on in, and I'll show you.' He smiled at her. He was wearing the same white trousers and gold-edged red waistcoat, but no shirt. Kat couldn't help glancing at his tanned upper body. There was still a boyish slenderness to his chest, but his arms were strong and well muscled. He raised the cord that stopped people from entering between shows, and Kat ducked under it. There was a change in him today, she thought. He seemed genuinely glad to see her, and touched her elbow lightly as he led her into the makeshift workshop behind the Panorama Palace. But some of his – she didn't quite know what to call it, his street hawker showmanship, perhaps – some of that had vanished. There was no come-see-the-wonders-of-the-world in his manner now; he looked and seemed quite . . . solemn, almost. All serious and sober. He showed her some plates of metal and glass with grey and black shadows on them and explained how they were coated with silver-salt and then inserted into one end of a box. At the front of the box was a glass lens which gathered the light and made the image appear on the plate inside the box.

'It's called photography,' he said. 'Photo means light, and it's the light which draws the image on the plate inside the—'

'God of my fathers, boy! What are you thinking of?'

Daniel's father stood in the workshop doorway, turban-less and obviously furious. Kat felt Daniel turn rigid beside her. He didn't say a word.

'Put those away! Do you want to bring the Mother-houses down on us?'

Daniel still said nothing. His silence was painful. He had turned quite pale underneath the market boy tan. Wordlessly, he began to put the fragile glass plates back into the cotton-wadded box they were kept in. He wouldn't look at his father, wouldn't look at Kat.

Something moved inside Kat, something deeper than pity. For a moment she didn't have to imagine what he might be feeling – she *knew*. A moment ago, he had been very much the grown-up, explaining complicated and wondrous things to Kat; now he had to stand there and be scolded like a naughty child. She knew there were tears in his eyes even though she couldn't see his face. And she knew that the humiliation was worse, a hundred times worse, because she was there to witness it.

She wanted so badly to make him feel better. To touch him, to take his hand. But she also knew he wouldn't want her to. Not now.

'Daniel has explained that photography is not something you can talk openly about in Breda,' she said, trying to defend him. 'I won't tell anyone.'

Daniel's father didn't say so outright, but she could tell how much he doubted that a girl her age would be able to keep her mouth shut about something so exciting.

'I would be grateful if you didn't,' he said. 'We abide by the laws and customs of Breda, as with all the lands we travel. If Breda's rulers feel that it will not benefit the people of Breda to learn about the possibilities of photography, then they must not learn about it from us.' There was still reproach in his voice, but Daniel's father was not oblivious to his son's averted face. He gentled his tone a bit. 'Daniel, won't you introduce me to your friend?'

Daniel did raise his head, then, but still would not look directly at anyone.

'Father, this is Katriona Trivallia . . . Katriona, this is my father, Samuel Sardi.'

It sounded so formal that Katriona had performed her best bredinari bow before she stopped to think about it. 'Most people just call me Kat,' she said, somewhat shyly.

'Be welcome, Kat. Perhaps you would do us the honour of sharing our midday meal?'

'I . . .' I can't, was what she started to say. She had promised Lu. But just then Daniel finally looked at her again, and there was something in his eyes that couldn't be refused. 'I would love to. Thank you very much.' Please, let Lu understand this . . .

When the noonday bells rang out over Breda, Summertown was almost empty. The remainder of this day was given to family meals and quiet commemoration, not the rowdy pleasures of the fair. Kat had to push aside mental images of the empty chair at the Ceuta table, and of Lu's offended face. At the Panorama Palace all props had been tidily put away after the last performance, and the Sardis agreed that it was warm enough to eat outside, in the little yard-like area between the blue caravan, the workshop, and the board and canvas wall of the Palace.

There were six of them. Daniel and his younger brother Seffi, the small curly-headed boy she had already met. Samuel Sardi, of course. Then there was Uncle Isak, who was in charge of the lights and the machinery, and

Kottas, who wasn't anybody's brother or uncle or anything like that, but seemed to be part of the family even so. Kottas was what most people called 'not quite right in the head'; his jaw hung a little too loose, and his face was oddly childlike even though he was a grown man, with a bushy black beard, broad shoulders, and great big calloused hands. He was the one who turned the huge rollers when Colmonte moved smoothly past the eyes of the marvelling crowd, and it was his strong back and arms that made it possible to change so quickly from Colmonte to Koronberk, and from Koronberk to the Wild Jungle of Katai.

'Kottas is the strongest man in Summertown,' said Daniel, clapping Kottas on the shoulder, and Kottas beamed at the praise.

And finally, when the last straggling fairground visitor had left, a delicate, dark-haired girl emerged from the wagon.

'This is my sister Sara,' said Daniel, with such gravity in his manner that he might be introducing the Bredani herself. Sara smiled shyly.

'Welcome,' she said, in a voice so soft it was barely more than a whisper. Her dark eyes met Kat's only for a second, then she lowered her gaze. She seemed almost afraid, as if she did not meet many strangers. The Sardi men clearly did what they could to protect her against the contempt the settled people of Breda had for travelling women. Kat couldn't help remembering what her own mother thought of 'women like that'. To Tess, they were cheap, no-good creatures, stealing and lying their way through life and sleeping with those who would pay. But Daniel's delicate sister, with her neat braids, lowered eyes and timid courtesy, was nothing like the shameless hussies of Tess's cautionary tales.

Kottas and Daniel brought some of the benches from the Panorama Palace out on to the grass, and Seffi and Sara set the table with a white tablecloth, brown clay bowls and spoons with black wooden handles. Finally Daniel's father came down the wagon steps, carefully holding the steaming black cast iron pot that had been simmering away on the stove all morning.

'And now, ladies and gentlemen,' he announced in his best ringmaster's voice, 'allow me to present: the renowned Sardi Gullyas!'

This food was different from the sort of dishes Kat was used to – a red soup, thick and spicy hot, with noodles and beans in it, and a side dish of thin flatbreads spread with something white and cheesy tasting strongly of garlic and black pepper. It burned inside her mouth even after she swallowed, and brought out little beads of sweat on her forehead and upper lip.

'Do you like it?' asked Daniel with an air of expectancy, and Kat nodded, even though her frank thought was that it was much too hot for ordinary folk. The Sardi family were made of sterner stuff than her, it seemed. Certainly none of them had to resort to the water jug as often as she did. Kottas watched her with growing interest.

'Five mugs!' he said triumphantly. 'That girl is really thirsty!'

Seffi spluttered and could not contain his giggle. The rest of the family, who had been busy not noticing how much their visitor drank, struggled with their composure. First Daniel's father succumbed, then Sara and Uncle Isak. Kottas joined in the laughter, loudly and delightedly, though he probably did not know why they were laughing.

'Kottas, I think that girl finds the food a little bit too hot,' said Isak, and they all laughed even louder.

All except Daniel. Palefaced, he rose to his feet in a rush, banging his spoon down so hard that a shower of little gullyas droplets spattered the white tablecloth.

'Why do you always have to be like that?' he shouted. 'Couldn't you even try to act like normal people when I bring my . . . when I bring a guest to the table?'

Silence fell. Or nearly so. Seffi still couldn't hold back his giggles. Kottas, though, had stopped laughing. He hid most of his face in his hands, but his eyes peeked out from between his thick fingers. Kat had no idea what to say. All right, it wasn't the world's greatest feeling to be laughed at like that, but did Daniel have to be quite that angry?

Kottas didn't like it either.

'Dani is angry mad,' he said with an anxious tremor in his voice. 'Dani is *very* angry.'

Daniel visibly tried to curb his fury.

'Come on, Kat,' he said with as much dignity as he could muster. 'Let's leave.'

Kat rose awkwardly to her feet. She didn't think storming off in a huff was the best thing to do, but she could tell that Daniel was too angry to listen to any well-meant advice from her.

Kottas had no such qualms. He simply stepped over the bench and put his arms around Daniel.

'Please don't be angry , Dani,' he said. 'Not that angry. It hurts. It hurts right here.' He brought his fist up to the base of his throat and held it there.

For a long moment Daniel stood passive in Kottas's embrace. Then he seemed to shake off his anger like a dog shakes out its fur.

'I'm not angry,' he told Kottas, patting the big man's arm. 'But laughing at a guest is really bad manners.'

'Yes, it is,' said Samuel Sardi, once more in control of himself. 'And I apologize. Katriona, please sit down. You too, Daniel.'

'You have pretty hair,' said Kottas, reaching out in the direction of Kat's curls. But someone had apparently taught him not to touch strange girls because he halted the movement almost instantly. 'It's all shiny, just like Roscha.'

'Who is Roscha?' asked Kat.

There was a slight pause.

'Err . . . Roscha is our horse,' said Daniel. 'The chestnut. She really does have a beautiful coat . . .'

'I see,' said Kat, grinning. 'So I have hair like a horse?'

'Yes,' said Kottas happily. 'Like Roscha. Roscha is really pretty. Just like you.'

'Thank you,' said Kat, meaning it. 'You're a very nice man, Kottas.'

*

After the gullyas soup there was tea, real tea like the one Simon served, and tiny sweetbreads with almonds for dessert.

'This is good tea,' said Kat, sighing contentedly. 'And very nice cakes,' she added hurriedly, so they wouldn't think the cakes were any less delicious in her eyes.

'One of the benefits of a travelling life,' said Samuel Sardi. 'Whenever we pass through Varas or Colmonte, we stock up on tea until our wallets ache.'

'I wish I could have tea like this every day.' A thought occurred to her. 'When you are in Colmonte, do you show Breda to the Easterners?'

Uncle Isak nodded. 'People want to see the world. It's what they pay us for.'

Daniel stirred a spoonful of honey into his tea. 'But in Koronberk and Colmonte, we make a small fortune taking people's pictures. So apparently, they will pay even more to see themselves.'

'Yes, Abel the music box maker told me you normally summer in Koronberk,' said Kat. 'But not this year?'

There was a moment's silence, and Kat had the sense that she had somehow brought up a sore point.

'We didn't have a very successful season there last year,' Samuel Sardi finally said, and left it at that. And Kat didn't like to pry any further.

'Thank you for a lovely meal,' she said instead. 'I'm sorry to rush off like this, but I really have to leave.' Lu would be spitting fire by now . . .

'No, wait,' said Daniel. 'We didn't even . . . Papa, there's something I have to ask.'

'And what is that?'

'Can we . . . I mean, will you . . . please take Kat's picture?'

Samuel Sardi frowned. 'Daniel, you know it is forbidden here. And when we are in Breda, we live by Breda's law.'

'It's not *forbidden*, Papa. There's no actual law against it.'

'No, but the Motherhouses ban it, so it's much the same thing.'

'But I promised—'

'You shouldn't have.'

'It's all right,' said Kat, seeing that Daniel was once more about to lose his temper. 'And Daniel, you didn't actually promise . . .'

Suddenly, Uncle Isak was on his feet.

'If you won't take that picture, I will!'

Silence fell like a curtain. Samuel Sardi made a strange warning motion with one hand.

'Isak, you know—'

But Uncle Isak did not let him finish his sentence. 'All this nonsense about demons and evil powers. Rubbish and narrow-minded superstition. What is the harm in taking a pretty girl's picture? Do you realize it has been months since I photographed anything at all? If this goes on, I won't even remember how. Motherhouses!' He hissed the word between his teeth. 'A flock of tight-arsed, frightened old *hens*!'

Kat gasped involuntarily. Not so much at the words – Cornelius had no fond feelings for the Mothers and called them worse things, at least when Tess wasn't around – but at the violence with which they were said. Uncle Isak, who had been friendly but a bit withdrawn throughout the meal, suddenly looked like a different person. The tendons in his neck quivered with fury. Until now Kat had assumed that Samuel Sardi was head of the household; now she was not so sure.

'Isak, you would make the girl party to something which is . . .' Samuel probably meant to say 'forbidden' once more, but thought better of it, 'something which is considered reprehensible in her country. Do you think that is right?'

'Do *you* think the way they live in this godforsaken country is right? Three days ago someone *spat* at Sara! I have no idea what we're doing here.'

'The children have to see their grandmother every once in a while . . .'

'Do they? She doesn't give a hoot about the boys. All she is interested in is getting her hands on Sara to stop what she calls 'indecent travelling'. To hell with their bloody grandmother, I say!'

Samuel Sardi rose to his feet, looking tired. 'In her eyes, we have done her a great injustice. She lost a daughter because of us. Because of me.' He bowed his head and rubbed absentmindedly at a spot on his black trousers. 'Take the damn picture if you feel you must. But please, let us end this conversation.' He turned away from the table and began to make his way towards the deserted darkness of the Panorama Palace.

Now it was Isak's turn to look dejected. 'Samuel . . .'

'Leave it.'

'Samuel, forgive me.' Isak shrugged helplessly.

Samuel Sardi stopped and turned around for a minute.

'You are my brother,' he said with an odd formality. 'There is nothing to forgive.'

Then he disappeared into the darkened hall.

'Is he sad?' asked Kottas with a worried frown.

'Yes, he is,' said Isak. 'But there is nothing we can do about it. Leave him be, Kottas. He'll come back in a little while.' He ran his hand over his balding scalp and rested it on the crown of his head, as if he felt a need to hold on to it. 'What about you, Kat? Do you feel that taking this picture is wrong?'

'I . . . No. I don't think so . . .' She hadn't really thought it through. But Merian's cousin Abel had said there was no harm in it. And Daniel wanted to . . . She felt a tickling sensation along her spine. No one had ever looked at her the way Daniel did. As if he couldn't *stop* looking. As if she was the best thing he had ever seen. So if he wanted a picture of her so that he could look at her even more . . . She glanced at him, and yes, he was looking at her right now, in that way of his.

Isak smiled, as if he could read her mind. 'Right. Let's do it, then.'

And so she had her picture taken. On the steps of the wagon, with Daniel next to her, resting his hand lightly on her shoulder. And while she sat there, waiting for the light to do its job inside Isak's little black box . . . while she sat there, feeling Daniel's touch on her shoulder like a blaze of heat . . . she couldn't help thinking about the first photograph she had ever seen. Daniel's mother and father on the steps of the wagon. Exactly like this.

BAD BLOOD

It took a while before the picture was finished, and then Daniel wanted to go for a walk, and it was the only time of the week when they were both free from chores and duties . . . In the end it was so late that Kat couldn't really present herself at the Ceuta doorstep. So it was not until next morning, at Weapons Practice with Master Haryn, that she had a chance to apologize to Lu.

Lu eyed her coldly with a look on her face that Kat had never seen her wear before.

'I suppose you couldn't tear yourself away from your gutter boy.'

Kat felt herself redden. 'Don't call him that! He's not—'

'He's traveller trash, Kat, out for what he can get. How can you be so stupid?'

'Stop it! He's nothing like that.'

'You think I didn't see you? With your hair down and a borrowed skirt, little Miss Mountain Beauty. What was I going to tell my mother? "Sorry, Mama, Kat isn't coming, she's too busy throwing herself at this circus boy she's found." That would have gone down really well, don't you think?'

Kat had become better at controlling her temper, usually. But this was not Meiles or DiCapra taunting her, morons from whom she expected such fare. This was Lu. And it hurt. It hurt so badly that the yellow beast inside her roared in rage, filling her stomach, her chest and her head with a molten anger that left room for nothing else.

In some distant part of her mind she never expected the blow to land. Lu was Lu, and infinitely better than Kat at this. But Lu apparently wasn't quite herself either, because there was no smart block, no smooth evasion. The hilt of Kat's training sword thudded into her face, and Master Haryn's star pupil keeled over into the dusty sands of the training ground, blood pouring down her upper lip.

Not that she stayed down very long. Kat was still staring at the blood with a mixture of horror and satisfaction – she had actually *hit* something! – when she abruptly realized that this was by no means the end of the fight. At the last minute she managed to raise the wooden sword into a clumsy defence, so that Lu's formidable strike was at least turned a little before it slammed into Kat's shoulder guard with a crack that echoed across the yard.

Fury claimed Kat and she forgot everything – forgot that it was Lu she was fighting, forgot all about positions, feints, counters and style. She threw herself at her opponent, ignoring blows that made her head swim, kicking and hitting with whatever came to hand – sword hilt, fist, elbow, knee, biting and scratching when nothing else would do.

It took three trained men to separate them. Master Haryn's journeymen, Tobin and Haral, held Lu, while Master Haryn himself got a grip on Kat's neck and arm that locked her helplessly in his grasp.

'Are you quite finished?' he said in a tone so searing that they might have been a couple of eight-year-olds he had had to pull from a playground scuffle.

Neither answered, but Lu hung her head like a puppy scolded by its master. Tobin and Haral let go of her; it was clear that any shred of temper had left her. Apparently, Master Haryn was not equally certain of Kat.

'Are you listening, Trivallia?' he demanded. 'Have we done with this show?'

'Yes,' she muttered. She couldn't even nod, the way he held her.

'Ceuta, go to the infirmary and have them look at that nose. Afterwards I want to see you. Trivallia, into my office. Now! I'll deal with you in a minute.'

He finally let her go. Lu was not completely steady on her feet, and Master Haryn detailed Tobin to go with her. On the whole, she was getting rather more sympathy than Kat, it was obvious.

As she waited her turn in the small enclosure that served as Master Haryn's office, she could hardly believe that this had happened. That she had fought with Lu. Would she *never* learn to control her damn temper? She felt like a worm. A miserable little worm. She couldn't fall out with Lu – Lu was her best friend! And what if she had been seriously hurt?

Unease gnawed at her, and although she was still damp with sweat and grimy with dust, she felt herself shivering. Why didn't he come? Waiting made it worse. She knew that whatever he said, whatever punishment he meted out, it had been richly earned.

Almost, she wished she had never met Daniel. Almost.

'So,' said Master Haryn, sliding into the chair behind his desk. 'Tell me what that was all about.' His dark, greying hair stuck to his forehead where the helmet had been, and a thin layer of yellow-grey dust coated his leather armour.

'Is Lu going to be all right?' asked Kat, staring nervously at his breastplate because she couldn't quite meet his eyes.

'I don't know yet. And I am still waiting to hear why you tried to flatten her nose.'

Kat wanted to protest, to say that she would never do a thing like that. But she *had* done it. Unreal as it felt, it couldn't be denied.

'Well?'

Master Haryn's eyes were grey, an oddly pale colour in his dark, weather-bitten face. Right now his gaze rested on her with calm expectation, unavoidable. But she had no answer she could give him. She couldn't tell him about Daniel and the blue wagon, and the Memory Day dinner she had missed. She shrugged, and looked down again at the stone floor of the Armoury. A silence descended, thoroughly unpleasant.

'Katriona?'

It was rare enough that Master Haryn used her given name, but not even that could make her raise her eyes. She just shook her head and bit her lip, trying to hold back hot, stinging tears. If only Lu hadn't said what she had about the skirt and her hair . . . It was true that she had done her best to look attractive. And Lu had made it sound cheap and ridiculous. It was easy for Lu to look good in the right way – she was tall and slim and had gowns and jewellery by the chestload, and she knew how to wear them too. While Kat . . .

A gloved hand swam into her blurred field of vision and touched her chin. Master Haryn forced her to raise her face to the light. She twisted free, but she knew he had seen the tears.

'Hold still,' he said. 'I need to look at your eyes.'

He made her turn her face into the brightest bit of sunlight and covered first one eye, then the other. Then he took off his gloves and pressed his fingers against her left temple, gently at first, then more firmly. Kat winced. It was where the hardest blow had fallen, the one that had made the world blur for a moment.

'Not a good spot,' said Master Haryn, 'but your eyes can still focus, so I think you've been lucky. Luckier than you deserve.' He looked at her for another few moments. 'So you won't tell me what is wrong between the two of you. Which leaves me no choice but to judge by what I saw. And what I saw, Trivallia, was an unprovoked attack by you.' He put his gloves carefully on the table, and she thought he was still waiting, still giving her time. 'It gives me no pleasure. Particularly not now, because I thought you were actually making progress. And there are plenty of people who will be only too pleased to say I told you so. You certainly don't need another black mark on your record, but you leave me no other option. You are banned from the Weapons Yard for two weeks, and I have to report your behaviour to Alcedina.'

Kat looked up in alarm. Not Alcedina! As if she wasn't in enough trouble with him already!

'Are you sure there is nothing you want to tell me?'

She knew he was asking for a way out. She knew that he actually liked her, and that he didn't want to see her punished for yet another breach of conduct. But there was still no answer she could give him, nor anything that she could say in her defence.

The infirmary smelled pungently of herbs and soap – not altogether pleasant, thought Kat, wrinkling her nose. Although her room was directly above it, she rarely set foot in the sick bay, and she heartily wished it hadn't been necessary now.

In the bed closest to the door was a man with one leg hoisted into the air by cords and pulleys. Awkwardly supporting himself on one elbow, he seemed quite intent on his two visitors, a couple of off-duty bredinari, and the game of cards they were playing. They barely looked up when Kat walked passed them.

Lu was lying in a cot at the far end of the room, with a wet cloth across the bridge of her nose so that very little of her face showed. It felt strange, standing above her like that, when it was usually Lu who towered above her.

'Lu?'

At first, there was no answer at all.

'Lu, I . . . I'm really, really sorry.'

Slowly, Lu raised a hand and pushed the wet cloth off her lower face.

'Go away,' she said. And the worst part was, she didn't even yell. There was no anger in her voice, just a tired stumble, as if she were close to tears.

Kat left.

'Trivallia. Enter.' The voice was cool, with no hint of welcome in it. Kat got up from the bench in the antechamber, nervously smoothing the wrinkles in her uniform. Then she walked through the open door to Alvar Alcedina's office.

He was seated behind a large desk and at first did not raise his eyes from the notes he was making. Kat came to a halt a fair distance from the desk. She felt no need to be any closer than she had to be.

She had been here before. Once when he threw her out of the Academy. Once when he had to take her back. And a couple of other times when she had brought herself to his notice in various unfortunate ways. She was painfully conscious that she was by no means his favourite apprentice.

He let her stand there for so long that sweat began moistening her palms and armpits, an unpleasantly clammy sort of sweat. When he finally laid down his pen to look at her, it was almost a relief, despite the icy coolness of his dark blue glare.

'Fighting again, Trivallia. Is that correct?'

'Yes, DomPrimus,' she muttered. In his presence, she always felt smaller and grubbier, and somehow dishevelled, even though she *knew* her clothes were clean and her hair tidily braided. He was so immaculate himself, in a uniform that looked as if it didn't even know the meaning of the word 'wrinkle', and his smooth dark hair might have been painted on. His manner made it easy to remember that he was the Bredani's own brother, and if any visitor should chance to forget, the Kingfisher coat of arms of the Alcedina family was there on the wall behind him, in tasteful blue and gold.

'I once made a decision regarding you, Trivallia.' He did not speak especially loudly, but his voice cut to the bone. 'Circumstances forced me to rescind it, but I have often wondered whether I was not right in the first place. Do you know which decision I am talking about?'

She nodded mutely.

'What then, Trivallia?'

She cleared her throat. 'DomPrimus is thinking of the time when . . . when I was expelled from the Academy.'

'Correct. I have sent you back to the borderlands you came from once before. I am exceedingly close to doing so again. But several of your masters have pointed out that you have in fact made progress since then, and their vote is the only reason why you are still here. But believe me, Trivallia, one more infraction, be it ever so trivial . . . and you are out. Irredeemably, irrevocably out. Is that clear?'

'Yes, sir,' she whispered. She barely had a voice left. Oh, Sweet Lady! Daniel. Daniel and his family, and Raven, and the sealed orders that she had read. If Alcedina ever found out . . . Her head hurt, a throbbing at her temples, as if the secret itself was pounding the inside of her skull, trying to get out. Please. Please let him not notice.

'Very well,' said Alcedina curtly and took up his pen again. 'You may leave.'

'Thank you, DomPrimus.' She gave him her best bow, though it made her head swim even more, and fled desperately from the lion's den.

UNKNOWN PERPETRATORS

he came out of the shadows, so abruptly that she nearly decked him out of sheer shock. But it was only Raven.

'Whoa there, little greyling,' he said, taking her quite gently by the elbow. 'I need your help with something.'

'What, again?' she snapped, none too kindly. She wanted nothing more to do with him, what with Alcedina's threat hanging over her head. It had been only two weeks since that uncomfortable interview and his warning was still crystal clear in her mind. Also, she was meeting Daniel before the evening show at the Panorama Palace, and she didn't want to be late.

'That's no way to greet an old friend,' said Raven in an aggrieved voice. She couldn't see his face clearly in the gathering dusk, and she was uncertain whether there was any real affront behind his words.

'You startled me,' she said, half apologetic.

'Yes, I noticed,' he grunted. 'And I didn't think you'd

got all dolled up like that just on the off chance that you'd bump into me.'

She immediately regretted her apology. What was it with men that they couldn't let her wear a dress every now and then without making all sorts of stupid comments? She had just made it through a barrage of off-colour jokes from the guards at the castle gate, all because she had borrowed Merian's skirt again.

'What do you want?' she said, feeling short of patience.

'What do you think? I'm not here just to gaze into your emerald eyes, girlie. I'm no great fan of redheads. But I want the use of the brain that lives under that flaming hair. Come along, for the Lady's sake.'

His grip on her elbow firmed, and she dug in her heels without thinking. They were still close enough to the gate that the guards might hear her if she yelled. Not that she was going to – too embarrassing, for one thing – but she didn't like the idea of moving out of earshot with a man who could probably 'pluck the feathers off a sleeping chicken', as Tess used to say of people she thought none too honest, but clever with it.

Raven let go of her when he felt her resistance.

'What's got into you?' he said. 'Anyone would think I was after your purse. I just need you to write something for me. I'll even pay you a few pennies for your troubles, if I must.'

In spite of herself, she hesitated.

'I'm . . . meeting someone,' she said.

His grin was visible even in the gathering shadows. 'You don't say. But where? It's not as if it will take you all evening to write a few words, and I've brought pen and ink and everything. Come on now, I've been looking for you for two whole days . . . So where are you going, girlie?'

'Summertown.' Nothing too revealing about that – hundreds of people met there every evening. That she was actually meeting someone Raven had been paid to look for by Alvar Alcedina himself . . . No, she thrust that thought out of her head for the moment, almost afraid that Raven's quick eyes might spot it.

'Summertown? Well and good. I'll walk you down there, we find a quiet spot and a mug of beer to go with it, you write a few lines for me and I pay you two marks. How about it?'

'Silver?' The question just popped out, and she felt like kicking herself. That was almost the same as agreeing!

'Two silver marks? Are you crazy? Do I look as if I crap gold every time I go to the shithouse? Copper, of course. All right, three marks then, and not a penny more. Come on, girlie, I know you could use the money.'

He was absolutely right. Her little trips to Summertown had not been free.

'Five marks,' she said, or perhaps it was her empty purse talking.

'Done,' he said, and slapped her shoulder. 'Damn, but you'd make a fine horse trader, girlie. Well, come on, then. Let's get on with it.'

She followed him through the now familiar streets of the north quarter, through the city gates and into

Summertown. They found a small beer tent, almost empty this weeknight.

'What's your drink? Winterbrew? Goldie?'

Kat eyed the barrels set up at the back and sniffed the air testingly. To someone brought up in an inn, beer was a serious business. 'I'll have a pint of black ale, if they have it,' she said.

Raven raised an eyebrow. 'Not quite a ladies' drink, now, is it? But if that's what you want, that's what we'll get.' He called to the landlord, and soon two steins of near-black ale were set in front of them, with thick honey-coloured froth on top.

'Your health,' said Raven, taking a hearty swallow. 'And now, to work!'

Obediently, Kat picked up the pen he provided, and began to write to his dictation.

Most of it was dull stuff – tedious accounts of prices of ore and seed and wheat and bread in the Southlands. It seemed Raven had noted and talked to every single Southern Rider, guard or archer that had come his way. He followed her writing carefully, to make sure she got the numbers right.

'I know how to read figures,' he said, 'so don't think you can leave anything out.'

'If you don't trust me, why not get someone else to do this?' she said, somewhat annoyed.

He scowled at her and took another draught of his beer. 'I don't trust anyone,' he said darkly. And his eyes, which most of the time were his friendliest feature, suddenly seemed so cold and mean that her heart skipped a beat.

'As for the persons wanted for questioning,' he continued, 'I have traced . . . Come on now, girl, write! . . . I have traced them back to Breda City, to Summertown, where they may be found in showing off so-called panoramas under the leadership of Samuel Sardi. If you have any orders for me, I'm staying at the the Golden Goose for the next eight days, after which my caravan leaves once again for the Southlands. In obedience and respectful regard, your loyal servant and all that nonsense – you know how it's supposed to go . . .' He raised his gaze from the beer. 'Girl? What's got into you?'

'Nothing,' she said. Her heart was pounding so hard it made her chest hurt. Daniel. He had found Daniel and his family. What on earth was she to do?

'Well, write it down, then. What am I paying you for?'

He was looking at her keenly, expectantly. Slowly, to keep her hand from shaking, she dipped her pen in the inkwell and finished writing.

'Good. Now read it back to me.'

She had to clear her throat a couple of times, but she made it through all the lists of prices and numbers and soldiers and the like.

'As for the persons wanted for questioning, I have traced them back to Breda City, to Summertown, where they may be found showing off so-called panoramas under the leadership of Samuel Sardi. If you have any orders for me, I'm staying at the Golden Goose for the next eight days . . .' and so on, through the last of it, with all the proper salutations.

'Good,' he said. 'Thank you. Here's your five marks.' He pushed the coins across the table, and she pocketed them automatically. The worn metal felt colder than usual against her sweaty palm.

'Thank you,' she said, getting to her feet.

'Aren't you going to finish your beer?'

The mug was still more than half full, but the thought of the strong, dark taste suddenly made her nauseous.

'You were right. It's no ladies' drink,' she managed. 'You finish it, if you like.'

'Hah! Can't wait to get to your sweetheart, more like. Ah well. I was young too, once. Run along, girlie.'

Gratefully she left the close air of the beer tent and stood for a few moments outside, beneath the streaky sunset skies, just trying to breathe again. *As for the family wanted for questioning, I have traced them . . .* The words were ringing inside her skull. She had said them out loud, pretending to read back his report to him. She had said them. But those were not the words she had written.

Daniel was waiting for her at the Panorama Palace.

'What kept you?' he said impatiently. 'You said you'd come as soon as you were off duty. Now there's nearly no time before the evening show!'

'I'm . . . I'm sorry,' Kat stuttered, still trying to breathe normally. 'Daniel, can we . . . can we go somewhere quiet? I have to talk to you.'

He smiled.

'You sound so serious. But if we hurry, we can sit for a little while by the brook. Come on . . .'

He took her hand. It felt so natural, and yet so odd. Even in the middle of the turmoil tumbling through her head, all her thoughts of Raven and his report and the part of it that she had faked, even in the middle of all that, she felt a warm thrill run through her because Daniel took her hand.

Just outside the Summertown gates, there was a path that ran along the palisades, across a hill and through a bramble thicket. And once through the thicket, there was a quiet spot by the brook where it was possible to pretend that Summertown and Breda City were miles away, and they were all alone in the soft evening dusk.

Daniel took off his woollen coat and laid it across the log they used for a bench. It was when he did such things that he made Kat feel like some sort of princess or great lady. Most days she worked her fingers to the bone, and she was quite used to being wet, dirty, sweaty, blistered and bruised from dawn to dusk. But when she was with Daniel, not even the night dew was allowed to touch her.

'What is it, then?' he said lightly. 'This serious business of yours.'

He said it so confidently, as if it could not possibly be any great calamity. Her throat closed for a moment, and she hardly knew where to begin.

'Daniel. Are you and your family planning to stay the whole summer?'

'Yes, of course. You know that.'

'It might be better . . . It might be best if you left. If you went somewhere else for a while.'

His smile vanished.

'What do you mean?'

'Just that . . . that it might be best.' She hardly knew what she meant. Only that she was dreadfully afraid of what might happen if they stayed.

'Are you trying to get rid of me?' He said it jokingly, but there was a hint of earnest hurt in it too. For a wayfarer like Daniel, it must be much too easy to believe that people would rather see him go than stay.

'No!' she cried, giving his hand a little squeeze. 'No. It's just that . . . Aren't you in danger here? In a place where the Motherhouses have so much influence?'

'Don't be afraid,' he said. 'As long as we do not take photographs openly, they leave us alone. Papa is good at talking to authorities. We get along.' Despite the assurance of his words, there was a momentary glimpse of worry in his eyes. Then his smile returned. 'And wayfarers help each other. Don't you worry. For people like us, Summertown is just about the safest place in the world.'

'I hope you're right,' said Kat softly. But she hoped for more than that. She hoped Raven would not realize that she had tampered with his report. She hoped that other Alcedina spies did not find Daniel and his family – the Sardis seemed to have no inkling that the single most powerful man in the country was looking for them. She hoped that Alcedina did not send for Raven to get a personal report. And that if he did, he would not wonder too much why Raven could not be found at the Cup and the Pitcher, as Kat had written in the report. Most of all, she fervently hoped that Alvar Alcedina would never ever realize that a certain bredinari prentice had anything at all to do with that faulty report . . .

Suddenly, Daniel's grip on her hand tightened.

'Look,' he whispered into her ear, so softly she could only just catch the words. 'Over there. By the bank.'

She followed his gaze a little way up the brook, to where the bank was nearly the height of a man. At first she could see nothing unusual. But then she caught it – a quick jewel-blue glint, a tiny hunting body darting across the darkened waters.

'Kingfisher,' she whispered. 'You don't see many of those. They are so shy.'

'They shy away from people, certainly,' said Daniel. 'Papa says they're anything but shy with each other. Jealous birds, they are.'

'Why do you have a kingfisher carved on your wagon?' she asked, thinking about how odd it was that the kingfisher should be the emblem both of Alcedina and the family he hunted.

'In one of our fairy tales, the kingfisher is a lucky bird,' answered Daniel. 'It helps a poor boy win the princess. I think that was on Papa's mind when he was building the wagon for Mama. He was a wayfarer, and not particularly rich, and she . . . well, she was used to living in a house much finer than any traveller's wagon could be.'

'How long ago did your mother die?' Kat asked quietly.

'It's been six years now.' Daniel lowered his head and looked into the water. 'I still miss her, but . . . I've grown used to her not being here any more.'

They sat in silence for a while. Kat looked at Daniel's bent head and felt an overpowering urge to make sure nothing bad ever happened to him again. Her secrets were choking her, but how could she say any more than she had?

'I hope the kingfisher brings you better luck in the future,' she said finally.

He raised his head and seemed to shake off his sadness.

'It's just a fairy tale,' he said. 'In reality, kingfishers are not at all sweet and helpful beings. If you are a small fish, they are lethal killers. And they defend their hunting grounds viciously, even against their own young. Sometimes the poor things actually drown.'

'You mean, they drown their own *children*?'

'Sometimes,' Daniel said, looking smug at the shock he had caused. 'If they think the young birds are after their territory.'

Kat shuddered and thought again of Alcedina's icy blue glare. Kingfisher blue. And it was certainly easier to see him as the merciless hunter than cast him in the role of helpful fairytale bird.

'Daniel, I think . . . I really think your family need to be very, very careful while you're here.'

'I tell you, we are. Why are you suddenly so concerned?'

She didn't know how to answer him. Couldn't, when

it came right down to it, betray everything her life had been about before she met Daniel: her apprenticeship, the corps, the silver hellhorse she hoped to ride one day.

'It was . . . a dream I had . . .' she finally said, evasively. Not an outright lie – she had had bad dreams aplenty lately.

'A dream?' He sounded sincerely startled. 'Katriona . . . you are about the last person I thought would be frightened by a *dream*.'

The half-lie made her blush and look down at her feet.

'Promise me you will be careful,' she said.

'We always are.' He rested his fingers lightly against her cheek. 'Look at me, Katriona. Let me see your eyes.'

She raised her head. She could never have enough of the way he looked at her. As if she was something *fine*. As if she was the most beautiful girl he had ever seen. His own eyes were so dark that you could lose your way in their darkness. His touch was so gentle it made her want to cry.

'Surely you can find better things to dream about,' he said teasingly, 'or else I'll have to help you . . .' And then he kissed her.

She had been kissed before. Birch, a good friend of hers from the Academy kitchens, had done it at the Landing Day party nearly two years ago. And Tarquin from the Academy had tried it last midsummer, when he had had a little too much to drink. This was different. She had never before been kissed by someone she *liked* so much.

Suddenly it all became a little too serious. She pushed him away.

'You must really think you are the bee's knees,' she said. 'Did you actually think you could make me dream of *you*?'

'I can try,' he said irrepressibly.

But there was no more kissing that night. In the distance, the Motherhouse bells started to chime, and this meant that Samuel Sardi was opening his doors to the first audience of the evening. Daniel cursed.

'I'm late. Damn. Please, Katriona, wait for me after the show. Please?'

'I can't,' she said, feeling miserable. 'I'm on foaling duty tonight.'

Daniel snapped to his feet in one long, frustrated motion.

'Why must it always be like this?' he said. 'Why is there never *time*? Old people run everything, and we get to decide precisely *nothing*.'

It was often that way with Daniel. His moods changed so quickly – all fun and happiness one moment, sheer fury the next. He could go from laughter to earnestness and back to laughter again in the time it took a more sedate person to take a deep breath. To Kat, who was used to living among people who had spent years polishing their self-control, it was quite a rocky ride.

They walked back to Summertown together.

'Goodnight, then,' said Daniel, when they reached the gates. 'If you're really sure you can't stay . . .'

'Goodnight,' she said, leaning her head against his shoulder. They stood together for a moment. Then Daniel sighed.

'Papa is waiting,' he said. 'May you dream better dreams tonight.'

She stood for a while, watching as he went in through the gates. He kept turning around to look at her, almost walking backwards for a while, at least until he bumped into a fat lady citizen of Breda, who gave him a real mouthful for his inattention. Kat couldn't hear his answer, but he had to put on his most charmingly subservient face in order to calm her ruffled feathers. Kat couldn't help laughing. She gave him a quick wave, and then turned to make her own way home, to the duties that awaited her at the Castle.

Dark had fallen now, and although there was an occasional street lamp, at least in the better parts of town, there were still long stretches where the only light came from the shuttered windows of the houses. Oddly enough, the darkness was at its densest closest to the Castle, where the Great Families lived. Here were few welcoming doors and windows, but rather walled orchards and gardens and wide grounds, and the streets were mostly unlit at night, as those that lived here could well afford to pay a servant to light their way, should they so choose.

On one of those long dark stretches, Kat suddenly heard footsteps right behind her. Before she had time to turn around, someone pushed her so hard that she stumbled forward cracking one knee against the cobbles underfoot. A painful jerk at her hair brought her head back sharply, and a cold metal blade was pressed against her throat.

'Don't scream,' came a quiet menacing voice by her ear.

She didn't scream. But she did throw her weight backwards, tipping both of them on to the hard cobblestones. There was a hiss of pain, and for a moment the coldness of the blade disappeared. She butted her head back, hoping to hit his face, and tried for an elbow to his stomach. Her head hit something hard, and the elbow something soft, but when she tried to roll free of him, he grabbed her hair again and pounded the hilt of his knife against her neck, at the angle where it met her collarbone. It hurt insanely, and her whole arm went dead. The next blow was to her head, right behind the ear, and after that things went rather mushy for a while. Someone was trying to haul her to her feet, and she bit weakly at the hand holding her mouth. Then she found herself forced against a wall, her good arm twisted behind her back and her face pushed bruisingly hard against the crumbling stone. She tried a kick and was punished by a knee thudding into the back of her thigh, numbing the whole leg. Her twisted arm was twisted even further, and most of the fight went out of her. He had her, whoever he was. At least he hadn't used the sharp end of the blade on her, so apparently he had no plans to kill her. Perhaps it was safe to yell for help, after all. Always considering there was anyone around to hear, of course. She gathered a shaky breath.

'Keep your bloody mouth shut,' he hissed, and pushed

her face even harder against the wall, so that the roughness of it grazed her cheek.

'Raven?' she gasped. 'Is it *you*?'

'Who else would it be? How many other people have you tried to swindle today?'

'I haven't—'

'Shut up, I said. I told you I wasn't stupid. Just because a man can't read and write it doesn't make him a complete moron. And you know what happens when my oh-so-perfect little scribe starts to make small mistakes when she reads stuff back to me? I get suspicious, that's what. And do you know what I discover when I follow her out of that beer tent? Damned if I don't see her swanning off, arm in arm with Sardi's eldest boy. How's that for a coincidence? Ought to interest our high and mighty Alcedina, don't you think?'

'It might. If you cared to let him know that you let a common courier read your sealed orders.'

She hardly knew where it came from, that cool, mocking voice. Or rather, she did. It was the same voice that had once driven her stepfather into a rage over and over again, knowing exactly where to hurt, what tender points to prick. But right now the voice was her friend. For one thing, it stopped her snivelling like a hurt child.

'Bloody *girl*!'

'That might interest him too. Don't you think?'

He let her go. For the first time since he shoved her to her knees, she could turn and face him. And what she saw frightened her. He really did look like someone who might use his blade to kill.

It was no cool, measured decision. She just opened her mouth to scream, as loudly and piercingly as she could. He jerked as if she had hit him. And before he had time to react, she pelted down the street, as fast as her still-numb leg would let her. Her boot heels cracked against the cobbles, echoing between the walls, and Merian's second-best skirt swished and flared around her legs so that she could feel the cool night air against her bare skin.

He used up a fair amount of breath cursing her, but he was still close on her heels in a few moments. She could hear him pounding along behind her, but she didn't dare turn her head. Ahead of her she saw Sari's Arch, which marked the old divide between royal lands and free lands around the Castle. To Kat, right now, it was the gateway to what she thought of as the real city, the part of town where there were houses and street lights and people like Agnes Tailor who might actually hear you if you screamed for help. She made a last desperate dash for the safety it promised.

He caught her just before she reached it. They both tumbled to the ground once more, but this time Kat was at the bottom, and Raven's bulk thudded into her with enough force to knock her breath away. She heaved and fought to get enough air to yell, but a squeaky wheeze was all the sound she managed.

Then she heard hoofbeats. There was such a roaring in her ears that at first she wasn't sure, but hoofbeats they were. Raven had heard them too, because he hissed a sharp 'Oh, *hell*!' between clenched teeth.

'If you rat on me, Alcedina gets the whole story, and to

hell with what it costs me,' he snarled into her back. 'So I think silence might be prudent for both of us. Don't you agree?'

She had no breath to answer him with, not even when he raised himself off her and stopped squishing her flat. For the moment she sensed only that she was safe, that he could not now use his blade on her and get away with it.

'Hello!' he called. 'Hello! Can you help us, please? A young girl has been attacked . . .'

Raven might be unlettered, but he was nobody's fool.

The hoofbeats, it turned out, came from the elegant hooves of five black horses from the Strigius Family stables.

'Sweet Our Lady, how terrible!' called one of the riders in a voice that seemed more excited than horrified. She was very young and wore her silver-lined black velvet riding habit with all the confidence of the supremely rich. 'Are you hurt, you poor dear?'

Kat still couldn't breathe well enough to speak, but Raven was perfectly willing to do the talking for both of them.

'Quite badly bruised, I think,' he said. 'There were two of them – they fled into that alley when I surprised them.'

'Aleksa, see if you can catch them. I'll take care of this poor wretch.'

'I hear and obey,' said one of the other riders with an ironic bow. 'The Maestrina has spoken. Come on, Sascha, you and I are going crook-hunting . . .' Sascha, it appeared, was the horse, for none of the others moved to join him. It wasn't until he was well into the alley that one of them reacted.

'Damn. I had better go with him, Ninetka. What if he actually catches them?'

The chances of that were extremely slim, thought Kat dryly, since they only existed in Raven's quick imagination. She glared up at the latter with sincere animosity.

'Here. Let's get you on your feet. You just lean on me, young miss . . .'

'I'd rather lean . . . on the devil himself,' she muttered, but so low that only he could hear it.

'Careful,' he said solicitously, and surreptitiously dug his thumb into a nerve in the arm he was holding. 'The young miss is lucky to have escaped worse.'

'Horrible, just horrible. We're not safe to walk the streets any more,' said Ninetka of the velvet riding habit. 'Oh, the poor dear is bleeding!'

The poor dear touched her face. She was, indeed, bleeding a little from her grazed cheek. A splitting headache was settling itself in her skull, and her collarbone still hurt almost beyond bearing. Superficial grazes and a few drops of blood were far down her list of priorities.

'Did you know your attackers? Did they rob you?'

'No, I – Yes! My purse is gone!' She glared at Raven, because obviously it could only be him. Apart from the five marks he had paid her to do his writing – and she couldn't really holler too much about losing those, she supposed –

but apart from them, there had been two copper pennies of her own. Damn him!

'A sad state of affairs,' said Raven, looking suitably dismayed. 'But perhaps Domnessa Strigius – for it is, surely, Ninetka Strigius I have the honour of address-ing . . .?'

'Do you know me?' said the domnessa, looking flat-tered.

'Who does not?' said Raven with admirable convic-tion, considering that Kat was fairly certain he had never heard of the woman before. But the others had called her Ninetka, and the black and silver riding habit and sheer quality of horseflesh made Strigius a very obvious guess.

'Perhaps Domnessa Strigius in her kindness will attend to the young miss? She is clearly somewhat shaken and should probably keep to her bed for a couple of days.'

'No, really, I'm fine . . .' objected Kat.

'Stuff and nonsense,' said the domnessa. 'Anyone can see you are in need of medical attention, and we just happen to have one of the finest physicians in Breda on our staff. Yakov, lift her on to your horse . . .'

'But . . .' Kat tried again, but Raven cut her short.

'She has suffered a blow to the head, I think. These things are not to be taken lightly, Domnessa.' He was still holding Kat's arm. It was obvious what he was up to. If he could lodge her firmly under the protective custody of the young domnessa for some days, he could finish his busi-ness here and get out of town before she had a chance to do anything about it.

Getting Raven out of town was an excellent idea,

119

thought Kat. It was what he might do before he left that worried her. Especially if it concerned Daniel and his family.

'The domnessa is too kind,' she said, trying to look healthy and clear-eyed and steady on her feet. 'But I am perfectly all right, and there are duties that await me . . .'

The last bit was a mistake.

'Child! You mustn't even think of working in your state! Yakov, help her.'

Yakov claimed her other arm. Kat took it back again.

'I really can't impose—'

'Yes, you can,' said Raven firmly. His grip had not shifted an inch. 'Go with the domnessa. You must not jeopardize your health.' There was a menacing undertone to the last remark that left Kat in no doubt as to its message; either she left now, with Ninetka Strigius, or Raven picked up where he had left off.

She gave in, temporarily at least, and let Yakov hoist her on to his well-mannered horse. Truth be told she needed his assistance – one arm was still quite dead, and her bruised knee felt hot and thick with swelling.

At that moment, Aleksa and his comrade returned from their 'crook-hunting'.

'They got away,' he gasped, out of breath. 'We nearly had them though.'

Somehow, Kat doubted that.

'Too bad,' said Raven without batting an eye. 'The city is hardly safe while such perpetrators lurk unknown in our streets.' The phrase rolled off his tongue as if he had been practising. 'But you, Domnessa, are a true angel of mercy. Goodnight.'

He bowed deeply, and walked off.

'What a brave fellow,' said Ninetka Strigius, following him with her eyes. 'You must be so grateful that he came to your assistance.'

'Oh, I am,' said Kat, biting her lip. 'And I shall do everything in my power to make sure he gets his just deserts . . .'

But he was already quite a long way off, and she wasn't sure he heard her.

The Strigius household could afford to pay for the best of everything. The sick bay was larger and better equipped than that of the Castle, and Domnessa Ninetka was probably not exaggerating when she claimed that the family physician was among the finest in Breda. With all that knowledge and experience at her disposal, Kat felt almost embarrassed that all she could bring to the show was a collection of minor and utterly commonplace bruises.

'What's this, then?' said the physician, pressing his fingers against her temple almost exactly the way Master Haryn had done some days earlier. 'These are not recent. Do you make it a habit to get attacked once or twice a week?'

'No,' said Kat somewhat sourly. 'I'm a bredinari prentice. At weapons practice, one sometimes collects bruises.'

'A fledgling bredinari? Well then, you probably know already that you are not seriously hurt.'

'I've been saying that. No one will listen.'

'Quite so. But you have had a fairly nasty knock on the head, and there is a deep contusion by your collarbone, which will impede motion of that arm for about a week. And on top of that, your bruise collection, as you call it, is an impressive one,' he said kindly. 'Also, you are a great deal more shaken than you are prepared to admit. All in all, young lady, a few days' rest is an excellent idea.'

'But—'

'No buts, please. Accept the generous offer of the domnessa. Those are your physician's orders. I am sure that Domnessa Ninetka has already sent word to the Castle to let them know where you are. To bed, young lady. Now.'

She lay alone in the sick bay waiting for the sounds of the huge house to subside. She knew that a property like this one would be well guarded, but she reasoned that the guards would be concerned with keeping people from entering rather than leaving. And she needed desperately to leave. She absolutely had to see Daniel.

She still did not know why a powerful man like Alcedina should take a personal interest in the Sardis, but she had no desire to see them arrested and charged with heresy, if that was what he had in mind. And what else could it be? The Sardis were not thieves and murderers – photography was the only remotely illegal thing they could be accused of, wasn't it? Was it really such a crime to catch mirror images on a plate of glass? It was hard for her to understand. She had felt no evil force at work when

Uncle Isak took her picture. But then, there were many things she and the Motherhouses didn't agree on, so perhaps she was a lost cause and well set on the road to heresy herself.

Not a nice thought, she decided. If the heresy was bad enough, one could be condemned and cast out by the Bredani, the way Ermine had been. *You, Creature, my land will not suffer you. The earth you walk on shall burn beneath your feet. The food you eat shall turn to poison in your mouth. All gifts of the land shall be denied you – food, sleep and comfort – from this time till you die.*

Was taking a photograph bad enough for that? Or having one's photograph taken?

She dozed for a bit. Her head and her shoulder throbbed in competition with each other, and she kept shivering as if she were cold. But the clean, soft nightgown they had given her was soon drenched in sweat.

She closed her eyes for a bit, and must have fallen asleep. When she woke, the house had settled into a nighttime quiet. She had no idea of the precise time, only that it must be late. Her body wanted sleep so badly it was an ache almost deeper than the rest of her hurts, but she was consumed with worry for Daniel and his family, a nagging anxiety that would not permit her to relax and rest completely. She sat up.

Ouch! And ouch again. Could someone lend her a new shoulder for a little while? And a new head too? The floorboards were cold under her bare feet. She needed shoes, and clothes of some kind, or she wouldn't get far. She checked a row of closets along one wall, but they were mostly empty. No signs of any clothing, neither her own nor something she could borrow.

Down one end was a storeroom, with a cot that was probably the physician's home-away-from-home when he had need. Under the cot was a pair of worn slippers, much too big but they would have to do. Shuffling along as quietly as she could, she peeked into the corridor beyond. It was an entrance hall of sorts, with a stairwell going up to the next storey. A single lamp had been left burning, with the wick turned down low, and on a hook under the stairs was a big woollen overcoat and a broad-brimmed hat. Just the thing. Or better than nothing, at any rate. The coat was long enough to brush her ankles, and with her hair shoved under the hat, she hoped she looked a lot less like a patient trying to escape her 'angel of mercy'.

The door gave a terrifyingly loud squeak as she opened it. Quickly, she slipped outside. The night sky was clouded, for which she was grateful – less light to see her by. She left the path and dodged into the deep shadows of some apple trees. The garden wall had to be over there, somewhere . . .

'Halt! Who goes there?'

The sharp call shattered the silence, and her heart gave a painful leap in her chest. For a second, she just stood there, frozen, hoping beyond reason that the shout was not directed at her.

'You there in the orchard. Step out into the light.'

She considered making a run for it, but thought better of it. The Strigius guards were probably armed with crossbows. And so far, she had done nothing wrong – just borrowed a coat and a hat. And some worn-out slippers . . .

'Into the light, I said.'

Resignedly, she stepped on to the path again, so that the light from the windows fell on her.

'Who the hell are *you*?' came an astonished enquiry.

'Kat Trivallia. A . . . a guest of Ninetka Strigius.'

'Let me have a look at you.' One of the guards, with the expected crossbow, stepped on to the path. As he came closer, she saw that he was one of the young men who had been accompanying Ninetka on her outing. What had she called him? Aleksa? He reached for her hat and she let him do it. Somewhere in the darkness, she knew, was another guard, and he probably had *his* crossbow aimed right at her.

'Oh, it *is* you,' said Aleksa when her red hair tumbled from the confines of the hat. 'Ninetka's little charity case. What on earth are you doing in the orchard this side of midnight?'

'I couldn't sleep. I just wanted to walk for a bit . . .'

'Couldn't sleep? All right, if you say so. But all the same, I think I'll just walk you back to the sick bay. This way, Miss.' He took her arm, lightly but firmly. 'I know my sister can be just a bit overbearing,' he said under his breath, so that the other guard might not hear him, 'but I still think fleeing her charitable attentions like this is a little impolite.'

'I don't mean to be ungrateful . . .'

'No. But you had other plans, didn't you? But please,

Miss, not tonight. I don't feel like chasing you all over town in order to rescue you once more.'

And there was nothing for it but to follow him meekly back to the sickroom.

'We don't usually need to lock up our guests,' said the physician dryly, 'and I have no intention of doing so now. But what else are we to do with you?'

Kat didn't answer. She just sat there in her borrowed coat and nightgown, feeling stupid.

'What is it that is so important that you can't rest for even one night under this roof? Surely not just a foal watch.'

Kat still made no answer. What was there to say?

The physician sighed.

'All right. I'll make a deal with you. I promise that you may leave this house in the morning without any inter-ference from Domnessa Ninetka. She will just have to find herself another pet project. In return, I want you to take these valerian drops and go to sleep with no further trou-ble. Is that acceptable?'

Kat finally raised her head. If she could leave in the morning . . . Perhaps a few hours would not make much difference. It was unlikely that Raven could barge in on Alcedina whenever he wanted to, and in the middle of the night. From the sound of it, he had to keep his contact with the Castle circumspect, or he would lose his useful-ness as a spy. Certainly, it would take more than an hour or two. It might even take him a few days. And she felt so battered and dizzy, and tired to the bone.

'Yes,' she said finally. 'I'll agree to that.'

Later, when she lay in her cot feeling the valerian like a heavy buzz in her lips, and in her arms and legs, she thought of Summertown and Daniel, who was probably fast asleep on his sleeping mat under the table inside the blue wagon. Tomorrow he must listen to her. This time she could not afford to let herself be put off with a few reassurances. *He* could not afford it, the Sardis could not afford it. Even if they didn't know it yet.

Don't let me be too late, she prayed, as the valerian dragged her down to a dark and heavy sleep.

ASHES

She woke several times during the night with her heart beating fiercely, as if she had had a nightmare, but she remembered no dreams. When dawn finally arrived, it was as if someone had drained the blood from her body and replaced it with lead. Grey and stiff-limbed, she lay in her cot, searching for the strength to move.

'So, Trivallia, how are you feeling?'

The physician entered quietly, letting in a brief chill breath of morning air along with him. Fine, she wanted to say. Just fine. But no sound came. Instead, to her horror, slow hot tears started to seep from her eyes, running down the sides of her face and into her hair.

'Where does it hurt?'

Her head and her shoulder were both still throbbingly sore, but . . .

'It's not that,' she croaked.

He sat beside her cot.

'Look at me,' he said, and like Master Haryn had done, he placed his hand first over one eye, then the other.

'You don't seem concussed,' he said. 'But Katriona . . . That is your name, isn't it?'

'Yes.'

'It is not just your body that can be battered and strained and exhausted. Sometimes your mind gets bruised as well, and there is no shame in that. You need to rest and give yourself a chance to heal. I think you ought to stay another day.'

'You said – you promised –'

'Yes. And I won't go back on my word. But Katriona, this is your body *and* your mind telling you that you have had enough. Listen to them.'

'There's something I have to do.'

'Can't it wait?'

'No.'

'How old are you? Fourteen? Fifteen?'

'Fourteen.'

'You're still a child. Leave whatever you think you *have* to do for the adults to deal with.'

Kat detested being called a child. Children were afraid of the dark. Children cried when they were hurt. The world was full of things children couldn't do or didn't dare.

'I am not a child,' she said through clenched teeth. 'I do what I have to do.'

The look he gave her seemed sad, though she didn't understand why that might be.

'As you wish,' he said. 'Someone from the Castle has come to see you. I'll let him in.'

It was Tarquin.

'Have you been in the wars again?' he said teasingly. 'Up to your usual no good?' Tarquin always teased. There was something oddly comforting about that, as if nothing could be truly difficult or truly serious with Tarquin there to joke about it.

'Watch it,' she said, 'or I'll give you a taste of the wars.'

He looked at her. She had wiped the tears hurriedly before he entered, but perhaps there were still traces.

'You are . . . all right, aren't you?' he said, suddenly less certain of himself. 'I mean, you're not seriously hurt or anything. Are you?'

'No,' she said, firmly. 'I'm fine.'

'Good. I've brought you a clean uniform. And a humongous piece of news!'

'What is it?'

'Not yet. Get dressed first. We have to hurry back to the Castle.'

'But there's something important I have to—'

'Kat, *nothing* could be more important than this. Oh, all right, I'll tell you. The lists are being posted today. At noon.'

'You mean that—'

'Yes! In less than an hour we shall know which of us is getting our hellhorse this year!'

Inside her head, everything froze. The lists. Now . . . or very nearly now. She had to know. She just had to. And anyway, it would be utterly impossible to explain to Tarquin that there might after all be something in the world more important than this year's hellhorse assignments. Particularly when you couldn't tell him what.

'Give me that uniform,' she said. 'If we hurry, we'll make it before noon.'

And after that, once she had seen the lists and before all the excitement had died down, no one would notice if she sneaked off to warn Daniel.

You won't be on them, she told herself, fumbling with the shirt and her useless right arm. Not after that stupid incident with Lu. Plus every other unfortunate thing you've been mixed up in this past year. Don't get your hopes up.

But the butterfly feeling in the pit of her stomach wouldn't go away.

The hall outside Studmaster Janek's office was crowded, and the apprentices were not the only ones eager to see this year's lists posted. Older, more experienced Riders were waiting too, albeit with slightly greater dignity.

'Oh, I'll die, I'll die, I'll *die* . . .' muttered Merian, pale around the gills, and probably the only person in the room desperately wishing *not* to see her name on the lists.

'I don't think you need to worry,' whispered Kat. 'They wouldn't give a hellhorse to someone who . . . to someone who feels like you do.' But what about me? she thought. What about an unruly and insubordinate Vale girl? Might she be considered for a hellhorse?

The noon bell rang, and a collective quiver of tension ran through the assembled crowd. Studmaster Janek's door opened on cue, and the Studmaster himself emerged to fasten two sheets of stiff parchment on to the waiting frames.

'Gentlemen,' he said, steadfastly ignoring the presence of the several 'ladies'. 'Gentlemen, the lists.'

Obviously not everyone could read the lists at once, and it was customary to line up according to rank and seniority, which of course meant the apprentices were at the very back.

'Not fair,' whispered Valente. 'We're the ones who are most nervous.' But even though it felt like an eternity, eventually their turn came.

And there it was.

Prentice H. Meilies, aspirant to filly out of Capra's Subito, from the Blue line.

'Meiles, you're here!' called Rubio.

Prentice L. Ceuta, aspirant to filly out of Medes' Corona, Yellow line.

'Lu! Lu, you're there too!' Kat turned to Lu and hugged her, fights and bloody noses momentarily forgotten. Lu just stood there with her mouth open, managing to look shocked and ecstatic at the same time.

'I'm there,' she whispered. 'Kat, I'm really there!'

And much further down, nearly at the end:

Prentice K. Trivallia, aspirant to filly out of Grane's Frost, Black line.

'We both are,' said Kat hoarsely, reading that unbelievable line once more. Grane's Frost . . . but that meant . . . that meant that *her* hellhorse, her very own hellhorse, was the daughter of Dorissa's Frost, the first hellhorse she had even ridden! 'Lu, I'm getting Frost's first foal . . .' Her head swam with vivid memories of that dew-bright morning – the speed, the sense of danger, the utter thrill. Stealing a ride on Frost had been the first step on her journey here, although she hadn't known it at the time.

'Congratulations, both of you,' said Merian, obviously happy on two counts – that her best friends were both assigned a hellhorse and that she herself wasn't.

And suddenly Kat and Lu were hugging each other like crazy, dancing about, as if there had never been a moment's bad blood between them. Kat's shoulder hurt like merry hell, but it didn't seem to matter. Not now.

'Katriona Bredinari . . .' said Lu.

'Yes, Lusiana Bredinari?'

'This calls for a celebration!'

And it was impossible to refuse, impossible to sneak off unnoticed.

It was early evening before she finally managed to make her way down to Summertown, and in front of the Panorama Palace a sizeable crowd was waiting to be let in. Samuel Sardi himself was on the door, politely blocking the entrance until the darkened space inside was ready. Kat pushed through the throng with the aid of a steady stream of excuse me's.

'Good evening, Master Sardi,' she said politely, trying not to show her relief at seeing him quite normal and free and un-arrested. 'May I talk to Daniel for a moment?'

'Hello, Katriona. Go on in – but not too long. He is getting ready, and as you see, the audience awaits.'

'Thank you. I won't make him late for the show.'

Daniel was setting up the system of mirrors and lanterns and flash powder that provided Samuel Sardi with his magical entrance.

'Kat!' he called happily when he saw her. 'I didn't think you'd be able to make it until the day after tomorrow.'

'That was the plan, but something happened. Daniel, I have to talk to you . . .'

'There you go again, sounding all serious. Have you had bad dreams again? I thought we'd taken care of that . . .'

He stood there in his stage costume, naked to the waist except for his scarlet waistcoat, looking like something out of an Eastland fairy tale. His fingers were blackened with soot from the flash powder bowls, and there was a dark smudge of it right next to his nose. She barely stopped herself from reaching out to rub it away. Why could he never be serious at the right time?

'There's more to this than a dream,' she said, and finally her anxiety seemed to reach him. He wiped his fingers on a grimy bit of cloth and looked at her searchingly.

'All right then,' he said. 'Sit down and watch the show, and we'll talk when it's over.'

'Thank you,' she said, relieved that he was finally listening. It made the hard lump in her stomach dissolve a little bit. 'And Daniel . . .'

'Yes?'

'Hold still for a moment.' She took the cloth from him,

found a reasonably clean corner, and wiped away the black smudge on his face.

His breath halted for a moment, and he gave her a look that made her stop what she was doing.

'What?'

His eyes gleamed in the pre-show darkness. He looked as if he was about to say something, but then he just shook his head.

'Nothing.' And then he kissed her, lightly and quickly, on the lips. 'Just watch the show. I'll see you later.'

The hexagonal hall was closely packed; not a single seat was free. A little unusual for a weekday night, Kat thought, but perhaps word of the fabulous panoramas had gone round. It might not be easy to persuade Daniel's father to give up such a good income. The Panorama Palace was heavy and difficult to put up and take down, and the hauling was probably no joy either. If they had to leave Breda and go all the way to Koronberk or Colmonte, it would mean weeks without earnings, and these would not be winter weeks, but the precious days of the high season . . .

The lights dimmed, and the buzz of conversation died away. Then came the first bright flash, and Daniel's father's six mirror images appeared on the walls.

'Welcome,' he called, making his usual bow. 'Let me take you on a journey . . . a magical journey to distant—'

Kat could not tell where it came from. But suddenly a rock whistled through the air towards one of the images, and Samuel Sardi's turbaned form smashed and dropped to the ground in a shower of glittering shards.

'Devil's work!' screamed a woman, rearing up from her seat. 'Black magic and devil's work!'

Part of the audience just stared at her in stunned silence. Others began to yell; some protested about crazy women ruining the show, others demanded to know what she was on about.

'What do you mean, devil's work?' asked a big man in a blacksmith's apron. 'It's just a couple of mirrors and a bit of paint!'

'Is it?' cried the woman. 'Is it really? Then what has happened to my daughter?'

'Ladies and gentlemen, please be seated,' said Samuel Sardi, trying to restore order. There were still five of him left. 'We will be ready to resume the show in moments . . .'

'There will be no more shows, you devil. Not after what you've done to my daughter with your filthy magic! Just look at her . . .' She pulled a young girl to her feet, and it was obvious there was something wrong with her. Her eyes were staring vacantly, and a trail of drool trickled from her gaping mouth and down her chin.

The huge oil lamp in the ceiling was lowered so that the room was once more lit almost to daylight brightness. Samuel Sardi disappeared from the mirrors and reappeared in the flesh, just one solid and reassuring version of him.

'My dear madam, I do see that your daughter is sorely afflicted, but it has nothing to do with this house. I have never seen her before in my life.'

'Is that so? Are you going to stand there and deny you and your devil kin made this demon image?'

Kat breathed in sharply, because the picture the woman held aloft was unmistakably a photograph. No paint had been laid atop to veil its sharpness. The metal plate held a clear, sharp black-and-white likeness, not of the daughter as she was now, but of the confident and smiling pretty young girl it seemed she had once been.

'So, devil. Do you deny it?'

Samuel Sardi's stunned gaze moved from the woman to the daughter and back again.

'See for yourselves,' said the woman, tossing the metal plate to the nearest onlookers. 'He has stolen my daughter's soul!'

'But I assure you, madam . . . photography is quite harmless and cannot possibly have caused your daughter's—'

'Devil magic!' screamed the woman, and now more voices joined in.

'Demon craft!'

'Soul stealer!'

'Filthy wayfarer magic . . .'

Just like that, the crowd went wild. Benches were overturned, several more mirrors shattered, people were shouting and screaming, some trying desperately to get out, others intent on getting to Samuel Sardi or the woman. Kat herself tried to reach Daniel's father, but in seconds he was completely lost from sight in a mass of human backs and legs, and a turning shoulder bumped her jaw so hard that she bit her own tongue. Somewhere a lantern was knocked over, and the smell of hot oil and smouldering canvas took the last remnant of sense out of the mob. They trampled over each other, stepping on soft bodies without compunction, and the screaming no longer had intelligible words in it. So many bodies were crammed up against one wall that the whole Panorama Palace rocked like a ship threatening to capsize. Kat was no longer thinking of Samuel Sardi or Daniel or anyone else – she thought only about not being knocked down and trodden to bloody bits, of fighting for breath, of trying to get out and get free.

Then the wood and canvas of the wall burst under the pressure, and it was as if a cork had been pulled from a bottle neck. People streamed out of the rocking Palace, out into the evening air and freedom. Kat stumbled over a fallen body, and the world became a chaos of legs and feet, kicks and shoves, and she couldn't get up, all she could do was curl up and try to protect her head.

It probably lasted only for some minutes. Then there were no more bumping knees and treading feet, and Kat wobbled to her feet again.

One side of the Panorama Palace gaped like an open wound. And inside, there were people who were not trying to get out. Instead, they were breaking everything they could lay their hands on – smashing benches, slashing canvas, shattering lamps and mirrors. Samuel Sardi was nowhere to be seen, but in the midst of all the destruction big Kottas was tottering about, crying like a baby and calling helplessly for the men to stop.

'Burn this devilry!' roared a voice in the mob, and while Kat was still just standing there, staring in numb shock at the general mayhem, he grabbed an unbroken lamp and smashed it against one of the panorama rolls, so that flames began to devour the Jungle of Katai, with all its vividly painted animals and plants.

'Burn it! Burn it!' The shout became a chant, and more canvas was tossed on the bonfire, painted and unpainted, along with broken benches and splintered tent poles, so that the flames roared up and turned the men into darkened silhouettes, feverishly feeding the fire, laughing and roaring and drunk on destruction.

Where was Daniel? Where was Daniel's father, and the rest of the family? Kat could still only see Kottas. Not quite knowing what she meant to do other than find them, she turned from the burning Palace and circled around it.

They were at the back, by the caravan. And they did not care what was happening to the Panorama Palace. They were fighting to save their home. The blue wagon, too, was ablaze, and the many buckets that were passed from hand to hand seemed to make little impression on the flames.

It was gone midnight before the last fires had been put out. The Panorama Palace was a sodden ruin, and of the blue wagon only a blackened shell remained. Samuel Sardi sat on a cot in one of the neighbouring caravans trying to breathe with two broken ribs and a face so battered it was barely recognizable. Next to him hunched Uncle Isak, whose hands had suffered terrible burns in his effort to save at least some of the precious glass plates. Without them it would not be possible for the family to recreate the panoramas. Without them, they would lose their means of making a living not just for a while, but forever.

'I . . . I'm so dreadfully sorry,' whispered Kat, and made herself look at Samuel Sardi's abused face.

'. . . not your fault . . .' he murmured thickly. His upper lip was a swollen mass of dark, dry blood. 'Where's Daniel?'

'I'll find him,' said Kat. She had barely reached the door before Uncle Isak snapped to his feet.

'Samuel, I never took that picture!' The words came in a burst, like something long pent up. But he had said them at least ten times while Kat had been there, and his brother's answers had the tired slur of reassurances repeated much too often.

'No. So you say.'

'I swear I didn't!'

'I believe you. Please, Isak, can you be quiet for a while?'

Kat closed the door gently behind her.

Daniel was looking at the blackened ruins of the blue wagon. Kat knew there was no real way to comfort him, that there were many things in this world that couldn't be made all better by a hug and a kiss. But she still had to try.

'Daniel . . .' she said, putting her arm around him.

He tore away from her with a ferocity that took her entirely by surprise.

'Stay away from me!' he hissed. 'Stay away from me and my family!'

His face was twisted with rage, and she had no idea what to do.

'I'm so sorry—'

'Oh, really?' His eyes blazed. 'You knew! You knew this would happen!'

'No, I – No, you misunderstand . . .'

He slapped her. His palm cracked against her cheek with all his anger behind it, and she was so stunned that she didn't even try to duck or parry.

'I never want to see you again!' he said, then spun on his heel and left.

ONE OF THEM

he couldn't really think she had had anything to do with it. He *couldn't* think that of her! She had to talk to him, to explain. It was all a horrible misunderstanding, she had to make him realize . . . but first Daniel wouldn't talk to her, and now the whole family had disappeared. Daniel and his brother and sister, Samuel Sardi and Uncle Isak, even Kottas had managed to dissolve into thin air. All that was left of the Panorama Palace now was a bit of scorched earth, and a pretzel vendor and an enterprising beer-seller were already putting up a booth in the empty lot. Soon every trace of the magical world of the Sardis would have vanished entirely.

'Can't you tell me where they've gone?' she asked the owner of the Tea Pagoda next door. It had been his wagon that had served as their refuge on the night of the fire.

'Don't know anything about that,' said the man curtly, but she felt sure he was lying. None of the residents of Summertown would speak to her any more – they had closed themselves around the Sardis like a wall, protecting them against the Motherhouses and the Castle and all other enemies. In their eyes Kat belonged on the wrong side of that wall, and there was nothing she could say to convince them otherwise.

'If I wrote a note, could you see that they got it?'

'Told you, don't know where they are. Sorry, miss, but will that be all? I have a business to mind.'

And there was nothing for it but to leave the Pagoda.

She was so discouraged that she just stood there. She could think of no more places to search, no more people to ask. Even Merian's cousin Abel had looked away uncomfortably when she had pressed him for news about the Sardis. Yet she couldn't make herself trudge back to the Castle once more without a glimmer of hope to show for her efforts. This would be her last chance for a long while, for tomorrow evening would see the beginning of her Primanotte, the first night of the long vigil that would make Frost's daughter *her* hellhorse.

She could hear the evening bells from the city towers. The streets of Summertown were getting crowded. Visitors strolled about, taking in the sights, while the Summertowners themselves were hurrying about their business, getting ready for the busiest time of day. A well-dressed merchant walked past with two muscle-bulging bodyguards in his wake. Then three giggling Breda girls, to whom the whole place was obviously enticingly forbidden and exotic. A white-haired old man was warming up his beggar's routine: 'Fair lady, spare a penny for a faithful servant fallen on hard times . . .' but the girl he was talking to hurried on without hearing the end of his chant.

The girl he was talking to . . . straight-backed and delicate, with neat black braids.

'Sara!' called Kat.

The girl threw a quick glance over her shoulder. It really was Daniel's sister!

'Sara, wait!'

Sara hesitated and paused, like a fawn uncertain which way to flee. But she did wait for Kat to catch up.

'Sara, I really, really have to speak to Daniel.'

Sara gazed at her, eyes huge and dark in her thin face.

'Daniel is very unhappy,' she said. 'More so than the rest of us. But he won't tell us why.'

'That's why we have to talk. He misunderstood something I said.' Oh, how trite and commonplace that sounded, and yet she couldn't think of any other way to put it. She just hoped Sara could see how desperately important it was.

'Walk a little way with me,' said Sara finally. 'But when I ask you to wait somewhere, you must promise not to try and follow me.'

'I swear,' said Kat, ready to agree to any condition as long as it held out a chance for her to see Daniel again.

But when they reached the Summertown gates, Sara suddenly stopped with a frightened little mew.

'There are guards,' she said.

'Yes, they come here quite often,' said Kat and couldn't quite see why it alarmed Sara so much. It was only good sense for the city guards to keep an eye on a place as lively as Summertown was wont to get.

Sara sent her an exasperated glance.

'You don't understand . . .' she said. And then she held out the canvas bag she was carrying. 'Here, take this. Meet me by the brook. Stay there till I get there, even if it takes a long time. Promise!'

Suddenly, Sara no longer seemed such a fawn. Her tone was harsh and commanding, and even though her hands were shaking, Kat could see a hard edge of courage that had not been apparent before.

Kat took the bag, even though she still couldn't understand Sara's concern. She peeked inside. Two flat metal boxes, somewhat soot-stained.

'Why—'

'If you want to see Daniel again, do as I say. They won't stop you – you are in uniform too.'

Some of Sara's reasons for worrying became clear. Kat noticed now that it wasn't just the usual town guards down there. They had been joined by two bredinari and a couple of castle guardsmen. So perhaps Sara was right, and it would be unwise for her to try to pass them with two boxes in her care that were in all likelihood full of illegal photographic plates.

'Hide them inside your shirt or something,' said Sara. 'They won't search someone like you. And wait for me at the brook, no matter how long it takes!'

Kat did as she was told. She stepped behind a tent and tucked the boxes inside her shirt, one box under each arm, with her belt holding them in place, she hoped. The metal was cold against her skin, and she hoped the guards would not notice the unusual thickness of her waistline. Then she approached the gate.

'Out fooling around, prentice?' said one of the Riders. 'Got a permit?'

'Yes.' Kat drew the yellow slip from her belt purse. The boxes felt huge against her sides, and she couldn't understand why the guards seemed not to notice.

'Well, that looks correct.' The Rider gave her back her slip. 'But why are you headed back already? The evening has barely started.'

'I'm skint,' said Kat, which was nothing but the honest truth. Raven had made off with her last remaining pennies.

The Rider grinned.

'That does take the fun out of things, doesn't it? Amazing how the Summertown welcome cools once they've fleeced you for everything you've got. Carry on.'

Kat couldn't help herself. Once she was clear of the gate and certain that the guards were no longer watching, she turned around to see how Sara managed. She had to wait for quite a while. Sara was being careful, it seemed. Lots of people passed through the gates unchallenged – fat farmwives, older men, caravan guards and pedlars. Only people matching one or more of the Sardis in age and general description were stopped.

'Hold on there, little lady,' said the Rider when Sara tried to move past. 'What's your name?'

'Sara Bonverte,' said Sara, not a shred of hesitation in her manner.

'Bonverte?' said one of the guards. 'You? I never seen someone like you around here before.'

'My grandmother is Maestra Angelica Bonverte,' said Sara quite coldly.

'Really? Makes it all the more peculiar that I haven't seen you.'

'Are you on such familiar terms with all the Bonvertes, then?'

'I know most of them,' said the Rider, 'and none of them talk like wayfarer trash!'

For the first time, Sara seemed uncertain. She couldn't disguise her accent, the liquid r's and the melodious lilt that Daniel also had. Breda folk didn't talk like that. Oh, Sara, moaned Kat silently. Couldn't you have picked some other name? Bonverte was a great house, well known to most of Breda.

'If you don't believe me, check the House Lists. Sara Bonverte. I'm there.'

'Well, what do you know, young lady? I might just do that.' The Rider made a curt gesture. 'Take her down to the Northern gatehouse. Send a runner for the Bonverte House Lists. If she checks out, let her go. If she doesn't, hang on to her. I'll be down later.'

Kat watched helplessly while they marched Sara down to the guardhouse by the northern gate. She couldn't even follow without drawing a lot of unwanted attention from the guards. What good and proper reason could a bredinari prentice have for taking such an interest in a traveller girl? How could Sara have been so stupid? To pick a name so famous . . . Angelica Bonverte was the maestra of a huge estate just north of Breda. Half the cider drunk in Breda's taverns came from the Bonverte orchards.

Wait for me by the brook, no matter how long it takes. All right, Sara, thought Kat. I'll do what you said.

But she was afraid it would be a long and fruitless wait.

It was still more spring than summer, and once the sun was down, the air had a real bite. A wet mist rose from the brook and the ground around it. If she was to be here half the night, she needed to do something to stay warm. She gathered enough twigs and branches for a small fire and managed to light it, despite the damp. A good thing she was not in skirt and shirtsleeves today. The grey leather uniform was warmer, and it meant she had at least a little basic gear with her, like the firestarters and a decent knife to cut tinder with.

No one came here usually. It had been one of the reasons why it was a favourite spot for her and Daniel. She thought of the kingfisher they had seen here only a few nights ago, when everything had still been . . . well, not all right exactly, but at least not the disaster it was now. She blinked back a few tears. Damn him. Why couldn't he have listened to her? Back then, before the fire. Or later, when she had tried to explain.

Her glance fell on the flat boxes, rescued at such terrible cost. Carefully, she opened one. Inside, set in a delicate wooden rack and protected by tufts of wool and shredded rags, were indeed the photographic plates she

149

had imagined. Some were cracked and discoloured, others still intact. She handled them all with respectful care, because she knew that Uncle Isak had sacrificed his hands to save them. One by one, she held them up and looked at them in the light from her small fire. Here, still, were the panorama views of Colmonte and Koronberk, and some of the marvellous beasts of the Jungle of Katai, though the beasts, it seemed, were not truly photographed in the wilderness but rather in some big vaulted hall where they were on display, stuffed and mounted on black platforms. Some had been lost, she thought, but most of them were here, waiting to be recreated. It was a comforting thought that something had been saved from the ashes, and she understood why Sara had risked discovery to come and retrieve them.

The second box contained mostly pictures of people. Kat shivered a little. She recalled the drooling empty-eyed girl. Could having your photograph taken really damage your soul in that way? She thought of the picture of her and Daniel, which was probably here in this box somewhere. No. She didn't believe it, didn't believe that these little glass plates possessed such evil powers. Something else must have made the girl ill. A brain fever perhaps? She did understand the woman's anger, though, at least a little. She might even understand why someone who had suffered such a loss could want to destroy the panoramas. But why burn the blue wagon? And why . . . why were the guards by the Summertown gate stopping and searching everyone who looked remotely like the Sardis? Was it because of the riots that night, or because of whatever

Raven had reported to Alcedina? Or both? She wondered what was happening to Sara, and hoped against hope that she would come.

She was holding a glass plate up to the light without really looking at it. Only gradually did she realize that she had stopped at this particular plate because it held a picture of someone she knew.

A somewhat plain young girl was seated stiffly on a chair, dressed in a huge frock, the skirt of which took up most of the bottom half of the picture. A man was kneeling at her side, holding her hand out rather pointedly, as if it was important that it was noticed in the picture. If one looked closely, one could see a ring on her finger. The man and the girl both looked oddly blank-faced, as if they weren't quite sure which expression was appropriate for the situation.

Kat had never seen the girl before. But the man was Alvar Alcedina.

Could *this* be why he was hunting the Sardis? Because Uncle Isak had taken a forbidden photograph of him and some girl? Would he leave them alone, perhaps, if they gave him the plate?

She looked rather thoughtfully at the glass square. So fragile. How could anyone think it could drain your soul? Did Alcedina really believe that? She thought of his icy, kingfisher-blue glare and the measured precision of his voice. No, he wouldn't be that superstitious. Not Alcedina.

Steps in the darkness. The rustle of a branch. Hurriedly,

she put the plate with Alcedina's picture on it back in the box and shoved the box behind her, out of sight.

'Who is it?' she called quietly.

'Me,' said Sara, stepping into the firelight. She seemed fragile and frightened once more, but did not look as if she had been hurt. 'Give me the boxes, and follow.'

'What happened?'

'They wanted to know who I was.'

'Yes, I saw – but how did you get away? Weren't they angry when they found out you had lied to them?'

'I didn't lie.'

'But you said—'

'I didn't lie!'

And that appeared to be all she had to say on the matter. She took the boxes and walked off, and Kat hurriedly kicked some dirt over the fire and followed as best she could.

They walked for several hours. Kat was beginning to wonder how she would ever make it back to the Castle in time for her morning duties. It was a dark and clouded night, and the paths Sara took were not wide and open to what poor moonlight there was. Often Kat stumbled across rocks and roots and swallowed a curse or two, but there was something about the straightness of Sara's back that did not allow for questions.

Finally they arrived at a tall stone wall with a gate in it.

'Wait here,' said Sara. 'I'll try and get Daniel to meet you. If he won't, I'll come back and tell you. But do *not* try to follow me.'

'No,' said Kat, well aware that she had made that promise once already. 'I'll stay here.'

And so she waited yet again, and this time there was no fire to keep her warm. She rested for a while with her back against the wall, but it seemed as if the stone was sucking any remnant of warmth out of her, and she soon got to her feet again. On the other side of the wall, apple trees crowded together and made it impossible for her to see if there was a building anywhere. At least the scent of the white blossoms made the wait a little more pleasant.

Apple blossoms . . .

Apple trees . . .

It wasn't till then that the thought occurred to her that Sara really had not been lying. What if this was the scent of the next Bonverte cider harvest? What if Sara really was Angelica Bonverte's grandchild? She remembered how Samuel and Isak had quarrelled the first time she had dinner with the Sardis. *The children have to see their grand-mother every once in a while . . . In her eyes, we have done her a great injustice. She lost a daughter because of me . . .*

If Sara was Angelica Bonverte's daughter's daughter, then her name really would be in the House Lists as Sara Bonverte. In Breda, no child bore its father's name. Fathers didn't matter – name and inheritance came only through one's mother.

Finally, there were light footsteps on the path under the apple trees. But it wasn't Daniel who appeared by the gate.

'I tried,' said Sara, 'but he wouldn't come.'

'But—'

'He said . . . he said he should never have trusted someone from the Castle. One of them. Kat, is it true? Did you have anything to do with . . . with what happened?'

'No! No, that's what I have to tell him. I tried to warn you, yes, but not against that. I knew nothing about that – how could I? It was nothing to do with the Castle.'

But Sara stood watching her with guarded eyes, and in her face Kat saw an expression she had come to know so well: the eternal distrust of the wayfarers. Like a wall, it was. The same wall she had come up against when she had tried to find the Sardis among the people of Summertown. Never trust a uniform. Never trust authority. Never trust someone from outside. Never trust one of *them*.

When she saw that wall in Sara's eyes, Kat finally understood that explanations were useless. Daniel meant exactly what he said. He never wanted to see her again.

'Master?'

Master Haryn buckled the last strap on his shin guard and straightened.

'Yes, Trivallia?'

'Master, can we . . . talk?'

She had not seen him since the day she had bloodied Lu's nose. The two weeks of her banning from the Weapons Yard were not yet over, and strictly speaking she was on forbidden turf right now. But he pushed open the door to his office and let her in.

'What's wrong?' he asked, throwing open a shutter to let in a bit of light.

She stared at the dust motes dancing in the morning sun. It was so hard to collect herself – she was confused and dizzy with everything that had happened, and she had slept only a few short hours in Merian's cousin's shop while she waited for the city gates to open. But there was one thing she had come to think about on the long walk back from the stonewalled orchard. If people like Daniel really couldn't trust 'someone from the Castle' . . . did she then want to be 'one of them'?

She would have liked to talk to Simon about it, but Simon was still assigned to the Northern courier route and it might be weeks before he returned. And after tonight, there was no way back.

'Master, what if . . . what if someone doesn't want to be a bredinari after all?'

Master Haryn froze in the middle of reaching for the second shutter.

'Why are you asking that?'

'Because I'm not certain any more. That I want to do it, I mean.'

He turned to face her, and she could see that she had actually succeeded in taking aback the normally impervious Weapons Master.

'Why this sudden doubt?' he asked.

She shrugged. It would be impossible to explain it all – Daniel, the photographs, the fire, and all the thoughts that had gone through her head on the walk home last night. Somewhere at the back of it lurked Simon too, with his ruined plans for a proper Resting Place, and DomFelix Strigius's words about borderlanders.

'It's your Primanotte tonight, isn't it?'

She nodded.

'But this . . . this is more than first-time nerves?'

'It's not . . . nerves.'

Of course she was nervous when she thought about it. But this was something else. A deeper uncertainty. Deeper and more dangerous.

'Katriona, from the first time I saw you, I have doubted a lot of things. Particularly whether you would ever learn to control that temper of yours. But I was never in any doubt that you knew what you wanted. It practically lit you from within, that damnable, stubborn, incredible will of yours. And I thought, with a will like *that*, there has to be a way. You will make a good bredinari. Not an easy and obedient one, but a good one. A bredinari who will serve to remind the high ladies and lords that they are not the only people in the world, and that there is a land outside the walls of this fine city. And believe me, Katriona, we need bredinari like that.'

It sounded almost like something Simon might have said. Not words she was used to hearing from Master Haryn.

'I don't know what doubts are plaguing you. It is hard to offer advice when you will not tell me the whole of it. But of one thing at least I am certain. Whatever it is, Katriona, you must put it behind you. When you enter the ligatorium tomorrow morning, you must leave this uncertainty at the gate. And if you cannot manage that, then you are indeed right to turn back now.'

His grey eyes rested on her – eyes that always spotted

every little imbalance, every tiny flaw. He was not a man who let his students take the easy way. Nor did he do so now. She had a decision to make, and he would not make it for her.

'Thank you, Master,' she said, and turned to leave.

'Good luck, Katriona.'

She knew he was right. As she walked into the Primanotte shrine that evening to prepare her mind and body for the seven days ahead, seven days alone with an untamed hellhorse, his words still rang in her ears. *Whatever it is, Katriona, you must leave it behind*. And so she took Daniel, and the blue wagon, and the fire, and the doubt, and the pain. She took them, and she buried them in a place inside, so deep that no one would ever find them. No one. Not even herself.

Then she closed the door.

MIDNIGHT

The Castle possessed six ligatorii, and they were all exactly alike. A yard, fourteen paces by fourteen, surrounded by a very tall wall. In the exact middle of the yard, a small square building, the refugium, protected by a solid five-foot fence. In the yard was sand and nothing else. Inside the refugium, there was a sleeping pallet, a blanket, a coiled rope and a week's supplies – water, bread and lentils for the Rider, hay and oats for the hellhorse. A box contained a few curry combs and a hoof pick, and a spade with which to dig a latrine. This was to be Kat's entire world for seven days.

It sounded so simple when Bruna read to them from the Book of the Binding and explained how each of the seven days should pass. The first day was the day of the Water Bond. This meant that the hellhorse was to come to the Rider and drink from the offered bucket. The next day was assigned to the Bond of Grass, which meant that the hellhorse had to accept that food, too, would come only from the hand of the Rider, when and where he wished it.

Then came the Bond of Hands, the Bond of the Voice, the Bond of the Mind, the Bond of the Rein, and finally the Rider Bond. All neat and regular, one day for each bond. And on the seventh day, the Rider would ride his hellhorse through the ligatorium gate, and the Binding would be complete.

Kat wished someone had read the Book of the Binding to Frost's daughter. Then perhaps she wouldn't have to sit here in the refugium on the third day of the binding, sobbing from helplessness and exhaustion, with a finger she thought was probably broken, and bruises just about everywhere. Three days had gone by, and she had nothing to show for it. Nothing. Not even the first and simplest of the bonds had she accomplished.

It had all gone wrong from the start.

At dawn on the first day she had been standing there, waiting, the way she was supposed to, so that the first thing the young hellhorse would see when its hood came off would be her – its Rider.

'They are quite confused at that time,' Horsemaster Bruna had explained to his apprentices. 'They have had very little contact with humans until that point, and now, suddenly, they are torn from their mother's side, choked by ropes and blinded by hoods, and led into this strange place that they have never seen before. Just stand there for a moment and let them feel that this is *your* turf, and that you are not afraid of them.'

So Kat stood, calm and relaxed, in that particular state of perfect equilibrium that Master Haryn called *posa*.

Without anger, without fear. Breathing easily, and with all doubts and anxieties safely stowed away. Merely waiting.

The ligatorium gate opened, and Horsemaster Bruna and six other Riders came in, dragging something that looked at first glance like a rolled-up tent. Kat stared, startled. Where was her hellhorse?

Then she saw that the bulky grey heap was moving. Something writhed beneath the canvas, and muffled bird-like cries issued from inside. Horsemaster Bruna straightened and looked directly at Kat. He could not speak to her, that would be against the rules, but there was a clear message in his eyes: Watch out!

They began loosening the ropes around the canvas bundle, and two hobbled hind legs shot out, striking a Rider's shinbone.

'Bloody devil!' he hissed, before remembering the ban of silence and choking back the rest of his curses. He made a gesture that clearly meant 'Carry on without me', and limped from the yard.

The six remaining men got rid of most of the canvas, so that a shiny, silvery-black body emerged. Bruna held down the hooded head with his entire weight while the others slipped off the ropes hobbling the front and rear legs. He jerked his head in the direction of the gate, and the others retired. Then he let go himself and sprinted for the exit with no trace of his usual dignity. The gate slammed shut, the last rope slithered over the top of it like a snake escaping from a basket, and the hood finally came off the horse's head. In one violent heave, the hellhorse got to its feet.

And this, then, was the moment when Kat was supposed to show it that 'this was her turf, and that she was not afraid of it'.

Somehow, she wasn't too sure the message got across. The instant the mare regained its sight and its footing, it screamed piercingly and charged the first living creature it saw.

Kat leaped to one side, threw herself on the ground, and rolled under the bottom rail of the fence, but the mare did not take kindly to having its prey snatched away. For the next half-hour it kept charging the fence, trying to kick or thrust its way through, screaming in fury all the while. The only thing Kat could do was retreat into the refugium and close the door, so that at least it wasn't infuriated by the sight of her. She sat there, waiting for its rage to subside, most of the time fearing it would do itself an injury, crashing into the fence like that, but as the day wore on and the attacks continued, she found herself wishing now and then that the monster would break its rotten, ill-tempered neck, so that at least there would be an end to it.

Finally the screaming stopped, and silence, blessed silence, descended. Kat warily eased the door open a bit and peered through the crack. The monster was pacing back and forth in front of the gate, having apparently understood that this was the way out, even though it had been blindfolded upon entering. It was the first time she had had any chance to study it. The first time she had been at ease to see more than hooves and teeth and fury. You may be an ill-tempered devil, she thought to herself, but at least you are a gorgeous ill-tempered devil.

Hellhorses developed more quickly than ordinary horses – they had to, to survive the predatory habits of their own kind – and so Frost's daughter already had her adult height, though she was little more than a year old. Only the slenderness of the body and the neck revealed that she had not yet come to full maturity. As with all hellhorses, the hide shone metallically in the sunlight, but with a darker sheen than most. Underneath the silver brightness, the skin was black as midnight. Blacksilver, they called this colour in the Castle studbooks, when it occurred, which was not often.

Right now the dark silver coat was grimy with dust and sweat, and Kat's fingers itched to brush it. But it would be a while yet before the mare would allow such attentions. Kat had to be content with enjoying the proud arch of the neck and the springy ease of its gait. And the tail! Kat laughed under her breath. All hellhorses carried their tails confidently high, but Frost's daughter just had to give it that little bit more . . .

The mare heard her laughter and spun round. It snorted and pounded the ground with one forefoot, but showed no signs of charging the fence. Apparently it had realized the futility of such antics.

All right, thought Kat. The Water Bond. Let's get started.

'Thirsty, horsey?'

The sound of her voice sent a quiver through the hellhorse, and it snorted once more. Other than that, there was no reaction. It stood staring at her, quite motionless, with golden tiger eyes like those of the marvellous jungle beasts of Katai. For a moment she saw the Jungle of Katai flare up and burn to ashes, but she caught the thought and buried it firmly along with all the rest of the things that had no time and place here. Here, it was just her and the hellhorse. Frost's daughter, hers to bind and tame, hers to name, hers to ride . . . hers, and no one else's.

'You and me, horsey,' she said softly, 'whether you like it or not.' And she turned to fill the water bucket.

A few seconds later, she was lying in a puddle of dust and water, flowing together to make instant mud. She hadn't even made it across the fence. The mare had held itself stock still until Kat began to swing her leg across the top rail and thus enter the yard, which the monster obviously considered its own territory. Then it charged. And it was lightning fast. Kat barely had time to swing up the bucket like a shield, so that the snapping teeth did not tear off her cheek. The bucket smacked into her nose instead, and she tumbled backwards, legs flailing, and hit the dust with enough force to wind.

'You rotten beast!' she spat, feeling the bridge of her nose. It was not easy to keep your inner balance when you were lying on your back in the mud, having been hit over the head with your own bucket. But if that was the way of it, she would just wait. Wait until the creature became really, really thirsty. Perhaps then it would be a little more willing to cooperate!

And so she waited. For hours. The noon bell chimed. The sun baked the sands hotly, then began its descent. Afternoon shadows lay across the yard. Still she waited. Not until evening, when she thought the beast had to be thoroughly parched, did she attempt the Water Bond once more. Wisely, this time, she pushed the bucket under the bottom rail first. The monster was glaring at her suspiciously, but kept its distance. Its nostrils quivered. Good. It could smell the water. She waited. It advanced a pace. She set her foot on the rail. It took yet another step. She swung herself up, so that she crouched on the top rail. A shiver went through the blacksilver body. It pounded the ground with its forefoot, once, twice. Slowly, she let herself slide down, so that she stood next to the bucket.

The hellhorse charged. This time, a hoof slammed into her forearm as she rolled under the fence. The bucket was overturned, and once more, water soaked into the dust. Kat cursed, nursing her arm.

'Damn you, beast!'

And that was the first day.

And the next. And the day after that. On the morning of the third day, Kat had caught her little finger between the hinge and the bucket as she had used it to shield herself yet again from the teeth of the beast. The finger swelled to three times its normal size and stuck out at an uncomfortable angle. It was then that she began to cry. She forgot all about equilibrium and calm thoughts and posa and just huddled inside the refugium, sobbing till her throat hurt.

If giving up had been possible, she would have done it.

But no one would come until the seventh day. The gate was barred from the outside. So she tore a strip of cloth from the bottom of her shirt and wound it round her pinkie and the next finger, so that one supported the other. The last scrap she used for a handkerchief and blew her nose with a blast like a signal horn. She would have killed for a cup of Simon's good tea, but the refugium had no such luxuries, not even a stove or a fire-place for the comfort of heat and hot water. She drank a cup of the water from the damned bucket, dipped the fingers of her good hand into it, and tried to cool her hot forehead.

It was the oldest of all ranking fights, she knew – the battle of the watering hole. The herd leader drank first, and the herd leader decided when the others would be allowed to drink. And Frost's daughter had no intention of letting a puny human girl be the leader of its herd.

But damn it all, it had had neither food nor drink for three days now. Surely it had to cool its temper just a little?

When the sun set, she had tried twice more. And twice more she had been attacked by Frost's mad beast of a daughter. The last time, she had made it a few paces into the yard and had felt a tired glimmer of hope when the monster decided to charge her after all. She was so exhausted that it made her clumsy, and this nearly proved fatal. The mare sank its teeth into her right shoulder as she was swinging herself over the fence, and the bucket slipped from her leaden fingers. She was jerked back and tumbled to the ground – on the wrong, dangerous side of the fence.

Her fall had made the horse loosen its grip, but Kat lay helpless on the ground at its feet. The bucket that had been her trusty shield was out of reach. She had no weapon, and no defence. Only her anger.

Oh yes, she was angry now. Fury sizzled in her veins, roared in her ears.

She got to her feet and screamed at the animal, using every term of abuse she had thought of these past three days. *Beast, monster, devil!* Gone was any thought of poise and equilibrium, any thought of self-preservation. She forgot that this was a hellhorse, with hooves like flint and teeth like knives, and a heart full of a predator's hunger. *Damn creature! Demon beast!* She made no attempt to hit it, she just shouted at it.

And the mare retreated.

Her rage subsided a little, and through the yellow haze of her fury Kat sensed that something had after all been gained. She was standing in front of the hellhorse empty-handed, and it did not attack. She strode back to the fence, seized the bucket and climbed inside. She dipped the ill-used dented thing into the water casket and filled it to the brim. Now. Now was the time.

But then she paused. She stood there motionless for a long, dizzy moment, her arm shaking with the weight of the brimming bucket. Her anger seeped away. And without it, there was no way she could gather her courage and her strength enough to go back outside. No way she could climb that fence again. No way.

That was when she cried for the second time. Not because she was hurt, but because she was frightened. Scared of the beast out there, and most of all, scared that she did not have the will and the nerve to do what she must do.

Darkness fell. Evenbells sounded from the Primanotte shrine, each chime pounding into her that she had failed, that this, the third day, was over now, and that she had not yet achieved even the first bond. Not yet, and not ever. The creature had defeated her.

Leadenly, she lay down on her pallet and curled up under the blanket. Her finger throbbed, and her whole body ached, particularly the bitten shoulder. But she was so exhausted that sleep claimed her after all.

She woke sometime later to a sound she had not heard before. The two previous nights, the mare had jerked her from her sleep again and again with her furious screams, like the call of some foreign seabird. But the whinny that woke her this time was different. This was not temper or fury. This was loneliness.

'Poor little horse,' whispered Kat. It hadn't asked for any of this. The yard, the walls, the dust, and the battle over that lousy bucket of water – that was all some human's bright idea.

She pushed the blanket aside and made the slow, sore journey to her feet. Fumbled in the darkness for the bucket she had filled and just left there. Walked outside with it, into the moonlight.

Frost's daughter stood in her usual spot by the gate. Even with her neck stretched to its limit, she couldn't see the outside, but perhaps the scent of grass and fields and freedom was stronger there.

'Horse,' she called, tentatively. Not because she imagined that it would come trotting up to her like a docile dog, more just to let it know she was there. It turned its head and snorted. Pawed the ground, but this time in a half-hearted manner. Three days without water. It must be dying of thirst. Literally. She pushed the bucket under the fence and laboriously made the climb again. The mare didn't move.

'Come and drink, horsey,' said Kat in her calmest voice, hoisting the bucket and walking into the centre of the yard. There she waited.

Step by slow step, the mare came nearer. The neck no longer arched quite so proudly. Searchingly, it extended its muzzle. The nostrils quivered.

'Wait,' said Kat firmly. The mare halted. 'Herd leader drinks first.' And she bent over and drank from the water, a few noisy, slurping swallows. Then she stepped back a single pace. 'Go ahead, then. *Now* it is your turn.'

The hellhorse walked the last few steps and buried its nose in the bucket. It drank and kept on drinking, until not a drop was left. And while it was still drinking, Kat finally put her hand on the soft neck, and the horse permitted it without so much as a single belligerent snort.

Kat ran her hand over the dusty silver-black coat. Dark and silky like mole fur.

'Midnight,' she whispered, and the mare's ears jerked a little. 'Midnight . . .'

When the sun rose, Kat had given Midnight four buckets in all, with suitable breaks in between to prevent colic. Now the mare was chomping away at an armful of hay, with Kat sitting next to her in the hay pile, yawning and humming by turns.

> 'Papa Barber he had gotten
> A leg of rotten mutton
> Which he paid for, the old glutton,
> With an old forgotten button . . .'

It was by no means the end of their troubles. It left, after all, only four days for the rest of the binding – teaching Midnight to obey spoken and unspoken commands, to permit every touch of her hand, to accept the halter without fighting it, and finally, to bear the weight of her Rider on her back. No, it certainly wasn't the end. But at least it was a beginning.

As the sun was beginning to set on the seventh day, Kat brushed Midnight's blacksilver coat till it shone. She picked up each hoof and cleaned it carefully. There wasn't much she could do about her own filthy clothes, but she washed herself in the last of the water and sacrificed yet another strip of cloth from her shirt so that her blackened and swollen finger might have a fresh bandage.

She looked around the refugium. It felt as if she had lived here always. She could hardly believe that tonight she would not sleep on that pallet, wrapped in that blanket, and that she might soon be treated to fare other than flatbread and cold lentils.

Outside, Midnight was neighing and pushing her chest against the fence – not to attack, but because she was lonely. She didn't like her Rider to be out of her sight. She no longer had a mother or a herd to comfort her – only this strange two-legged herd leader.

'I'm coming. Don't fret,' murmured Kat and collected the simple rope halter she had made for her horse. As she opened the door, Midnight stopped neighing and instead made the odd deep humming sound that was her usual greeting now.

For the last time, Kat climbed the fence around the refugium. She couldn't help thinking about all the more or less elegant ways she had cleared those rails during the past week.

'You weren't exactly easy, you know that?' she told the hellhorse. Midnight blew into her face, a soft warm cloud of hay-scented breath. Kat rubbed her withers with one hand so that the golden tiger eyes half-closed in enjoyment.

She could no longer see the sun, though there was still some daylight left. It had to be nearly time though. She slipped the halter over Midnight's narrow head, put a foot on the bottom rail of the fence, and slid on to the smooth, warm back. Only a little later, she heard the sound of the gate being unbarred. Midnight stiffened, and her ears quivered like antennae. Kat thought calm, equable thoughts. Then the gate opened.

The mare took an eager step forward, but Kat halted her with a command.

'Stand!'

Horsemaster Bruna entered. His face revealed nothing, but Kat could tell by the deliberately calm way he walked that he had by no means forgotten the fury Frost's daughter had displayed the last time he had been close to her. When he saw the hellhorse standing there, stock still under its Rider's command, a small smiled touched his lips.

'Prentice Trivallia,' he said in formal tones, 'your Master asks if you have completed the Seven Bonds.'

'Master,' she said in the same formal way, 'I have.'

'Then as your Master, I ask you to prove it.'

This was the time for Kat to ride her hellhorse through the gate and bring it to a halt. A gentle walk would do. But Kat suddenly thought of the speed with which Bruna had sprinted for the gates that first morning. And an impish spirit took hold of her. She squeezed Midnight's flanks with her calves, so that the hellhorse leaped forward at a full gallop. Bruna's face showed a moment's horror before he sprang to one side, out of the horse's path. To him, it must seem as if the creature was bolting, out of control. Then Kat showed him that this was by no means the case. The moment she was through the gate, she gave Midnight the cue they had so painstakingly practised, and the horse came to a complete and utterly controlled halt, less than a pace away from Bruna.

'Beast,' he hissed, and it was not the horse he was talking to.

'Master, your prentice asks if the test is accepted?'

'Yes,' he said, running a finger across his damp brow. 'Damn your eyes, yes. And don't you ever pull a stunt like that again.' Then he cleared his throat and returned to the formality of the ritual.

'The test is accepted. What is the mare's name?'

'Midnight.'

'Midnight?' He looked surprised. Normally, apprentices called their first hellhorse dashing and exotic names like Lazuli or Azure. And Kat had toyed with names like that before entering the ligatorium. But the moment her hand had touched the mare's neck, she knew that they would not fit Frost's daughter. Only one name did – a simple one, perhaps, but true to the dark, free spirit of this horse.

'Then let this be writ into the studbooks: that in the eighteenth year of Cora Duodecima's rule, Trivallia's Midnight has entered into the service of the corps. The binding is complete.'

And then Kat could let herself slip from Midnight's back and lead her into the Riders' stable, where a stall strewn with clean straw awaited, and water and oats. She stayed with her horse until she was sure that Midnight had settled into her new surroundings. The hellhorse exchanged a few snorts and whinnies with her neighbour through the bars, but she was a very tired hellhorse, and once she had eaten her oats and munched a few mouthfuls of hay, the movements of her jaw slowed. Her eyes closed, and the rise and fall of her flanks became calmer and more regular. Kat's new hellhorse was asleep.

Outside the stable, Merian was waiting.

'Sweet Lady be thanked,' she said, giving Kat a long hug. 'I've been soooo scared. I heard the Riders talking after they had brought it to you. They said it was a vicious devil . . . Are you all right?'

'I'm fine,' said Kat. 'Master Rodrian will have to look at this stupid finger, but other than that I'm fine. And Midnight is no devil. How are the others doing?'

'Lu is through her second day, and they say it is going well. At least there are no screams. My gods, how yours screamed! Didn't it drive you up the wall?'

Yes, thought Kat, but didn't say so. 'It wasn't that bad. What about Tarquin?'

'Still kicking his heels and biting his nails – his Primanotte has been put off twice now. Heavens, I'm glad it's not me. But come on, let's take you to Master Rodrian and then get you some dinner. Go on, tell me what it was like . . .'

Having the four-day-old fracture set was no picnic, but once Master Rodrian had fixed it up with a proper splint, a lot of the pain went away. Kat had thought she would eat her head off the minute she was served anything other than cold lentils, but she was almost too tired to eat at all. She hugged Merian again, and teased Tarquin a bit to make him forget his nail-biting. Then she went to her room and fell into her alcove still wearing all her filthy clothes, and seconds later she was sleeping so deeply that she would not have woken if Midnight herself had been kicking in the door.

THE SUNDERED HEART

For a week only one thing mattered to Kat, sleeping or waking. She dressed herself impatiently in the mornings, tearing at drawstrings and buttons, eager to be out of her room and across the Weapons Yard and the Riders' Yard and into the stables. The most delightful sound in the world was the quiet nickering Midnight greeted her with when she heard Kat's footsteps or her voice. The most beautiful sight in the world was Midnight's narrow, dark head as it poked out over the door of the stall. And the sweetest sensation of all was the feel of Midnight's silky muzzle against her cheek.

'You've gone bonkers,' sighed Merian, when, for the third time that week, she had to drink her evening tea seated on a bale of straw in front of Midnight's stall. 'Can't you leave the poor animal alone for five minutes?'

No, Kat couldn't, at least not as long as she had any choice. And poor Merian was much afflicted because five days later, Lu emerged from the ligatorium with her Stala and exactly the same bewitched expression in her eyes. And the week after that, it became Tarquin's turn.

'It will get better eventually,' said Bruna comfortingly, when Merian complained. 'Or at any rate, less intense. But these first few weeks it really is important for the hellhorse and the Rider to be together as much as possible, to strengthen their new bond.'

For the first months, no one else was supposed to feed or water Midnight, and no other hands were supposed to touch her. *Her*. It was no longer remotely possible for Kat to think of Midnight as 'it'. Did a mother say 'it' of her child? And though Midnight's young back should only bear her weight for perhaps half an hour every day, there were so many other delightful ways to spend time with her, and so many new things to learn.

But when Talis Day came round, with the whole city getting ready to party, and Kat was showing signs of wanting to spend that night, too, in Midnight's company, Merian put her foot down.

'Too much hellhorse is injurious to the brain,' she declared. 'Valente, help me!'

'You take one arm, I'll take the other,' said Valente. 'A bath, a comb and some clothes that don't stink of horse, and then it's off to town with us!' And they made good their threats and dragged Kat from the stables despite her protests. It ended in a water fight and a lot of giggling, squealing and towel-swatting.

'Just like the old days,' said Kat, wringing water from her hair and trying to catch her breath.

'Old days!' harrumphed Merian. 'You mean three

weeks ago when you could still walk and talk and act like a normal person?'

'Something like that,' admitted Kat with a grin. But actually it had been more than three weeks since she last felt like a 'normal' person. Old times meant back before things went wrong between her and Lu, back before she had ever met Raven and – and everything that had happened since. Before Daniel. But no. Don't think of him now, she admonished herself. In fact, don't think of him ever again.

'Do you want to borrow my skirt?' asked Merian.

'No,' said Kat, a little too sharply, then tried to soften it. 'No thanks, I mean.'

Once, there had been two peoples in Breda – the Bredans and the Talisians. But they had lived together for so long now that nobody could really tell whether a person was mostly one thing or more the other. On Talis Day, everyone became highly Talisian and sang old Talisian songs and danced old Talisian dances, wearing canary yellow scarves and weird hats with garish hatbands that would probably have had a real Talisian from the old days howling with laughter. But there was one point on Talis Day Eve when everyone became solemn.

Because Talis didn't exist any more. The land from which the Talisians came had perished, choked by poisonous fogs and poisonous ice, and the Talisians had had to save themselves by sailing away to find new homes. And at sunset on Talis Day Eve, every single human being in Breda, man, woman, and child, went to the nearest river or lake with a candle to be set in a tiny wooden boat and pushed on to the darkening waters. The candles were lit in remembrance of those who didn't make it to the ships. And everyone watched in silence as thousands of candles bobbed and fluttered for a while, and then went out. No one left the bank until the last small flame had burned out, and while waiting in the darkness, it was the custom to think not only of distant Talis, but of one's own dead as well.

When Kat was a little girl, it had always been her grandmother she thought about – the *real* Katriona that she was named for. Now there were other dead who pushed forward, wanting to be remembered. Anna Weaver, who had died from an arrow through her chest in Ermine's valley. And Ermine himself, who had become one of her dead because she had held the sword that killed him. She could see him so clearly that it felt as if she might reach out and touch him. *Hold it firmly*, he had said, *pointed at the heart*. And then he had smiled, a smile like a young girl's, and leaned forward, without warning, without hesitation, until the blade pierced his heart.

She felt silent tears on her cheeks. And it wasn't just Ermine she was crying for. She wept for Isak Sardi's burned hands, for Daniel's pain and mistrust. She wept for older things – for Cornelius whom she had never called her father, and who would never ever believe that he was loved and needed and had a place at the inn except that Tess needed a strong man to keep robbers and ruffians from the door. She felt a sudden stab of longing and homesickness for the Vales, for the twins and Little-Cor who were growing up without really knowing her, for Nicolas who was suddenly big enough to write letters, for Mattie, her best-loved sister, who was becoming older and stronger and learning everything she needed to know to take over the inn from Tess one day.

And Tess . . . who could be sharp and hurtful like the crack of a whip, and then the next moment put her arms around you and whisper, *You are the stubbornest child I have*, so that you knew you would always be hers, no matter what you did, no matter where in the world you were.

The last candle had been swallowed by the waters of the Breda River. The Silence went on for another few moments. Then the fiddlers in the crowd struck up the old Talisian tune 'The Sundered Heart', which started very slowly and sadly – 'My loved one has left me, my loved one has gone away . . . one half of my heart will weep in sorrow forever . . .' and then became faster and faster – 'but the *other* half of my heart would love to dance with you . . .' until it was a sizzling dance tune with a beat so rapidly accelerating that it was nearly impossible for one's feet to follow, and nearly impossible not to try.

That was the signal that started off the festivities. People danced as best they could and laughed breathlessly when they could follow the tempo no longer. Those who had given up cheered those still bravely trying to stick with the devilish tune all the way to its crackling finale. There were usually one or two who wouldn't give in, but this was a battle always won by the fiddlers, because they simply kept going until the last dancer succumbed. Shame on the fiddler who could not move his fingers more quickly than a dancer could move her feet!

Kat didn't last long – she never did. But Merian! Merian kept at it, feet flying, skirt whirling and cheeks ablaze with the heat, but in the end she was the only one in their part of the crowd still dancing. The fiddler gave a demonic smile and upped the tempo another impossible notch. His fingers flew, the bow leaped across the strings, and in the end even Merian had to quit. The fiddle laughed at her, laughed at all of them, but when the final furious note had been sounded, the fiddler took his instrument from his chin, bowed to the audience, and kissed Merian smack on the lips.

'Nice try,' he said, grinning.

'Nice playing,' she replied. 'And next year . . . *next* year, we'll see who gives in first . . .'

'It will be my pleasure,' he said. 'At least you are a bit of a challenge!'

People applauded, and there were coins passed not just to the fiddler, but to Merian as well.

'Great,' said Tarquin. 'Now I know who is buying the first beer!'

He dragged Merian, Kat and Lu along to the nearest beer tent, and Merian willingly bought the three jars her tips would pay for.

'We'll have to pool our money for the rest.'

'Once you've caught your breath, we can find another fiddler for you to challenge,' said Tarquin, his eyes firmly on the profits. 'There's money to be made from this!'

'Oh, really?' snorted Merian. 'They're not *your* feet.'

'Stuff and nonsense! You enjoy it, don't you? And you're brilliant at it!' He looked at her admiringly. 'Light-footed as a fawn, graceful as a butterfly—'

'Oh, shut up,' said Merian. 'Flattery will get you nowhere. "Graceful as a butterfly" . . . For the Lady's sake, Tarquin, are you implying I used to be a caterpillar?'

But she did after all challenge three more fiddlers, at three different inns, and if the tipping wasn't quite as good as the first time, the profits were decent all the same. Tarquin won nearly four marks in all on various bets he made.

'Enough,' moaned Merian after the last dance. 'I'm exhausted. Next time, *you* do it.'

'I don't have quite your talents,' said Tarquin, counting his winnings. 'Better ones, mind you, but not your nifty feet . . . Fourteen, fifteen, sixteen . . . three marks and six-teen pennies. What do you say to that?'

'That it's your turn to buy the beer,' said Valente dryly.

Tarquin muffled a burp. 'Haven't we had enough for now? If Merian won't dance any more, we could all go to Summertown and have some fun with the rest of the money.'

'Excellent suggestion,' said Valente. 'Hurry up, you lot, before his shopkeeper's soul gets the better of him and he regrets the offer.'

The others got up, but Kat stayed on the bench.

'Kat? Aren't you coming?' said Lu.

'No,' said Kat. 'But you go ahead. I'll stay here for a bit.'

'But . . . we'll never find each other again in this crowd. Come on, Kat.'

Kat shook her head. 'I'm meeting Birch,' she said, 'at the Golden Goose.' It was the first name that came to her mind.

'We'll walk you there, then. And if you change your mind, bring Birch along to my cousin's stall. We'll look in every once in a while to see if you're there.'

They went outside. The streets were jammed with people, and from every other house the sound of laughter, music, stamping and clapping poured from open windows and doors.

'My heart is sundered in twain,' sang Merian. 'My loved one has left me, my loved one has gone awaaaayyy . . .'

'Oh, do be quiet, Merian,' snapped Kat. 'Your dancing is better than your singing.'

A look of surprised hurt passed quickly over Merian's face. Then she must have realized what was going on, because she reached out and gave Kat a one-sided hug.

'Think of Midnight,' she said. 'Think of Birch. *He* likes you. Forget about that stupid traveller boy and dance with someone else.'

'If he can dump someone like you, he's not worth having,' said Lu, putting her arm around Kat's waist. 'I knew it right from the start . . .'

Lu meant well, but Kat wished she would keep her mouth shut.

*

They came to the Golden Goose, and Kat had to go in and pretend to be waiting for Birch.

'Here,' said Tarquin, putting a handful of pennies on the counter. 'Have a jar while you're waiting.'

'Thank you.'

'You just take care of yourself,' said Merian. 'See you later!'

'Yes,' said Kat. 'Maybe. If Birch wants . . .' She had no intention of going to Summertown ever again.

She stayed where she was until she was sure they would be out of sight. Then she reached for the money on the counter.

But the barmaid beat her to it.

'What'll it be?' she said, in a voice that made it obvious that you didn't just pick up good money once you had laid it down on *her* counter.

'A small cider,' said Kat reluctantly. Where had she seen that face before? She had never set foot in the Golden Goose. The only reason the name had popped out of her mouth was because of the business with Raven. This was the place he had mentioned in his report.

Sweet Lady! she suddenly thought. Suppose he is still here? No, surely he wouldn't be. But the mere idea made her anxious to be gone, and she wished she hadn't ordered the cider.

'Coming up!' The barmaid reached for one of the glasses hanging on a rack behind her. Her movements were quick and deft, and it was just as well. It was clearly party time at the Golden Goose, and business was brisk. 'That'll be two pennies . . .'

Kat paid. What was it about that face? Smooth, brown hair, brown eyes, and that small cleft in her chin . . .

Then she nearly choked on her cider. She knew where she had seen the barmaid before, but it was no wonder it had taken her a while to recognize her. The eyes that danced from one customer to the next were far from vacant, nor was the mouth slack and gaping. The girl was laughing one moment, acerbic the next, returning the teasing remarks of men and women with a quick and witty tongue. All the same, there was no doubt. The girl who had served her cider was the same drooling wretch that had started the riots at the Panorama Palace.

It was a miraculous change, and not the sort of miracle that Kat believed in. She was certain that the girl had never been afflicted, that the whole thing had been one big act. But why? Why rouse the Panorama audience to all that violence?

Kat finally let her mind return to the evening she had shied away from so determinedly. Uncle Isak had kept on declaring that he hadn't taken the photograph. And there had been an unusually large audience for a weekday night, she remembered. The house had been crammed. And they had been *very* quick to go wild. So maybe it wasn't just the girl who was playacting. Maybe the whole thing had been a charade from beginning to end.

Kat surreptitiously eyed the girl who was serving beer to a group of caravan guards down one end of the long counter. She had not shown any recognition at the sight of Kat, but then, Kat hadn't been at the centre of events that night. Samuel Sardi's bloodied face. Uncle Isak's burned hands. The blackened remains of the blue wagon. How could anyone purposely plan such destruction? And *why*?

She finished her cider. It was a long way to Bonverte, and she had promised herself it was not a road she would ever walk again. But the Sardis had to know about this. *Had* to.

'There's a bredinari at the door, maestra. A Prentice Trivallia. She says it's urgent . . .'

Like the rest of Breda, Bonverte was celebrating, and it had taken a while before someone had come to let her in. But finally a slender, fair-haired girl had appeared. Kat knew better than to mention the Sardis, so she had asked to see Daniel's grandmother instead. The girl had led her to the big hall presently serving as the ballroom. The music, of course, was 'The Sundered Heart', and Angelica Bonverte's fingers kept time, drumming gently against the glossy waist of her blue-green gown as she watched the dancers. Then she turned to cast a measured look at her unexpected visitor.

'What can be so important that she sees fit to interrupt the Talis Festival?'

'If the maestra could give me just one moment of her time,' begged Kat. 'It's about . . .' but she couldn't say 'son-in-law' to a woman who probably considered marriage to a mere man a gross offence against the Locus Spirit. *She only cares about the girl*, Uncle Isak had said, and so Kat thought that would be the best card to play. 'It's about Sara.'

Angelica Bonverte's gaze rested on her for a few seconds.

'Sistina!' she said to the girl who had opened the door to Kat.

'Yes, maestra?'

'Turn up the lamps in my office and tell Caspar I need him. Sober, please.'

'Maestra . . . it might be a little too late for that,' objected the girl tentatively. 'The sober bit, I mean.'

'Then tell him to stick his head under the pump till the mists clear. Now!'

'Yes, maestra.'

Angelica Bonverte collected her skirts and swept into motion like a ship setting sail. 'Well?' she said. 'Do you want my time or not?'

Kat gathered the wits the woman's forceful presence had scattered.

'Yes, maestra,' she said, as if she had been turned into some kind of echo of Sistina. And she followed Bonverte's unchallenged mistress out of the great hall, up the stairs and into a room nearly as grand as the hall downstairs. Sistina had lit a few candles hastily and was now struggling to raise again the enormous chandelier that she had had to lower from the ceiling in order to turn up the wicks. Something about her reminded Kat of Mattie, her sister back home. Her slenderness and the fair hair, of course, but perhaps also the softness of her manner.

'Will this do, maestra or should I fetch—'

'Yes, yes. Quite sufficient. Get me Caspar.'

'Yes, maestra.'

Angelica Bonverte seated herself at her massive desk but made no move to offer Kat a chair.

'Well?' she said, inspecting her guest in a manner that made Kat think of Alvar Alcedina. 'What is this about Sara?'

At least, thought Kat, she didn't say 'Who is this Sara?' She took that as a good sign.

'Maestra, it is terribly important that I be allowed to talk to Sara or . . . or some other member of the family.'

'Which family might that be?'

'The Sardis. Please, maestra, it is absolutely—'

'And what makes you think I know anything of this . . . Sardi family?'

Oh no. Not a helpful sign after all.

'Maestra, I *know* that Sara is your grandchild, and Seffi and Daniel. I *know* they are here. Somewhere.'

'I know no Sardi family.'

It was said in rock-steady tones. The dismissal in Bonverte's voice, body and glance was absolute. Kat might more easily scrape her way through a mountain with her fingernails, she thought. She stared helplessly into the old lady's crannied face.

'But maestra—'

'Caspar?'

'Yes, maestra?'

He must have been waiting in the hallway outside – his presence was instant. He was a big man, obviously no pushover, and his wet hair bore witness to the fact that he took his maestra's orders very seriously indeed. *Tell him to stick his head under the pump till the mists clear.*

'See this young lady to the gates.'

'Yes, maestra.'

'Wait.' Kat's thoughts raced feverishly. 'What if I wrote a letter . . . a letter to Sara. Perhaps then the maestra might after all . . . see that it was received?'

The old lady considered it. Then she waved Caspar off, and pushed a sheet of paper and a pen and inkwell towards Kat. 'Write, then.'

And Kat wrote.

> To Sara and her family.
>
> I have seen the girl from the night of the fire. The one who was crazy. But she is not realy crazy, she was just pretending. Take care. Someone wants to hurt you, but I dont know who. I realy dont. Please tell Daniel that it wasnt my fault. And go away from Breda as quikly as you can it is not a safe place for you.
>
> Greetings from Katriona. Please be safe.

She blew gently on the ink until it had dried, then folded the letter. *To Sara*, she wrote on the outside. She couldn't make herself write Sara Bonverte, and she didn't want to insult the old lady by writing Sara Sardi. She took the stick of sealing wax from the pen tray and held it above the flame of one candle until it started to melt, then let a few fat red drops seal the letter. She had no fancy signet ring or brooch to press into the wax, so she merely scratched a clumsy K with the blunt end of the pen.

Angelica Bonverte held out her hand, and Kat gave her the sealed letter.

'Caspar,' called the old lady once more.

'Yes, maestra?' As quickly as before.

'Now you may see Prentice Trivallia to the door.'

'Yes, maestra.' Caspar bowed politely and stepped aside to let Kat precede him. But as Kat was about to leave the room, something made her look back. And she saw that the old lady was already breaking the seal and was preparing to read the letter.

'No!' said Kat, outrage flaring within her. 'It's for Sara!'

Angelica Bonverte did not even favour her with a glance before she let her eyes run over the short, desperate lines.

'Your spelling is hardly adequate,' she said acidly. 'I thought they taught you better at the Academy.'

And then, with a cool and steady hand, she held the letter into the flame of the candle until it flared.

'No!' Kat leaped forward, but Caspar had seen it coming. He grabbed her by the collar, and then by one arm, and though she struggled and tried to kick him, holding her back was no great challenge for a man as large as he was.

'I shall deal with my family's affairs without interference from strangers,' said Bonverte's maestra as the last flickering remnants of Sara's letter scattered on to the flagstone floor like flakes of black snow. 'Caspar, see to it that she does not intrude again.'

ACTS OF TREASON

Rain was slithering down the window-panes – a soft, wet summer shower, falling almost vertically because there was no wind. Kat stared at the letters on the page, unable to see much sense in the words they formed.

'*And if a person takes the mount or draught beast of another without permission or proper lease . . .*' Her eyes moved from the book to the window and the silver tracks of the rain almost without volition.

'Kat? Come on, blast you . . .' Lu elbowed her none too gently. 'We have to know all seven codices by tomorrow. Or do you want to sit through Lawmaster Taurus's classes all over again?'

'No, but . . . you read for a while, then.'

Lu heaved a sigh and drew the heavy law book across to her side of the table. 'All right. One more page. But then it's your turn!'

'OK.'

Ordinarily, the thought of any test, written or oral, was enough to give Kat mild heart failure and cold sweats. She knew how far behind she was, and just how much she didn't know. Book learning did not come easily to her; she had never had her own tutor the way most of the other apprentices had, only Tad who had tried to teach her her letters back home in the inn's kitchen, in moments snatched from the rigours of potato peeling and stew-making. Master Valentin said she had a quick mind and would catch up eventually, but he was not her examiner tomorrow. Lawmaster Taurus was, and he was no kindly judge, they said.

She ought to be in a state of near-panic. But it all seemed so . . . unreal. It had been three days now since Sara's grandmother had read her letter and burned it. During that time she had been able to think of very little except Daniel and his family, Raven, the crazy girl who wasn't crazy after all . . . Everyday chores like kitchen duties and homework seemed utterly unimportant. Who cared which five conditions applied if some man took a horse? Who could worry about the distinction between theft and robbery and unlawful possession? Words like 'malice' and 'volition' and 'previous knowledge' wriggled through her mind like tadpoles, refusing to line up and come together in any sort of order.

'Codicil 3.1: Rights of cultivation,' said Lu, looking at her expectantly.

Kat made a grab for her wriggling thoughts, and rattled off what she could remember. When she got to the end she heaved a sigh of relief. It seemed the cramming she had done had had some effect after all.

'Acts of Treason,' said Lu. 'You forgot Acts of Treason.'

Kat gazed vacantly at the wall. Acts of Treason?

'But if Acts of Treason have been . . .' prompted Lu.

'But if Acts of Treason have been done to the land and its spirit . . .' she ground to a halt once more, and Lu had to help her along.

'Be it the felling of trees . . .'

'Be it the felling of trees, the burning of woodlands, starvation and exhaustion of the soil, the damming or channelling of streams, or any other ravaging of the Locus Spirit, then the maestra of that place may punish the offender blow with blow, burn with burn, starvation with starvation and thirst with thirst, until proper penance and reparation have been made to the land.' Kat looked up, a faint curiosity stirring in the midst of the rote-learning. 'Do they really *do* that?' she asked. 'I mean, actually burn people or starve them?'

'Not to the death, I think,' said Lu hesitantly. 'At least, I've never heard of that happening in modern times. But everyone knows that Maria Esocine's grandmother once branded some poor man who had burned down her peach grove by accident.'

Kat shuddered. In her mind's eye, she saw Isak Sardi's crippled hands. Did someone imagine that was a fitting punishment for making forbidden images? She felt the opposite. She wanted the arsonists to feel just a little of the pain they had caused Daniel and his family, inside and out.

'Let's take a break,' she said. 'My mind is spinning. Isn't it almost suppertime?'

'Not quite,' said Lu. 'We have at least half an hour. If

we put our minds to it, we can get through one more codex.'

'If we put our minds to it . . .' Kat sighed. 'You know, if we put our minds to it, I bet we could feed the monsters and still make it to supper.' She put on her most alluring voice. 'Think of poor Stala, alone and bereft, pacing her stall and just waiting for you to appear – you, the only love of her young life . . .'

'Kat, they'll test us on this tomorrow!'

'But why should the horses suffer today? Come on, Lu, my head is already twice as big as usual with everything you've crammed into it today.'

Lu cast a dubious glance at the law book, but Stala won a pretty easy victory over the codicils.

'All right,' she said. 'But if they fail you tomorrow, it's your own damn fault.'

The risk of failing first year Law was the least of Kat's problems right now. But she didn't say anything to Lu about that.

They were very nearly late. The supper bell had chimed for the last time, and most of the Riders, masters and apprentices resident at the Castle were already standing by the benches, awaiting permission to sit. Today Dom-Felix Strigius herself presided over the meal, and Kat ducked her head involuntarily when that grey gaze fell on her. Was it her imagination, or did Lisabetta Strigius *and* most of the other diners stare at her and Lu with particular reproach for their belated entry? Nervously, she tucked a wayward strand of hair behind her ear. She did not quite have Lu's sure touch with the braiding, and right now her red mop was particularly frizzy due to some hasty ablutions at the stable's rainwater barrel.

'Be seated, gentlemen,' said Lisabetta Strigius, and Kat sank gratefully down on the bench among the other apprentices. But even there she had no peace from prying eyes. Right across from her was DiCapra, and he was smiling a particularly ill-omened smile, the way he only did when he had thought of some wonderful new way to irk her. He could barely wait until the soup bowls had gone round and Lisabetta Strigius had led the brief grace to Our Lady which was customary at castle meals.

'Ready for the test tomorrow, Trivallia? Or was that why you were late?'

'As ready as you are, I should think,' she replied calmly. 'Even though my mother didn't have to pay for extra tuition for me.'

DiCapra's smile didn't falter, but she knew the sting had gone home all the same. Hah! she thought. It's a stupid man who accuses his neighbour of smelling before he has washed his own shirt. And DiCapra had a particularly bad memory when it came to the convoluted phrases of the codicils. Worse than Kat's.

'Now, I happen to have a family who *can* pay for my education . . .' he began.

'And isn't that fortunate, when there is so much educating still to be done?'

He ignored her interruption.

'However, that wasn't why I asked. I just thought you

might find it a little *difficult* to concentrate. As matters stand.'

Kat stiffened with her spoon raised halfway to her mouth. How could he know . . .? No. He couldn't. He couldn't possibly have got wind of Daniel and Raven and all of that. Daniel, perhaps, if Merian or Lu had spoken out of turn, but the rest . . . No. It couldn't be that. She forced herself to sip her soup as if nothing was wrong, but it could have been dishwater for all she cared.

'What are you talking about?' she said as evenly as she could.

'Ah, so you haven't heard the news?' DiCapra's smile warmed even more, and Kat's temper stirred ominously.

'I have better things to do than listen to castle gossip,' she said coldly, biting into the slice of rye that came with the soup.

'Oh, I do beg your pardon, maestrina,' he sneered. 'It's just that I thought you and Simon Jossa were friends.'

Simon? What did *Simon* have to do with anything?

'What do you mean?'

'Oh, I'm sure I was wrong to think you'd be interested. On a purely friendly sort of basis, of course.'

Kat fought down an urge to drown DiCapra and his awful smile in the beet soup. 'What is it about Simon? Go on, DiCapra, I know you are just dying to tell me.'

'No, no. Far be it from me to pester you with unwanted gossip.'

She knew he liked toying with her. The more heated she became under her uniform collar, the more he would enjoy it. That was the only reason why she managed to hang on to her temper.

'Do as you like,' she said, deliberately blowing on the next spoonful with apparent unconcern. 'Tell or don't tell. I'm sure I'll hear it from someone else, sooner or later.'

DiCapra gazed at her from across the table, smile firmly in place.

'Well, if you must know, I heard they brought him in this morning. Bound hand and foot. And on a common service nag.' DiCapra appeared to consider his catalogue of expressions and settled for a look of warm, insincere pity. It looked only slightly contrived. 'He is down the Hole now, while they discuss whether to charge him with acts of treason, or merely with desertion and ordinary oath-breaking.'

Kat dropped any pretence of not caring. It was all she could do not to leap up and run out – possibly without strangling DiCapra first, but not necessarily.

'Who said that?' she breathed.

'Oh, everyone knows by now, I should think. I heard it from a cousin in the guards. Poor Jossa. They had treated him rather roughly, it seems. But I do hope you won't let a small thing like this disturb your concentration for the test tomorrow. After all, it's not even certain that he'll hang.'

She made no conscious decision to get up. Suddenly she was standing, with Lu hanging on to her right arm with such force that she later discovered five finger-shaped bruises. The only thing on Kat's mind was a burning desire to shut DiCapra *up*, to stop those horrible mocking words which could not be true – *could* not. She managed to get one knee on to the table despite Lu's grasp. DiCapra flinched and drew back so suddenly that his soup bowl clattered to the floor.

'Sit down, Kat,' said Lu through clenched teeth, hanging on still harder. 'Don't make it this easy for him. Tarquin, help me!'

And then Ben Tarquin had her other arm, and between them they manhandled her down on to the bench again.

'You know I don't usually threaten people,' said Tarquin, soft-voiced. 'But one more word out of you on this subject, DiCapra, and Kat won't need to take you on. There will be three or four of us lining up for the pleasure.'

'Oh, dear,' said DiCapra. 'Such splendid ferocity. Let me just check – am I shivering in my boots? No, I don't think so.' But he kept his mouth shut all the same through the rest of the meal.

'Merian, help me clean up this mess,' said Lu, tackling the soup stains on the table. 'If we're really, really lucky we might still get out of this without anyone getting any black marks for it.'

But just as Lisabetta Strigius rose and formally ended the meal with another traditional gratitude, one of her clerks came over to the apprentice table.

'Apprentice Trivallia? DomFelix Strigius wishes to see you in her offices. Now.'

THREE QUESTIONS

For some reason, Kat was looking at Lisabetta Strigius's nose – perhaps because she couldn't quite make herself meet her eyes, but still found it rude to look away. It was not a particularly remarkable nose – a little thin and sharp, perhaps, with a deep furrow on each side. The silence went on and on, and the fly buzzing at the window seemed to buzz very loudly.

'How old are you?' asked DomFelix Strigius in the end.

'Nearly fifteen, DomFelix.'

'I see. Practically of age, then. We shall have to stop calling you "little Trivallia".'

'I'm not that little any more.'

The furrows round the Strigius nose quivered a little. Kat could not tell whether it was amusement or irritation.

'No, I don't suppose you are.'

'With respect, DomFelix, I just want to see him for a moment. To make sure he is all right . . .'

'Yes, I understand. But quite frankly, I think it will do you no good to be further involved at this stage.'

'Involved in what? I don't even know what he is accused of, and why.'

The long, elegant fingers of Lisabetta Strigius were drumming gently against the tabletop.

'I understand you have bound a hellhorse to you now?'

'Yes, DomFelix. Midnight.' Kat didn't understand this change of subject, but answered willingly enough. Even in the midst of all this, the thought of Midnight was a small flush of pleasure. But then she thought of Simon's Grizel. How had they separated them? Had they had to drug Grizel, the way it had been necessary with Frost when Dorissa disappeared? How utterly awful Simon must feel.

'No way back, then. You are bredinari, body and soul. And nearly of age.'

The gentle drumming stopped. Lisabetta Strigius's hands rested quietly on the table, and there was a decisive edge to her voice when she spoke again. 'Very well. I shall let you see him. On one condition. You must pose him three questions on my behalf. Ask him when there is no one else within earshot. And when he answers, bring his reply directly to me, *and no one else*. Do you understand? It is more vital than you can possibly imagine.'

Kat nodded. 'But . . . why doesn't the DomFelix ask him herself?'

'I must not be seen to interfere directly. But no one will wonder at your coming to see him.'

'I have to tell him that it's you who are asking.'

'Certainly. Jossa will in any case easily guess that questions such as these did not come from you. And the way things are for him now . . . well, he is not disposed to trust very many people, I imagine. Trying to mislead him would be a bad start.'

'And the questions, DomFelix? I would like to talk to him tonight, if possible.'

'No, you will have to wait until tomorrow morning, when the guards have changed. I'll make sure one of them will let you in and leave you alone with him then.'

'But DomFelix . . . I am to be tested by Lawmaster Taurus directly after breakfast.' It sounded absurd right now, but if she didn't show up all hell would break loose, and there would be a lot of unwelcome questions.

The DomFelix considered it for a while.

'You must make time to see him before breakfast,' she said. 'Then you go to your test as you normally would, and after that, you come to me. It is better in any case that you do not go directly from Jossa to my door or vice versa. And if anyone asks, Trivallia, this conversation has been solely about your unfortunate behaviour at supper. And you can tell whoever cares to know that you are to scrub my office floors tomorrow by way of punishment.'

This sounded more and more like one of Master Aurius's 'discreet assignments', but for some reason, Kat's troubled heart was eased a little.

'Can the DomFelix do anything to help Simon?' she finally nerved herself to ask.

'Perhaps. Perhaps, Trivallia. But it depends entirely on the answers he can give me. There. I have written the questions out for you, but you must learn them by heart. When you have, give me back the paper. No, do not leave the room. Just sit there as you memorize them.'

It seemed a very complicated way of asking a few questions. Why couldn't the DomFelix just tell her? It was almost as if she was afraid of saying the words out loud. Kat didn't protest though. She just took the slip of paper and read the words that the corps' second-in-command had penned in her neat, precise hand.

Does he know whether the rumours regarding an impending marriage for Madalena Bartelin are true, and if so, does he know to whom she may be affianced?

Does he know of any person of rank from the Bredani's circle, or from the army of the corps, who may have journeyed to the Southlands within the past eight months?

If his answer to either of the first two questions is affirmative, does he know of any reliable witness who may testify to such a journey or such an alliance?

Typical Breda posh style, thought Kat as she struggled through the wording. If she had written that note, it would have looked quite different: *Who is going to marry Madalena Bartelin? Has anyone important been to the South-lands lately? Were there any witnesses?* But such straightforward language wouldn't do, she supposed, if one were Alvar Alcedina's second-in-command and born to one of the highest families in Breda to boot.

The cool gaze rested on her. There was no finger-drumming or any other sign of impatience from the

DomFelix now, yet somehow her whole stance gave Kat the overwhelming impression that she had better finish up and be done. Fortunately she had had a lot of training in learning things by heart, and despite the complicated phrasing, this was child's play after the tortuous codicils of the law books. But what did it mean? Why was Lisabetta Strigius so inordinately keen to know about some Southland woman's impending marriage?

'DomFelix?' Kat decided to risk the wrath of the lioness. 'What has all this got to do with Simon? And what's so important about that engagement?'

The furrows around the thin nose grew deeper.

'You ask too many questions. Do you know the wording?'

'Yes.'

'Then see to it that you don't forget. And be *sure* that no one else overhears. Is that understood?'

'Yes, DomFelix.'

'Right. Be off. And come back after your Law test tomorrow.'

The news spread rapidly through the Castle. Simon Jossa was locked in the Hole, and the charge could cost him his life. Merian, Lu, Ben Tarquin and Valente came together silently to form a sort of protective guard around Kat. No matter where she went and what she did for the rest of that long day, somehow, at least one of them was always near. And DiCapra, who despite Tarquin's warning could not let pass such a wonderful opportunity to stick his barb into Kat's frightened heart . . . well, DiCapra had a most unfortunate fall on the steps leading up to the girls' baths. He bruised his knee badly enough to need a visit to Master Rodrian, and though he swore somehow he had been *made* to fall, neither Lu, Valente nor Ben Tarquin had seen anything unusual on the steps, they said.

'It was simply an accident, Master,' said Valente, having accompanied the limping DiCapra to the hospital wing with all the solicitous care of a dear friend. 'He tripped and fell, that's all.'

'I see,' said Master Rodrian, who had indeed seen the results of such accidents before. 'And where was the little Trivallia when this . . . accident . . . occurred?'

'In the library reading room, Master,' Lu replied readily. 'We have our tests in Law tomorrow.'

'You are sure about that? Trivallia was nowhere near? What say you, Prentice DiCapra?'

'She wasn't there,' admitted DiCapra unwillingly. 'But—'

'Well, then, my suggestion, DiCapra, is that you spend the rest of the evening quietly in your room, preparing for tomorrow's test. That way, we will have no more *accidents*. Isn't that so, Lusiana?'

'Yes, Master,' said Lu piously.

'And pass my regards to Trivallia and tell her that concentrating on her work may well be the best cure for the . . . worries that nag her.'

'Yes, Master. Goodnight.'

*

Kat really was sitting in the library reading room, gazing dutifully at the pages of the law book. But if she had found it difficult to concentrate before, now it was utterly impossible. Simon! She felt tears burning behind her lowered eyelids, and her throat tightened at the thought. *They had treated him rather roughly, it seems.* Damn DiCapra and his spiteful tongue! What did that mean? Had Simon resisted them, or had they given him a beating just because they felt he deserved it? Was it a bruise or two, or . . . worse? And what on earth had Simon been up to, to lay himself open to such charges? He was no traitor, but . . .

'Simon. have you been stupid?' she whispered so quietly that it was barely a breath. He was the one always telling her to be careful. Think, he always said. Use your head – not just your heart and your hands.

All bredinari learned a high degree of composure, but Simon made an art form of it. Hands, face, body, voice – always so carefully controlled, and she had learned that he was most expressionless precisely when his feelings ran high.

'Did you say anything?' Merian looked up from her book.

'No.'

'Do you want me to make some tea? Or ask Karolin if we can have some cider?'

'No, thanks.'

'Oh, Kat . . . Say something. *Do* something. Don't just sit there wearing your stone face. Do you want to see if they'll let us in to talk to him? Maybe there is someone we know in the guards down there.'

'No, I . . . I'll try tomorrow. Before breakfast.' She felt the woodenness that Merian called her stone face harden and set. She couldn't help it. She tried to soften it with words instead. 'But . . . thank you. You've all been . . . I mean, this is all so nice of you.'

'We're your friends. Friends do stuff like that. If you let them do it, that is. Are you sure you don't want to talk? Or is there anything else you'd like us to do?'

'No, that's . . .' and then a thought did occur to her. Merian, who was so clever and knew just about everything it was possible to know from books . . . 'Merian, why do people marry, down in the Southlands? What does it mean?'

Merian looked at her as if she had just turned into a large green frog.

'Why do you want to know?' she asked suspiciously. 'Or are you planning to run away from it all and marry a Southlander?'

'I just thought . . .' Well, what did she think? She couldn't tell Merian about the three questions the Dom-Felix had posed. 'You know my stepfather, Cornelius, is from the Southlands, and he married my mother, but I think it means something else to him than it does to her.'

'I bet it does,' said Merian dryly. 'In the Southlands they talk prettily about the husband being "helper and protector" to the wife, and there are a lot of chivalrous rituals so that he has to open doors for her, and hold her cloak, and never sit if she is standing, and stuff like that, and he has to address her with such awe and admiration that you'd think she was Our Lady herself . . . but I've heard that they think it unwomanly to take an interest in such mundane things as the household and business accounts, or the hiring or firing of staff, or to make any decisions at all, really. And the high ladies hardly dare set foot outdoors for fear of being thought promiscuous – you know they are supposed to stick with just one man all their lives, unless he dies on them? So what it amounts to is that it's the husband who really rules the house in most respects. I guess that is the closest a man can get to owning a place.'

'Is that why they have this Regent thing?'

'Yes. He marries the queen and runs the country on her behalf.'

'What does she do, then?'

'Oh . . . I think they like it if she has a lot of children. And she is supposed to be a sort of mother to all children in the country, and do good things for orphans, and stuff like that.'

'And when one of her daughters becomes queen . . . whoever she chooses to marry suddenly gets to be Regent?' Kat thought that was a ramshackle way of running a country.

'Oh, but there's not much choice involved. In the Southlands, marriages are most carefully planned. And unless your last name is either Martlin or Horsalin, your chances of ever marrying a queen are nonexistent, really.'

'But . . . what if she wants someone else?'

'Like I said, it's not her choice. The heir will marry

whoever the current Regent picks for her – the Regent and the Regency Council, that is.'

'What if she doesn't like him?'

'I think she has to marry him anyway.' Merian grinned. 'Remember how close I came to having to marry someone I most definitely didn't like? If my mother hadn't thought of sending me here, it would have been very hard indeed to turn down the honourable proposal of marriage from the Matriarcha Sechuan's brother. In Colmonte, that sort of thing is considered *entirely* normal.'

'I'm glad I don't live in Colmonte then. Or the Southlands, for that matter.' But then Kat remembered that she was not particularly happy to be living in Breda right now, and she could feel her face become mask-like again.

Merian sighed. 'Are you sure you don't want a cup of tea?'

'No, thanks.' Kat closed the law book. 'I think I'll go to bed. This isn't doing any good.'

'Goodnight, then. And if there's anything . . .'

'Yes.' She had to force her lips to move. 'Thank you. And goodnight.'

Lying in her alcove, she thought of Simon, asleep in the Hole. Or trying to sleep, perhaps, like she was. Was he scared? He must be. No one, not even Simon, would be able to slumber peacefully with the threat of a death sentence hanging over their head. What on earth had he done that they could talk of *treason*?

Her head ached. It had begun in the library, as she was

sitting there pretending to study for her test. There was a tight throbbing in her skull, and whenever she closed her eyes, strange white flames danced on the inside of her eyelids. She considered asking Clerk Angia for a little hops and valerian – it might help her sleep. But she was afraid of oversleeping too. It would be catastrophic if she didn't wake in time to visit Simon before breakfast and ask him the three strange questions posed by Lisabetta Strigius. And it felt wrong, somehow, to pamper a mere headache, when Simon was in the Hole and might . . . might be sentenced to . . .

She closed her eyes again. The flames were still there. They twisted this way and that, and acquired faces. 'Some of us never come back,' whispered a flame wearing Simon's face. And Ermine smiled and died, and Anna Weaver died with an arrow through her chest, and Dorissa rode off and never returned, and a smiling DiCapra placed a noose round Simon's neck, while Grizel screamed like a mad horse, and the flames were eating the Jungles of Katai and Uncle Isak's hands. In the middle of it all stood a form, dark against the whiteness of the flames, and the flames flickered and became embroidery on the hem of a midnight blue cloak, white stitching against blue velvet, fluttering in the wind, but there was no sound, no rustling or whistling or any sound at all, just dark silence. She walked a path through this darkness, a path among black apple trees, but the branches had thorns like roses, and they tangled her.

'Give me your hand,' whispered a voice, and she reached for the velvet cloak. A cold grasp held her, and suddenly she had no hands. It didn't hurt, there was no pain full of blood and bone splinters, there were merely no longer hands at the end of her arms. And still she was stuck, tangled and spitted by crooked branches with pale white petals and long black thorns.

'Free me!' she called, and the voice whispered an answer.

'Give me your heart.'

'I don't know how,' she said, struggling in the grasp of the thorns. 'You will have to take it yourself.'

Ice touched her chest, and there was a fierce tug, and suddenly everything was silent, inside and out, impossibly silent, because her heart had stopped beating. She no longer heard the quiet beating of her pulse, because the blood in her veins had stopped moving and there was no longer any reason to breathe. She had no hands, she had no heart. A chill wave washed through her, spreading outward from her chest, a hundred winter days at once, and branches, thorns and petals all shattered like glass in the cold.

Am I dead? she asked, but with no sound, because she no longer had breath to speak with.

'We all die,' said the voice. 'And it is not so bad. You are free now. You see clearly.'

It was true, she could see much better now. She could see in the dark. She saw them fetch Simon from the Hole. He walked slowly and reluctantly; they had to push him forward out into the Gallows Yard where the scaffold waited. She could see his mouth move, shouting, but she heard no sound. She wanted to touch him, but had only stumps, no hands. It's not so bad, she wanted to tell him. We all die. But Simon didn't want to die – he fought and struggled and tore at the noose they put around his neck. She watched quietly, with no fierce beating of her heart, because she had none. Why does he fight it so? she asked of the velvet-cloaked figure at her side.

'He doesn't know any better. But soon he will be free, like you.'

She waited patiently. It took a while, but finally the frantic kicking ceased. Simon hung quietly at the end of his rope, and the hangman left.

Simon! she called. But there was no answer. Simon, you are free now. It is not so bad. You are like me. But Simon didn't move, didn't speak, with or without words. She climbed on to the scaffold and tugged at the dangling body as best she could with her stumpy arms. Simon's eyes were open, but he saw nothing. He was not free. He just wasn't there any more. He was nothing. Gone. Dead. More dead than her.

You cheated me! she shouted at the velvet cloak. I am not dead at all – this is not death.

'You are dead enough to suit me,' said the velvet figure, and she suddenly thought she glimpsed a face deep in the shadow of the hood – a face she knew. But then the figure turned away, and she was no longer sure.

Give me back my hands! she called. Give me back my heart!

'Too late. You asked me to take them.'

Give them back!

But the figure melted into the darkness, heedless of her silent cries.

She fell to the ground at Simon's lifeless feet and discovered that it is possible to weep, even though one is half dead and has no heart left at all.

When she woke, she knew at once that she was alive. Her heart was pounding loudly, her pulse was a steady throb in her ears. All the same she slowly drew her arms from beneath the blankets and held out her hands in front of her. She stared at them for a long time. In the daytime they were tanned and marked by hard work, full of small cuts and threaded with the tiny dark lines of ingrained dirt, nearly impossible to get rid of. Now, in the patch of moonlight from the window, they looked strangely pale and bloodless, as if they were the hands of a ghost. Her headache was worse. She climbed out of the alcove to get herself a glass of water from the washstand. There was an ugly, metallic taste in her mouth, like a remnant from her nightmare. She lay down again, but it was no good. Every time she closed her eyes, the white flames were waiting. Finally she wrapped the blankets around herself and settled in the window. It was not a proper window seat, but the sill was just wide enough to sit on and broad enough that she could curl up, knees almost to her chest.

She didn't want to sleep any more. Or at any rate, she didn't want to dream. She stayed where she was, leaning carefully against the smooth glass, until a hint of dawn crept across the fields outside. Then she rose, dressed carefully for the day, and went to see Simon.

The Hole was not quite as dark and miserable as it sounded. The castle jail might be located in the cellars, but the walls were whitewashed and some morning light did get in through the semicircular peepholes. But the walls were massive, more than an arm's length deep, and there was a damp smell of pee and old hangovers – this was where castle guards and other staff members ended up if they were 'challenged in a state of inebriation', as the regulations called it.

From time to time, the cell housed people whose crimes were more serious. Some might have sold off castle equipment and pocketed the profits. Or it might be that a fight had ended in injuries or worse. But members of the bredinari corps were not frequent inmates, and it was rarer still to see someone charged with something so heinous as treason. Perhaps this was why they had put Simon in the remotest cell, far from the stairs and the guardroom and several empty lock-ups from the nearest drunk and disorderly charge.

The turnkey was grouchy and in no mood to leave his armchair and a steaming mug of something much stronger than tea, judging by the heavy pungent scent.

'Hell of a time to come calling,' he snarled.

'Sorry,' said Kat. 'I don't have time later.'

'Just because His High-And-Mightiness is a bredinari,

it doesn't mean that the rest of us are at the beck and call of the likes of you!'

'Sorry to bother you,' said Kat, trying to look suitably regretful. Obviously, the orders from Lisabetta Strigius had not been well received.

The turnkey muttered something inaudible and banged his keys against the bars of the cell a couple of times.

'Hey, Jossa! Got a visitor.'

The cell was not large – only just long enough for a man to lie on the brick shelf that served as a bed, and only so wide that he could touch both walls at the same time. There was a latrine bucket with a lid, and that was that. Not even a blanket. Kat's stomach contracted. This was where Simon had to stay for days? Weeks, maybe?

He was lying on the bed shelf, curled up on his side, and at first there was no reaction to the turnkey's call. Then he slowly raised himself on one elbow and looked towards the door. It was hard to tell who or what he had expected, but it seemed Kat wasn't it. His shoulders slumped as some kind of tension left him.

'Kat,' he said, neither pleasure nor disappointment evident in his voice. 'You shouldn't have come.'

'But I'm here anyway,' she said calmly. Simon had always thought that it would be best for her not to see too much of him, as if it might somehow incriminate her – now more than ever, of course. 'And it's not really up to you.'

She looked at him stubbornly, and saw a brief smile flash across his face. He had shaved off the beard so that the scar on his chin was visible again – the scar she had once given him. It was now accompanied by a swollen lip and a bruise on his cheekbone, but other than that he did not look particularly mistreated.

'What does a man have to do to rid himself of you? Not even jail will serve, it seems. Hob, do me the favour of throwing her out. This is no place for a girl.'

Hob the Turnkey grasped her elbow.

'You heard the man, Trivallia. Off you go.'

'No!' Kat freed herself. 'I haven't even . . . look, I have to talk to him . . .'

'You said you wanted to see him. Well, you've seen him. Now leave him alone. If he doesn't want to talk to you, that's his right.' This time he took hold of her upper arm in a firmer grip.

Kat jabbed her elbow into his chest, spun around and punched him just below the shoulder with her left hand, one knuckle extended, so that she hit the precise point that would deaden his whole arm.

'Kat!' Shock flattened Simon's voice.

A pained noise came from the turnkey, more than a grunt but less than a roar.

'You little bitch!' he hissed, ready to strangle her if his flushed face was anything to go by. But Kat had backed away and stood poised, ready to counter any move he made. She could have gone for his throat with that strike, and he was well enough trained to know it. You could practically see the calculation that went on in his head. He could probably take her down, but not without some damage to himself. And if she went all out for the places that would hurt the most . . . He rubbed his dead arm, not thrilled at the prospect. He could of course summon reinforcements from the guardroom. Yes, he could do that – if he were willing to suffer months of taunting because he had proved unable to handle a fourteen-year-old girl on his own. And he *had* after all had orders from above saying that the vicious little bitch should be allowed to see Jossa.

'Have you gone completely mad?' snapped Simon, who recognized a combat stance when he saw one. 'Stop it, Kat! If you hit him one more—'

'Me?' said Kat acidly. 'I'm just a puny little girl. Why would I go around hitting a big strong guard like him? Unless of course he *touches* me. Indecent behaviour towards a prentice, turnkey. How many days in the Hole for that?'

Hob the Turnkey swore under his breath. He had not considered that angle, obviously. And even though everyone knew that Trivallia was a hothead and no innocent little lamb-to-the-slaughter, still . . .

'Bloody hell, Jossa. Can't you just talk to the girl? It's too damn early for all this hassle.'

'Let her in then,' said Simon resignedly. 'She won't leave us in peace until you do.'

Hob unlocked the door, and Kat entered the cell. The door itself was so low that even she had to duck, but inside there was more headroom.

'Stupid bitch,' muttered Hob, slamming the door shut with a clang that echoed down the passage.

Simon was standing now, very straight and stiff,

giving her his coldest glare. There was not the least hint of any smile now, and she could tell she had actually managed to shock him.

'And what was all that in aid of?' he said icily. 'Do you want to move into the cell next door?'

'No, but—'

'Or perhaps you think Hob will be so charmed by your gentle nature that he will fail to report this?'

Kat shuffled a foot. 'He won't say anything. Too embarrassing.'

'You may be right. In which case you are luckier than you deserve to be. And it certainly doesn't excuse your behaviour. Just how good does it make you feel to hit a man and make sure he can't hit you back because you're a girl?'

'Just how good does it make *you* feel to betray the service and your country? *I'm* not the one charged with treason here!'

She heard the words snap out of her mouth and was instantly horrified. This was certainly not what she had planned to say to him when she had sat hunched in her window nook most of last night, thinking about him. She almost expected him to hit her. But of course he didn't. Not Simon. He just looked at her with that peculiar lack of expression she knew so well.

'Simon, I'm sorry. I know it's not like that at all . . .'

'Don't apologize. You are right. You are not the traitor here. And I wouldn't want you to become one. So perhaps you had better leave now.'

'Stop it, Simon. Don't talk like that. I know you didn't do what they say you did. You'd never betray Breda.'

'No? I think that depends on which Breda you mean. A Breda that cares not one whit for Jos and Grana and the Vales . . . A Breda that barters away lands and people as if they were nothing more than mere property . . . such a Breda I might well betray.' His eyes took on a strange vagueness, as if he had forgotten that she was there, and who he was talking to.

'What do you mean? Barters? Simon, what's going on?'

He closed his eyes for a moment and when he opened them again, his gaze was once more alert and present, with his superior self-control in place as if the slip had never happened. Or nearly so. Sweat filmed his forehead, she now noticed, and when he spoke, the words came more rapidly than they usually did, almost feverishly so.

'Nothing. Forget I said that. Look, you've seen me, and you know now that I'm all right. I don't blame you for being worried – I can just imagine how the rumours must be flying. But the charges are likely to be simply insubordination and fraud, not treason. So there is really no need to look as if you are expecting an invitation to my funeral any moment. Sorry, but there it is.'

'Simon. Did you hurt your head?' He talked too much for Simon, and she didn't like that vagueness that had been in his eyes.

'A little, perhaps. Nothing too alarming.'

'People are saying that they . . . roughed you up.'

'And so you came running to defend your poor abused

friend? Sorry again. The rumours were grossly exagger-
ated. I . . . fell off a horse, that's all.'

'You? You never fall off.' Other people fell off horses,
not Simon. He was from Jos, where children rode before
they could toddle. 'Simon, how bad is it? Really, I mean?'

'Not bad, I tell you. Go. You'll miss breakfast.'

'The hell with breakfast,' she hissed, getting desperate.
'Simon, talk to me! It's me, for the Lady's sake, not
some . . . well, not someone else. Tell me what's going on,
and don't give me that I-fell-off-a-horse rubbish!'

He looked at her silently for so long that she started
wondering about his head again. His eyes did not seem
vague this time, but she could make no guess at what he
was thinking. Then suddenly he smiled, so easily and
with such warmth that it was hard to believe that this was
a man sitting in a cell awaiting judgement.

'No,' he said lightly, and crouched down on the bed
shelf. 'This time, Kat my sweet, you do *not* get your own
way. Hug me or hit me, if you have to. But this . . . this I
will not let you interfere with. You are a wonderful girl,
Kat, loyal and strong and stubborn, and I . . . I am very
fond of you. That much, at least, you should know. And
now you must walk away. Get out of here. Go to Midnight. Go to Lu and Merian. And breakfast, if there is any
left. Go away, and do not come back. Next time, Hob
might be a whole lot less understanding.'

She hated the way he said it as if he were saying goodbye. As if he had given up and did not expect to see her
again. Ever.

'I'm not letting you off so easily,' she said, softly, because she didn't quite trust her voice.

'Goodbye, Kat.'

'No. I have a message.'

'So?'

'Yes. From DomFelix Strigius. Three questions.'

'Tell the DomFelix that—'

'Three questions, I said.' And she reeled them off, not letting herself be interrupted. 'Does he know whether the rumours regarding an impending marriage for Madalena Bartelin are true, and if so, does he know to whom she may be affianced?'

'Tell her that I—'

'Does he know of any person of rank from the Bredani's circle, or from the army of the corps, that may have journeyed to the Southlands within the past eight months?'

'There is no way I—'

'If his answer to either of the first two questions is affirmative, does he know of any reliable witness who may testify to such a journey or such an alliance?'

He was on his feet again. His face was still flatly expressionless, but she knew that had Grizel been there, she would have laid back her ears and struck sparks with her pounding hoof.

'Have you quite finished now?' he asked tonelessly.

She nodded, struck dumb. His anger was like a wall – a wall of fire. Despite the flatness of his tone, despite the blankness of his face and the careful stillness of his body, despite everything he was doing to hold back his rage, the wall was there, a silent roar of flame.

'Then you may tell DomFelix Strigius that I do not barter with people who risk the lives of children.'

'But Simon—'

'There's my answer.'

'But she might be able to help . . . Simon, at least she is willing to try . . .'

'No. She is willing to risk you, so that she may win a point or two in a power game. That is the extent of her willingness.'

'She's not like that—'

'They are all like that. All the high and mighty, those who come of the Seven. It may not be their fault, it may be the way they are brought up that destroys them. I've said it before, Kat, but it is absolutely vital that you *listen* this time. Stay away from them. Do *not* trust them.'

'But I think—'

'No. Don't believe her. She will use you and throw you away. Do not for a moment think she will protect you at any risk or cost to herself.'

'Simon, not all borderers are alike, despite what people here think. Perhaps the same is true of the Seven.'

He grimaced in something that only retained the shape of a smile. 'I used to think so. I used to believe in the exceptions. Once, I thought that there were people here who actually meant what they said when they talked of serving *all* of Breda, not just this small power-riddled corner of it. I got wiser. As a matter of fact, I have just had a whole lot of wisdom pounded into me. And I don't want you to pay for the same expensive lessons. If I won't play along, she can't use you, and I'm not playing. She can earn her filthy little points on her own – I will *not* let her use you.'

The way things are for him now, he is not disposed to trust very many people, Lisabetta Strigius had said. And it was clearly no exaggeration. What had happened, who had let him down, to make him lose his last remnant of trust in the 'high and mighty'?

'But it might be your only chance . . .' whispered Kat, tears burning her eyelids.

'Then I will just have to do without that chance,' said Simon. 'Go, and give her my answer. And then stay away from her. And from me.'

'I can't do that!'

'Yes, you can. And if everything goes wrong . . .' he hesitated. 'Katriona Teresa-Daughter, have I ever told you my clan name?'

She shook her head.

'My clan is Chekessa, and my name is Simon Ravi da'Chekessa. Say it.' His eyes did not leave hers.

'Simon, why—'

'Say it!'

There was a force of will in him so strong she obeyed without thinking.

'Simon Ravi da'Chekessa,' she whispered. And he nodded slowly, and the glow of his will died down.

'If you can make it to Jos, my clan will take you in in my name,' he said. '*Remember* that. Chekessa. It's a place you can always go. A home if you need one.'

'But—'

He shook his head. 'There is nothing more to say.'

He put a hand on each side of her face and kissed her on the forehead, a gentle and oddly formal kiss. 'My sister will like you. And Daniel Sardi is a complete and utter idiot.'

He released her, and she stood as if turned to stone. Daniel? How had Simon heard about that? Had Lu been telling tales? Or Merian?

'How—' she began.

But Simon had said what he felt needed saying on that subject. He lay down on the bed shelf and folded his arms across his chest.

'*Tam'kora atavisa,*' he said, and closed his eyes.

'Simon!'

There was no reaction. She knew what he was doing. He was leaving her. He could not go into another room and close the door behind him, so he went into himself instead. The door was shut all the same. She could scream and yell now, and he would not hear her. She could touch him, shake him even, and it would do no good. The door would remain shut until he himself saw fit to open it.

'That's not fair,' she whispered, 'running out on me like that.'

He had said goodbye. It was clear he did not expect to see her again, whatever the charges. He had decided not to take the hand held out to him by DomFelix Strigius. And he had decided that Kat could no longer afford to be his friend and fight by his side.

'But you don't get to decide everything around here!'

she murmured, looking at his tanned, closed-in face. She touched the graze on his cheek. It was warm, but not burning with infection. She pushed a damp lock of black hair off his glistening forehead, but then she suddenly felt shy, touching him like that, when he wasn't really there.

Tam'kora atavisa, he had said. She knew that expression. It was the clan tongue, and it meant *Take care of my heart till I see you again.* It sounded so reassuring. She tried not to remember that it was this phrase he had written in the Memory Book when he knew Dorissa had died.

LESSONS IN LAW

'Congratulations!' Lu was trying to hug her and pound her back at the same time. 'That was *great*! Honestly, I didn't think you could do it. You looked half dead when you went in, and I thought—'

Kat never found out what Lu had thought. At that moment Lawmaster Taurus's door opened, and the Master himself came out. He had a grey cloak around his shoulders, and some parchment rolls wedged under one arm, and the corners of his mouth twitched with disapproval at Lu's enthusiastic lack of decorum.

'An adequate performance, Trivallia,' he said curtly. 'Albeit somewhat . . . absent-minded. I feel bound to impress on you that next year's studies will require something more than mere rote-learning.'

He looked at Kat, clearly expecting some response, but it wasn't until Lu jabbed an elbow at her that she managed a meek 'Yes, Master.'

Master Taurus raised an eyebrow and primped his mouth with even greater displeasure. 'Surely one has not been so careless as to inebriate oneself on the night before the examinations?'

'No, Master.'

'It's just lack of sleep, sir,' said Lu. 'There were so many codicils to keep straight, we were up half the night.'

'I see.' The Master looked sceptical. 'Who is next? Prentice DiCapra? Enter. Or is he also incapacitated by sleepless nights?'

'Not at all, Master,' smiled DiCapra, nearly succeeding in concealing the shoddy state of his nerves. And as he passed Kat, he whispered: 'When a mountain peasant with dirt for brains can do this, *I* have nothing to fear.'

For once, Kat was completely impervious to DiCapra.

'I have to go now,' she told Lu, 'to scrub the floors of DomFelix Strigius's office.'

'I'll help,' said Lu. 'We'll be finished much quicker that way.'

Kat shook her head. 'It's not supposed to be quick. It's my punishment for what happened in the dining room yesterday.'

'Oh. Well, I'll see you later in the stables then.'

'Sure. Pat Midnight for me, will you?'

'Are you joking? She'd take my hand off if I tried.' Midnight was still not very amenable with anyone other than Kat.

The office floor in question was an ordinary wooden one, but painted in white and grey squares to look like tiles.

Kat slowly washed one square after the other, waiting for the DomFelix to turn up.

'While we're young, Prentice,' said the aide in some irritation. He wouldn't let her be alone in the room, but stood behind her, stiff-backed and stiff-legged, keeping a grumpy eye on every stroke of the brush. Did he imagine she would wipe her nose on the drapes, or make paper hats out of important documents? 'I don't have all morning to waste on you!'

'I don't want to do a sloppy job,' said Kat, and turned the brush over to use the handle, so that she might scrape at a spot that had no doubt resided there since the founding of the Castle. 'The DomFelix said she wanted it clean, not just half-clean.' And if the DomFelix did not appear soon, this would no doubt end up the cleanest floor in Breda. What was she to do if the aide lost all patience with her and threw her out?

'Thank you, Mikélin,' said a cool voice behind them. 'You may leave now. Did you speak to Master Aureus about next month's assignments?'

'Not yet, DomFelix.'

'Then pray do so. He will be in his office now.'

There was a whiplash sharpness to her voice, and Kat wondered if she disliked the man. If she did, why did she keep him on as her aide? But perhaps that was merely the way they talked to each other. The aide, in any case, left the room, and the door closed behind him with a muffled thud.

'So, Trivallia. What did he say?'

Kat straightened slowly, still holding the brush.

'He didn't say anything, DomFelix.'

'Nothing? He must have said something.'

Kat looked down at the very clean floorboards. She couldn't quote Simon's words to the DomFelix. *Tell Dom-Felix Strigius that I do not barter with people who risk the lives of children.* She couldn't say that!

'He wouldn't answer the questions,' she muttered in the end.

'Why not?'

'He was . . . very angry.' Like a wall. A wall of fire.

The DomFelix was standing at apparent ease, her back straight but not ramrod. Yet Kat could sense a tension in her, a sort of complete attention, like a hunting dog waiting for the signal to fetch the prey.

'How did he look? Was he . . . Were there any apparent injuries?'

'A few bruises. I think he had hurt his head a little.'

'But he was alert? He knew what you were saying?'

Kat nodded. 'Yes. It wasn't that bad.'

Lisabetta Strigius walked slowly to the window. With perfect control, she crossed her arms and gazed down at the people and beasts crossing Riders' Yard.

'Has he understood the seriousness of the charges laid against him? What it might cost him if they were proved?'

Kat's eyes stung, as if she might be about to cry.

'He understands,' she said softly.

'And yet he will not answer? *Why?* Is he mad? Or is he trying to raise the price? If that is his game you may assure him that it is a very dangerous one. I am not in the habit of letting myself be pressured.'

Contempt lay like hoar frost on those last words. And so Kat said it after all.

'I was to say that he does not barter with people who risk the lives of children.'

A jerk went through the DomFelix, a visible one. She turned to look at Kat again, and for a moment she reminded Kat of Chief Cook Karolin the time she had been bitten by a pike she had thought already dead. Then her composure returned, like a mask slipping into place.

'Put down that scrubbing brush and sit down, Trivallia,' she said. 'You and I need to talk if we are to save Jossa's stubborn neck.'

Kat sat hesitantly in one of the chairs by the desk. Lisabetta Strigius remained at the window for a moment more, then she joined Kat at the table.

'I have a feeling you and Jossa understand each other quite well,' she said. 'Better than . . . than someone born and bred inside these city walls might hope to. So I will tell you exactly what he has done. And then, perhaps, you may tell me *why* he did it.'

Kat nodded. But she felt far from certain that she knew Simon as well as the DomFelix supposed, nor that she would necessarily tell her everything she did know and understand about him.

'As you no doubt recall, Jossa was transferred away from the Thora Vale Resting Place this spring.'

Oh, yes. Kat remembered that. The house that Simon and Remus had worked like beasts to restore and turn into a refuge for the wayfarers now housed a mob of Lodge Brothers, and, if the letters from home were to be trusted, a rather drunken mob too, who acted as if they owned the town and hassled the ordinary people of the Vale so that no one went near the place without a very good reason.

'As you also know, he was angry about this dismissal. Since then he has been on courier duty, and by order of the DomPrimus himself, none of his routes took him near the Vales.'

Kat knew that too. He had been sent north for nearly a month, to Luna and beyond, into the Northlands, so far that he had been able to smell the sea, he claimed. On the table in her room were two delicate blue shells he had given her when he returned.

'But then, some weeks ago, one of the other Riders broke a leg, and the routes had to be reshuffled. And suddenly Jossa's name was on the southbound routes again. How that came about . . . well, that is one of the questions you might ask him. It certainly was *not* by orders from above.'

For the first time Kat was surprised, and also a little shocked. Simon had not said a word about going to the Vales. Surely he would have said. Surely he would have offered to carry a letter . . . It was true she had been busy and that they had not seen much of each other, but still . . . She could feel the DomFelix's eyes on her, but she didn't say anything.

'Ah . . . Perhaps he didn't tell you that,' said Lisabetta Strigius dryly, and Kat swore under her breath. Did the woman have magus eyes? Could she see straight into your soul? It almost felt that way.

'Jossa left immediately, heading for Thora Vale. How long does that trip normally take, Trivallia?'

'Six days.' Six days to get there, one day's rest, six days coming home. On a hellhorse, that was. An ordinary horse would take nearly twice that long.

'Six days, yes. But Jossa did not report to the Thora Vale Station until ten days later. How did he spend the extra four days? That is another question you might ask.'

'Grizel might have been lame,' said Kat. 'Something like that. It's not a crime to be a little late.'

'No. But when the next courier took over the mailbag from Jossa, he discovered that the seal had been broken and that two of the tubes were empty.'

'That doesn't mean Simon took it,' snapped Kat, without thinking.

'Theoretically, it might have been someone else,' said the DomFelix, 'if not for the fact that Jossa revealed knowledge of the contents of one of the letters to the Bredani herself.'

'*What?*'

'Yes. On Talis Day, the day he returned from the southern route, he asked for an audience with the Bredani, and was granted one because of the part he had played in the capture and death of Tedora Mustela. I do not know what was said – I was not myself present – but the Bredani was much outraged by his behaviour, and when he revealed knowledge of affairs of state that he should not have had . . . questions were raised. Eventually, Alvar Alcedina issued the order for his arrest. But by then he was gone, with his hellhorse. It took them three days to find him.'

Kat sat completely still on her chair, as if she might fall off it if she moved. What on earth had Simon got himself into? What was so important that he had risked every-thing to go to the Bredani herself? And why had he run afterwards?

'What does Simon say?' she eventually asked.

Lisabetta Strigius held out her long slim hands in front of her, as if she wanted to assure herself that they were clean.

'Not a lot. He says he did not break the seal, but he will not reveal the source of his knowledge either. Nor will he explain why he was four days late coming into Thora Vale. Or where he was going when he ran. And that is the reason why they may yet accuse him of treason. Several of Breda's neighbours would pay handsomely for the intelli-gence he had acquired. What if he was headed for one of them, to sell his knowledge?'

'No,' said Kat firmly. 'Simon wouldn't do that.' Unless . . . His disturbing words in the cell came back to her. *A Breda that barters lands and people as if they were mere property . . . Such a Breda I might betray.* But not for money. Surely not for money.

'What *would* he do? Who is he, Trivallia? What does he love and what does he hate? When will he lie and when speak the truth? What comes easy to him and what would he never do? Tell me *who he is!*'

Suddenly Kat thought that Lisabetta Strigius looked like a woman appraising a horse before a race. Lungs, legs, temperament, breeding. Was it worth betting on? And perhaps that was exactly what the DomFelix was doing right now – assessing Simon to see if he was worth betting on, or if she would be a fool to risk anything on his behalf.

'Simon is a clansman,' said Kat slowly, feeling that to reveal even this much to the cool appraising gaze was a sort of betrayal, though surely the DomFelix already knew what the clans were. 'Clansmen do not lie. They may not always tell you everything they know, and if you choose to misunderstand they do not necessarily feel they have to correct you. But Simon would never tell a direct lie. And he would never sell anything that mattered just for the money. And . . . and also, he would never betray a friend.'

'And Breda? Would he betray his country? His duty?'

'No,' said Kat, adding in her own mind, not the Breda he believed in. Not the duty he felt he had. The DomFelix looked at her with eyes like a storm cloud; dark grey and cold and slightly threatening. But Kat did not back down. Simon was no traitor. Not to the things that mattered.

For a while, the only sound was the light drumming of the DomFelix's elegant fingers. Then that stopped too, and the silence was complete.

'Very well,' said the corps' second-in-command, and reached for two yellowish sheets of paper. 'We will make one more attempt. This is a pass so the guards will let you in again. And this one is an oathsman's vow of service. If Jossa signs this declaration, he immediately becomes the sworn oathsman of the Strigius family. Do you know what that means – you who have just passed an examination in Law with Master Taurus himself?'

Kat had to think for a moment. Then it hit her.

'It means that he . . . that he cannot be executed, other than by the direct order of the Maestra Strigius.'

'And that a Strigius Lawmaster must be present at every interrogation, every trial and every sentencing.' Lisabetta Strigius signed the document herself with a swift, practised signature. 'It will ensure him a significant degree of justice and much better treatment than some nameless borderman would otherwise get.'

He is not nameless, thought Kat fiercely. His name is Simon Ravi da'Chekessa, and his family may well be more ancient than yours. But she bit her lip and kept her silence, because Lisabetta Strigius was right. In this city, in this castle, Simon was nameless in every significant respect, because his name was not one that meant anything here.

'And what must he do in return?' she asked miserably, because she could not imagine that such a paper was without price, and she was so very much afraid that the price was not one that Simon was willing to pay.

'Nothing. This is his, no matter what else we agree on. I want to ensure him a fair trial. And I do not believe he has done anything he deserves to die for. Give it to him freely. And once it is in his hands . . .' the fingers took up their habitual drumming, 'you might perhaps ask him my three questions once more. Do you still remember them?'

Kat nodded. They would no doubt stay engraved in her memory long after every last codicil had fled.

'But whether or not he decides to answer, the oathsman's certificate is his.'

The DomFelix rose to her feet. The interview was clearly at its end. Kat folded the certificate carefully and secreted it in one of the hidden compartments of Cornelius's old belt. The pass for the guards she tucked inside her waistcoat – it was nowhere near as vital. Then she collected her bucket and her brush and pushed the door open with her shoulder.

Outside in the antechamber, the aide was busily putting some papers in order.

'Mikélin,' said DomFelix Strigius, once more with that deadly sharpness in her voice, 'am I mistaken, or did I give you an order?'

'I needed to get the paperwork straight first,' said the aide in hasty apology. 'DomFelix knows how Master Aureus detests a disorderly presentation.'

True enough, thought Kat, who had had to present a report to Master Aureus more than once. His demands for precision bordered on obsession.

'That may well be,' said Lisabetta Strigius, 'but he also detests lateness, so get over there. And Trivallia . . .'

'Yes, DomFelix?'

'You may return tomorrow to scrub the antechamber's floor. And in future I would like to see you behave yourself with discretion, correctness and decorum – in the dining hall and elsewhere.'

For a moment, Kat had honestly forgotten what the DomFelix was referring to. Then she remembered that the floor scrubbing was supposedly her punishment for the incident with DiCapra and the beet soup. And she knew that the wording was also the DomFelix's way of giving one last order: keep your mouth shut, don't draw unwanted attention, and come back tomorrow with Simon's reply.

'Yes, DomFelix,' said Kat obediently, and followed on Aide Mikélin's heels out into the fresh air of the Riders' Yard. He barely glanced at her and walked as if he had a stick up his back. Probably he didn't like her very much. Or perhaps he was always like that.

NO BLOOD

The guardroom was stuffy and full of smoke. Hob the Turnkey reclined in his armchair, feet propped on the edge of the fireplace, snoring so mightily that his upper lip actually fluttered. Kat cleared her throat a couple of times, but soon realized that it would take more than that to wake him. The mug that had contained something stronger than tea this morning was on the floor where it had fallen from Hob's limp hand. He had not done all his drinking alone though – three pewter tankards sat on the table, still mostly full. Kat sniffed – mulled wine, it seemed, spiced with cloves and spirits. Perhaps it was no mystery that Hob had felt the need for a nap. If she woke him now, he would be as grumpy as a hibernating bear and about as safe. Better to leave him alone and have her talk with Simon undisturbed, even though it meant they would have to talk through the bars. She tiptoed past him towards the crooked whitewashed passage to the cells.

The Hole was awfully quiet, she thought, apart from

the muffled subterranean roar of Hob's snoring. The man who had been in the first cell this morning had been released, it seemed, and the next couple of cells were empty as well. But as she turned the corner, she saw three men standing outside Simon's cell. The door was open, and Hob's big bundle of keys dangled from the fist of one of the men. Simon, however, showed no signs of making a dash for freedom. Instead he stood in the middle of the cell, and the way he was standing made a whole chorus of alarm bells go off in Kat's head. Perfectly poised, completely attentive – the state of readiness that Master Haryn called posa. The first man through that narrow door would regret it.

This had occurred to the men outside in the passage, and none of them was volunteering.

'We just want to talk to you, Jossa,' said the tallest. His voice was muffled and a little indistinct because he was masked – a Lodge Brother owl mask. 'But there's barely room to stand let alone sit in that bloody cell. Let's go to the guardroom.'

'Where is Hob?' asked Simon softly.

'In the guardroom. Come on, now.'

'Thanks, but I think I'll just stay where I am.'

'Aren't you tired of that filthy Hole?'

'Not that tired.' Simon suddenly raised his head the tiniest of fractions – nothing Kat would have noticed if she had not been noticing *everything* about him right then – and she knew that he had seen her.

'Aren't there any other guards?' he said, and Kat realized that was meant as a message to her. Find the guards.

Get help. But there were no guards apart from snoring Hob.

'Why are you so nervous, Jossa? One would think a bit of conversation would help pass the time. This place would give me the creeps if I were stuck here all alone.'

Kat backed slowly down the passage, as silently as she could. Maybe she could shake some life into Hob. Maybe she could find some other guard. Or guards, preferably. Whatever the three owl brothers were up to, Simon was convinced they meant him nothing good.

Hob showed no signs of returning to consciousness even though she shook him so vigorously that he slid off the chair and on to the floor. She let go of him and ran up the stairs to the first floor of the guards' quarters, but the bunk rooms that were normally full of off-duty men sleeping, card-playing or beer-drinking were completely deserted. Where the hell had they all got to? She ran along the corridor, slamming open every door, and found not a single guard, asleep or awake, on duty or off. Where were they? Up another flight of stairs, yet another door, and another . . . still no one. And then, blissfully, behind the third door, a guard. And one she knew.

'Ola!' She could have kissed him. 'Where is everyone?'

He looked up from the piece of wood he was whittling away at. 'Behind the barn,' he said. 'There's a cockfight on.'

'Come on!' She grabbed his arm, trying to pull him to his feet.

'But it's no place for a girl,' he protested. 'And anyway, it's against regs.'

'Not the cockfight!' she snapped. 'The Hole! Hurry! There are three men there, three owl brothers, and they want to . . . want to . . .' What did they want? She didn't really know. 'They've drugged Hob Turnkey, and I think they want to hurt Simon.'

Finally he seemed to realize that she was serious.

'Ah well, we'd better take a look then,' he said calmly and got to his feet with exasperating slowness.

'Hurry up!'

'Yes, all right, on my way . . .' but apparently he saw no reason to run or make undue haste in any other fashion, even though Kat dragged and chivvied him along. She felt like a sheepdog nipping at the heels of a very big, very slow-witted sheep. It seemed to take forever to walk down the corridor and down the two flights of stairs to the Hole. Ola paused at the sight of Hob's slumbering body on the floor, and for the first time a certain tension asserted itself in him. He caught Kat by the shoulder.

'Stay behind me,' he said softly. 'And if I say run, you run like hell. Try the guardroom proper – it's further, but at least there ought to be someone there who is both on duty and capable of walking a straight line.' He straightened his own uniform and walked down the passage with a firmness to his step that clearly announced that this was authority on the move. Kat followed, a somewhat smaller and less awe-inspiring shadow. She couldn't see much except Ola's wide back. But the moment he turned the final corner, he called out a smart and very loud 'Halt there! Desist!' that echoed between the bare cellar walls.

She glimpsed a masked face – why was the man kneeling? – and heard the thuds and scuffling of combat.

'Desist, I said!' roared Ola, even as another voice was hissing 'It's the guard!' Ola pulled his truncheon from his belt, but one of the owl brothers had moved more quickly, and suddenly Ola bent forward sharply, pitching on to his hands and knees, and there was a spray of blood against the whiteness of the walls.

'You moron! No blood, he said.'

Kat stiffened, staring at Ola's kneeling form. Then she saw Simon, kicking and hissing, with his head turned oddly back and to one side. A rope – they had a rope around his throat, and even though he had managed to get a hand inside the noose it was only a matter of time before—

'Run!' moaned Ola before slumping completely to the floor, but she had hesitated too long because Simon was standing there being strangled. One of the owl brothers let go of Simon's untrapped arm, then leaped across Ola's fallen body to catch hold of her sleeve just as she was turning to flee. She kept twisting, jabbing at his midriff with her elbow, but he was wearing a padded leather jerkin and the blows had little effect. Turn, keep turning – he was trying to seize her rather than strike her, he knew he was bigger and stronger than her. One more turn, don't let him catch hold . . . and then a swift kick to the knee, releasing a stream of curses . . . back, back, stay out of reach or he'll have you . . . There wasn't time to see how Simon was doing, but at least he had only one opponent now. Simon, you are on your own, I'm quite busy with this one . . . Another half-turn, and then the kick, the one absolutely perfect kick, a slow lazy feel to it though she knew she was moving very quickly indeed, there, just beneath the edge of the owl mask, very difficult when one was no taller than she was, but for once she got it right, it was just high enough, just hard enough . . . The mask went sailing through the air and the man went down like a falling tree. Blood poured from the broken nose into his grey beard, but she was not the first one to break that nose, and that broken-nosed face was highly familiar . . . Raven. What was *Raven* doing here? But there was no time for the whys and wherefores. She threw a quick glance Simon's way and could see that he had managed to trap his opponent's arm between the bars of the door, but Ola, Ola lay ominously still on the floor and had already bled far too much . . . Run, he had said, and it was still the most sensible thing to do, to get help before it was too late for Ola and perhaps also too late for Simon.

She was turning to sprint down the passage when a flash of movement caught her eye. Something thudded into her shoulder, turning her whole arm numb. She stumbled, ran a few tottering steps, but something was wrong – she brushed against the wall and screamed in pain. She didn't understand what had happened, only that something hurt, that she was dizzy, that something . . . something was stuck in her upper arm. Something black and square. A knife, she realized – the hilt of a knife. Behind her Simon was yelling something, but there was such a buzzing in her ears she couldn't hear him properly, and her legs weren't obeying orders either.

She stumbled to one knee, and before she could find her feet again someone caught her by the neck and hissed: 'Stay here!' right beside her ear. A terrible new tearing pain in her arm released a stream of hot, greasy blood down past her elbow and on to her hand, and she was swimming at the very edge of consciousness, but not quite so far gone that she couldn't feel the cold edge of steel against her throat or hear the hissing voice make its threat:

'Hold still, Jossa – or else . . .'

Then all sounds did disappear for a while, and when they came back, she knew that time had passed, because suddenly she was lying somewhere else, propped on her side against something not a wall and not a floor. Bars – it was the bars of a cell.

'What the hell do we do now?' said the hissy voice.

'A little hard to make it look like suicide now, isn't it?' Simon's voice was raspier than usual, but quite calm. Calm and flat like always when the fat hit the fire.

'Shut up, traitor. You'll dangle yet. And if I had ten more of your kind, they would hang right next to you!'

'Of my kind? Which kind is that?'

'Just shut your trap. Right now the girl has a tiny chance of making it out of this alive. You want to spoil that for her?'

'No,' said Simon softly.

'Then shut up and do as you're told.'

Simon went quiet. Kat carefully opened her eyes. She could see nothing other than brownish straw and a white-washed cell wall, and she couldn't move at all. Her head was huge and leadenly heavy, and her throat was afire with thirst. Something still seeped from the knife wound – she could feel it moving slowly down her arm.

'What's keeping him?' This was Raven's voice – apparently he had regained consciousness. 'We haven't got all day. Pollo can't make that cockfight last forever.'

Then there were footsteps and a new voice, cold and strange.

'The carriage is ready. There are blankets within. Can the girl walk?'

'I don't think so,' said Raven. 'She bled a lot.'

'Then Jossa will have to carry her. Get moving. And see that you follow orders this time!'

The footsteps retreated again.

'You heard the man, Jossa. Take the girl. And don't get clever, all right? You know what will happen to her if you try.'

'Kat?' Simon's face swam into her foggy field of vision. 'Can you hear me?'

Yes. She meant to say yes, but her lips were so dry. She managed a sound only at the second attempt. 'Yes . . .'

'I have to pick you up. I'll be careful, but . . . it will probably hurt all the same.'

She nodded, and tried to brace herself. But when he lifted her injured arm she couldn't help gasping, despite the care he took.

'Why do you have to drag her along?' said Simon between clenched teeth. 'If I promise to go along quietly can't you just leave her be?'

'Sorry, Jossa,' said Raven. 'She was the one who helped

246

you escape, don't you see? Wouldn't be very convincing with her still here, would it? Come on, now. If you don't take her, I will. And I don't have quite the tender feelings for her that you do.'

No, he probably didn't. Not after that kick . . .

'It's not so bad, Simon,' she said. 'It's mostly that I'm so horribly dizzy.'

'You lost more blood than is good for you,' he said. He loosened her belt and secured her wrist with it so that the injured arm wouldn't dangle. Then he slid one arm under her knees and the other beneath her shoulders, and heaved to his feet. It made the world waver and reel even more and the arm began to throb heavily. But with her good arm around Simon's neck it felt a little less as if she was constantly falling.

They did not go up the stairs and into the yard, the way she had expected. Instead, Simon had to carry her through some cellar passage, deeper even than the Hole. Here there were no windows, not even a peephole now and then, but only the light of the lanterns the owl brothers had brought along flickering across slate grey stone walls glistening with damp. There was a smell of rotting turnips that went straight to her queasy stomach, then another flight of stairs, this time going up. Then suddenly there was daylight again, fierce and blinding after the dimness of the cellar.

'Here,' said the one with the hissy voice, and strange hands seized her, much less gentle than Simon's had been. She hit her head against some hard edge, and had to close her eyes for a moment.

'Inside,' ordered Raven. Not her, she was already inside – it was Simon he meant. 'Get down on the floor – and stay there!'

Simon lay down meekly next to her, in the space between two carriage seats. It was probably the finest vehicle she had even been inside, Kat thought, with blue velvet cushions and gold trimmings against polished black wood. But she didn't get to see much of it before Raven threw a blanket over her head and seated himself on the bench, planting both feet solidly on her legs. There was a creaking and a rocking as yet another man got on. Then the door was slammed shut, the driver clicked his tongue, and a lot of hoofbeats – more than two horses, it sounded like – racketed against the cobbles. With a jerk, the carriage began to move.

THE DOVECOTE

Suddenly it was evening. She didn't know how that had happened. She was no longer lying on the floor of the carriage, jarred by every motion, but in a much softer nest, surrounded by a smell she would know any place and any time: the scent of newly mown hay. A barn, she thought – a barn or a stable. She opened her eyes and looked up into a dim space full of fluttering, cooing shadows. Not a stable then, or rather, a very peculiar kind of stable; this was a dovecote. Part of the domed ceiling had collapsed, and through the jagged hole the sunset made pink and orange bars on top of the wall.

Sunset. Time to feed Midnight and settle her for the night.

The thought abruptly cleared Kat's mind. She was here, not at the Castle. Someone had planted a knife in her upper arm and the chances of making it home to feed Midnight her evening oats were slim indeed. Actually . . . actually, she didn't think much of her chances of seeing Midnight again. Ever.

That was when fear finally took hold of her. There hadn't been time before, or waking moments enough. She breathed in rather suddenly, a snuffling sort of sob.

There was a rustling in the hay near her.

'Kat? Are you awake?'

Simon. Relief rushed through her. She was simply so happy to see him, so happy to know that he was still alive, that they were still together.

'Yes,' she whispered, almost soundlessly because her throat and her mouth felt glued together. 'Is there anything to drink?'

'Water, a whole bucketful.' He put his arm around her and helped her to sit. Down here at the bottom of the cote it was already dark, and she could barely see his face. She fumbled with her left hand for the mug he passed her.

'Drink as much as you can. You need it, after bleeding so much. Can you hold it yourself?'

She nodded. The water was lukewarm and tasted metallically of bucket, yet she couldn't get enough of it.

'Feeling better?'

'Yes.' She wiped her mouth with the back of her left hand. 'Not nearly as dizzy as I was before.'

Simon covered the bucket with his leather waistcoat.

'Otherwise we'd get pigeon droppings in it,' he said. 'Let me have a look at that arm while there is still a little light to see by.'

She discovered that someone – Simon, probably – had bandaged her arm. Thinking back, she did recall it in a vague sort of way. It had hurt, and he had shushed her . . . how long ago? Daylight, at any rate.

Simon pushed back her sleeve all the way to the shoulder and unwound the top layers of bandage.

'It seems to have stopped bleeding,' he said. 'I had better loosen this a little, then.'

She nodded. The first layers weren't bad, but when he got to the bits that were stuck together with caked, dried blood, it hurt like hell, even though he used part of their drinking water to soak it loose. She clenched her teeth and didn't cry out, but a couple of tears slid down the side of her nose all the same. She hoped it was too dark for him to notice.

'I have to try and clean it,' said Simon when the bandage was finally off. 'I know it hurts, but . . . but it will be so much worse if it gets infected.'

She nodded again, silently. If she had tried to speak, he would have heard the tears. He filled another mug from the bucket and used the old bandage as a washing cloth. It took a very long time, she thought.

'I think we'll use a bit of your shirt this time,' he said. 'It's a good deal cleaner than mine.'

She pulled her shirt tails out of her pants with her good hand.

'Hack away. You can use this.' She handed him the tiny penknife Merian had once given her for her birthday.

'Good! They didn't find that.'

It was only now she realized that the pass and the oath certificate from DomFelix Strigius had gone, together with the somewhat larger knife that became part of the uniform once one had passed the Seven Bonds.

'It's so tiny, they must have missed it.' And it had been

in its usual place in one of the hidden compartments in Cornelius's old soldier's belt.

'Sharp enough though,' said Simon thoughtfully, sawing away at the bottom part of her white uniform shirt. You could practically hear the gears clicking over in his mind, weighing up the possibilities.

The last touches of sunlight vanished from the dove-cote while Simon was still securing the new bandage. The pigeons above them grew quieter. One by one, they tucked their heads under their wings and went to sleep. She shivered.

'Are you cold?'

'A little.' Quite a lot, actually. She felt chilled through and through, from the bones out. Perhaps that too had something to do with the wound. Perhaps warmth had run out of her with the blood she had lost. It had been just past midday and warm when she had gone to see Simon in the Hole for the second time, and her grey woollen uni-form cloak was still hanging on its peg by the door in her room. Pity. She could have used it now.

'They might have left us a blanket,' Simon said, 'but I suppose we are lucky to have the hay. Here, lean against me – it might warm you at least a little.'

Very carefully he put his arm around her, and she was suddenly reminded of Daniel and the evenings they had spent sitting together almost like this, on the log by the brook outside Summertown. Where was he? Had Alce-dina's men found the Sardis or were they still safe? And was he still angry with her?

'Simon?'

'Mmmmh?'

'Did they say anything about . . . about what is going to happen?' *You'll dangle yet*, the hissy voice had said to Simon – but perhaps he wasn't the one who gave the orders.

'I'm not sure they know themselves,' said Simon evasively. 'Things didn't go according to plan exactly.'

No. The plan had been for Simon to be found dead in his cell, a rope around his neck. A convenient suicide.

'Simon, couldn't you just tell me what it's all about? I'm in it now. You can't keep me safe any more by *not* telling me.'

'They might still let you go, Kat, if you are not a danger to them.'

'They'd never believe you if you said you hadn't told me anything. And . . . it's worse not knowing. Not knowing what the hell is going on, or why we are here. Why did you go to the Bredani? And could you answer those three questions the DomFelix asked you – if you wanted to?'

He thought about it for a good long while, but in the end he sighed.

'I suppose it doesn't make much difference now. But I thought . . . I thought it might interest the Bredani to know that Kernland troops have moved into the Vales – with no move made to stop them.'

At first she didn't understand. Soldiers from Kernland in the South was nothing out of the ordinary in the Vales – as a matter of fact, her own stepfather Cornelius was one of them.

'You mean . . . mercenaries? Caravan guards?'

'No. I mean four regiments of the Regent's own forces.'

'Under Kernland command?'

'It looks that way.'

'But . . . what did the Bredani say to that?'

'Nothing. She already knew. It was part of the terms of the sale.'

'*The sale?*'

'Oh, they don't call it that. They call it "a treaty to secure the defence of the ore transports and end the reign of bandit groups in the area". But to the people of the Vale, what it really means is that they will wake up one morning next spring to discover that they have suddenly become a Kernland province.'

Kat sat frozen for several minutes while her mind split into two different kinds of thoughts. One lot had to do with the inn and Tess and Mattie and Tad and Cornelius. Were there Kernland soldiers stationed in the Vale? Perhaps even at the inn? And was Cornelius pleased, or had he become so much the Breda man that it made him angry? The other kind of thoughts were strangely cool and logical, as if she was in the midst of a debate in one of Master Valentin's classes. Why did Bredani Cora Alcedina Duodecima enter into this treaty? Was it legal? What were the long-term consequences? She could almost hear Master Valentin's dry voice outline the issues for a history paper, but these were not distant events in Breda's past – this was here and now, and she was sitting here not quite bleeding any more as a result.

'How on earth can the Bredani do this? Is it even legal?'

'Best not to ask such questions out loud,' said Simon bitterly, 'or you'll end up in the Hole. But it just *might* have something to do with a certain chest of gold – ten thousand marks, to be precise. And with the cost of keeping an armed force in the Vales large enough to do something effective about gangs such as Ermine's.'

'Ten thousand marks. In gold . . .' it was an unimaginable sum.

'Yes. From the Regent to the Bredani.'

'Yes, but . . . but she can't *sell* the Vales . . .' In Kat's mind resounded the words that every maestra swore each and every Memory Day, fifty-two times a year: never to abuse the land, never to make herself master of it and trade with it as if it were a dead possession anyone might own. Of all the crimes she had had to learn about in Law class, rape of that land was the most severe. And now Simon was telling her that the Bredani . . . the maestra of maestras . . . that she would . . . 'But she *can't*. She can't *sell* a whole region!'

'Of course she can't. Officially the ten thousand marks are a gift from the Regent and have nothing whatsoever to do with the Three Vales Treaty. And *officially* the Vales are still part of Breda. The Regent is merely "helping" his neighbour defend and control her unruly Vale peasants. Very convenient for everyone concerned, except perhaps for the Vale peasants.'

'But Simon – how do you know all this?'

She could just make out a crooked smile in the near-darkness. 'Some of it emerged during my unfortunate meeting with the Bredani. But the bit about the money . . .

well, believe it or not, most of that comes from your mother. And I couldn't very well reveal *that* to the lords and ladies of Breda City. Some Kernland captain had become bewitched by her charms – and that does tend to happen, doesn't it?'

Kat nodded. Oh yes. Men in love with her mother was nothing new.

'Well, this captain confided to her that he was a very important man. He was guarding a transport of gold – ten thousand marks, no less – headed for the Bredani herself.'

'So that's where you were those four missing days.'

'Yes. Remember what your mother said back in the spring, about there being too many Kernland men in the Vales? Well, it didn't take long to discover that most of them were soldiers. So Tess was right, as usual. She has always had a keen sense of what goes on around her.'

'So you didn't—'

'No. I did not break any seals, or open any dispatches. And I severely doubt that information of that kind was in my very common mailbag. That was all a set-up. But that's another matter.'

'Why did the DomFelix want you to answer those weird questions? About Madalena Bartelin's engagement, and all that? Nothing about a pot of gold there.'

Simon sighed. 'I think she is trying to work out if anyone in Breda stands to gain from this deal. The Bartelin family is one of the most important families in Kernland, like one of the Seven here. And whoever gets to marry her will be the master of a very major estate.'

Kat shook her head slowly. 'A man? A master of lands? That doesn't seem quite . . . right.'

Simon smiled crookedly. 'It's the way they do things there. They think Bredans are the ones that are crazy, leaving it all to the women.'

'And another thing. Why would the Kernlanders—'

But Simon was no longer listening. In one abrupt movement he was free of her and on his feet, listening tensely.

She heard it too now. Hoofbeats. Galloping hoofbeats approaching in the dark, then breaking pace to trot a few paces and then halt completely. There was the scraping of a bolt being drawn, and then the low square door of the dovecote opened.

'Out!' barked Raven. 'No, not you, Jossa – just the girl.'

GLOWING COALS

Simon wouldn't let them take her.

'Leave her be!' he yelled, but the owl brothers didn't care – one of them grabbed her by her injured arm so that she grew dizzy and couldn't hold back a cry. There was a thud, and she caught a glimpse of Simon in motion. For a moment he just seemed to hang there in midair, then Raven grabbed her and she didn't see the rest of the move. Simon was good, she knew that, and he knew a lot of clansman tricks that were not taught at the Castle, but there were too many, five of them this time, and in the end it was Simon who lay on the floor of the dovecote, moaning and unable to rise.

'All that for a silly girl,' said Raven contemptuously. 'You're a fool, Jossa.'

Simon didn't answer, and then the dovecote door was slammed to, and she could no longer hear or see him. Immediately after that she could see nothing at all, as some sort of a sack was pulled over her head and lashed around her neck, as if her head was a head of cabbage they wanted to take to market. She was handed up to a rider who turned out to be Raven to sit perched on the saddle-bow in front of him.

'Sit still or you'll get hurt,' he said into the back of her neck, and despite her fear of what might lie ahead at the end of her ride she had no wish to fall either, not like this, blind and bound and with a shoulder already throbbing badly enough to make her sick to her stomach.

They didn't go very far, perhaps a mile or so. Then Raven slowed to a trot, and the hoofbeats echoed among stone walls for a while before he halted completely. New hands seized her and pulled her from the horse, and when she stumbled and couldn't keep her feet, she was simply slung over someone's shoulder like a bedroll. Let go of me! she wanted to shout, but she could barely breathe, and dizziness was threatening to overwhelm her. Then he did let go of her, and she slumped on to a wooden floor with an audible thump.

'Here she is,' said Raven. 'The Vale girl.'

At first no one answered. The floorboards moved under the weight of a heavy body, and she sensed someone standing right next to her, but the thump had stolen away her last remnant of breath and she lay without moving, waiting for the world to settle and for things to become just slightly more bearable.

'Take off the hood,' said a voice she could not remember having heard before. But the tone, the rise and fall of the accent . . . she knew that very well from her stepfather. The man was a Kernlander. One of the Regent's men, perhaps?

Hands fumbled at the rope holding the sack together, then the rough cloth rasped against her cheek and her head came free. She could see only slightly better. The room was so dark that she could only just make out two solid legs a few hands' breadths away from her face.

'Put her on the chair. No, gently, please – I hear she is injured.'

A fat lot you care, she thought bitterly, while once more she had to let herself be lifted and manoeuvred like she was luggage. Don't stand there sounding all sympathetic when you're not!

But actually the voice was strangely gentle, and when someone raised the wick of a lamp just a little, the face she looked at was a round, moon-like one, in no way fierce or brutal. Moonfather, she thought – the man who sits up there in the moon deciding when the oceans must rise and when they must fall . . . so mild to look at, but with a power no mere human can understand. Perhaps this was true also of this odd being. Certainly it was hard to look away once he had caught your eye.

'Wait outside,' he told Raven and the owl brothers, and Kat thought they moved very quickly to comply, almost as if they were uneasy in his company. He seated himself on a stool in front of her.

'Katriona,' he said, 'I want to ask you a few questions.'

Questions? she thought. What questions? What might a moonfather such as this want to ask that she could answer?

'What's your mother's name?'

She was prepared for much, but not for this. Why did he want to know what her mother was called?

'Why do you want to know?' She was rude on purpose, not giving him any 'sir' or 'master', though clearly he was no commoner and certainly of higher rank than she.

'Please, just answer me,' he said. 'The question isn't hard.'

She tried to take his measure, but found it difficult to tell what he might do. Such a big, soft face, and yet she didn't trust his mildness. Perhaps it was not a good idea to anger him so soon. There would be questions later, no doubt, that she would have to try not to answer. Questions about Kernland troops and ten thousand marks of gold, for instance.

'Tess. Or Teresa di Ranunculi, if you want the formal version.' Tess. Tall and dark and beautiful, sharp as a whiplash and warm and soft like velvet at the same time. All of a sudden she missed her mother terribly, so much that she had to blink away a couple of tears.

'And your eldest brother. What is his name?'

'Eskill . . .' But she hadn't seen him for a long time – he had left home like boys do, just joined a caravan one day, and that was him gone . . . They saw him at the inn every now and then travelling through, and sometimes there were letters which he had got someone to write for him. He had never quite got the hang of letters himself. And Kat, who was only home perhaps once a year, had not seen him since she was eleven.

'And the next eldest?'

'Dan . . .'

And so it went. He asked about all her siblings, and when she answered, it was as if he drew them into her head so that she saw them all so clearly: Mattie with her blonde braids and her serious expression, concentrating fiercely on whatever she was doing at the time, whether it was patching a sweater for one of the little ones or doing the dishes with Tad . . . Mattie, who would be innkeeper in Kat's stead, now that Kat had left and gone 'travelling' like no proper woman should . . . Nicolas, cheeky freckle-face, and at the same time irresistible when he came to you with a shy smile, presenting some thing he had found, a snail's shell or a bit of quartz that glittered like a diamond . . . Tim, Little-Cor, Tessa, Rose . . . she felt such a longing for all of them, and at the same time she started to become afraid. Were they safe? It didn't feel that way. She began to get a sense that something threatened them, something bigger and more dangerous than the ordinary hazards that Cornelius and Erold Blacksmith might be able to protect them against. And as if that was not enough, Moonface started to ask about her friends at the Academy.

'I'm sure you have found lots of good friends there too, haven't you?'

Mild and soft and with no hint of threat in his voice, and yet . . . and yet she dared only nod, not say the names. She resisted him so that he had to say them out loud himself, and he knew them all – knew that Lu and Merian and Valente meant something completely different to her than Meiles and DiCapra . . . Even Birch he knew about, though

263

Birch was 'just' a kitchen boy and did not normally have anything to do with the higher-ups.

How could he know so much about her? She had never seen him at the Castle – she would have remembered that face. And the way he talked . . . He had not lived in Breda long, she thought – he sounded as if he had just arrived from the South. It was eerie and very frightening.

And yet he did not make any threats. There were no veiled hints about 'not wanting them to get hurt', the way she imagined it would have gone if Raven had been in charge here. But still . . . still . . . she was sweating. Her arm hurt fiercely. And she was sitting here, feeling horribly heartsick and terrified, without him having laid a finger on her or hurt her in any way. Normally when she was frightened anger came hot on terror's heels, and she used that anger to ignore the fear. But he did not invite anger, this terrible mild, moonfaced man.

'Wh-why do you ask?' she finally stuttered. 'What do you want with them?'

'What do you mean?' He looked mildly surprised. 'I am just trying to get to know you, that's all. I have no reason to hurt them.'

She didn't believe him. There was a tiny inaudible 'yet' attached to that sentence. No reason to hurt them – yet.

'You also you know a family of travellers, don't you?'

While Kat was still considering whether that little *yet* was only in her own ears, and not in the room at all, the next question sneaked up on her, softly as if on cat's paws.

She felt her head begin to nod before she caught herself, and barely managed to bite back a 'yes'.

He watched her mildly.

'The Sardis. You know them too, don't you?'

Was that what this was all about? Not about ten thousand marks and treacherous treaties at all, but still Daniel and his family and their illegal images?

'I don't know what Master is talking about . . .' she muttered, suddenly very polite without meaning to be.

And at that moment, the instant the lie crossed her lips, it was as if someone had placed a lump of glowing coal inside her hand. She screamed and looked down, totally convinced that she would see her skin crackle and blister, but her palm was undamaged, her fingers painfully hooked like a bird's claw but not burned at all.

Suddenly she recalled that first day at the Academy when Master Ahlert had put an iron sphere in her hand and asked her questions she had to answer before they would let her in. Simon had later told her that if she had been untruthful then, the iron would have become hot in her hand. She sat as if turned to stone, staring at her hand, empty and dirty and unharmed, while at the same time it still felt as if an ember was lying in her palm, burning her skin. Now she knew why the owl brothers had been in such a hurry to leave. Magus. Moonface was a magus, and so strong – she swallowed at the thought – so strong that he didn't even need an iron sphere.

He was still looking at her with his mild, calm face. How could he – how could anyone – remain so unaffected seconds after hurting another human being so badly?

'Well? Do you not know a travelling family by the name of Sardi?'

She looked down at her hand. It still stung, and the thought of holding the glowing coal once more – even though it wasn't really there – was unbearable. In any case, he already knew. She had betrayed herself to him already with her reaction. So she nodded.

'Please, Katriona . . . will you not say it aloud, so that I may know your thoughts?'

She looked at him, finally angry after all. She hated him and his stupid moonface; she hated the soft Southern voice that lied so badly about the man inside. She simply couldn't understand that it didn't show. That there was not in that fair gaze and that round face one single trace of glee or mockery or evil.

'Say it out loud, Katriona,' he said, as if he were coaxing a shy child to greet a visitor.

'They had a stall in Summertown,' she said. 'It burnt down.'

'And then? What happened to them after that?'

'I don't know,' she said, thinking that was nearly true.

Not nearly enough, it seemed. This time she didn't scream, being better prepared, but she couldn't suppress a shudder or prevent tears from coming to her eyes.

When the pain waned enough for her to open her eyes, she looked at her hand again. This time it was not undamaged. In the middle of her palm, between the thumb and the little finger she had broken, there was a large wet blister the size of a pigeon's egg. She looked at it in disbelief, hardly knowing what was worse – feeling such pain without any visible signs of harm, or getting a burn from something that wasn't even there. From *nothing*. From magic.

'What happened after the fire, Katriona?'

Her thoughts leaped this way and that, like a herd of confused goats. Wasn't there something she could tell him? Something that didn't endanger the Sardis?

'They weren't in Summertown any more.'

Truth. And no burning coal. But also not enough for him.

'No. But where did they go, Katriona?'

She wished he would stop using her name all the time. It sounded as if they were friends or family or something. And the mere thought of belonging to him in any sort of way gave her a slimy slug-like feeling all over.

I don't know, she wanted to say. But she didn't dare.

'After the fire . . . after the fire, Daniel said that he never wanted to see me again.'

'And you haven't seen him since?' He still looked like a mild and round moonfather, but for the first time there was a searching, prying power in the soft voice. Just as well that she could answer that question with complete honesty.

'No. I haven't seen him since.'

Let that be enough, she begged silently. Let him stop now and not ask anything more.

He did actually remain silent for a while, cocking his head as if he was still listening to what she had said.

'Or heard from him? Katriona, have you heard from him or about him?'

'He wouldn't talk to me.' Again, a truth. 'None of the Summertowners would. And they wouldn't tell me where he was.'

Again he was silent for a while. Then he rose – surprisingly graceful, considering his size – and crouched down right in front of her, his face inches from hers.

'I think you are not being entirely honest, Katriona,' he said sadly, as if she was his much-loved daughter caught in a lie. 'I think you are trying to hide something from me.' He put his hand on top of her blistered one, and a shudder went through her from head to foot, and all the way to her fingertips. 'Tell me – where are the Sardis now?'

He watched her face very, very intently. And he would feel it if she so much as tried to clench her hand. But I don't know where they are now, she told herself firmly. They could be anywhere. Long gone.

'I don't know where they are now,' she told him, and met his gaze without hesitation. And even though Bonverte sat at the back of her mind and made her palm smart sharply, only the tiniest of tremors shook her hand.

He did not let go of her with his gaze, nor did his hand leave hers. His grasp was light, and yet it felt as if she had her hand trapped in a door. Would he never stop? Perhaps he could feel what she was holding back. There had been that near-truth that had not been true enough. *What happened to them after that?*

'Katriona. Is there anything about the Sardis that you haven't told me?'

Holy Lady. What a question. Impossible to dodge. She sweated, and stayed silent.

And he calmly repeated the question.

'Do you know anything about the Sardis that you haven't told me?'

And of course she did. The photographs. Bonverte. That the crazed girl had been a fraud . . . There were a thousand things she hadn't told him.

'I can't tell it all,' she said in despair. 'How can I tell you every little thing? Uncle Isak cooks a great gullyas. They have a horse called Roscha. How can I tell you *everything*?'

Slowly he straightened, but his hand stayed on top of hers.

'Stay here,' he said. 'You cannot rise from this chair until I tell you that you can.'

And finally he let go of her aching hand and stepped away from her. She now realized that what she had thought of as the end wall of the room was in reality a screen made of lacquered wood and a faded silky material that might once have been royal blue. Moonface disappeared behind the screen. There was a rasping sound of a light being struck, and then a soft glow turned the screen partially transparent. Someone had lit a lamp back there, and she could see indistinct shadows flicker across the faded silken screen. Someone was sitting there, she thought – someone had been sitting there the entire time. Listening.

They did not talk. Obviously they didn't want her to hear what they might say. But there was the scratching sound of a pen on paper, so probably questions were being asked or instructions given. Who was it? Who was lurking back there, afraid to let her hear even the sound of a voice?

You cannot rise, he had said. Not may not, or must not. But she could try, couldn't she? Or perhaps it wasn't worth the bother. Why should she? She was comfortable enough . . . and then her thoughts came to a screeching halt. It felt like the time one of the guests at the inn had become so drunk that he had tried to touch her between her thighs. Sweet Lady, but Cornelius had been livid! That was one man who would never set foot at the inn again. She dearly wished that Cornelius would come and grab Moonface and throw him out 'head over arse', as he himself used to call it. Moonface might only have touched her once on the outside, and only on her hand, but he had done something much worse. He had touched her inside. Where her will lived.

How dare he! She wanted him out of her head, now! No way was she going to let him tell her what she could and could not do. No way was she going to allow him to muck about in her head as it suited him. On your feet. Come on, Kat. Now!

It felt strange to fight herself in this way. A bit like forcing oneself to walk in a straight line and speak clearly when one was very, very tired or had had too much beer, like at the Midsummer party last year. But when one was used to controlling a hellhorse by willpower alone – and a hellhorse like Midnight to boot – then no way was a filthy magus going to tell her 'Sit!' like she was his damn dog. No way in hell. No.

She got up. It sounded so easy, but it wasn't. Her legs felt numb, as if they weren't really a part of her body, and it was hard to keep her balance. But she got up and walked towards the screen. Every single step was difficult but it felt good, it felt wonderful. You don't own me, she thought triumphantly. I am not your dog.

Not until she reached the screen did she hesitate. Someone had gone to a great deal of trouble to stay unseen and unheard. Some secrets were dangerous to know, and this might be one of them. But . . . the pen was scratching across the paper, and the two shadows were bent over their silent conference. She might be able to sneak a look without them realizing.

Cautiously, she dropped to one knee. Master Haryn had taught her never to stick out her head at the enemy's eye level if she didn't want to be seen. Slowly she leaned forward and peeked around the edge of the screen, until she could see . . .

A back. A back covered by a blue velvet cloak with gold kingfishers embroidered round the edge. She clutched at the edge of the screen with one hand. It was not very solidly built, it seemed, because her movement caused it to rock ominously. And when she tried to steady it with her one good hand, the whole thing came crashing down on top of her.

The man in the blue cloak spun like a cat.

'What the hell . . .'

But he did not finish his sentence, just stood there

staring down at her with cold rage in the kingfisher blue gaze that she knew much too well.

'You were told to stay seated,' said Alvar Alcedina in an acid tone. 'For once in your life, could you not have obeyed an order?'

THE BRAVEST PIGEON

Once, when Kat had been absolutely livid with her stepfather, she had taken his dearest possession – a blue-and-white china mug that his old regimental chief had once given him – and smashed it against the flagstones of the floor back at the inn. While she had stood there looking down at the shards, hundreds of tiny porcelain splinters that no one would be able to glue back together, a thought had gone through her head: So. Now there is no turning back.

That was the way she felt now. She had seen Alcedina and the world could not be put back together again, any more than the splintered goblet. If Alcedina, a man who ranged nearly as high as the Bredani in her world and only just below Our Lady herself, if *he* was . . .

He didn't look like a villain. The dark hair was combed with smooth precision, his face looked calm and clean-shaven, his uniform was utterly immaculate. He looked like the perfect bredinari. And his voice was no sharper than it had always been.

'On your feet, Trivallia.'

Life returned to her numbed body. She could think, she could move. She rose, and then thought – might as well try. She took three fast steps to the door and tore it open.

Raven stood in the doorway, filling it entirely.

'Where do you think you're going?' he said.

Nowhere, obviously. She turned to face Alcedina and Moonface.

'Does the DomPrimus wish for the interrogation to be continued?' asked Moonface.

'No,' said Alcedina coldly. 'There is no need for circumspection now. We might as well be direct.' He nodded to Raven. 'Take her back to Jossa. And if she does not tell you where the traveller family is hiding . . .' his blue eyes caught Kat's with such force that it was almost like being stabbed again, '. . . if she still won't talk, hang him.'

Kat nearly choked.

'But I tell you, I don't know!'

There was no hint of pity in his ice-blue gaze. 'If that is true, it is very unfortunate for Jossa,' was all he said.

They had brought torches. The flames licked against the whitewashed walls of the dovecote and blackened them with soot, and the pigeons were roused to flutter uneasily below the dome of the roof.

'Easy now, Jossa – unless you want the girl to get hurt,' said Raven in his meanest voice.

Kat struggled to warn Simon, to tell him to fight for his life, but the hissy-voiced man had put his big paw over her mouth, and a muffled wordless cry was all she could manage.

Simon stood still while they tied his hands behind his back. Not even when they tossed a long rope over one of the roof beams did he resist.

'Take the girl outside,' was all he said to Raven. 'There is no need for her to see this.'

'That's where you are wrong,' said Raven. 'This whole show is for her benefit. Well, Trivallia? Anything you want to tell us? Or do we finally get to hang this dog?'

Only then did Simon look surprised.

'What is it you want her to tell you?' he asked.

No one answered him. Hissy Voice took his hand away so that she was free to talk, but her throat was completely choked up. She could feel the tears streaming hotly down her grimy cheeks. If it had been possible, she would have run away from this. She couldn't betray the Sardis. She couldn't let them hang Simon. Both were impossible. But one or the other would happen – she could see that just by looking at Raven. There was no trace of warmth in his brown eyes now, and she knew he was not bluffing. His hands shaped the noose with practised ease. One of the men holding Simon kicked him to his knees, and they held him there while Raven forced the noose over his head and tightened it round his neck.

'Well?'

If only she could faint. If somehow she wasn't there, surely they wouldn't hang Simon? But now, when faintness would have been welcome, even the dizziness had evaporated and she saw Simon's dark, bent head with crystal clarity, she saw every twist of the rough hempen rope, the hands holding him, the dark beam above. Her throat was aching so badly she wasn't even sure she *could* talk.

'I must say I'm disappointed, Trivallia,' said Raven. 'I didn't think you would let down a friend like this.'

'Wait . . .' she begged. 'For the Lady's sake, how can I tell you when I just don't know?'

Raven ignored her. 'Sorry, Jossa,' he said. 'But that's women for you. Heartless bitches. Cold. Unfeeling. And they tell me this is a damn unpleasant way to die too.'

He put his full weight on the rope and hauled so viciously that Simon's body was jerked into the air several feet off the ground. *Now* he fought, kicking and writhing, but he was as helpless as a fish at the end of the fisherman's line, and it was just like the nightmare, with her watching while they hanged Simon, watching without doing anything, without hands, without heart, but still not quite as dead as she thought she was.

'Stop,' she choked. And when they didn't seem to hear her, she screamed at the top of her lungs: '*Stop!* Stop it! I'll tell you. I'll tell you . . .'

Raven slackened the rope, and Simon collapsed on the dovecote floor, gasping and heaving and retching for air.

'Speak then, sweet maiden,' said Raven coolly, 'if you wish to save your knight errant here. Where are they?'

'I don't know where they are now,' she began, and then hurried on quickly as he made a move to tighten the rope once more, 'but I know that they . . . that they went to Bonverte for a while.'

Raven snorted.

'Did I ask for a bedtime story? And do I look like a piddling wean who'll believe any fairy tale you tell me?' He jerked on the rope again, so that Simon struggled desperately to his feet.

'It's true,' screamed Kat, her voice hoarse with despair. 'Samuel Sardi married Angelica Bonverte's daughter. Sara is her grandchild . . . You can check the House Lists – it is *true . . .*'

She was crying all out now, her breath bubbling in her nose, her voice shrill and hoarse at the same time. And Raven slackened the rope again, almost reluctantly, it seemed.

'Bonverte. Well, I suppose we had better take a look.' He let go of the rope and Simon fell to his knees. A shove pitched him forward into the hay. Raven strode across his fallen body and came right up to Kat. His hand gripped the back of her neck like a vice, and he forced her face right up close to his own, so near that she could feel his breath.

'I hope you don't think you can fool me, my sweet. Or do you reckon I'm just a dumb old caravan guard?'

Kat couldn't even shake her head.

'No,' she whispered. 'I know you're not stupid.'

He nodded. 'Good. Goodnight, then. And don't worry. We'll be back.'

*

They took the torches. Darkness descended. The sound of hoofbeats faded and Kat could hear only the great, heaving sobs she couldn't seem to stop.

'Kat?' It was Simon's voice, though not quite as flat as usual. This was the second time today someone had tried to hang him, and she supposed it took its toll, even on a stiff-necked clansman from Jos. 'Your little knife is hidden in the hay just in front of the door. Could you please cut my hands free?'

Raven and his comrades had not bothered to. They hadn't even taken the trouble to rid him of the noose. She did as he asked, crying all the while. The tears just wouldn't stop. It was as if someone had knocked a hole in a dam – they just kept on pouring out. Simon rubbed his wrists. They were dark with blood because he had struggled so fiercely to free himself.

'Kat. I know it's hard, but you have to pull yourself together,' he said finally.

'Why?' she cried. 'Why should I? What good would it do? First they find Daniel and his family, and then they come back here to finish the job. They'll kill us – you know they will.'

'Stop it. We're not dead yet.'

'As good as! I saw him. There's no way he can let me live now . . . and anyway, he never liked me!'

The last bit came out in a childish wail, and she knew she was being hysterical, but she couldn't see the point right now in facing death bravely, with a smile and a joke on your lips, especially not after having served the Sardis up to them on a silver platter. No joking matter, this. There was really nothing to laugh about. .

'Who? Who never liked you?'

'Alcedina, damn it. Who else?'

Simon grew quite, quite still.

'Alvar Alcedina? You saw him? Are you *sure*?'

'Of course I'm sure! He was hiding behind a screen, but I overturned it.'

'So it is him.' Simon's voice came softly in the dark, as if he was talking more to himself than to her. 'I had hoped . . . I had hoped that the enemy would be some-one . . . smaller.'

'What does it matter?' said Kat. 'There's nothing we can do either way.'

'He is brother to the Bredani herself,' said Simon thoughtfully. 'She has been ill, and her strength is not what it was . . . Of course she has listened to his advice. Of course she has left a lot up to his judgement. Sweet Lady! It has been so easy for him . . . but I'm still not sure exactly what his game is. He's not the one getting ten thousand marks in gold . . .'

'What do I know?' sniffed Kat sourly, thinking he'd do better to worry about his own future, and hers. 'Perhaps he is the one who gets to marry Madalena Bartelin. I'm sure *he* would like to be the master of an estate.'

She was shocked into frozen stillness when Simon seized her by the shoulders in a fierce grip.

'What did you say?'

'Oww! Simon, my arm!'

'Sorry.' He let go hastily. 'But don't you see it? It's

brilliant. He marries her and gets to rule all of the Bartelin estates – and believe me, that's not pennies, it's practically half a province – and in return Regent Jakobus has the Vales served up to him on a platter, with free access to the mines in Orevale, and an easy route of attack if he ever decides to invade the rest of Breda. And all the while the Bredani is convinced that her brother is only thinking of her and the country, with their best interests at heart. If she knew what he was really up to, she might not take his counsel so easily. If only we could prove it. But he wouldn't be so stupid as to leave any witnesses, at least not this side of the border. And anyone trying to accuse the Bredani's own brother of treason had better have *very* solid evidence.'

At long last Kat had stopped sobbing and had begun to think instead.

'Simon . . . Simon, there *is* proof. At least, I think there is.'

'What do you mean?'

'The picture. The photograph. Isak Sardi took a photograph of Alcedina. With a very young girl in a very big dress. And with a ring on her finger. Simon, what if that girl is Madalena Bartelin? That would certainly explain why Alcedina has been looking high and low for the Sardis!'

'A photograph . . .' Simon's voice was hardly more than a whisper, as if he was afraid that the chance would vanish if he spoke of it too loudly.

'It's like a mirror image, sort of. It's not painted, it's real. It's the light that make the picture, and what is in the picture is *true*, not made up by some artist.'

He nodded. 'Yes. I know what a photograph is. It's illegal here, but not in Kernland. But . . . how could Alcedina be so careless?'

'Uncle Isak says that most photographs are made on a metal plate, and that way there is only one. If there was only one, and he had that himself – then Alcedina might not think it so dangerous. And perhaps he needed proof of the engagement, so that she couldn't just run off and marry someone else once the treaty was signed. But when Isak takes a picture he uses a glass plate, and that way he can make as many copies as he likes. Perhaps someone told Alcedina that glass pictures were different from metal ones and could be copied . . . and perhaps that was when he started looking for the Sardis.'

Simon nodded slowly.

'Any educated Kernlander might know. Photographs are far more common there. It could even have been Madalena Bartelin,' he said. 'Maybe she wanted a copy of the picture for herself. Kernland women are brought up to believe they have to fall in love with the man they must marry, even though they rarely get to choose him themselves.'

'Weird.'

'Yes. But Kat – was it true, what you told them about Bonverte?'

'Yes. Simon, I didn't dare lie. They . . . they would have done it. Raven doesn't bluff. He would have killed you.'

Simon touched his throat. There was only a little bit of moonlight coming in through the broken roof, but the marks were still evident, dark and deep and ugly.

'Yes. I believe he would have. But it means that we have very little time now.'

'Why? What can we do, except wait for Raven to come back? I'm in no hurry for *that* to happen.'

'We just have to hope that Angelica Bonverte can keep Alcedina at bay for a little while. He can't after all just move in and arrest her, the way he could with some nameless traveller family. Meanwhile, we must get hold of that photograph before he does!'

Simon picked up the rope that had been used to hang him. He looked at her in a strange measuring fashion.

'Simon, they locked us in. Or didn't you notice?'

'I've been envying those pigeons all day,' he said. 'Haven't you? But I'm too big, I think.'

Too big?

'For what?' she asked, confused and wary at the same time.

He gazed upward at the hole in the roof. There was a jagged bit of night sky visible and a solitary star.

'Do you think you might squeeze through that hole?' he asked.

'Possibly. But I don't have wings. How do you propose to get me up there?'

'Well, look what our hosts have been considerate enough to leave us. A fine, long rope . . .'

Moments later, she was dangling midway between the floor and the ceiling while Simon stood below, hoisting her up as if she were a flag and he a sailor.

'Mind your head when you get to the beam,' he said.

And then she was up there, in the fluttering world of the pigeons. They beat their wings and scolded sleepily at her intrusion as she perched cautiously on the cross-beam. She slid along inch by inch until she was directly below the hole.

'It's not very big . . .' she said dubiously.

'Give it a go,' said Simon encouragingly. 'Tie the rope to the cross-beam as a safety line, then go through the hole feet first.'

All well and good, but that meant she had to stand on the cross-beam, and she was feeling dizzy again. She clutched at the broken wall and felt a nail break. She eased one leg through the opening, and then the other. She pushed herself backwards, so that more and more of her went through the jagged opening. Her bottom was a tight squeeze though.

'Simon – what if I get stuck?'

'You won't,' he said with admirable conviction.

If I can do this, she thought – if I can only do this, I'll never again complain about being small! She wriggled, and her hips slid out on to the roof dome. And then gravity suddenly took hold and did the rest of the job. She slithered, banged her sore shoulder against something, banged her head . . . and then she was outside and still sliding, then falling abruptly into space. Her stomach turned, and she thought for a moment that she would crash all the way to the ground and surely die . . . Then the rope caught and broke her fall halfway down the wall. She could see the dark ground no more than four or five feet below. She fumbled Merian's small knife from her belt and cut herself loose. Though the last fall was not a long one, it jarred her shoulder so badly that she nearly fainted again. But she was down. She was free. They had done it.

She sat for a moment in the wet, cool grass until the throbbing of her arm and head had receded a bit. Then she got up and unbarred the door to let Simon out.

'You are the bravest pigeon I know,' he said, and put his arms around her in a warm but careful hug.

LIKE AN EGG

Splat! Another drop from the huge green ferns shattered against the back of her neck, just above the collar. It was almost worse than being soaked all at once – like a big animal drooling on her. But she and Simon had to be grateful for the cover of the green fronds they were huddled under. Only a few steps away, so close that Kat felt as if she might reach out and touch his ankle, stood a castle guard.

I think I know what it is like to be a hunted animal, thought Kat. No rest. No sleep. No help anywhere. And there was no doubt that she and Simon were the prey the guard was hunting. He and his partner had just had a loud discussion about what to do with the reward if they caught 'the bastard who stabbed Ola'.

'I hope we catch him,' he said. 'He'll get what's coming to him then!'

'Just finish up!' rumbled his partner. 'What are you trying to do, piss a lake? If we don't get a move on, we have *no* chance of that reward.'

Oh yes, thought Kat. Finish up and ride away!

The guard shook himself, laced his trousers, and remounted his horse. Then he and his partner moved on, and Kat and Simon could climb out of the ferns, cross the road silently, and dodge into the shrubbery on the other side.

They could not travel on the road – it was too dangerous. Instead they had sneaked through woodlands and orchards, and fields of maize on stalks taller than Kat. She knew they had to go as far as they could while it was dark, but her arm throbbed with every step and her legs felt wobbly and unstable, as if they were not properly attached to her body.

'Simon?' she whispered finally. Why she was whispering she didn't quite know – there was no one around to hear her.

He stopped, and turned to look at her.

'I don't think . . . I'm sorry, but I really don't think I can walk much further.' She ducked her head and stared at the ground, feeling a peculiar kind of shame – as if she *ought* to be able to walk or run for days for something as important as this.

'You've done very well to walk this far,' he said. 'Let me feel your forehead . . .'

But she pushed his hand away.

'Don't be nice to me,' she said through clenched teeth, 'or I'll start bawling again.' Once she started to cry she knew her last few remnants of strength would flow out of her along with the tears.

He just nodded. That was the wonderful thing about Simon – he *understood* things like that.

'Wait here,' he said. 'I'll try to find a place where we can rest safely for a while.'

Gratefully, she slid down on to her haunches and rested her back against the low stone wall that surrounded the maize field.

She didn't dare close her eyes – doing so brought waves of dizziness, and if she passed out here, or fell asleep, she wasn't sure Simon would be able to rouse her again. Instead, she rested the back of her head against the cool, damp stones of the wall and looked straight up into the sky, dark blue like Alcedina's velvet cloak, but somewhat more reassuring to look at. To the east there was a glimmer of false dawn – not yet a real sunrise, but it was not far off. The stars were already beginning to fade.

'Come on, Kat. It's not far.'

She started. She hadn't heard Simon approach. Perhaps she had after all managed to sleep for a bit, eyes wide open and staring at the stars.

He had to help her to her feet.

'You're shivering. Are you cold?'

'No,' she said. 'It'll be better once I get going.' And it wasn't cold, not really, although she felt chilled through.

Simon had found a hawthorn bush, part of a hedge that separated the maize field from a less rich pasture dotted with grazing sheep. At first she just stared at it dumbly. She had imagined a goat shed or a hen house, but of course the castle guards and Alcedina's men would search such obvious hiding places right away. The thorn bush was better. Simon held the prickly branches to one side so that she could crawl under them. There was a space in there, close to the root, where one could lie concealed as if in a green cave. Simon had collected a pile of ferns for them to lie on, and she collapsed gratefully on to the makeshift bed.

'Drink something before you sleep,' he said, 'or you'll wake up with a headache.' He had dragged the bucket along from the dovecote because it was the only container they had. She drank greedily of the cool, clean spring water he had found to fill it with. Then she curled up again, closed her eyes, and sank into a deep black hole of sleep.

Someone had hold of her arm.

'Kat . . . Kat, you have to wake now.'

It was Simon's voice, but it sounded strange – as if he were standing at the bottom of a well. Why was he so far away?

'Kat. Come on!'

This time he was closer. She prised her eyes open. Sunlight dappled his face; it was clearly daytime, and not even the dense cupola of hawthorn branches could keep out the sun. They were in a tearing hurry, she and Simon. At first she couldn't remember why, but the sense of urgency was sharp within her. Then all the reasons came flooding back, and she recalled only too clearly. She had betrayed the hiding place of the Sardis, and now she had to try and get to them and save them and the picture before Alcedina hunted them down.

'Do we have to leave now?' she said, in a voice that came out thick as porridge.

'It's not that,' said Simon. 'Listen . . .'

For what? Insects were humming. Somewhere above them a lark was singing. A dog barked – a series of short yaps, as if it had caught the scent of something.

As if it had . . .

'The dog? Is it our scent?'

'Dogs, plural. Hounds, actually. And yes, I'm afraid they have our scent.'

At that moment, the barking dissolved into a chorus of howls that sounded as if an entire pack of bloodhounds was right on their heels.

'They're coming,' she hissed. 'Simon, what do we do?'

The hawthorn bush might shield them from human searchers, but not from the hounds. Kat saw them in her mind's eye – a flash of snarling, snapping black shadows with cruel jaws and drooling fangs. Black? Why did she think they were black? But they were, at least in her head.

'How are you feeling?' Simon touched her cheek testingly, like Tess did when she wanted to check you for fever.

'What has that got to do with anything? Do you think the bloody dogs care?' Her voice shook.

'We're not that far from Bonverte. You just have to

continue north for an hour or so. And stay away from the roads.'

'"You?" What's all that "you" business? What are you planning to do?'

He smiled faintly. 'Play the hare. Just stay here until you can no longer hear the dogs.' He began to edge his way out from under the bush.

'Simon. No!'

'It's the only thing that might work. Get that picture, Kat. Nothing else really matters.'

The branches fell, and he was gone. She could hear his rapid footsteps and the sound of the corn stalks slapping wetly against a running body.

'That's not fair!' she whispered. She knew what he meant by playing hare. He would give the hounds something to chase and try to lead them away from her. 'Simon, they'll catch you!' She saw those black shadow hounds again, and they grew more and more monstrous to look at, with ember eyes and fiery jaws and fangs the length of a hand. Fangs that could tear and slash at a soft defence-less body like knives. And all the while she was supposed to lie here, cowering against the ground like a leveret?

But he had left her no choice. If she left their hiding place now, there would merely be two hares instead of one. And then there would be no one left to find the Sardis and get hold of the picture that might save Simon from being hanged and the Vales from becoming a Kernland province.

There was a new sound from the hounds – an ominous howl. She knew they had seen Simon now. Then there was some not-so-distant shouting, and the crack of a long dog-whip. She closed her eyes and prayed. *Sweet Lady, let him get away. Don't let them catch him* . . . But Simon was tired, he was on foot, and his hunters probably had horses – at least some of them. And all she could do was lie there and listen – she couldn't even see what was happening. Both the shouting and the baying grew more remote, and finally she couldn't hear either any more. And she still didn't know whether they had caught him, or he had miraculously managed to escape them.

It was quite hot now, the midday heat. From one of the thorny branches, a pale green aphid dropped on to her arm. She brushed it away. The world stayed silent, apart from the insects and the birds and the soft rustle of the maize. *Stay here until you no longer hear the dogs*, he had said. And *Get that picture*.

Nothing else to do now. She hoped she might at least manage that much.

Cautiously, she pushed her way out from under the hawthorn. She peered at the sun and decided that north had to be *that* way . . . along the maize field and then up through the hilly pastures. What if she couldn't find Bonverte? It was one thing to get there by following the road, but she had to go cross-country, zigging and zagging among the fields. It was a good thing those apple orchards were as huge as they were – hard to miss if she was anywhere near them. And perhaps she would be able to travel parallel to the road some of the way.

She left the bucket under the hawthorn. She had enough to do just dragging herself along, she thought. But

291

it wasn't long before her throat began to feel parched, despite the fact that she had drunk her fill before leaving the hideout. The sun hammered at her skull, and she took off her leather waistcoat and used it as a sort of scarf until that became too hot to bear too. Her feet were boiling in her boots, and she finally gave up and kicked them off. Barefoot, she continued her journey, with the waistcoat and the boots in a bundle under her good arm. It was strange to feel grass and dirt and rocks under the soles of her feet again. Back home, she and the others had run around barefoot through most of the summer, but when she arrived at the Castle, she was informed that that sort of thing 'wouldn't do'.

She started up another hill. Here, too, there were grey and black sheep grazing among tufts of heather and tall yews. She found a cluster of blueberries, and suddenly remembered how shrunken her belly was. She picked as many of the black-blue berries as she could hold, and ate them as she walked. One by one she put them on her tongue and pressed them against the roof of her mouth until they burst with a tart pop. The more slowly she managed to eat, the better she would be able to fool her stomach into believing it had had a full meal.

As she reached the crest of the long hill, she paused to get her bearings. Down there she could see the wide glittering loops of the Breda River, partially hidden by dark clumps of trees. Over there was the dusty white line of the road. Two ox-carts were making their way along it, headed for the city. One of the drivers saw her and waved. She waved back, and then realized with a burst of panic how stupid it was to stand like this, visible for miles. She was not used to thinking like a hunted beast. She withdrew hastily from the hilltop and walked along the ridge a little lower down, in better concealment. But it was good to have seen the road about where she thought it ought to be. She knew where to find Bonverte now, she thought. Only a couple more hills, and she would be there.

But when she finally reached the top of the last hill and looked out across the orchards of Bonverte, relief was short-lived.

The big gates that had closed so massively behind her the night Caspar threw her out . . . They weren't there any more. A bit of wreckage hung from one hinge, that was all. And when she looked more closely at the great house where she had had her interview with Angelica Bonverte, she saw that many of the windows were blackened and broken.

'You were wrong, Simon,' she whispered. Alcedina had wasted no time in getting what he wanted, and the power of a well-known maestra had not been enough to stop him. He had attacked directly, and Kat had come much, much too late.

Mechanically, she walked towards the house anyway. It looked deserted. Above the chimneys two black crows circled, and their hoarse cawing somehow made the place feel even emptier. Was there anybody left at all? Or had Alcedina killed or arrested every last one?

She paused when she reached the ruined gates. What had happened to them? In Weaponry and Armament class, she had learned of siege engines that might batter down defences such as these, but no ramrod she had ever heard of could turn solid oak into kindling like this. Splintered debris was scattered all over the place, and only a few broken boards still dangled from the twisted hinges. What could have made such a hole? She stepped through the arc of the gate. Inside, the yard between the house and the stables was a chaotic sight. A cart had been overturned and someone had tried to set it on fire. Most of its load of large stoneware cider jars lay scattered in thick grey shards on the cobbles. The contents had long since evaporated, but a heady smell of fermented apple juice still hovered, strong enough to be noticed even in the midst of the charred stench of burned straw and smouldering roof beams. Most of the stable doors were wide open, empty of beasts and people, and a set of saddlebags lay slung on the ground where someone had dropped them or flung them. From behind one of the few doors still closed came a frightened, lonely whinny, but Kat headed for the big house instead. Somewhere there had to be a living human being who could tell her what had happened.

Inside, too, the signs of violence jarred her senses. The big mirror on the end wall lay shattered, and one door had obviously been hacked open with an axe. Brownish spatters and stains on the doorframe and the wall could only be dried blood. Kat wasn't inclined to continue her investigation in that direction. Instead, she turned to the room she had always instinctively thought of as the heart of any house: the kitchen. If there were no people there, she felt, then the house really was deserted.

She found it downstairs, in a sort of high cellar. At one end was the huge fireplace where the meals were cooked. And although there were now no leaping flames under the copper kettle that hung there, there were embers, and a thin trickle of steam coming from the kettle's spout. There was still life somewhere in the ruins, it seemed.

Then her attention was caught by some round flat-breads hanging on a stick, like wheels on an axle. There were so many – surely they could spare just one? Her stomach, which had been relatively somnolent since the blueberries, roared like a monster demanding food, now! She eased one of the breads off the stick and bit into it. It tasted heavenly. Just about anything did if one was hungry enough, of course, but bread in particular.

Her enjoyment was rudely interrupted. Something huge and bear-like seized her from behind and literally lifted her into the air by her collar.

'Thieving brat! Haven't you had enough? Didn't you get enough loot the first time round, you and your pack of murderous brutes?'

The flatbread dropped from her trembling hands, and she struggled to breathe, let alone answer.

'Didn't steal anything!' she managed hoarsely. Well, she took the bread, of course, but . . . 'Just the bread. I was hungry!' Oh, that didn't sound very good – like one of Breda's little pickpockets caught red-handed. She tried again. 'Caspar, let me go. I haven't done you any harm, have I?'

It had to be Caspar, of course. No one else had the

approximate height and strength of a full-grown bear. She remembered him well from that awful Talis Night.

'You tell me,' he growled. 'You tell me where you and your filthy gang hide yourselves, and I might let you go.'

Gang? What gang?

'What are you talking about?' She tried to wriggle free, without much hope. But suddenly his grip did loosen, and she could feel him swaying like a tree in a storm. He let go of her, crashed into the table, and then sat down abruptly on the bench beside it. He was in a bad way, she could see. All of one side of his face was such a swollen mess of bruises that the eye was almost invisible. The grip on her collar must have been left-handed, because his right was strapped to his chest with splints and bandaging, and only the tips of his fingers showed.

'Caspar? What happened here?'

'As if you didn't know . . .' he rasped and tried to get up again, but he was clearly too weakened and too groggy.

'I'm telling you, I don't know anything,' claimed Kat, not quite truthfully. 'Tell me!'

'That night . . . that Talis Night when maestra threw you out. You were here to spy, weren't you? To check the gates, to see what was worth stealing, to see where our defences were weakest. Bloody murderers!'

Murderers? 'Who is dead, Caspar?'

He didn't seem to hear. He was staring down at his hands, the bandaged and the unbandaged one.

'Who would have thought it?' he muttered. 'This close to Breda . . .'

Kat felt like shaking him.

'*Who is dead?* Is it . . . is it Daniel? Sara? Uncle Isak?'

'What has the world come to, when the Bredani can't even protect us right here in the midst of the heartland?'

Then she did shake him. She caught hold of his arm and jerked at it, trying to make him look at her, make him answer her.

'Was someone killed? Caspar, tell me!'

He turned his big, misshapen face. Tears were running freely down both cheeks, despite the fact that only one eye was properly visible.

'Sistina is dead,' he said, as if he still didn't quite believe it himself. 'My little Sistina, who never hurt anybody in her entire life . . .' Suddenly he pounded his left fist into the tabletop. 'I *told* her. I told her to stay in the kitchen, I told her to hide. Why couldn't she just do what I said?' A huge sob shook his massive body, and he held both hands up, even the damaged one. 'Do you know how tiny she was? I could circle her waist with my hands, like this. What could she do against a brute of a bandit almost as big as me? He swatted her like she was a fly.' He seized Kat's wrist and appeared to have momentarily forgotten that she was supposedly an accomplice of the robbers. 'At first you couldn't even see that there was anything wrong with her. She lay still, but she looked all right. But then . . .' he wept unashamedly and without inhibition, as Kat had rarely seen any man cry, '. . . when I wanted to lift her up . . . just lift her . . . her head . . . it was quite flat. In the back, I mean. Like an egg dropped on the floor. Like an egg . . .'

His body heaved with each sob, and Kat had tears in her eyes as well. She could barely remember Sistina – the girl who had let her into Angelica Bonverte's study. A slender, fair-haired girl, soft-spoken and not very tall. She had looked a bit like Mattie. Kat was relieved that it wasn't Daniel or any of the other Sardis who had been killed, but you would have to be made of stone to stay unmoved by Caspar's grief. Clumsily, she put her good hand on his shoulder and stroked his back, as if he were a horse she was trying to calm.

A woman appeared in the doorway, carrying a large basket.

'I found four of the hens, but I couldn't—' she stopped abruptly, catching sight of Kat. 'Who are you?' she asked, suspicion sharp in her voice.

Kat didn't quite know how to answer.

'My name is Katriona,' she said. 'I came to . . . to talk to the Sardis, if that's possible.'

The woman snorted. 'Them! Traveller riff-raff, if you ask me. I wouldn't be at all surprised if this whole mess was all their fault. Invite one cockroach, and the whole damn swarm will descend on you.'

Kat sighed and decided not to battle her prejudice.

'What happened?' she asked. 'I asked Caspar, but . . .' she indicated the big man with a flap of her wrist. He was still crying uncontrollably, but with hardly any sound. Only a faint whimpering 'Aaaahh' escaped him every time he heaved another breath.

The woman's face softened.

'He is not himself,' she said. 'And he should be in his bed. Come on, Caspar, let me help you up the stairs.'

But Caspar shook his head and wouldn't budge.

'You're too big for me to carry,' she said. 'At least drink the tea this time.'

He didn't react. She sighed, then pointed at Kat.

'Make yourself useful. Fetch me some more water from the pump outside.'

Kat did as she was told, despite the sense of urgency that made her want to scream at every second she wasted. She had the feeling that she might get some answers out of the woman if she didn't push too hard. Patience, she told herself – patience.

When she returned Caspar's weeping fit had ebbed somewhat, but it was clear that it had taken its toll. He slumped forward over the table, and it seemed only a matter of time before his poor abused head would sink on to the arm he was using for balance.

'What are we going to do if he falls asleep at the table?' asked Kat.

'Let him sleep. I would like to get him to lie down on a proper bed, but he won't, and that's that. I don't see how the two of us can force him, do you?'

Kat shook her head. Trying to move even his unconscious body would clearly be impossible. If he fought them . . . well, best not to attempt it.

'He is so used to being big and strong, he doesn't know how to deal with the fact that there are things he can't do. And Sistina . . . Well, it is hard for a man like him to accept that he couldn't protect someone he loved so dearly.' She poured fresh water into the kettle and gave the embers a rather violent poke.

'What happened?' said Kat one last time.

'Robbers,' said the woman briefly. 'Six or seven, we think. They wore hoods – we couldn't see their faces, only their eyes. And we . . . Well, one doesn't *expect* that sort of thing this close to the city. Way out in border country such things may happen, but not here . . . and we had a good solid gate, and a couple of men like Caspar . . . Well, he *is* the biggest, of course, but Enok and Bastian aren't exactly puny either. We thought that was enough. But the gate . . . they did something to it. There was a noise like a peal of thunder, and wooden splinters flew through the air, and then there was suddenly no gate any more. Black magic, I shouldn't wonder. So what can you do? We tried, but it wasn't enough.'

'And the Sardis? What happened to them?'

The woman raised an eyebrow. 'Friends of yours, are they?'

Something in her expression told Kat that she wouldn't gain much in the way of respectability if she said yes.

'I know them,' she said cautiously. 'And . . . they have something I need.'

'Is that so? You know, funnily enough those murderous thugs were asking after the Sardis too. But I can give you the same answer I gave them. They aren't here, and they haven't been here since four days ago when they left.

Where they've gone, the Lady only knows. Or perhaps you would do better to ask the Devil.'

Kat felt her knees weaken suddenly and had to sit on a stool by the fireplace. It was a relief to know that Alcedina and his 'robbers' had not caught the Sardis. But now she was as ignorant as he was, with no place to start looking, and unlike him, she couldn't go around freely asking if anyone had seen a travelling family – three men and three children, and possibly a horse called Roscha. What on earth could she do now?

At that moment, hoofbeats echoed through the yard upstairs.

'That will be maestra and the others, back from the hunt. I hope they caught the bastards!'

Kat rose reluctantly. However unpleasant, she would have to face Angelica Bonverte once more, and hope she would get better answers this time.

She climbed the steps to the yard. The sunlight was still harsh and white, and after the dimness of the kitchen, she had to squint to see anything at all. The yard, which had seemed so deserted a moment ago, was now teeming with horses and riders. She looked around for the upright figure of Angelica Bonverte, but couldn't see her anywhere. Only very slowly did it dawn on her that the riders were not Bonverte robber-chasers, back from the hunt. They were city guards.

'Right, lass, tell us where those bastards went,' called their leader, a black-bearded captain she knew by the name of Korbett. And then he recognized her.

'What the hell . . .'

She spun and leaped for the cover of the stairway, but she knew it was too late.

'Trivallia! Come back here!' he yelled, and then, when she threw herself down the steps instead of obeying, 'Strega! Bartel! Go get her!'

THE GALLOWS AT DAWN

bob the Turnkey slammed the cell door shut.
'Better get used to it,' he said maliciously. 'I won't
be needing this key again any time soon.' Then he
departed and left Kat in the dark, alone except for the
mice that rustled in the straw on the floor. Or were they
rats?

It hadn't taken them long to catch her. She had hoped
to find some kind of back door, but she never got far
enough to know if there was one. After a brief struggle in
the stairwell she was dragged back to Korbett, barefoot
and dirty and with a new graze on her cheek because
Bartel had pushed her face a little too roughly against the
wall.

'Where is Jossa?' asked the captain, and she was glad
to hear that, because it might mean they hadn't caught
him yet.

'How should I know?' she said sourly. Her arm was
throbbing worse than ever after the manhandling Strega
and Bartel had subjected it to.

'Insubordination will get you nowhere,' snapped Korbett. 'If I were you, I would be *really* cooperative right now, the way things are for you.'

'I can't tell something I don't know, can I?'

His nostrils flared. 'If that's the way you want it.' He turned to his men. 'Search this property and the hills beyond. He must have sent the girl ahead to check the lie of the land.'

They searched, but of course without finding Simon.

'Where is he?' asked Bartel, closing his fist around her arm – fortunately not the damaged one. 'Where is the bastard hiding?'

'Told you. I don't know!' Her head felt like an overripe pumpkin, ready to explode. She had had a headache to begin with, and Bartel's efforts had not improved matters.

'Take her back to Breda,' said Korbett. 'A few days in the Hole will loosen her tongue.'

They fetched the last remaining Bonverte horse from the stable – the one that had whinnied in such a lonely voice earlier on. It was a wretched sway-backed gelding, so old that its muzzle was going grey.

'Tie her hands to the saddle,' said Strega. 'She certainly won't outride us on *that* nag.'

And then they headed back to Breda, Kat slumped on the old horse's back, not taking in much of what went on around her. But as the walls of the city came into view, she eventually realized that something had changed.

'Summertown is gone!' she exclaimed.

'Not quite,' said Strega, who had the dubious honour of being her escort. 'But there isn't much left, that's true.'

'Why? Did Alcedina – I mean, were they made to leave?'

'Not that I know of. Come on, Trivallia, can't you get that waste of oats to move just a little bit faster?'

'It's ancient,' she said. 'If you try to make it gallop, it'll drop dead before we reach the walls.' Nor was she in any hurry. What would they charge her with once they reached the Castle? Just helping Simon to escape, or would there be worse accusations? Murder? Treason, even?

As they got closer, she could see that there were still some Summertowners about, but they all seemed busy dismantling their stalls and loading things on to carts and wagons. It didn't make any sense. Why now, right in the middle of the busiest season?

'Why are they leaving?' she asked.

'How the hell should I know? Traveller scum drift in and away again as it pleases them. Now, would you please talk a little less and ride a whole lot more!'

And then they were at the city gates.

'Well, well,' said the guard on duty there. 'You got Trivallia too! That means both rats are in the trap. They brought in Jossa less than an hour ago.'

Kat's heart sank. So they had caught Simon after all. The only good thing about that was that it must have been the city guards, not Alcedina's men, or the only thing they would have brought back with them would have been the memories of a stealthy execution. And then her heart sank even further, to lodge somewhere in her stomach. Alcedina's men . . . Weren't they all Alcedina's men? If the

DomPrimus had told her to do something, a few days ago she would have done it with alacrity, no matter how strange the order might appear. He was her commander-in-chief, after all, and brother to the Bredani herself.

If I could only talk to the DomFelix instead, thought Kat, looking down at the gelding's bony neck. She's our only chance now.

'Strega? Whose shift is this? Alcedina's or Strigius's?'

'What do you care? Either one'll carve strips out of your back. Does it matter whose hand is holding the knife?'

More than you know, she thought. *Much* more than you know. But she didn't say it out loud.

Hob the Turnkey roared with laughter the first time she asked to see Lisabetta Strigius.

'Oh, right. I'll just ask Her Ladyship to nip down here to the cells for a nice little chat. Do you fancy she has nothing better to do than talk to a jailbird like you? No, you can bloody well rot here until it pleases the high lords and ladies to have you dragged out of here. And believe me, that won't be for a long, long time.'

And so she was left in the dim twilight of the cell. Sometime later he came by with a tin mug full of water and a bowl of gruel, but he still wouldn't listen to her pleas. His taunts grew less humorous and more cruel as his irritation increased.

'Just shut your face, Trivallia, or I'll shut it for you.'

Time passed. She ate the gruel and drank the water.

Through the small peephole, she heard the sound of the evening bell. It felt as if the rest of the world had just forgotten about her. Was Lu feeding Midnight? Oh, if only she could put her arms around that slender neck and rest her cheek against the sleek hide – the softest, the most gorgeous in the whole world! A couple of tired tears trickled out of the corners of her eyes. Why did all this have to happen? All she ever wanted was to be Midnight's Rider. Why couldn't she just be a prentice like Lu and Valente and the others?

It was cold here, in shirtsleeves, with no shoes or a cloak. There wasn't even a blanket. And she was so thirsty. One lousy tin mug was nowhere near enough to quell her raging thirst.

'Why can't I sleep?' she muttered to herself. She didn't want to be awake any more. She was so tired of hurting, so tired of being tired. And she didn't want to think the dark thoughts that kept intruding all the same. Did hanging hurt? She remembered how Simon had fought the rope back in the dovecote. It had looked neither peaceful nor painless.

There was yet another rustle in the straw on the floor. A mouse, she hoped. She didn't want to fear rat bites on top of everything else. *It's a mouse*, she told herself, as if she could force the unseen creature into that more innocent shape by the power of thought itself. Mouse or rat, in the end she did sleep, and nothing bit her. It wasn't exactly a peaceful sleep all the same. Several times she woke, heart thudding and sweat cold on her brow, because she thought she had heard someone yell. Perhaps it was herself, because when she lay listening, the Hole was quiet except for the scurrying of its smallest inhabitants.

'Get your butt out of bed, Trivallia!'

Hob's voice woke her from her latest doze. Confused and woolly-brained she sat up, trying to make out what time it was. Morning, judging by the slant of the sunlight. Night had somehow come and gone without her noticing it. She was thirstier than ever, and her headache was so strong it nearly made her throw up.

'Can I have a little water?' she asked. 'I'm so thirsty.'

'Not now,' he said. 'You are wanted by the powers that be.'

Powers? Did he mean Alcedina? A tremor began somewhere deep in her stomach and worked its way up and out until it reached her hands and knees.

'Alcedina?'

'Just get a move on. We haven't got all day!' He slammed the door open and grabbed her arm. 'Forward march!'

It was her injured arm. She marched.

He dragged her along the passage, through the guardroom, up a short flight of stairs, and into a small whitewashed room not much bigger than the cells, but a lot sweeter-smelling, and furnished with a table and a chair. He closed the door on her and left her there. She stood there barefoot on the cold stone floor and wasn't sure whether she should tremble with hope or with fear.

Something trickled down her arm, and she couldn't tell whether it was sweat or blood. Had Hob torn the scabs on her wound when he grabbed her? She felt cautiously around the edge of the bandage, but then there were steps outside and she had to give up her investigation.

The door opened, and DomFelix Strigius came in, followed by her stiff-backed aide. He put some papers on the table and then moved to stand so that he blocked the door.

'Thank you, Mikélin. That will be all.'

This clearly didn't suit the stiff lieutenant.

'Is it wise of the DomFelix to be alone with—'

With what? A traitor? A dirty border brat? A possible assassin? Kat never found out, because the bredinari second-in-command froze her aide with a look so glacial that it brought his objections to a stuttering halt.

'Thank you!'

It didn't mean thank you at all – even an ignorant borderer could tell that much. It meant shove off, and be quick about it. Mikélin shoved, and Kat was left alone with Lisabetta Strigius.

'Sit,' said the DomFelix, having regarded her for a moment. 'You look as if you might fall otherwise.'

Kat looked dubiously at the only chair in the room. She couldn't sit and let the DomFelix stand!

'Just sit, Trivallia. I mean it.'

Kat did as she was told. She felt woozy enough to keel over at any moment, it was true.

'Jossa's case has been up before the Council.'

Kat's head pounded feverishly. She hardly dared look at the DomFelix.

'What . . . what did they say?'

'It was . . . almost inevitable, Katriona.'

'What did they *say*?'

'Death. He is to be executed.'

'Death? But . . . but he didn't . . . he isn't . . .'

'He confessed.'

'*What?*'

Lisabetta Strigius peeled two sheets of paper out of the pile in front of her and held them out to Kat.

'Read.'

Kat read. 'The undersigned hereby admits to the truth of the following charges . . .' and there followed a long list: homicide and attacking an officer of the Bredani, treason against Breda's common good, attempts to evade justice . . . and at the bottom a signature. Simon's.

'He signed it!'

'Yes.'

'But . . . he can't have done!'

'It seems he did.'

A horrible thought occurred to her. 'Did they *force* him to sign?'

'I don't believe so. When I saw him last night, he had only superficial bruises. I tried to talk to him, but there was only one thing he would say to me: "See to it that Trivallia walks."'

'But he . . .' Kat frowned. 'Has he . . . Does DomFelix think he signed this for my sake?'

'I wouldn't know. But it does make it that much harder to keep you locked up, if he accepts all the blame.'

'He's playing hare again!' said Kat angrily.

Lisabetta Strigius raised a perfectly shaped eyebrow. 'I beg your pardon?'

'Yesterday, when the hounds nearly had us . . .' she interrupted herself. 'It doesn't matter now. But didn't he say anything to the DomFelix about . . . about a picture?'

'A picture? No.'

Kat took a deep breath. And then she told the Dom-Felix about the photograph that Uncle Isak had taken.

'And you think the young girl is Madalena Bartelin?'

'If she isn't, I can't see why the Sardis have been hunted so ruthlessly.'

Kat could see that it was not a new or shocking thought to the DomFelix that the bredinari commander-in-chief might be the spider who had made the web that Kat and Simon were now caught in.

'The DomFelix has known about this for a long time, haven't you?'

Lisabetta Strigius straightened her back and looked tired for the first time.

'I've had my suspicions. But no proof.'

'The picture is proof!'

'Only if we can get hold of it. And the Sardis seem to have vanished from the surface of the earth.'

'Not quite,' said Kat, slowly raising her head. 'I think I know where to start looking.'

'Where?' The question came fast and sharp, like a jab of an awl. And that very speed made Kat hesitate.

'Can the DomFelix get me out of here? And get me Midnight?'

'Midnight?'

'My hellhorse. If the DomFelix can do that, then . . .' She took a deep breath and made a promise she wasn't sure she could keep. 'Then I'll get you that picture.'

'Trivallia, why do I get the sense that you don't trust me?'

The DomFelix's glare was almost as penetrating as that of Moonface, but Kat set her jaw and refused to look away.

'I'm not the problem,' she said. 'But there are others who are less disposed to trust someone like the DomFelix. Or anyone else from the upper ranks of the Castle.'

Lisabetta Strigius slowly shook her head.

'I can't just let you go when the DomPrimus of this corps has personally ordered your arrest.'

'The DomPrimus of this corps is a liar and a traitor, and people are getting killed because of him. *Simon* is going to be killed because of him! Isn't there anyone with the guts to take him on? Are we all that *pitiful*?' Kat stopped herself seconds before she accused the DomFelix personally of being a coward afraid to risk anything to bring Alcedina down. But although she didn't actually say the words, she rather thought Lisabetta Strigius heard them anyway. An unfriendly silence descended.

Kat could hear her own breathing, fast and tense. She tried to slow it.

'DomFelix. When . . . when will they . . .' she couldn't actually say the words *hang Simon*, she found. But the DomFelix caught her meaning all the same.

'Tomorrow at dawn.'

It was a kick to the stomach. 'So soon?'

DomFelix Strigius smiled, a bitter grimace that had nothing to do with humour.

'Alcedina gave the order himself. And when Alcedina gives an order, it is obeyed in a timely fashion.'

Tomorrow at dawn. Tomorrow!

'DomFelix . . . help us. Please! We *have* to stop this.'

Lisabetta Strigius folded her hands behind her back. For a moment, she herself looked like a prisoner.

'He knows I am here,' she said, and Kat was in no doubt that 'he' meant Alcedina. 'My own aide reports to him. Trivallia, there is very little I can do for you and even less I can do for Jossa.'

'That's it, then? You are just going to let him die? Without even trying . . .'

DomFelix Strigius tapped a signal at the door, and a key rattled in the lock from outside.

'In this game, there is no such thing as *trying*,' she said. 'You win or you lose. Not all pawns can be saved. You should be pleased that you yourself are still alive. I may yet manage to keep it that way.'

Kat was on her feet now herself, so furious she could barely breathe.

'Simon is no pawn,' she shouted. 'And this is no game!'

But Lisabetta Strigius didn't even look back as she left.

Back in her cell, Kat took stock of her surroundings. She had to get out, if she had to dig herself through those walls with her fingernails. But here there was no convenient hole in the roof, and there was no one she could get to drug Hob and steal his keys. Might she fake some kind of illness so they would take her to the infirmary? Or might she somehow fool Hob, or overpower him, or bribe him? He would be no easy victim after what she had done to him to get to talk to Simon the first time. She yanked at the bars that blocked the peephole with her good hand, but they didn't shift a hair, and in any case she was probably too big to fit through that narrow opening. She wasn't even sure why they bothered with bars. To keep contortionists from escaping?

If only Simon had been here in the cell next to hers, so that they could talk and make plans and come up with something. Anything. Anything would have been better than to just sit here while the minutes and the hours ticked by, and the hour of Simon's death rushed closer.

But he wasn't in the Hole at all – he was in a special cell up at Old Castle, right next to the Gallows Yard. Could he actually see the scaffold when he looked out of his peephole? She didn't know. But when the hangman tested his equipment tonight, she was pretty sure he would be able to hear the sharp crack of the trapdoor, and the thump as the sandbag jerked at the end of the rope. She kicked at the straw on the floor of the cell and tried to think of something else, anything other than that sharp metallic crack. She had never seen or heard a real human being hanged, but last year they had executed a murderer *in absentia*, as they called it, when they had to hang a dummy instead because the real killer had escaped and was laughing at them from the other side of the Westland border.

Her thirst was a torment to her. If only she could have a little water, she might be able to think more clearly. She took her tin mug and started banging on the bars of the door.

'Hob! Hello!'

She had to bang away for quite a while before the turnkey hove into view.

'Stop that racket, girl. What do you want?'

'Please, Hob, I'm so thirsty. Can I have some water?'

'Please, is it? Well, well, well. A night in the Hole certainly helped your manners, didn't it?'

Kat bit back a sour reply and waited silently. He grinned.

'Well, since you ask me so nicely. Give me that mug.'

He went back to the guardroom and returned minutes later with a full mug. Kat felt she could almost smell the water, like a thirsty horse could. He steered the mug through the bars.

'Thank you, Master Turnkey,' she said, reaching for it. But at that moment, Hob let go of the handle and the mug clanged on to the stone floor, spilling its contents in a pool at her feet.

'Oooops!' he said.

'You did that on purpose!'

His grin broadened. 'What makes you think that?'

'Give me another!'

'Sorry. It says in the rules I have to provide the prisoner with one mug of water three times a day. Ain't my fault if the prisoner is butterfingered.'

'You bastard!' she yelled. 'It was you! *You* dropped it!'

'Tut tut, Trivallia. Whatever happened to your manners? I'll bring you another, don't sweat. At the noon bell precisely. And if you ask me very prettily.'

He went back up the passage, paying no attention to the invective she hurled at his back. And by and by Kat realized that all that shouting would only make her thirstier. She shut her mouth and crouched to dip her fingers in the spilled water so that she might at least wet her lips. But the pool had already gone, leaving only a damp spot. Damn Hob Turnkey and her own lousy temper! The noon bell . . . probably not for hours yet, she thought.

She kicked angrily at the useless damp patch on the floor. And then she started thinking. Where had the water gone? It was hardly hot enough for it simply to evaporate, and there wasn't enough straw to soak it up that quickly. There had to be a drain . . .

She dug into the filthy, foul-smelling straw with a will. A drain. Yes, indeed. A shallow gutter ran from the middle of the room to a square hole in one corner, blocked by an iron grille. Kat hooked her fingers around the bars of the grille and hauled at it. It shifted minutely, with a sort of squeaky moan. But even when she sat down, put her feet against the wall and pulled with all her might, it stayed stubbornly in place. She had to give up after a while because the pain in her arm was making her dizzy.

Her hands shook. Feverishly, she fumbled Merian's little knife from her belt. Hob hadn't bothered to remove it, thank the Lady. Or perhaps that was no oversight. A lot of people, with Alcedina at the head of the list, would be applauding vigorously if this prisoner did everyone a favour and hanged herself from the bars of the cell. Well, she wasn't about to oblige them. Instead, she dug the blade of the little knife into the crack between the grille and the side of the drain, and tried to loosen the rust. She scraped and prised and prodded, trying to rid the drain cover of the ingrained filth and corrosion of decades.

Finally, she made another attempt. She braced her feet against the wall and hauled until she thought her arm would come off. The grille moved. It shifted. It—

And then she was lying on her back in the straw, having done her best to knock herself out with a drain cover. Her jaw and nose hurt – another ache to add to a growing list of pains. But the drain . . . the drain was open.

Just a hole, now. A square dark hole, four or five hands wide. It didn't look big enough. But she had thought the same of the opening in the dovecote roof, and she had been wrong. She rooted about in the straw until she found a bit of brick that had come off the wall. She weighed it in her hand, and then dropped it down the drain. It rattled down the shaft and landed with a plop in what must be water, further down, so far that she couldn't see any glitter on its surface. Where would she end up if she managed to wriggle down that narrow shaft? How deep was the water? Would she fall into a pool of sewage and drown, or was there actually a way out somewhere down there?

While she was considering the possibilities, she suddenly heard voices. Hastily, she pushed the grille halfway back over the drain and covered it with straw. She could hear Hob grumble at whoever it was who had disturbed his mid-morning nap. Then a long-legged, frizzy-haired figure showed up at the cell door.

'Lu!' A wave of happiness washed over Kat in the middle of all the horror and pain.

At first Lu didn't reply. She just stared at Kat, and Kat suddenly felt very battered and dirty and worn because she could see that Lu was horrified at the way she looked.

'Kat. What happened to you?'

'Long, long story. I'll tell you later. But Lu, has Hob gone?'

Lu backtracked a couple of paces so she could see round the bend in the passage. Then she nodded.

'Yes. He went back to the guardroom.'

'Good.' Kat quickly took off her waistcoat and handed it to Lu through the bars. 'Take this. And listen, I need you to do something for me. It's terribly important . . .'

The noon bell sounded. Come on, thought Kat. Bring the bloody water! But Hob Turnkey was nowhere to be seen. Kat was sure he was late on purpose. She cursed under her breath, and not just because she was thirsty. She couldn't try to squeeze through the drain until he had been and gone. What if he found her halfway down? She would be stuck looking like the Legless Lady of some carnival freak show and there would be no escape after that – that much was certain. He would probably chain her, the way they did with the more troublesome prisoners.

Finally she heard his steps outside.

'Well, Trivallia? Feeling thirsty?'

'Yes, Master Turnkey.'

'Then ask me nicely – so that I can see your manners have improved.'

Damn the man. But there were more important things at stake than her pride.

'Good Master Turnkey . . . give me a little water. *Please* give me some water.'

He grinned from one ear to the other.

'Now, *that*'s my girl. Give us the mug then.'

Kat pushed the tin mug through the bars and watched while he filled it from an earthen jar.

'Here. And let it never be said that Hob Turnkey is not a caring master to his prisoners . . .'

She was almost afraid to reach for the mug. What if he played the same trick on her again? But he didn't. She drank greedily and emptied the mug in a few long swallows.

'Well, doesn't a man get a pretty thank you? Or I might forget about the bread.'

'Thank you, Master,' she said, adding silently, And may you one day rot in your own jail.

He pushed the end of a loaf through the bars, and she took it. She wasn't particularly hungry – her stomach felt odd with the water sloshing about, even though it had eased her throat wonderfully. But she knew the bread would be needed. If she couldn't eat it herself, she knew someone else who would appreciate it – if everything went well. And if Hob Turnkey would ever slink off back to his den.

He was watching her suspiciously, almost as if he had

caught something of what was going on in her mind. But finally he nodded.

'See you in a couple of hours. In the meantime, you might practise a few polite phrases. Honoured Master Turnkey and Good Sir might come in handy if you want a decent meal tonight.'

How she wanted to stick out her tongue at him, like she did with Meiles and DiCapra when they were being particularly irritating. But she checked herself. And finally he went away, and she was alone again.

She pushed back the straw and removed the grille. Now that it was time, it suddenly looked a lot narrower. Was it possible at all?

'Oh, Simon. Do you really think I can do this?'

But the noon bell had sounded, and she had less than a day and a night before they would hang him. Impossible or not, she had to try.

She went feet first. Then the hips – again a tight squeeze, but she managed to wriggle through. She probed with her naked toes but could feel nothing but the slimy sides of the drainage shaft. The hardest bit was to raise her arms above her head and let herself start sliding. What if she got stuck? Stuck down there in that stinking tube of a pipe, stuck until she could no longer heave a breath? Panic fizzed inside her, and for a moment she almost felt the shaft contract around her, as if she were inside a giant animal preparing to swallow her. She grabbed for the edge of the drain with one hand and scrabbled with her feet, trying to get back up into the world of air and light. But there were no footholds, and her fingers couldn't hold their grip. She fell, sliding and plummeting in turns, till her feet hit water and then stone.

She was standing upright in cold water up to her calves, her upper body still caught in the bottom part of the shaft. But there was more room further down, she could sense it, and she managed to slide to her knees, so that she was finally out of the shaft and into . . . well, another shaft. Or rather, a large pipe filled with cold sewage water flowing lazily past her. The dark was punctuated by some tiny, tiny pinpricks of light, probably from shafts like the one she had just dropped through. Other than that, it was blacker than a beast's belly. Somewhere there was a plop and a swish, and she tried not to think of rats.

She had to go on her hands and knees – there wasn't room to do anything else. And although instinct said to go upstream, not down, down was still the direction she chose. Sewage had to come out somewhere, didn't it? Possibly in the river, which would do nicely.

She started crawling. Not quite on all fours – her injured arm couldn't bear it. Instead, it was a rather uneven rhythm, hand – knee – knee, hand – knee – knee. It was not a lightning progress, and her knees quickly became very sore. The seeping sewage sloshed disgustingly around her thighs and elbow, and any incautious move caused it to splash into her face.

Just how long was this damn pipe? She heard a splashing somewhere, as of water falling, but couldn't quite determine how far away. She paused when she reached one of the pinpricks, but as she had suspected, it came from a shaft much like the one she had descended through. No chance to climb up those vertical walls. Nothing for it but to continue, hand – knee – knee, hand – knee – knee . . . until suddenly her hand came down on nothing, and she pitched helplessly forward, half-somersaulting to land on her back in more water, deeper this time, deep enough to submerge her completely, so that she swallowed an involuntary mouthful of stinking sewage. Spitting and spluttering, she sat up.

More light here – at least a little. Daylight trickled down from high-up grilles and shafts with some regularity, and she was able to stand almost upright. Brown foam drifted on the surface, and a little further on she saw quite clearly a swimming rat – a smooth black head with a V-shaped wake. Right now, she wouldn't have minded losing her sense of smell entirely.

The bread she had kept inside her shirt was a sodden mass now. She threw it away. The way she felt, she wasn't sure she'd ever want to eat again. She waded forward through the water, still following the current down. And now she could see more light and hear an even stronger splashing, like a waterfall.

Out. Oh, Sweet Lady, I want out of here. She increased her speed. The bottom of the pipe was greasy and slippery with silt, and there was a limit to how fast she dared go. But oh! To be able to straighten up completely, to be able to breathe air that wasn't thick with filth and decay. She rounded a bend in the pipe and daylight embraced her, daylight so strong that she was blinded by it and had to stop for a moment, squinting and trying to see.

Slowly, vision returned. It was just as well that she had halted. Ahead of her was a steep drop from which the water was splashing down into a basin fed by several other pipes like her own. On the other side of the basin was a big square opening blocked by a sturdy grille.

She hesitated. Did the grille open? Or could she perhaps squeeze through the bars? Once she let herself slide down the drop into the basin, return would be very difficult. On the other hand, she didn't much fancy struggling all the way up the pipe again, on the off chance that she might find a shaft she could climb.

She squatted, and shuffled to the edge. The drop was not quite vertical but nearly so, and a moment later her foot slipped and she could no longer break her fall. She slid sideways down the last part of the tube and only just remembered to shut her mouth tight. Who knew how deep that basin really was?

Deep enough. She went completely under again, and what was worse, a strong wide current seized her and dragged her under even further, down towards some invisible outlet. She struggled frantically to get free of it and back to the surface. It was like being a fly in a sink from which someone had just pulled the plug. She was flung against a wall but could get no grip on it, then down she went again, and one foot slid into the sinkhole, disappearing as if into the maw of some devouring beast, but she managed to push off the bottom of the basin with the other, swimming upward as strongly as she could. Her head broke the surface for the first time since going under, and she hooked her good arm over the rim of the basin.

She hung there for a while, just clinging to the rough stone. Air was a wonderful thing, she decided. Even air full of gutter gases and sewage spray.

It wasn't easy to shuffle up on to the rim. She could still feel the pull of the undertow, and only one of her arms was in good working order. But at last she paddled round to the grille, got a good grip on that, and managed a graceless bellyflop on to the edge. She rolled over and lay against the rusty iron bars, looking out into freedom.

It was a steep drop. Far below she could see the Ridderpond, a partial moat round the base of the Castle. The noonday sun glittered on dark water, at least where it wasn't hidden under a mass of water lilies and green pond scum. A couple of ducks paddled about quite peacefully – a mated pair, it seemed.

There was a hinge on the grille. It was meant to open, probably so that the system could be serviced. But it had been at least a couple of decades since someone had felt the need, thought Kat. The two bolts looked as if they had rusted permanently shut sometime before she was born. She put her hand through the grille and pulled at one of them, but she was not surprised that it didn't shift.

Exhausted tears slid down her cheeks. Unless she got the grille open, she might as well have stayed in the cell. At least it was warmer there. And less wet. And sometimes, one was even fed and watered. She gave the bolt another tug, but it was no good and she knew it.

Merian's little knife – best birthday gift ever. With numb fingers she got it out and started chipping away at the rust, flake by stubborn flake. Red-brown dust floated down on to the ledge she perched on.

It took forever. If it hadn't been so important, or if there had been any other way, she would have given up on it. But there was nothing else she could do, and so she scraped and chipped, scraped and chipped, while the sun slid over the Castle walls and her shirt gradually dried.

Clang! The first bolt shot free, so suddenly and un-expectedly that she nearly lost her balance and tipped into the basin again. She shook the grille, but one was not enough – she had to get both of them open. Now that she knew it was possible, she did less chipping and more tug-ging, out of sheer impatience. Finally the second bolt started to budge, less suddenly than the first. She pushed at the grille.

It stayed stubbornly shut.

She pushed, harder this time. Still nothing. Not even when she leaned against it and pushed with her whole body did it shift.

She wept in frustration and helplessness. It couldn't be true. She had struggled with the damn bolts for hours, and the damn grille still wouldn't open! Meanwhile, Simon was hours closer to his death. She hit the bars with her good hand, hard enough to cause more flakes of rust to loosen. Damn the thing!

And then she felt more like hitting herself over the head instead. Of course the grille was made so that it swung inward! Only sewage rats like herself needed to get out – most people would need to get in. She could have pushed from now till midwinter. Pulling – now, that might be more effective . . .

Even then it was no walk in the park – the hinges, of course, were as rusty as everything else. But she succeeded. And she was free. Or she would be once she made it to the bottom of the wall.

Climb or jump? She tried to estimate the drop. No steeper, certainly, than at the swimming hole back home, where she and Mattie and the boys used to plummet from the fat branch of a willow tree and into the sun-warmed waters. But she didn't know how deep the Ridderpond was, and it might be dangerous if it was too shallow. Besides, her shirt was nearly dry now. She would attempt the climb.

She eased herself down, feet first. There were cracks in the masonry big enough to provide a foothold here, a foothold there. It was difficult mostly because she was virtually one-handed, but once she reached the rock at the base of the wall, it became easier. Less steep here, and with a bit of shrubbery one could hang on to. She made it down to the edge of the Ridderpond without falling. And, fortunately, without being seen.

And then she realized she would have to get wet after all. She could hardly use the drawbridge, now, could she? So she had to lower herself into the still, dark water, startling the placid ducks. They were the only ones to raise a quack of alarm, thank the Lady. She made it to the other bank, pushing through weeds and water lilies, and got out, trying to wring at least some of the water from her hair. Well, the pond was a lot cleaner than the last bath she had taken, so maybe her smell was a little sweeter now.

At that moment the afternoon bell rang out, which meant she had to hurry. Not just because of Simon, though that was the greatest urgency of all. Soon Hob would bring the evening meal to her cell and discover there was no one there to greet him with Good Sirs and Honoured Master Turnkeys. She couldn't help grinning at the thought of his expression when he found her gone. But he would raise the alarm promptly and the hunt would be on.

TO ACT WITH HONOUR

her shirt was brown with sewage stains and stank to high heaven, one sleeve had come unstuck at the shoulder seam and the other was torn almost as badly. Not even the leather trousers had escaped damage. Her right knee poked out, and they were no longer a distinctive grey but a rather indeterminate brownish black, stiff with dirt and no less foul than the shirt. Her hair, too, was filthy, and stuck to her skull limply instead of giving her her usual halo of red frizz. She looked more like a beggar than a bredinari prentice now – and that made it much easier to slip through the streets unrecognized. As soon as people caught a whiff of her stench, they took pains not to look at her. Not even the guard at the North Gate cared to examine her very closely.

Summertown was now completely gone. Only flattened, yellowed grass and some shallow drainage ditches revealed that this had ever been more than summer pasture for the couple of black-and-white goats now grazing there. She crossed the open space quickly, and made her way into the small wood and down to her and Daniel's special place by the brook.

'Lady be thanked,' said Lu, leaping to her feet. 'I thought you'd never get here.' And then she was interrupted by a piercing whinny, and a slim, blacksilver hellhorse tried to tear herself loose from the branch Lu had tied her to. Kat didn't say a word to Lu. She just headed straight for Midnight and threw her arms around the slender neck.

Midnight snorted and sniffed and snorted again, perhaps to be sure that it really was her Kat underneath that stench of drying sewage. Kat merely stood with her cheek against the soft, smooth neck, feeling such a sense of relief that it was as if someone had lifted a mountain off her shoulders.

'Hello, beastie. Hey, little horse. You gorgeous monster.' The words hardly mattered – all she really needed to do was let Midnight hear her voice.

'Gods, how you stink,' said Lu. 'Was it hard?'

'Not easy,' said Kat, but she didn't feel like telling anyone about the shaft that had felt like the gullet of a huge beast, or the rats, or the sucking abyss at the bottom of the basin. 'And my beastie? Did she come quietly?'

'This helped,' said Lu, patting the slightly too short waistcoat she was wearing. 'She could smell your scent on it. Also . . . we don't really know how clever they are, do we? Perhaps she knew we were coming to meet you.'

'What about the castle guard?'

'Nothing. I told him I was taking Stala out for a practice ride. Luckily, they don't know one hellhorse from the other.'

Kat sniffed. Midnight was nothing like Stala – they weren't even the same colour. How could anyone mistake Midnight's deep blacksilver hue for Stala's greysilver coat?

'Did you bring my clothes?'

Lu shook her head. 'I couldn't get near your room without being spotted. You'll have to borrow some of mine. And if you've finished clutching that precious beastie of yours, might I suggest a bath? You really do *stink*!'

Kat gratefully removed her filth-matted clothing and washed herself in the clean, cold brook. The bandage around her arm was as unsavoury as the rest. Once the water had soaked into it and loosened it a bit, she set her teeth and eased it off the wound.

'Kat! That arm – that's a sword cut, surely!'

'Knife,' said Kat briefly, her jaw still set against the pain. The edges of the wound were very reddened and swollen. Not a good sign. She scrubbed it with the soap Lu had brought, even though it made her eyes water. Then she washed herself all over once more. There were minor cuts and bruises everywhere, and the soap stung, but it felt heavenly to be clean again.

'Are you sure you don't want me to come?' said Lu dubiously. 'You look like hell.'

'It's no good,' said Kat. 'Bad enough that you come

back without the hellhorse you rode out on. Even the stupidest of guards will smell a rat if you then try to get through the gates on the *real* Stala a moment later.'

'I suppose so,' said Lu, but she still looked worried.

'Besides . . . there's no time, Lu. The way I'm going to ride tonight . . . I don't think even Stala could keep up.'

'She's just as fast as Midnight,' said Lu, instantly leaping to an outraged defence of her darling.

'*Nearly* as fast,' said Kat with a grin. She wrung out her hair as best she could and started dressing. Lu's trousers were miles too long, but she managed to fold up the bottoms. The boots were worse. Lu had long slender hands and feet, and her boots pinched at the instep and were much too loose elsewhere. A good thing she would be mostly riding, not walking.

Lu helped bandage her arm again.

'Try to be careful with it,' she said. 'It looks awful.'

'I'll be as careful as I can,' said Kat, 'but there are more important things at stake than a hole in the arm.'

'Perhaps so,' said Lu, 'but if you don't rest it a bit, you'll fall off Midnight from blood loss and sheer exhaustion, and what good would that do?'

'Yeah all right, you've made your point. I'll try.'

She slipped on Lu's shirt, her own waistcoat and Lu's long grey cloak.

'Here,' said Lu, handing her a small bundle and a leather flask. 'Sausage, bread and a bit of cheese. And water. You look as if you haven't eaten for days.'

'I almost haven't.' Kat gobbled up some of the food

right away, and tied the rest in a bundle at her saddle-bow. Then she was ready to ride. She gave Lu a quick hug.

'Thank you,' she said.' I'm glad you're my friend. And I'm so, so sorry about your nose.'

Lu's nostrils flared. 'Don't think I'll lower my guard with you again,' she said.

Kat swung up on Midnight's back, somewhat less smoothly than usual due to a variety of hurts.

'Take care,' said Lu. 'I don't want to have to pass second-year Law without you.'

Kat nodded. Her throat choked up for a moment, and so she didn't actually say anything. She just raised her hand in a sort of wave. And then she turned Midnight on to the path and took off, heading north on the Caravan Road. The way the Summertowners had gone.

Never had she ridden Midnight so hard or so long. Even though the hellhorse mare had grown stronger over the summer she was still very young, much too young for what Kat was asking of her. But she ran willingly, one dusty mile after the other. Afternoon became evening, and there was still no sign of the Summertown caravan. An odd light lay across the road. Huge and red, the sun was sinking into heavy black clouds, and distant lightning siz-zled across the sky. Midnight flicked her ears every time thunder rolled through the valley, but continued on, though she was tiring now, her neck caked with sweat and dust.

'We must be halfway to Essford now,' murmured Kat comfortingly. 'They surely can't have gone much further with those heavy wagons.'

A soft drumming came closer and closer, and suddenly she could see the rain approach like a silvery curtain. Grasses bent before the shower, and the dust of the road rose in little bursts where the first heavy drops fell. And then everything was water. Midnight halted, snorting disgustedly, and Kat lost her breath for a moment. The rain was no longer drumming, it was hammering. It pounded them so hard that Kat felt as if she was being knocked to the ground. All of a sudden, it was as dark as if it were the middle of the night and not early evening.

Kat took a moment to get used to the dense weight of the rain. Then she bent forward so that she could talk directly into the mare's flattened ears.

'I know you are tired. And I know you don't like the rain. But we have to go on, at least for a little while.'

Midnight blew through her nostrils and shook her head to clear her ears of the rain. Then she set off again, not at a gallop, but at a relaxed trot. Kat didn't urge her to go faster. There was still the way back to be considered.

It was still raining when she finally reached the camp of the Summertowners. She was soaked to the skin, and Midnight was so tired that both head and tail had lost their proud bearing.

It was just a camp. None of the fantastic buildings had been erected, not here. The only touch of magic was in the paintwork on the wagons. No boring brown or black here. Blue, gold, red, green – no, one wouldn't mistake this for an ordinary trader's caravan.

Kat slowed Midnight to a halt and peered through the rain. She had found them. The question now was, could she make them trust her? She shook her feet free of the stirrups and slid to the ground. Her borrowed boots squelched around her ankles, and she hoped she might be able to take them off soon, at least for a little while.

'Who goes there?' called a voice through the rain. Well, well – the Summertowners posted guards now. Good for them. And good for her, too, it turned out, because the guard was none other than Merian's cousin Abel. She felt like hugging him.

'Abel, you have to help me,' she said.

'Kat?' He stared at her incredulously. 'What are you doing here?'

'I absolutely have to talk to Isak Sardi. It's a matter of life and death!'

Big words, but never more justified. Simon's life, Simon's death, and a whole lot else besides.

'Why would you think he is here?' said Abel, and even though he was Merian's cousin, even though he knew her . . . still, there was that edge of suspicion in his voice. That lack of trust in 'them'.

'Why else would the Summertowners suddenly up and leave? Midseason? Abel, it's me and I'm alone. What harm could I do to you?'

'For starters, that monster there would trample me in

335

seconds if I laid a hand on you,' said Abel, eyeing Midnight with due caution.

'She is very tired, and meek as a lamb at the moment. Abel, I beg you. Help me.'

'Merian says you don't lie,' said Abel, as if to himself. 'Even Sara Sardi says that you hold to your word, even when it is hard for you.'

Kat stood still, not wanting to ruin things. She could tell that he was weighing one thing against the other, her uniform and the authorities and the distrust on one side against the verdict of Merian and Sara. Finally he made up his mind.

'At least come in,' he said, 'before we both drown.'

Nearly all wayfarers took good care of their animals, and the Summertowners were no exception. Soon Midnight was stabled under a sturdy canvas roof next to two solid draught horses who eyed their alien new stable mate rather nervously. A good thing that Midnight was tired, thought Kat, as she poured a ration of well-earned oats into a borrowed bucket.

'Rest, little beastie,' she whispered softly, and then added, rather more firmly, 'and behave!'

Midnight snorted and twitched her ears, and then dug hungrily into her oats. A straw-lined blanket ensured she wouldn't cool too quickly. It was in any case not cold – a heavy humid heat hung around them still, despite the sun having set.

She had hoped that Abel would take her to the wagon that the Sardis were living in, but he was still cautious. He brought her to his own small caravan and asked her to wait. Shortly after, he returned with Isak Sardi.

Kat hadn't seen him since the night of the fire. She couldn't help but look at his hands, still swathed in bandages.

'Katriona,' he said, in the same soft lilt that Daniel had, and she nearly cried at the sound. But she pulled herself together.

'Thank you for agreeing to see me,' she said.

Isak Sardi merely nodded, sat down on Abel's bench and stretched his long legs. 'Abel said it was important. And who would ride such a long way in such weather, else?'

'Isak . . . I'm horribly sorry for your loss and your pain.'

'Thank you. But surely it is not your fault?'

'I had nothing to do with the fire,' said Kat. 'And I tried to warn you, because I knew my DomPrimus was looking for you.' She forced herself to meet the calm eyes, brown like Daniel's. 'But I did . . . I did do something. I revealed who Sara's grandmother is. In a way, it is my fault that Bonverte was attacked. And that – that Sistina was killed.'

'That is a hard burden to bear.' Isak wasn't judging her, not yet. He was waiting for an explanation. Kat threw herself into it.

'My only excuse is that I had to do it to save a friend's life. But he is still in danger, and has been falsely accused of treason. If you don't help me, he'll – they will hang him. At dawn.'

She cast a desperate glance at Isak, but he wasn't saying anything, neither yes nor no. She just had to soldier on.

'All the bad things that have happened to you this summer, all this evil – I know why it happened and who is behind it,' she said.

'So?' Isak didn't sound as if he entirely believed her. 'An explanation would be nice.'

'You took a picture—'

'I *didn't* take that picture! I never saw the girl before in my life!'

Kat looked at him in confusion. Then she realized that he was talking about the photograph of the 'crazy' girl.

'I know that. Not that picture. Another one. Of a Bredan man and a young Kernland girl. I think her name is Madalena Bartelin.'

'I don't remember that,' said Isak. 'When did that happen?'

'Probably last autumn. Or a little earlier, perhaps. In Koronberk.'

'We took pictures by the dozen there. *They* don't think photography is a sin.'

'I saw it in the box with the glass plates. And I would be eternally grateful if you would give it to me.'

'Why?'

She told him. It took a while, but he sat quite still throughout and did not interrupt her once. 'And the crazy girl,' said Kat finally. 'The one who started the riot. She is not crazy at all. She's a barmaid in Breda. I'm sure someone paid her to act like that. And I'm sure it was

Alcedina's men who saw to it that everything was burned so thoroughly. He was hoping to destroy the picture.'

'This man,' he slowly said, when she had finished. 'This Alcedina. If you get that picture, you can bring him down? Is that what you are saying? He will pay for what he did?'

'Yes. And an innocent man will go free, and the Vales will be saved from the Southerners. I hope.'

He suddenly smiled. 'You don't deal in small change, do you? You really think you can accomplish all of that with one little photograph that I took?' He got up suddenly, without waiting for an answer. He was a tall man and had to bend his head to avoid hitting the ceiling of Abel's little wagon. 'Come along then,' he said. 'The family needs to talk to you.'

Abel suddenly smiled. 'I acted with honour then,' he said, oddly formal. And Isak answered him with equal formality.

'Yes, brother of the road. You acted with honour.'

And Kat suddenly knew that if Abel had been wrong – if he had led Isak into a trap, or revealed his whereabouts to Kat for no good reason that Isak would approve of – it would have cost him his place in the community of the wayfarers. Isak's formal words meant Abel was still a part of that community. She was relieved. It was probably not easy to manage on the roads without a place in that brotherhood.

'It's the red-haired girl,' said Kottas gleefully, and gave her a bear-hug that nearly made her wounded arm fall off.

Or at least it felt that way. But it was nice that someone in the Sardi family was unequivocally glad to see her.

'It is a good thing that you have come,' said Kottas seriously. 'Daniel is sad without you.'

He is probably not much happier *with* me, thought Kat, but she didn't say so out loud.

The Sardis were living in a red wagon, a small and simple one that did not come close, for comfort or practicality, to the blue one they had lost. In this rain, no one stayed outside voluntarily, so the small space was cramped and crowded, and privacy was distinctly lacking. Sometimes, when she had imagined seeing Daniel again, these were not quite the circumstances she had fantasized about.

He was sitting on the kitchen box next to his younger brother Seffi, and he wouldn't meet her eyes. She could see only his black hair and bent neck. And she had no idea what to say to him.

'Give me the picture files, Sara,' commanded Isak. 'There is something I have to take a look at. And meanwhile, Kat has a story to tell you.'

Kat threw him a miserable glance, but he was already busy rummaging through the glass plates. She swallowed, and launched into her story about Alcedina and everything he had done, and why. She was certain that when Daniel heard of the betrayal of Bonverte, that would be it. He would despise her and never talk to her again. Ever.

'Is this the man?' asked Isak in the midst of it all, and held out the glass plate with Alcedina's image on it.

'Yes,' she whispered, almost unable to speak at all. 'Will you let me have it?'

'Soon,' said Isak. 'There is something I have to do first.' And then he was gone, a tall slightly stooped man striding off into the rain.

Kat battled on, to the dovecote and the rope and the attack on Bonverte. She couldn't look at any of them then, just stared down at her bruised and dirty hands while she told them of Alcedina's deeds and of Simon, now waiting for the dawn in his cell by the Gallows Yard. On and on she went, until there was nothing left to say.

The silence grew. Sara, who had been embroidering a ribbon, had long since stopped sewing. She sat quite still now, watching Daniel. He was still looking rigidly at his feet.

'Daniel,' said Samuel Sardi after a while, 'have you nothing to say to Katriona?'

Daniel shook his head. But for some reason, Samuel wouldn't let him off the hook.

'Daniel, my son, I think you have. And I know you will act with honour.'

There it was again, that formal expression. What did it mean this time?

It made Daniel look up, at least. His face was deathly pale and his eyes beseeching.

'Papa . . .'

But Samuel Sardi had risen to his feet. 'Sara. Seffi. Kottas. Come on – we will go to see Abel for a little while.'

Sara put down her sewing, gave Daniel's hand a tiny squeeze, and obediently followed her father. Seffi took Kottas by the hand and went too, without a word. And then Kat was alone with Daniel, and the wagon that had felt so cramped was now longer than the road to Breda City. She wanted to go and sit next to him, to take his hand, or touch his curly hair, but she didn't dare. Nor did she know what to say. And she had not the faintest idea what Samuel Sardi meant by 'acting with honour'.

'Daniel . . .' she finally managed.

'Katriona . . .' he said, at exactly the same time. It would have been comical if he hadn't been so deadly earnest. And if she hadn't felt so small and scared. She didn't feel like laughing at all.

'Katriona,' he repeated, 'I must ask you to forgive me.'

Forgive? She looked at him in confusion.

'Forgive what?'

That seemed to startle him.

'I hit you,' he said, as if surprised that it needed saying. 'I hit a woman!'

Woman. The word nearly made her blush in the middle of everything. But for the rest . . . Whatever she had expected from him, this was not it.

'You were angry. You thought I had hurt your family.'

'There is no excuse. If anyone had hit Sara in that way I . . . I would have half killed him, I think.'

Kat smiled involuntarily.

'It's a good thing, then, that my brothers are not like you,' she said. 'And if I want to get back at someone, Daniel, I do it myself.'

Daniel shook his head. 'But you didn't. You didn't hit me back. You didn't even duck.'

'You surprised me.'

'So do it now.'

'What?'

'Hit me. So we are even.'

It was too much. On top of everything else that had happened, at a time when Simon might only have a single night left to live, and everything was down to her . . . here she was with a traveller boy who wanted her to hit him so that they would 'be even'. She began to laugh rather hysterically. Daniel's expression switched from penitent to offended in a second.

'Is that so funny?' he said. 'We're talking about my honour!'

Kat would willingly have stopped laughing, but she couldn't. Her laughter was like a tight jerkin she couldn't pull off. It was stuck on her and went on and on, even though she didn't really think it was funny any more. And somewhere along the way, it veered into tears.

'Kat? What's wrong?'

What was right? Where to end? Where to begin? He put a worried arm around her shoulder.

'Not that one,' she squeaked. 'It's wounded.'

'Wounded? What happened?'

'Someone stuck a knife in it.'

That shook him. Perhaps he finally understood why she couldn't get excited about a mere slap to the face.

'Kat, I . . . how . . .?' But he didn't know what to say,

and his bewilderment for some reason calmed Kat down. She wiped her tears with the back of her good hand.

'Daniel. Forget the slap. I've . . . I've done you much graver harm. I betrayed you to Alcedina.'

'To save a friend. This Simon. I understand that.' Then his face changed again. 'How old is this Simon Jossa?'

Why did he want to know that?

'Are you jealous?' she exclaimed. 'Daniel, he is old. Grown up, I mean. Twenty-something, I think.'

'That's not so old. And you like him, I can see that.'

'Yes! I like him! He was my first friend after I left home. He . . . he is willing to risk death for me, to hang for me. Of course I like him! And what is it to you? You said you never wanted to see me again!'

Jealousy vanished from Daniel's changeable face. Suddenly, he looked only sad and tired.

'You care more about him than you do about me,' he said. And as he said it, Kat knew that it was true. Daniel was . . . sweet, and she had been very much in love with him. And perhaps also a little bit in love with the way he looked at her. But Simon. She wasn't in love with him. He was too old, too grown up. And he would definitely think that she was much, much too young. But she did love him all the same. Like she loved Tess, and Tad, and Cornelius, because she had finally realized that she actually loved her stepfather. She loved Simon like that. And perhaps also, just a little, with a particular sort of Simon-love, which was a feeling like nothing else in the world.

'Save him,' said Daniel, so softly she could hardly hear him. 'Go and save your Simon.' He took her face between his hands. They felt very warm. And then he kissed her gently on the mouth. 'Fare well, Katriona.'

'Daniel . . .'

'You don't have to hit me if you don't want to. Good luck. Perhaps I'll see you next summer.'

THE GALLOWS YARD

idnight needed to rest before making the trip back to Breda. And however impatient Kat was – and she could barely lie still, thinking of Simon and Alcedina, and of whether anyone had worked out where she had gone and why – however impatient, she too had to rest or Lu's gloomy prophecy would come true. Abel shared his dinner with her, then lent her a bunk in his caravan. If she had had to stay with the Sardis, she wouldn't have closed an eye.

It was pitch dark in the wagon when Abel woke her.

'Kat,' he whispered. 'You had better get going. Riders are coming.'

'On hellhorses?'

'It looks that way. They are still some distance away, but you can see the horses gleaming in the moonlight.'

She fumbled into her clothes. They were not much drier than they had been when they had been hung to dry by Abel's small stove. And where were Lu's boots?

'Is it safe to light a lamp?' she asked.

'Better not if they haven't seen us yet.'

'Abel, if they come asking tell them I've been here but rode off again.'

'But they'll come after you.'

'Yes. But if you lie to them, they might burn your wagon down. Or the Sardis'.' And Simon was not the only one who knew how to play the game of hare.

Midnight did not grumble at being saddled again, even this late. She just blew her warm breath against Kat's throat and nibbled at the collar of the drying shirt.

'You are the best, the strongest, the fastest hellhorse in this world,' whispered Kat, tightening the girth. She sincerely hoped this was not empty praise, because the mare would need every ounce of her speed and stamina if she was to beat three grown hellhorses in the race for Breda.

The attempt had to be made. No, it had to succeed. Nothing else bore thinking about. Kat swung up, made sure Uncle Isak's gift was securely in place in its bag around her neck, and then eased Midnight into a walk to warm up the stiffened muscles gradually. Hurrying too early could lose her the race.

She stayed away from the road at first, to avoid being seen by the oncoming Riders. Midnight had to leap stone walls and ford streams, and Kat didn't like that, but at least the moon shone clearly and brightly and the rain had stopped.

Then the light changed as big dark clouds came rolling in, hiding the moon. Her cross-country route became too dangerous – she couldn't ask Midnight to jump obstacles she couldn't even see. They had to take to the road again.

'Trivallia! Trivallia, halt!'

The shout came only minutes after Midnight had set hoof on the gravel of the Caravan Road. She turned and saw three hellhorses behind her, with three Riders. So close! Had they been to the camp already, or had they caught a glimpse of her and turned back?

'I can't stop,' she shouted back at them. 'I have a duty.'

'Stop, I say,' said the foremost Rider. 'Alcedina orders it!'

She wasn't sure how far they'd go, what they would do, at Alcedina's orders. But she couldn't stop, not now.

'I ride for Breda,' she called, 'not Alcedina!'

And she closed her legs around Midnight's warm flanks and asked her to run.

Darkness and moonlight, galloping hooves. Midnight was tired. She had already borne Kat longer than ever before. Nearly two days' travel for an ordinary horse. And now Kat demanded that she do it again, after less than four hours of rest. It wasn't fair, and it was much too hard on a young horse's legs and back. But Kat had no choice and could do nothing except lean forward and try to make herself as small a burden as possible.

And Midnight ran! How she ran. Willingly, bravely, long after the joy of running had worn out and only the will not to be caught was left.

Kat looked back. They were still there, the three silver

shadows. But the distance had not grown less. Midnight was doing it. They weren't catching up.

The road was no longer white but moonlit grey. Poplar trees cast knobbly shadows on the wet grass. Clouds chased across the sky, and somewhere beyond the river there was still thunder.

Midnight's stride was becoming shorter and less certain. Kat was whispering ceaselessly, telling her how brave and strong she was, asking her to keep going. Just a little further. Just a little longer. Go on, my darling, my blacksilver treasure, just a little bit more. Please. And Midnight ran on.

With a hiss, something long and black shot past Kat's leg. She knew at once what it was. She knew that sound, had been shot at with a crossbow before. A new hiss, another bolt, this one on her other side, close enough to nick her boot. Too low, thought Kat. Was she almost out of range? She looked back. Two of the Riders had paused to reload, the third was still coming on, full tilt. And then shock thudded through her heart, because she knew now why they were aiming low. They were trying to shoot Midnight.

'Stop, Trivallia!' shouted one of the crossbow Riders. 'Or we'll drop the horse from under you.'

No. Not that. She couldn't bear the price.

She nearly reined in Midnight. But if she stopped, Simon died. It was that simple. And perhaps, perhaps Midnight could outrun even their bolts. She bent further over the foaming neck.

'*Run*,' she begged. 'Run for your life!'

She knew she was asking for Midnight's last reserves, the last remnant of strength that no one had the right to demand. But somewhere in the depths of her stubborn soul, the hellhorse mare found yet another ounce of speed, a new wealth of courage. If only they could get out of range – and their pursuers couldn't ride and shoot at the same time, not with crossbows. Not if they wanted to hit anything.

Then a violent jerk went through Midnight. She screamed, and stumbled. Kat pitched forward with barely enough time to curl up, and hit the ground rolling. She tumbled over and over before finally lying still, while the world went black and red around her.

Midnight!

The thought drove her to her knees, though everything was still spinning. She looked across the road. The mare was lying on the grey gravel, flat and still. All of the slender, sweat-soaked body silent and still. Kat crawled to her side.

'Midnight,' she whispered. 'Midnight!'

One flank trembled. The mare was still breathing, and at first Kat could discover no wound. But then she saw it. Under the blacksilver quarters, a pool of dark blood was spreading.

The three silver Riders came on, more slowly now, because they knew their prey could not escape.

She knew all three of them. One was Marco Esocine, a Rider close to Alcedina. He was the one who had shouted at her. The second was Prentice Meiles. And the third was Lisabetta Strigius.

Kat sat by her fallen hellhorse and watched them coming.

When they reached her, they split up, one in front and one on each side, so that she was surrounded by sweating hellhorses.

'Prentice Trivallia,' said Lisabetta Strigius with no expression whatsoever, 'it is my duty to arrest you and take you into—'

'You shot my horse,' said Kat. 'You shot Midnight.'

And then came rage.

Like a giant wave. A wave that yanked her to her feet and rolled on through her and out of her, wild and unstoppable, like lava, like the thunder that was still rolling through the valley.

Lisabetta Strigius's hellhorse screamed and crashed backwards, as if someone had slashed it across the muzzle with a whip. Meiles's young mare simply turned and ran. And Marco Esocine had to throw down the crossbow and clutch at his mare's neck as she danced on her rear hooves and leaped, reared and leaped again, then turned so quickly that Esocine was catapulted off, sailing vertically through the air to slam into the trunk of a poplar tree. He slid down to the ground and lay unmoving. DomPrimus Strigius's mare was still down, kicking and writhing with her Rider trapped under her. Then the animal managed to roll to its feet, but it stood still with one leg tucked up in an awkward, wounded fashion.

Lisabetta Strigius remained on the ground.

Kat slowly approached. Anger still rumbled within her, and the wounded hellhorse took a nervous limping step to one side. Lisabetta Strigius's face was pale and drawn. Her legs and hips looked all wrong, twisted in a way that might be possible for a rag doll but shouldn't be for a living human being. But her eyes were open and conscious.

'What was that?' she whispered.

'I got angry,' said Kat.

'Sweet Our Lady! And the hellhorses . . .'

'They felt it, I suppose.'

'Felt it. Yes. I suppose they did.' A thick cough shook her chest and shoulders, and she gasped for breath. Something inside her had been broken and crushed – something vital.

'The DomFelix . . . shouldn't have shot Midnight,' said Kat.

'No. Clearly a mistake.'

'Why? Why did the DomFelix come after me?' Even now, Kat could not drop the honorific. It was too deeply ingrained.

'That's the way the game is played,' said Lisabetta Strigius, in almost the same tone of voice as in the Hole this morning. A weird sort of resignation passed over her pain-ridden face. 'One makes a move, and if it fails . . . one must agree to the winner's terms.'

Kat shook her head. 'I told you. It is no game.'

She cast a glance at the sky. To the East a pale hint of dawn coloured the sky. She could see the walls of Breda now, and if she was to get there before it was too late, on foot now . . .

'I will send help when I can,' she said.

'Do that,' said the DomFelix, and coughed again, in the same thick, painful manner. They both knew that she might be dead before help reached her. But for Kat it was much more difficult to leave Midnight, still breathing but otherwise not moving at all.

She walked. She *couldn't* run. It was all she could do to set one foot in front of the other. In front of her the sky grew paler and paler, and she tried desperately to hurry. Soon they would wake Simon, offer him one last breakfast, then take him to the Gallows Yard.

'Sweet Dear Our Lady,' she prayed as she walked, 'please let me be in time. Please. Please let me get there in time.' But the walls of Breda were still distant. Hopelessly distant.

'Iiiiiiyyyyyahhh. Iiiiiiiiiyyyyyyyahhh!'

A sound behind her. A sound she knew.

She spun on her heel.

Along the road, at a stiff and tired jog, came Midnight. And while Kat was still standing there, frozen with relief and joy, the mare screamed again, a shrill offended call. Why did you leave me?

'Oh, beastie . . .' whispered Kat, and stood where she was until Midnight reached her. For the second time that long day she threw her arms around the hellhorse's neck, not caring that the movement sent a jab of pain through her arm. 'I was so afraid . . . I was so very much afraid . . .' and then she remembered the blood, the blood pooling under the mare's quarters. She released her grasp of the neck abruptly. The mare had a long bloody furrow where the bolt had grazed her but the muscle was not penetrated, and it must have been the fall itself that had kept her winded for so long.

'Sorry, horsey. You deserve better than this. But if we don't do it, we'll be too late.' And she put her foot in the stirrup and mounted her tired, injured hellhorse once more.

Midnight set off at a trot as soon as she felt her Rider settle. The springiness of her stride was gone, but there was only a slight lameness. And even Midnight's trot ate the ground quickly enough to bring Breda's walls closer with significant haste.

When they were nearly at the gates, Kat asked for a canter and got it.

'Courier!' she called out sharply, and the guard, seeing a hellhorse at a gallop and a uniformed figure on its back, rushed to open the gate without hesitation.

'There has been an accident down the road,' she called over her shoulder as she passed. 'Make sure help is sent at once!'

'Yessir!' he barked, not noticing that the order had been given by a mere prentice, and a fourteen-year-old girl at that.

Midnight's unshod hooves clattered up the cobbled streets towards the Castle, and Kat saw to her dismay that the morning sun was already touching the top of the sandstone walls. Dawn – that was now. Was Simon already in the Gallows Yard?

'Courier!' she snapped at the castle guard, and he too

had been trained to jump when he heard that word. Through the darkness of the gate and into the first yard . . . Midnight veered hopefully towards the water trough, but there was no time . . . they trotted on, through another gate, into the Ridderyard, and right along a row of columns . . .

The Gallows Yard was packed despite the earliness of the hour. Mostly guards and Riders, but there were curious townsfolk too. On a special dais Kat saw Alcedina, immaculate as always. And with a shock she recognized the woman next to him. Greying dark hair, a thin face with deep shadows under the blue eyes, and on her embroidered dress the kingfisher that was the mark of her family. Cora Duodecima, ruler of all Breda. The Bredani herself had come to witness Simon's execution.

And Simon? At first she couldn't see him anywhere, and a stab of fear went through her heart. Was she too late? Had they already . . . done it? But then she caught sight of him on the steps to the scaffold, a guard at each side and his hands bound behind his back. A start went through him as he saw her, and the guards had to yank him up the last step.

But she had no more time for Simon now. It was enough that he was alive. She steered Midnight straight for the dais and people moved aside as best they could. No one willingly got in the way of a hellhorse.

At the foot of the dais, Midnight stopped and stood on four stiff legs as if she never meant to move again.

'My Bredani,' called Kat, her voice cracking with tiredness. 'I have a report to make.'

A murmur spread through the crowd. Kat clearly heard a voice whisper: 'It's that nutcase Trivallia . . .'

Alcedina was already on his feet.

'Guards!' he snapped. 'Seize her. Put her back in the Hole and see to it that she stays there this time!'

A guard did seize her ankle, but she kicked her foot free. 'No. I have to talk to the Bredani!'

'Is this not the little prentice who killed the false maestra?' The Bredani's voice was not overly loud, but it cut through the din with no trouble. 'Let her approach.'

'Cora,' said Alcedina to his sister, 'it's not safe, the girl is a lunatic, there is no knowing—'

'You worry too much, Alvar. I want to speak to her.'

At her gesture, a bodyguard took hold of Midnight's reins, rather nervously. Kat slid to the ground. She had to hold on to the saddle for a moment, as her knees threatened to buckle beneath her. Another bodyguard knelt to let her use his thigh as a step, the way he would if he were assisting a grand lady into a carriage.

'My Bredani,' began Kat. 'I have a most important thing to give you.' She took the glass plate from the bag around her neck and held it out, her eyes not on the Bredani but on Alcedina. 'This is a picture of—'

Even though she had been watching him, his speed surprised her. One hand shot out like a striking snake and seized her wrist, while the other plucked the plate from her grasp.

'Devilry! How dare she bring such filthy unlawful magic into the sight of the Bredani!'

And he threw the glass plate down, to shatter into a hundred sharp little pieces. 'Guards! Seize her!'

'Wait,' cried Kat. But it was not her word that made the bodyguards of the Bredani freeze in their tracks. The Bredani herself waved them off with a firm gesture.

'You are so hasty, Alvar. What picture was that?'

'A photograph, madam. The devilry of media illusion.'

'It is not devilry,' said Kat. 'The light itself makes the picture. And it may be unlawful here in Breda, but this picture was taken in Koronberk, quite legally. And the people in the picture are Alvar Alcedina and Madalena Bartelin!'

A flash of cold lightning from Alcedina's blue eyes.

'A lie you cannot prove, little miss,' he said.

'Is that so?' said Kat. 'What, then, is this?' And this time she was faster than Alcedina. The picture, one of Uncle Isak's clear accurate copies, finally reached the Bredani's own hands. 'I made two,' he had said, when he gave her the glass plates. 'With such a costly thing, it is good to have more than one.'

Silence descended. Not many people in the crowd understood what was going on up there on the dais with the 'high and mighties'. But the Bredani's face had altered the second she saw the two people in the picture.

'Simon Jossa is no traitor to his country,' said Kat quietly. 'He did everything he could – he risked everything, even his life, for Breda's sake. But is the Bredani quite sure the same may be said of Alvar Alcedina?'

The Bredani looked thin and tired. It was easy to

believe the rumours of her illness, and Alcedina put a hand on her arm, as if to support her.

'Cora, you mustn't think—'

'Is it true, Alvar? Are you affianced to Madalena Bartelin?'

'Do not believe such witchery,' he said in an oddly gentle voice such as Kat had never heard from his mouth before. 'Sit down, Cora. You mustn't strain yourself.'

And the Bredani did sit. Her hands clutched the picture so that her knuckles showed white, but she sat. Alcedina cast a glance at Kat that made her feel like an ant he was about to step on. Hopelessness turned her knees weak again, but she wouldn't give up.

'Listen to me—'

A hand grabbed her arm in the exact place where the wound was.

'We have heard enough,' said Raven, dragging her from the dais with one swift pull. A knife glinted in his other hand. 'Now, you just be quiet and let the hangman do his job.'

It wasn't the knife that prevented her from shouting. She couldn't breathe, couldn't stand. She clutched at Raven's knife arm simply to stay on her feet.

Suddenly a narrow hellhorse muzzle pushed between them. Yellow teeth flashed and Raven dropped the knife, stumbling backwards. Too late, though. Midnight had him by the tunic and was shaking him like a terrier shakes a rat.

'Master Hangman,' called Alcedina from the dais. 'Proceed.'

'No . . .' Kat's voice was a mere whisper and no one heard her. The hangman put the noose around Simon's neck.

'Thus be done the will of the Bredani—'

'*No!*'

Kat turned dizzily. The Bredani was on her feet again.

'It is not my will,' she said. She walked to the edge of the dais and looked out over the crowd. Her hands were still holding the picture of Alcedina and Madalena Bartelin. 'My will is that this man be freed!'

A sound went through the crowd. Some cheered, others looked disappointed. The Bredani seemed not to notice any of it. 'Master Hangman, loose his bonds.'

The Hangman obeyed his Bredani. He swiftly removed the noose and cut Simon's bound hands free.

Simon doesn't even look happy, thought Kat, inside a strange bubble of stillness. Just confused and almost . . . lost. As if he had manned himself up to die and didn't know what to do now that it wasn't necessary any more.

'Cora . . .' protested Alcedina. But the Bredani had not finished yet.

'Jossa shall live,' she said. 'He has served Breda faithfully and well. While you, Alvar . . .' she took two steps towards her brother and looked him straight in the eyes, 'you have betrayed my trust. You have betrayed your duty and your country.'

And then the words of the outcasting sounded across the Gallows Yard, words that made Alcedina an outlaw and a peaceless man in all of Breda:

'*You, Creature, my land will not suffer you. The earth you walk on shall burn beneath your feet. The food you eat shall turn to poison in your mouth. All gifts of the land shall be denied you – food, sleep and comfort – from this time till you die.'*

Silence was nearly total. Not one of the many people assembled stirred a foot or made a sound. Alcedina looked as if he could no longer feel the ground beneath his feet. He merely stared at his sister.

'You can't do this,' he said finally, his voice hoarse. 'You can't mean this. I am your brother!'

'The Bredani has spoken,' she said, and left the Gallows Yard.

Kat didn't see her go. She had sunk to the ground with her back to the dais, and with each beat of her heart the darkness moved a little closer.

She knew where she was even before she opened her eyes. The sharp smell of spirits and herbs was unmistakable. The infirmary. Just below her own little room. For a few moments she lay there, trying to work out how she felt. Her arm was sore, and somehow heavier than usual, but it no longer throbbed quite so fiercely. She still had a raging thirst. And the rest of her felt as if someone had run her through a thrasher.

Then she suddenly remembered.

'Midnight!' She prised open her gluey eyes and tried to sit up.

Hands held her back.

'Easy. Lu took care of her. For once, your little monster was too tired to put up a fight.'

'Simon . . .'

He had a fresh batch of bruises and was still quite pale, but there was something in his face . . . Life. Expression. A sort of eagerness. As if he had finally cast off his flat mask. Something had happened.

'Simon, what has happened?'

He looked, of all things, bashful. 'What do you mean?'

'Something has happened to you.'

'I had the noose around my neck and was still saved. Can't I be permitted a little simple relief? I'm only human, you know.'

'No. It's something else. Something more than that.' She was absolutely certain.

His smile grew wider. 'Damn, but you are no easy woman to fool. All right, then. Because it's you. Because I owe you . . . everything that is owed. But you have to keep your trap shut about it, at least for a little while. It's not official yet, and all hell will break loose once people find out.'

'Find out *what*, Simon?'

'The Bredani has a mind to make me the next Dom-Primus of the corps.'

'*What?*'

'Yes, isn't that a bit of news? A borderman, and from Jos! Can you imagine the look on their faces?'

'And you'll take it?'

Simon nodded, completely serious now. 'Yes. At first I . . . well, I refused. I had had enough of the corps. I was only trying to work out how on earth I was going to buy Grizel free from the service, so that I could take her back to Jos with me. But then . . . she is a clever lady, our Bredani. She said that that was a shame, but at least she would like my counsel on how to guide the new Dom-Primus. She made me write a list of things I thought needed changing. More Resting Places in the borderlands, for instance. Bredinari who are more than errand boys for the Seven. Fewer regulations. More conscience. I wrote. My list grew longer and longer. And all the while she just smiled. And in the end she said, very gently, "And how will you feel, Rider Jossa, if you are not here to make those changes happen?" And so I was stuck with it.'

He didn't look stuck. He looked like a racehorse waiting for the tapes to go up.

'I'm glad,' she said. 'Really glad.'

Simon snorted. 'Yes, I suppose you would be. But you can bet your stipend that there are a *lot* of people who will be less than pleased.'

'Simon. What happened to Alcedina?'.

'Last seen riding post-haste for the Kernland border.'

'She didn't let them lock him up?'

'No. Perhaps that was too much to ask for – her own brother. But he is cast out, and he can no longer live in Breda. And I am not sure his welcome in Kernland will be as warm now that he no longer has the confidence of the Bredani.'

'But he is still engaged to Madalena Bartelin?'

'Until someone manages to remove him from the picture.'

The picture. She thought of Uncle Isak, of Daniel, and of the other Sardis. They had so much rebuilding to do.

But at least they no longer had Alcedina hanging over their heads like a sword waiting to fall.

'And DomFelix Strigius?'

Simon looked away. 'She died last night.'

Kat closed her eyes. A couple of tired tears seeped out and down her cheeks to her ears. She wasn't quite sure why she was crying. Perhaps because Lisabetta Strigius was now, like Ermine, one of her dead. One of the ones she had to think of every Talis Eve, as she lit the candle in her little boat and set it on the still waters.

'She said it wasn't your fault.'

'But it was.'

Simon took her hand. 'You didn't do it on purpose, did you?'

'No. I just got angry. But Simon . . . if I *had* been able to do it on purpose, I still would have done it.'

He didn't say anything. He just held her hand for quite a long time.

Ten days later they unsaddled Lisabetta Strigius's mare and released it on to Hellhorse Mountain, like they had once done with Frost. It was Simon who presided over the ceremony, one of his first official duties as DomPrimus. As he had predicted, his promotion had not gone unopposed. Some of the opposition was open, some rather more covert, and a lot of people just gossiped and complained. Lu and Kat talked about it later that day, in the stable with Midnight and Stala.

'Did you hear Wrestling Master Medes? "Put a beggar on a horse . . ."' Lu tried to imitate the snide male voice.

'People will talk. But I know he is going to make a fine DomPrimus.' Kat still had one arm in a sling, but this didn't stop her from using the other to brush Midnight's smooth hide. The mare wriggled her upper lip in a grimace of delight.

In Stala's stall, Lu was quiet for a while. Kat knocked the dust from her curry comb by tapping it against the partition.

'Don't you think it's a good thing for the corps?' she asked when Lu still didn't say anything.

'Perhaps. Yes, I suppose it will be. But there'll be a lot of trouble.'

'So? Who says the quiet life is always best?'

Lu laughed. 'Spoken like a true bredinari. And if it was peace and quiet I wanted, I certainly wouldn't have picked you for a friend!'

Kat unhooked her healing arm from its sling and leaned over the top of the partition. 'Thanks a lot,' she said, and pulled her fingers through the brush so that a cloud of Midnight's dust settled on Stala and Lu instead.

'Kat! I was nearly finished here!'

'A good act cannot be performed too often,' Kat said virtuously, starting on Midnight's other side. 'But hurry. When we've finished, I challenge you to see who'll get to the black oak first.'

'You're not even supposed to ride yet!'

'Says who?'

'Our new DomPrimus, for one.'

'Him!' Kat snorted. 'What does he know about it? I'm perfectly fit. And Midnight has been completely healed and ready to run for days now.'

The last part was certainly true. So a little later, when they swept across the South Fields towards the old black oak, it was Midnight who reached it first, several lengths ahead of Lu and Stala.

'Well?' said Kat. 'Who is the fastest hellhorse in Breda now?'

'That creature is no hellhorse,' said Lu, still out of breath. 'That's a wind devil. A Nightmare. An evil spirit disguised as a horse.'

'No,' said Kat, patting the shiny blacksilver neck. 'It's just Midnight.'

Read the start of Kat's adventures . . .

SILVERHORSE

Lene Kaaberbøl

And at that moment the horse turned its head and looked at her.

Horse? No. No horse had such eyes . . . golden, with black slits for pupils. The eyes of a predator that hunts at night.

Kat shuddered, despite herself. Old tales of ghosts and magic stirred inside her, and she felt herself drawn helplessly deeper and deeper into that fierce golden gaze.

From the moment Kat first encounters a silver hellhorse in the rain-swept yard of Crowfoot Inn it is her burning ambition to become a bredanari – a keeper of the peace and rider of these magnificent creatures. But Kat's terrible temper, a dangerous secret and a shadowy outlaw all threaten her dream.

STAR DANCER

BETH WEBB

The omens warn of great evil to come. But there is a promise too: a shower of stars will mark the birth of the Chosen One who shall stem the tide . . .

On the night of the dancing stars, the prophesied child is born somewhere in the land. The druids begin their search for the enchanted boy, unaware that a baby named Tegen is also drawing her first breath . . . a girl who grows up with magic in her steps.

It is only years later, when the oldest and most honoured druid is dying, that Tegen is finally declared the rightful Star Dancer. But can she defeat the dark and demonic forces that are hell-bent on destroying her?

**STAR DANCER begins an enthralling
fantasy sequence set in a stunning
but harsh prehistoric landscape.**

DRAGON KEEPER

CAROLE WILKINSON

Ping is a slave in a remote royal palace at Huangling Mountain. Her cruel master neglects his duties as Imperial Dragonkeeper, and under his watch the Emperor's dragons have dwindled from a magnificent dozen to a miserable two. Soon only the ancient and wise Long Danzi remains. Ping has always been wary of the strange creatures living in their dark pit – but in a moment of startling bravery she rescues Danzi and the mysterious and beautiful stone that he protects.

Now fugitives, Danzi and Ping race across the kingdom, fighting enemies at every turn. But as they come to the end of their journey Ping must prepare for a heartbreaking loss – and a truly thrilling revelation . . .

The first part of an enthralling, magical adventure set in the exciting and colourful world of ancient China

THE BLACK BOOK of SECRETS

F. E. Higgins

When Ludlow Fitch suffers an unspeakable betrayal he runs from the rotten, stinking City. On the night he enters Pagus Parvus a second newcomer arrives at the remote village. Joe Zabbidou, a mysterious pawnbroker who buys people's deepest, darkest secrets, is searching for new customers – and for an apprentice. Shadowy Ludlow seems perfect for the job.

But as he begins his new life recording the villagers' fiendish confessions, Ludlow's own murky past threatens to come to light . . .

Shortlisted for the Waterstone's Children's Book Award

THE TRIBE

Valerie Bloom

The birds should have told us. They should have been silent in the trees, not singing and squabbling as if it was just an ordinary day. The sky should have worn his angry face and the sea should have been boiling with rage. But none of these things happened, so we had no warning. And we were not prepared . . .

Maruka isn't like the other girls in the tribe – she likes to hunt with her bow, deep in the forest. But she wishes she'd stayed in the village the day the Kalinago tribe came and stole her mother.

Two years later giant white sails loom on the horizon and an even deadlier enemy wades ashore. Maruka's tribe welcomes the pale-skinned men but is repaid with treachery. Her world is falling apart, but Maruka won't give up – even if it means turning to her old foe, the Kalinago . . .

A selected list of titles available from Macmillan Children's Books

The prices shown below are correct at the time of going to press. However, Macmillan Publishers reserves the right to show new retail prices on covers, which may differ from those previously advertised.

All Pan Macmillan titles can be ordered from our website, www.panmacmillan.com, or from your local bookshop and are also available by post from:

Bookpost, PO Box 29, Douglas, Isle of Man IM99 1BQ

Credit cards accepted. For details:
Telephone: 01624 677237
Fax: 01624 670923
Email: bookshop@enterprise.net
www.bookpost.co.uk

Free postage and packing in the United Kingdom